Chapter 1

"The Wolf stood tall, ignoring the wound in his side, staring defiantly at the man who... who stood before him. The Butcher laughed, reaching down and drawing his pistol, pointing it straight at The Wolf. The brave captain st..."

"He's not gonna die, is he?"

"Shhh, just listen to the story and you'll find out. Now... Where was... Ah! The Wolf stood up, and smiled. 'You can kill me,' he said, 'but humanity will live on. That spirit is something you can never defeat.' The Butcher hesitated, hearing another voice ring out behind him."

"'As long as we stand together, nothing can stop us.' The Hawk proclaimed as she strode..."

"I like her."

"I know you do, sweet. ...The Hawk proclaimed as she strode out of the darkness, holding her silver badge out in front of her like a shield.

"What's proclaimed?"

"...said."

"Ah.... I like this story."

"You keep telling me that, sweet."

"Well I do. Its good. Is that the end?"

"I've read this to you a million times, you know how it ends. We'll finish it off tomorrow night."

"Do they win?"

"Go to sleep, Jana."

"...fourty years since true unification, and the Ashkan Union has weathered all storms. The celebrations are scheduled to take place in two months time in the grand city itself, with the Councillors representing all major peoples and worlds of the twelve to attend! Even Councillor Ostroy, proud representative of you, the envoy listening to this, is slated to..."

"Jana, will you turn that shit off?" called a gruff voice.

Jana flicked a switch, and the radio fell silent with a final distorted shriek. The skimmer fell silent, the only sound the muted roar of the twin engines through the aircrafts outer hull. Glancing at the cabin-view screen beside her, she thumbed the switch on her headset.

"Happy now, Karl?" she said, hearing her voice repeating behind her over the internal comms.

She glanced back at the screen, watching as one of the eight or so machinists in the passenger bay raised a tin cup in acknowledgement.

"Much obliged."

"Watch that you don't get any of that stuff on my seats, or I'll set this thing down right here and you can walk the rest of the way." she retorted.

"Jana, I've been drinking in skimmers before you even learnt to walk, let alone fly the damn things."

"Alright then." She grinned, and turned back towards the front window, lowering her visor against the brightness of the sun reflecting off the red sands that surrounded the craft. The dark silhouette of Verkat already sat on the horizon, like a black mountain against the surrounding sands.

Jana leant sideways in her seat, craning to see out of the side window as a set of tracks caught her eye. Far below her skimmer, a ragged line of figures struggled up one of the rock-strewn dunes. One of the Bolvar caravans was making good progress today. If they were lucky, they might make it to the city district within the hour. Some people made strange choices, she mused as the figure passed far below her. Flying wasn't the best thing in the world, it was noisy, uncomfortable, and… well… noisy, but its not *that* bad. And it beats riding across the freezing desert any day of the week. She glanced back over her shoulder, seeing if she could still catch sight of the figures, half tempted to swing down and offer them the chance to change their mind.

But they wouldn't. If they did, they wouldn't be Bolvar, not really. Stubbornness was what made them… *them*.

That being said, she was glad that Verkat had stayed a Class Three. Class Two planets and cultures were permitted heavy machinery and modern weaponry, and she couldn't imagine the locals getting hold of advanced technology like guns. Or skimmers, for that matter. It seemed like the Bolvar were still a little backwards for that kind of responsibility. Even with the Ashkan Union enforcing inter-tribal peace, the locals still primarily resorted to bloodshed to resolve their conflicts. Many of the younger tribe leaders bore brutal scars as a result of the inheritance duels that had become commonplace in recent years.

It would work eventually, Jana thought to herself. With time maybe they would come to appreciate the value of stability and peace.

A voice crackled sharply in her ears, making her jump "Siren-class vessel, we are monitoring your approach. Please stand by."

There was a pause for a couple of seconds, then the voice came again, buzzing unnaturally through the cheap headphones.

"Jana! Good to hear from you again, long time no see. Done anything interesting since this morning?"

She grinned. "Yeah, yeah, nice to see you too, Control. Where's my landing spot?"

"Look, I'm just trying to chat. It's been a really slow day."

"We can chat once you tell me where my landing is, so these bums can get to work on time."

"They're valued employees, not bums. So I've been told, anyway." There was a rustling from the other end of the line. "Platform 6E. It's all yours."

"Great, thanks." Jana pulled on the steering column, bringing the skimmer round towards the plumes of smoke rising from the Union-segment.

She flew high as she approached the city, bringing the Skimmer around in a wide arc over the outskirts as she headed towards the landing platforms. The mess of low mud buildings and lavishly decorated tents began to give way to the Union Spire itself, a mass of grey concrete and steel that rose out of the city below.

As the skimmer neared the segment, Jana could see the landings hove into view. The area was busy with workers; carrying, loading and unloading. Most wore simple blue or green overalls, stained a dusty red by the fumes from the plants. A pair of Legionnaires, the military security arm of the Union, strolled slowly across one of the walkways above the platform, their heavy grey-green coats fastened tight against the bitter wind that swept across the upper reaches of the city.

Jana pulled the craft in above the platform, and gently dropped the engine power until the skimmer hit the deck with a jolt. She removed her headphones, and a discordant chorus of 'Thanks Jana!' echoed from the rear compartment as the workers jumped the few remaining feet down onto the platform.

She reached out, grabbing the headset off the dashboard and holding the microphone to her mouth.

"Please remember to take any personal belongings with you, because if I find any I *will* keep them forever."

She looked up as someone tapped her on the shoulder.

"Just got to scan the dataslate, then you can be on your way." muttered the overseer; raising his slate by way of explanation, its screen a mess of figures and icons.

"Don't have one." said Jana. "We've got to do it manually for this craft."

The overseer let out an audible sigh. "Marija. Really? I've heard about this skimmer from the others."

"Sorry." Jana shrugged. "Although if you want to make sure no-one ever suffers the terrible fate of manual registration again, you could always arrange a new one for me. Maybe one of those shiny new Greyhawk freighters, they look nice?"

"You wish." The overseer chuckled, scribbling a few notes on the slate. "You'd think the top brass would want their best skimmers on show for the locals, wouldn't you? Seems like this disaster-in-waiting might leave a bad impression."

"The locals wouldn't know a Shearwater from a Peregrine, I doubt they'll notice the difference." Jana said with a smirk. "Half of them still describe me as a 'flying sky-devil'. Pretty sure the Union made the right call this time, you might as well use the rubbish somewhere people will think its gold."

The overseer pursed his lips thoughtfully.

"This one of the old models then? Must be bloody ancient if it doesn't have slate access."

"Its older than I am, that's all I know really. It still uses radio, for crying out loud." Jana flipped the transmission switch back and forth a few times by way of demonstration, then shrugged.

The overseer sighed. "Alright, I'll take care of it." he muttered, with an exaggerated eye-grimace. "Go and get something to eat, we'll be an hour or two."

"I assume the canteens are all out of everything?" Jana said, clambering out of her seat and stepping aside as the overseer ducked into the flight deck past her.

"Mhm." the man murmured, clearly intent on his work. "Pioneer should arrive in a couple of hours, but it'll take days to get all the supplies properly distributed either way. What we have left still beats the city though."

"We'll see about that." Jana said, intent on ignoring the man's advice.

The streets of Verkat were a strange place. Once you stepped outside of the Union administration, it was like walking into a whole new world. It was possible to, within a few hundred steps, walk from a small, grey-walled office in the administration into two flamboyantly-dressed Bolvar elders as they brought their prize steeds to market.

This was precisely what Jana had done.

The occupation of Valmeer was recent; within Jana's own lifetime, in fact. The Bolvar at the time were still pre-feudal, isolated within a thousand squabbling tribes across a million miles of tundra, deserts, arctic forests and salt-plains. The Union was doing its best to accommodate them, to raise them up to the modern standard of living, but progress was slow. The Bolvar mindset was still, at its heart, pre-medieval, and any attempt to introduce advanced technology to the planet had immediately resulted in the eruption of violent conflict.

The elders chattered at Jana, their dyed and elegantly styled facial hair blowing in the cold wind that whispered down the streets of the tent city. Jana listened to them as best she could, nodding encouragingly whenever one of the two managed to slip a few words of Imperial Ashkan into the mix. She was an Envoy after all, she had a job to do.

One conversation filled with mumbled half-sentences in the Bolvar tongue later and Jana was alone again, watching the two Elders meander their way back into the thronging crowds that made up the market of Verkat. She grinned to herself. She liked talking to the Bolvar. They had a… directness to them that most people didn't. They never minced words, they never lied unless there was money to be gained, and they were always helpful and polite. It was a refreshing change after spending six hours digging through the Union administration system trying to get a replacement seeker light ordered to just be able to talk to someone who called a spade a spade, or a flying sky-devil a flying sky-devil. It wouldn't last forever, of course. Things changed. People changed. The Envoy families were doing their job. These days even the most isolated of the tribes spoke at least a few words of Ashkan.

With a final glance towards the Union spire, Jana went in search of some lunch. She wasn't one for crowds, usually, but at this time of day most of the locals would be out at the cattle market anyway, so with any luck the outskirts would be almost empty. Quieter than the pilot's canteen, either way. More civil too, probably.

Within the hour, she was back in the air. She had the radio on again, and was lost in the music, carrying out the minor adjustments needed to keep the skimmer airborne almost without thought after so many years of practice. She gazed out of the front window, idly watching the caravan she had seen earlier pass below as the grey mass of Verkat disappeared slowly over the horizon behind her.

The radio crackled. "Jana, you there?"

"Yeah, what?" she replied sharply, a little irritated about being drawn out of her reverie.

"We've picked up a heat signature in sector South-14. Looks like one of the first sons might have wrecked his bike or something like that, judging by its size. I'll get a couple of POF guys out there to check up on it in a bit, but for now you might want to divert if you want to avoid a face full of smoke. Plus if there has been an accident and you fly over it they're bound to pull you in to write a report on it, and I wouldn't wish the 'Observed Non-Fatal Incident Report Form' on my worst enemy, let alone you."

Jana, straightened up in her seat a little.

"Hold up, control. If I'm flying over it anyway, shouldn't I go and help?"

"Well, technically you're not qualified to actually *help* at all, you only have a... 2nd level medical qualification. And normal procedure is typically to divert..."

"Really, control? Someone could be hurt! Let me at least go down there and take a look."

"Jana, I..." the voice sounded hesitant.

"*Please?* I promise I won't try to put out any fires or set any broken bones while I'm down there." Jana wheedled.

There was an exasperated gasp from the other end of the line.

"You know my other pilots don't give me this kind of crap? Why can't you just be lazy like the rest of them?"

Jana laughed at that.

"I didn't have any plans this evening anyway. Let me have a bit of fun, at least."

"You need to get yourself some hobbies. Fine, fine..." the voice subsided into mumbling for a moment. "I've put it in the system. Sector South-14. I would give you more detail but I imagine you'll see it from up there anyway."

"And this is why you're my favourite air control manager." Jana smiled, checking over her maps. "I'll be about ten minutes. Let me know when the POF are incoming, maybe I can help them out." She twisted the steering column, bringing the Siren into a lazy arc as she turned south.

"Please don't try to help the occupationary forces when they show up. Messing with the military is more trouble than its worth."

"Psh." Jana sniffed. "If we can't trust them then who can we trust? Besides, I'm not about to start wrestling legionaries in the sand, control. Just, you know, if one of the local boys needs a hand..."

"Alright, sure, if they ask for your help I'll let you know, how about that?"

Jana smiled fondly.

"Gotcha control. Ten minutes. I'll talk to you if anything changes."

The heat signature was a wreck. One of the engines had ignited, sending a plume of black smoke coiling into the sky above like some vast serpent. To Jana's relief she could see figures picking their way through the wreckage. The figures looked up when they heard the roar of the engines, and one began to run towards her as she landed on a patch of flat ground. She threw open the rear hatch remotely, and unbuckled the belts that held her in her seat. Stepping down onto the exit ramp, feeling the chill breeze blowing through her hair, she waited as the figure approached.

He looked Ashkan, from what she could see. Beneath the thin layer of red dust that covered most of his form, Jana could make out a gaunt, narrow face, sporting a short coarse beard. His clothing was rugged, looking like something the trekkers wore on their march across the plains, all thick cloth and heavy boots.

"You looked like you need a hand!" she shouted at the man with a friendly smile, trying hard to make herself heard over the dying roar as the engines wound down.

"You're not wrong." he called back as he scrambled up over the last few feet of soft sand, muttering curses as the ground shifted and slipped under his boots.

"What happened? It looks pretty bad from here." Jana said as she reached for the man's shoulder to steady him as he stumbled over the lip of the incline.

"The engine catching fire is what first caught my attention."

Jana chuckled. "Speaking as an expert, that is usually a bad sign."

"We thought so too." the man replied, drily.

"How many of you are there?" Jana asked, squinting her eyes at the figures below.

"Three, including me."

"Is everyone alright?"

"All fine, yeah." the man said, watching his friends toil through the wreckage below. "I don't suppose you feel like giving us a lift to the nearest platform?"

"Sure, but... Don't you want your skimmer? I can call you a maintenance patrol, then you can try and get it fixed up..."

"No thanks, a lift will do just fine. She's not going anywhere for now. We can sort it out once we're not in the freezing desert anymore." He turned away slightly, and held up a hand to his earpiece. "Nadir? It's me. Get up here, quickly."

They waited together, staring down at the two figures below. "Name's Kristof, by the way." said the man, not looking away from the crash site.

"Jana." said Jana. She stared down at the two figures, who had begun to toil up the slope towards them. She shivered for a moment, pulling her jacket tighter about her shoulders.

"I should probably get the engines warmed up." she muttered, half to herself.

She turned, clambering back into the warm interior of the skimmer, leaning into the cockpit from the doorway and flicking the ignition switch. She paused for a second, listening to the rising whine of the engines before heading back outside as the other two figures crested the dune.

The first man was Varian, which immediately piqued Jana's interest. There were no Varians native to Valmeer, and only Ashkans could be envoys, meaning that this man must be a recent arrival. He had the black hair and pale skin common amongst his people, giving him an almost ghostly appearance amidst the freezing sand of Verkat's desert. The man ran a hand through his long, coal-black hair, shaking some of the clinging dust out of it with a muttered curse before looking up and, catching Jana's curious gaze, treating her to a broad grin and a wink.

The second man was tall and broad shouldered, standing nearly a foot taller than Kristof. Around his shoulders hung a battered old greatcoat of the kind that Legionnaires wore, the usually bold red and green of the Legions leeched out of the fabric by the passage of time, leaving the coat a sickly grey-green tone. The man's face was stern, with a heavy brow and thickset nose. Streaks of silver ran through his beard and hair, the trials of age beginning to take their toll.

"Is that a Siren-class?" the Varian said looking up at the skimmer above them, his words inflecting strangely both due to his strong accent and the smirk played across his lips. "I thought they had decommissioned these years ago."

The man in the legionaire's coat looked up with a grimace. "With good reason, if I remember right."

Jana frowned at that, feeling a little defensive despite the fact that the man was really completely right.

"Nadir." said Kristof, addressing the first man, "We set to go?"

"Can't think of a better time, myself." the Varian responded.

Kristof turned back to Jana with a gentle smile.

"Well then. After you, Jana."

Chapter 2

17th Ledas, 2052.33 Core Time – Electronic Messaging Certificate

Captain Bastian Wulfe,

Having heard the latest reports of the conflict brewing on Carth, the administration has allocated a Commissary (1st Class) to your case. The individual in question is scheduled to arrive in around three days local time as the Pioneer Interstellar Freighter passes through your system.

I understand that your men and some of the locals may have reservations about the Commission, but the situation has been deemed sufficiently dangerous to warrant their attention.

As per regulations, you are to surrender to them any and all authority they require in pursuit of their mission to them.

You have been performing admirably, captain. Continue to do so.

Forwards as one,

Adran Massri, Commissary (2nd Class), Ashkan High Command.

"Look Jana, you're not in trouble. But you did help a group of armed criminals escape."

Jana leaned back in her seat, giving a long, drawn out sigh. The sands of Verkat rolled by far below, the midday sun now beating down upon them, lending the ground a ruddy reddish glow. The day had been going so well, too…

"Well I wasn't to know, was I? That's *your* job, if anything!"

"You think my arse isn't in the fire here too?!" there was an exasperated sigh from the other end of the line.

"Look Jana. South 17, alright? Some guys will come over to ask you a few questions, and then we can all go home."

"Fine, control."

"Oh, and get that access panel open when you land. They'll need the registration codes for the skimmer."

"Can't I just write this shit down Control? It's pretty tiresome to have to open the panel every time…"

"You know the rules Jana, no reproduction of serialisation codes without explicit authorisat…"

"Sorry I asked, Control." muttered Jana sullenly, rolling her eyes as the lecture continued.

She cursed irritably to herself as she swung the skimmer around towards the South-17 station. This shit went on your record, innocent or not. She'd just unwittingly shafted her chances of a new skimmer for the next year or so.

"Try to do a good deed and look what you get." she muttered to herself.

She wasn't worried, she was annoyed. Union justice was overbearing, but fair. Finally a benefit to the endless bureaucracy, oversight and surveillance, she thought, revving the skimmer's engines as she cut in low over the platform. The skimmer set down with a clank and a dull hiss as the hydraulics took its weight.

Jana leaned back in her seat, kicking at the ignition switch on the dash with her foot, causing the engines above her to splutter and die, winding down with a long, descending whine. Jana sat there for a moment, foot kicked up on the dashboard in front of her, staring out across South-17.

Verkat-South-17 was busy, bustling with folk from all walks of life. It was one of the more commercial platforms, and it showed, with a huge variety of people, goods and services passing into and out of the hub every hour. Hawkers cried their wares, trying to lure in workers, pilots and whatever tourists were clueless enough to get drawn to this desolate part of the planet in the first place. Workers toiled back and forth, loading and unloading, stocking and piling, their thick jackets drawn close against the biting chill of the wind on the unprotected walkways between the platforms.

Jana sighed as she exited the skimmer, casting a glance over the thronging crowds. No-one paid her the slightest attention, and even fewer seemed interested in coming to ask her any questions.

She sighed again, inwardly cursing Control, the Union and anyone else in the immediate vicinity.

"Union efficiency, ladies and gentlemen." She muttered under her breath, drawing a set of tools out of the maintenance panel beside her and dropping down onto the concrete. "Best in the solar system, if only for no other *bloody* options."

She tried to be positive, she really did. The Union had done a lot for her. For everyone. But the Union didn't make itself easy to defend, especially out here. As she started unfastening the maintenance hatch, Jana began to wonder what it must be like in the home system, on Ashka itself or even one of its moons. *They probably didn't have to wait three weeks for a seeker light replacement, at least* she thought bitterly.

"You a pilot?" rang out a voice from behind her. Jana glanced up sharply from her work.

The girl who had spoken was young, late teens at most. She was short, her head barely reaching to Jana's shoulder. Her long black hair had been pulled back behind her head into a ponytail, leaving a single strand hanging down across her cheek. She was also, Jana noticed, not dressed remotely for the weather. Ashkan style, too. Probably a tourist.

The girl stayed, watching silently, one hand idly toying with the hanging strand of hair as she did so, the other folded across her chest.

Jana looked up, catching the girl's eye. She paused, raising an eyebrow inquisitively.

"You know you're not supposed to be here, right?" she muttered, her words muffled through the two screws she had wisely decided to hold between her teeth as she worked.

The girl shrugged, still eyeing Jana carefully.

Jana sighed, straightening up and balancing the two screws carefully on the wing above her.

"What's up?" she said over her shoulder, beginning work on the lower corner of the panel. "You like skimmers?"

The girl paused thoughtfully for a moment, then nodded.

"Yeah."

Jana grinned, forcing herself to put aside her bad mood as best she could.

"I get that. I used to be the same." she held out a hand, beckoning the young woman closer. "Come on, I don't bite."

Not like I can get in much more trouble anyway, she thought as the girl stepped up beside her.

"Thinking of being a pilot? You must be about that age, right?" Jana asked, as she turned back to her work, digging the screwdriver into the third socket.

The girl shrugged.

"I thought about it once."

She looked up at the skimmer, leaning back a little to do so.

"Do you go far?" she asked.

"What, flying? Not far, no. Mostly just shuttle people to and from their work, really."

The girl looked a little disappointed, stepping back as Jana hauled at the panel, pulling it clear with a metallic clank, its sudden weight driving her' back a few steps.

"That's what I thought."

Jana placed the panel on the ground with a grunt. Turning around, she saw two figures making their way across the platform towards her, dressed in the grey and green of the legions.

She turned back towards the girl.

"Well, I hope this has been educational. I've got a couple of people to talk to, but you can keep looking if you feel like it. Try to stay out of sight, if anyone sees you on the commercial pad they'll throw you out."

The girl smiled a tad shyly. "Thanks. Very nice of you."

A voice rang out from behind Jana. "Miss Schleifer?"

Jana turned around, forcing herself to smile.

"Yeah, that's me." she said, beaming at the two legionaries who stood in front of her. She glanced back over her shoulder.

"Alright, get out of…"

The girl had already vanished.

Jana cursed as the screw slipped out of her grip, skittering and bouncing away down the wing of the skimmer. She stared intently at it as it bounced away, watching every glint and glitter of light as it spun off into the darkness. She sighed deeply. That was going to take some explaining. Opening the access panels unsupervised was not technically allowed, otherwise known as strictly forbidden, but if they weren't going to fix the heating system for her she wasn't about to freeze to death without a fight.

It had been a long day, and it didn't seem like it would end any time soon. POF had wanted a written report of the incident. A few forms to fill in. The usual 'how dare you take on unauthorised passengers without prior approval' speech, delivered in the same grey monotone voice. She hadn't heard from Control yet though. Hopefully he'd made it through alright.

Jana shivered involuntarily. It was getting late, and the cold was beginning to bite as the sun sank towards the horizon. Jana scooted around and slid down the wing, landing on the rough concrete with a scuffle, throwing out a final glance for the errant screw as she tucked the screwdriver into her inside pocket. It had been a long day, all in all.

She ambled around the side of the craft, idly running a finger along the worn metal plates that covered its surface. It was doing well for something older than she was. Well, not *well* exactly. But it still flew, and that was the main thing.

She reached up, leaping up into the main hold of the craft with a grunt of exertion, glancing around the dingy interior as the lighting flickered to life. Even in here there was a chill to the air; the heating system hadn't been working in weeks. Every time she asked they promised to send someone out to fix it, but no.

She glanced at the locker's front, where words had been roughly scratched into the metal below the official-looking serial number.

Jana's stuff, hands off!

It had seemed a funnier idea at the time.

Jana reached into the locker, and pulled the coat off its hanger. After a moment's hesitation, she put the cap on too.

She strolled back outside, shrugging the jacket tighter around her shoulders against the chill. She paused, staring back across the concrete platform towards the control centre. Figures were approaching across the concrete, two of them. Jana narrowed her eyes, squinting into the darkness as the figures came into view.

The first was a young man whom she recognised. Hassan, or Hasir… or something like that. Local boy. He was supposed to be a guard of sorts, but she didn't think she'd ever seen him do much actual guard-work beyond sitting behind a desk with his feet up manning the booking system. Still, a nice enough guy.

The figure who accompanied him was shorter, though not by much. The woman's face was thin, almost gaunt, her hair buried somewhere in the shawl she wore draped over her head as some kind of makeshift hood against the wind. A black legionary coat hung around her shoulders, the colour reserved for the Legion officer-class and specialist divisions.

"Are you Ms. Jana Schleifer?" the woman asked, without looking up from her work. Her accent was hard and clipped, definitively Ashkan, although with a trace of something else that Jana found hard to place.

Jana glanced at Hasan, raising an eyebrow. The guard barely acknowledged her, briefly meeting her gaze before glancing away with a quick shake of his head.

"That's me." said Jana. "Can I help you with something?"

There was a pause for a few moments. Jana glanced between the two figures in slight bewilderment, waiting for one of them to speak.

Hasan stepped forwards, speaking in a low voice.

"The commissary would like a word about what happened this morning."

"An Inquisitor?" said Jana, taken aback. She leaned sideways, throwing a suspicious glance past Hasan towards the woman.

"A *commissary*." The inquisitor said, glancing up and fixing Jana with a withering stare. "First-Class. I have a few questions that need answering, if you would be so kind."

"This is about those guys this morning?" said Jana. "I've already given a report to Control, I'm sure they would let you see it. I've been interviewed already, too. It should all be there all there."

"They would have no choice but to let me see it. However, I usually prefer my questions answered face-to-face." said the inquisitor. She stepped forwards, past Jana, pulling down her hood and gesturing towards the skimmer.

"May I? I would prefer to conduct the interview out of the cold, if possible."

Jana hesitated, glancing at Hasan in confusion.

"…Yeah, sure."

As they stepped towards the skimmer, Jana spoke again to the two newcomers.

"So, how can I help you… What do I call you, anyway?"

The inquisitor gave a short, tight-lipped smile, extending a hand towards Jana.

"Atesca Seratov, Commissary First-class. Although just 'Commissary' will do for now."

Jana paused mid-handshake, throwing a suspicious glance at the woman.

"You're joking."

"I assure you that I am extremely serious." Atesca paused. "I gather you have heard of me."

"My mum served under you at Carth. I used to be such a fan. Read all the stories over and over. Used to pour over every release as it came in. The Wolf, the Hawk and the Butcher, I used to love all that stuff." Jana paused for a second, lost in the memories. "I assumed…"

She faltered, catching Atesca's gaze. The inquisitor sat there silently, unmoving, her eyes watching Jana intently as she spoke. Jana felt herself withering slightly under the intense stare, and fell silent.

"I'm sorry, you said you had questions?" she said quietly.

Atesca smiled again, although this time it seemed a little warmer. "I am glad that I could have such a positive effect on you. But yes, I did have questions."

She paused for a second, and Jana once again felt that strange sense of being *measured* as the Inquisitor's gaze bored into her.

"Perhaps we could continue this conversation inside?" Atesca said, gesturing towards the skimmer with a single incline of her gloved hand.

Jana had no choice but to agree.

Chapter 3

"Captain, I gather that you are in command of the Carth divisions?" the inquisitor asked quietly, her voice so low as to almost be a purr. Or a growl, thought Captain Wulfe.

"Active command, yes" he replied. "Logisitical command is delegated to..."

"I am well aware of where the head and heart of this operation lie, Captain." Commissary Atesca cut in, her youthful features twisting into the faintest hint of a smile. "It is my job to be aware, after all."

"And to what do we owe the pleasure of your company, Commissary?"

"Your operation is not the only one in Carth with a head and a heart, Captain. I believe your men have named him 'Butcher'?"

Wulfe frowned. "The Union reporter from high command decided on the name, I..."

"He is the reason you have the pleasure of my company. Although, I'm sure we can all hope, it will not be for long."

"Miss Schleifer, could you describe the event again for me? Please take your time, and ensure you do not leave out any details."

Jana nodded nervously. The Siren's hold suddenly seemed very small indeed. The inquisitor paced steadily around the interior, boots striking the metal decking with dull, rhythmic clanks as she did so. Her hands were thrust deep into the pockets of her black greatcoat, her eyes wandering with an almost idle curiosity around the skimmer's interior.

"I... I was flying my usual route, and got redirected to investigate a heat signature a few miles off it by command. There was a downed skimmer, maybe a Kestrel or an Osprey, judging by the..." Jana paused, stumbling over her words as she withered under the inquisitor's glare. "...a Kestrel, I think. There were three guys out with it. One was called Kristof, the other was... Nadir, I think."

The inquisitor's footsteps stopped in front of Jana's locker, and Jana heard a faint chuckle from behind her.

"And the third?"

Jana shrugged. "They didn't say. He didn't say much at all."

Atesca appeared from behind her, sweeping past almost silently to take a seat opposite Jana on the rough steel benches that lined the walls.

"Could you describe them to me?" she asked earnestly. "All of them?"

"I…" Jana hesitated. Describing people was surprisingly hard, she realised, as she stammered her way through the descriptions. Clothing was easy. Hair, too. But a face? There weren't enough words in the language nor enough details in her mind.

"Sorry, it's just…" she paused. "It's hard to remember details."

Atesca paused for a moment, her gaze lingering on Jana for a moment as if deep in thought.

"Don't worry yourself, Miss Schleifer. It is in both our interests that we cooperate to help you remember as much as you possibly can. We are both on the same side, after all."

The inquisitor sat forwards a little, folding her hands in her lap and tilting her head to the side a little as she spoke.

"Perhaps we should get some background on you." she said, her voice warming slightly from the cold, clinical tone she had previously adopted. "I gather you are a first generation envoy family?"

Jana nodded. "Yes. I was born on Ashka, I think. Or Taynia. We migrated here when I was three."

"Taynia. Yes." Atesca murmured. "The moons of Ashka are a common source of envoys. I gather your mother was in the legions?"

"I… yes. Medicae Divison." Jana stammered, hesitating a little. "You're very well informed, inqu… commissary."

"This is very basic information, Miss Schliefer. I would not be doing my job if I had not read your registration file before my arrival." The inquisitor looked up, and Jana followed her gaze out across the bare expanse of sand-dusted concrete that formed Bay 17.

"This bay is always this empty, isn't it?" Atesca said. It sounded like a question, but Jana suspected the Inquisitor already knew the answer. She nodded silently in response, and the two of them listened to the night winds whistling around the hull of the skimmer.

"And yet you still operate from here. Every night, from what the booking system showed me."

"When I first started out Command told me to. They wanted someone on the outer fringes, I think." Jana shrugged. "These days I'm used to it. Better me than someone else, I think."

The commissary smiled at that, seeming to almost stifle a chuckle as she turned back towards Jana.

"Very dutiful of you." she said. "I meet many of the Union's worst types in my profession, it makes a change to see someone willing to sacrifice for another's gain."

Jana grinned nervously. "Thank you. That means a lot coming from you, commissary."

"Anything for a fan." the inquisitor replied drily, though a conspiratorial smile hovered about the corners of her lips. He leant in then, fixing Jana with that piercing gaze once more.

"Think for me, Miss Schleifer. Start from the beginning again. The very beginning. Picture the day. Picture the scene. You would be amazed at what the human mind can reconstruct given the correct building blocks..."

Jana felt herself slowly warming to the Inquisitor as the two of them spoke. The sick fear in the pit of her stomach had begun to recede. In fact, she could hardly remember why she had been worried at all. This was an Inquisitor. They were on the same side, after all.

She recounted her day once more, speaking about the morning scheduling issues, her encounters at the market in Verkat, the redirection on the route home, the figures emerging from the smouldering skimmer...

Atesca sat forwards in her seat.

"...he was tall." Jana continued, struggling with the words. She could feel the inquisitor's gaze on her, unwavering, taking in every move she made. "Ashkan, definitely. His clothing wasn't local either. He had a coat like yours, but green."

"Details, Jana." Atesca said, her voice gentle. "What did he *look* like? Picture it."

Jana closed her eyes, drawing them away from the inquisitor's piercing gaze. She was tired. It had been a long day, and despite her nervousness she was having trouble focussing. "He hadn't shaved in a while. Fairly long hair..." she stumbled for a moment, then opened her eyes again with a sigh.

"Is that all?" the inquisitor asked quietly. Jana's felt her eyes drawn almost magnetically back to her.

"That's..." Jana paused. She had been sure that was it. She had been ready to say it. But now that the inquisitor had asked, there had to be more. Something small, at least. She looked up, and caught Atesca's gaze for a moment as she hesitated.

The inquisitor grimaced, and made to stand up.

"Wait!" Jana blurted, her heart thudding in her chest as the inquisitor paused and glanced up expectantly. She was getting unusually worked up about this, she thought. Must be nerves.

"He knew about skimmers. He identified the Siren when he saw it."

The inquisitor relaxed her posture a little, settling back into her seat.

"This was the Varian?" she asked levelly.

"Yes! Yes." Jana replied eagerly. She was feeling nauseous, but she barely cared anymore.

For a moment, the skimmer's hold was completely silent. Jana stared at the inquisitor, hanging on her every word.

Slowly, like the dawn sun creeping over the horizon, Atesca smiled.

"Thank you, Miss Schleifer."

Jana smiled back silently for a moment. She could hear a voice in the back of her mind speaking urgently to her, but right now she didn't care what it was saying. Atesca was what was important right now.

"I must say," the inquisitor rose to her feet, striking an imposing figure as she turned towards the Siren's hull doors. "that I had hoped for more from our conversation, Miss Schleifer. But thank you for your cooperation."

Jana felt her heart sink in her chest as she watched a frown creep across the inquisitor's features. There had to be something that she could say. Something to make Atesca happy again.

The voice in her mind was screaming now. She still didn't care.

"The other one... the one in the coat... he... he was tall! Six and a half foot at least!"

Atesca turned, and smiled. Jana smiled back eagerly as the nervousness withdrew for a fleeting moment, revelling in the rush of joy that coursed through her veins. She felt drunk. Delirious. Sick to her stomach.

"And you're sure there isn't anything else you can remember? Any details you may have left out before?" Atesca's voice cut through the haze, sharp as crystal.

Jana shook her head, eyes locked with those of the inquisitor. She was baffled. Why would she have left anything out? They were *friends*.

The inquisitor sighed quietly. The expression of disappointment only crossed her features for a few seconds, but to Jana it felt like an eternity. How could she have done this? Atesca had trusted her. Asked for her help. And Jana had let her down.

She had a headache. She felt like she was about to vomit.

Jana watched, aghast, as the Inquisitor rose to her feet.

"That will be quite enough, Miss Schleifer."

Jagged flashes of pain broke through Jana's mind. She felt her knees give way as she tumbled sideways onto the metal flooring of the skimmer's hold. She clutched at her head with numb fingers, trembling uncontrollably, trying desperately to make the pain stop as the darkness rose to envelop her.

Chapter 4

19ᵗʰ Ledas, 2067.34 Core Time – Electronic Messaging Certificate

Commissary Massri

I want my objection to the Commissary's presence registered. I have Carth balanced on a knife-edge, and the Commissaries are not exactly well-liked amongst the locals. Her presence is tossing a lit match into a powderkeg.

Captain Bastian Wulfe

(Message Access Requisitioned by Com. A.Seratov 20ᵗʰ Ledas, 2068.42 Core Time)

Blackness.

Jana jerked awake.

She was sat on the floor of the skimmer's hold, her head resting against one of the rows of benches that lined the walls. Her head swam, a persistent, piercing headache throbbing in her temple with every heartbeat.

Words surfaced in her mind as she shook her head to clear it, every clipped syllable sending another stab of pain through her head.

"I trust you to be careful, legionary. Her memories are significantly more valuable to me than you are. Do I make myself clear?"

Jana shook her head again, struggling to sit up, her eyes still fixed on the two figures. There was a metallic clink from behind her as something brought her hands up short. A sick fear beginning to rise in her heart, she stared about, bleary-eyed, trying to take stock of the situation.

Her hands were cuffed behind her, locked around the supporting beams of one of the steel-backed benches that lined the walls of the skimmer. Atesca and Hasan stood in the doorway, Atesca stepping in close as she delivered her orders in a low, commanding voice.

Noticing Jana's movement, Atesca glanced over. For a moment, she caught Jana's gaze, before turning back to the guard once more.

"Am I understood?"

Hasan nodded his head, a look of grim determination on his features.

"Of course, Commissary."

Jana struggled to stand upright as the Inquisitor turned to leave, feet scrabbling on the floor for purchase as she tugged against the bench's supports.

"Hey. Hey!"

Atesca paid her no notice, stepping wordlessly out through the skimmer doors and dropping onto the concrete below. Jana gave an irritated snarl as she gave up, dropping back into a sitting position beside the bench, clattering the cuffs against the bar in a fit of frustration.

She stopped, watching carefully as Hasan walked past her, taking up position in the skimmer's side doorway, his fresh, unused rifle slung over his shoulder. He stood with his back to her, staring fixedly out across the concrete plain of the landing field.

"Hasan?" she ventured, quietly.

She stared up at his back hopefully, but the skimmer remained shrouded in the same oppressive silence.

"Hasan. Come on, you know me."

The guard remained motionless, avoiding her gaze as he stared out across the empty landing bay. His grip shifted on the butt of his rifle for a moment, but he gave no sign that he had even heard Jana's voice.

"Just talk to me. Please."

Hasan turned his head, throwing a quick glance over his shoulder at Jana. As he met her eye, he silently shook his head, before turning away once more.

"Where's she gone, Hasan? What does she want?" Jana could feel a note of fear creeping into her voice, as much as she tried to suppress it.

"I don't fucking know, alright? You think she'd tell me? I don't know!"

Despite her own panic, Jana could hear a faint tremor of fear in the young guard's voice. It was not comforting.

"Look, just let me go." she pleaded, slowly. "You can come too. Don't do this."

"Do you know what the penalty is for disobeying an inquisitor?" Hasan said quietly, his back still to Jana.

"No, I don't. Hasan, please…"

"I don't know either. I don't want this. I didn't want to be involved. I just want to go home." He turned round, meeting Jana's pleading gaze with a sorrowful shake of his head. "I'm sorry Jana. I really am."

"Hasan you son of a bitch, I've known you for six years! You can't let them do this to me! Please!" she lashed out with a kick from her prone position, the cuffs bringing her up short as Hasan took a step backwards, out of her reach.

"Coward." she spat the words. "They're going to fucking kill me and you're just going to watch?!"

Hasan looked back once, the fear and distress plain in his expression as he walked away, taking position at the far end of the room, beside the skimmer's open doors.

Jana let out a noise somewhere between a sob and a snarl, her terror and frustration finally breaking to the surface.

She twisted her head around, trying to get a good look at the cuffs, raising her hands to do so. Single locking. Looked like steel. Titanium, maybe. If she could get something into the lock it was possible she could just crack them…

The screwdriver.

She paused, rolling her shoulders thoughtfully as she felt its weight shifting in her inside pocket.

Out of the corner of her eye she saw Hasan straighten up, squinting off into the darkness as he unshouldered his rifle. A voice called from outside, muffled by the hull of the skimmer, and Hasan stepped out, shouting something in response.

Without a moment's hesitation she rolled herself onto her side, reaching her arms around as far as the cuffs would allow to try and reach the pocket. With a muffled curse she struggled upright again, this time craning her neck down, trying to catch the elusive tool in her teeth. A nervous sweat had begun to set in, the horrible feeling of helplessness still sitting in a deep knot in her stomach.

She froze as she heard an unfamiliar sound against the skimmers hull. A faint scrape of metal-on-metal, followed by a faint electrical whirring. She glanced up quickly, terrified that Atesca had returned, but the skimmer remained empty. She fell silent, frozen, willing her beating heart to be still as she listened intently. Snippets of conversation carried on the air, muffled by the thick steel plating that covered the aircraft.

She shuffled upright, straining her ears for the distant voices that drifted by on the cusp of hearing.

A pair of heavy footfalls hit the ground behind her.

She spun around as best she could, drawing back from the noise with a frightened whimper.

Kristof grinned at her, raising a finger to his lips.

The skimmer was silent for a moment, as Jana stared silently at Kristof, her lips moving soundlessly as she forced herself to stay quiet. The man had his head cocked, listening intently to the faint voices coming from outside.

Jana jumped again as something slammed into the outer hull, hard, the dull clang reverberating around the skimmer's bare interior.

Kristof winced.

"Sorry about this." he said with a grimace.

"You… What…" Jana spluttered, managing to somehow be incandescent with rage and crying with relief at the same time, the surge of emotions rendering her almost speechless as she stared up at Kristof.

"Who *are* you people?" she blurted.

Kristof hesitated for a moment, then stood up, raising a hand to rap it sharply against the side of the skimmer.

"We're a problem." he muttered.

Jana heard another set of footfalls as a figure dropped through the emergency access hatch in the ceiling. Nadir stumbled slightly as he landed, his grip shifting on the armful of equipment he held as he struggled to keep it balanced.

Jana looked back quickly as Kristof moved away, stepping towards the open skimmer doors.

"Hey!" she hissed, stamping a foot on the floor. "Don't just fucking…" she slumped back against the seat with a resigned sigh as Kristof disappeared through the doorway.

"Don't worry, he gets like this sometimes." said Nadir as he knelt beside her. "He's all business right now."

Jana's eyes had wandered to the tool Nadir held in one hand. She glanced up at him suspiciously.

"What's that?"

"Laser cutter, I hope. That's what they told me when I bought it, anyway."

Jana's eyes widened slightly, despite herself. "No." she stated flatly, shuffling around as best she could to get her hands out of the man's reach. "No, no, no. I've seen those things working. You'll take my bloody hand off."

The man sighed theatrically, rolling his eyes a little. "Things would be so much easier if everyone just assumed I knew what I was doing." He glanced down at the tool for a moment, giving one of the dials a slight adjustment, before looking up and shrugging at Jana. "Look, do you want to get out or not?"

Jana gave him a hard look for a moment.

"Fine."

"Lovely." the word dripped sarcasm. "If you could just lean forward a bit for me, so I can get at your hands?"

Jana complied, struggling into a more upright position. She felt Nadir take hold of the cuffs.

"Why did you…" She gasped as a searing pain flashed through her wrist, the skimmer's hold briefly lit up with a flash of dazzling blue light. She felt the metal break apart as her hands suddenly became free. She scrambled around to face Nadir, clutching at the angry red mark on her right forearm.

"See? Flawless." Nadir said, his ever-present smile creasing with worry as he drew back from Jana's furious glare.

"That really fucking hurt." said Jana breathlessly, eyes darting around the skimmer's interior. She began to pull herself to her feet.

"Do you want the other side off?" Nadir said, pointing at the second half of the cuffs that still hung forlornly around her left wrist. "You can keep it on if you want. It's a bold fashion statement…"

"Do it." Jana said. She held out her other wrist and turned her head away, screwing her eyes tightly shut.

Nadir took hold of her hand. "Don't worry, I've got the hang of it now."

There was a pause.

"Probably."

There was another flash of light, followed by a metallic tinkle as the ruined cuffs fell to the floor.

Jana sighed with relief, scrambling to her feet, clenching and unclenching her fists in an attempt to relieve the stiffness in her joints. She glanced at Nadir, crouching to retrieve her cap from the floor beside where she had been sitting.

"Why did you come back?"

The man shrugged, busily packing the cutter back into the small leather bag he carried over his shoulder.

"Depends who you ask."

They both looked up as Kristof stepped through the doorway, the larger man Jana had seen earlier close behind.

"We'd better get in the air. Are you ok to fly, Jana?"

Jana nodded quickly. "Yeah."

"Then go. We'll just get away from here as quietly as we can, and we'll just have to pray they don't notice we're gone until it's too late."

Jana scrambled into the cockpit, her heart still pounding. Her hands skimmed over the controls almost without thinking, and her heart rose slightly as she heard the familiar deep roar of the engines as they fired up. She was in control again. Free. If the inquisitor tried to catch her again at least she could just crash the fucking thing…

She paused. They wouldn't try to catch her. Not anymore. Jana wasn't too clear on the specifics, but she knew that bad things happened to those who ran from the law, especially inquisitors. Bad things of the permanent sort. But what choice did she have?

Bright orange light flooded the cockpit as Jana lifted the Siren into the air. The sky had turned a vivid crimson as the sun dipped slowly below the horizon, the occasional cloud scudding low through the atmosphere. As the light faded, trails of light began to blaze across the desert as hundreds of skimmers turned on their visibility systems.

"South-17, Jana!" came Kristof's voice from the hold behind her. "There's someone we need to pick up."

"South…" Jana stopped, one hand scrambling for her mic and flicking the switch to internal broadcast.

"Were you fucks following me?" she said, hearing her voice echoing, amplified in the room behind her over the roar of the engines.

"Seems to me like you were lucky we were." came the reply.

Jana struggled to think of a response.

Chapter 5

"The Carth revolt was the first real test of the freshly formed Ashkan Union, a conflict that boiled for almost four years before its eventual conclusion with the death of the revolt's leader, the so-called "Butcher" of Carth. Interestingly, the revolt itself served mainly to strengthen the Union's hold on the newly-acquired systems, primarily due to the callous and increasingly vicious tactics employed by the revolutionaries over the course of the conflict. At risk of throwing more praise to a man already drowning in goodwill, Captain Bastian Wulfe deserves every bit of recognition he has received for his valiant efforts at containing that conflict and preventing the tendrils of insurrection from creeping outwards into the Union at large."

-   Sari Veth, "The War for the White City", 2084.72.

Jana dropped down from the skimmer, pulling her coat tighter about her as the cold bit deep. Nights were cold on Verkat, where the atmosphere wasn't yet thick enough to store heat for long periods of time.

Due to the late hour and the cold, Platform South-17 was a little emptier than before. Two men in black uniforms hurried past, dragging a heavy-looking crate between them. A carrier roared overhead, settling further along the platform as more uniformed porters hurried towards it. One man stood atop a pile of grey crates, stamped with the seal of the Union, his voice carrying on the wind as he called down to the workers assembled below.

She looked around as Kristof dropped down behind her.

"Alright, let's go." he muttered, casting his gaze across the bleak surface of the station.

As he strode off along the platform Jana hurried after him, dodging between the figures that crossed her path on errands of their own.

"What am I looking for?" she muttered, catching up with Kristof and falling in beside him.

"Who, not what. She'll find us, you just focus on looking inconspicuous."

"Yeah, but what do they look like? Just in case I see them."

Kristof grinned. "If you see her, you'll know. She tends to look a little out of place in these parts of town."

Jana nodded slowly, a faint suspicion beginning to form in the back of her mind.

"Hey, Kristof!"

Jana spun around, temporarily blinded as she stared into the headlights of one of the grounded skimmers. She stared into the crowds, searching for the source of the voice.

Her suspicions were confirmed as a familiar figure stepped from the crowd.

The girl who had approached Jana looked different now. Less withdrawn. The shyness had vanished, and there was an alertness to her now, an energy to her movements that seemed to give a twinkle to her eye and a spring to her step.

Kristof grinned as he spotted her. "Hey Cass." he said as she approached, ruffling her hair playfully.

"Did you get them?" he added, a momentary look of concern flashing across his features.

"I got 'em" She patted a small bag she carried over her shoulder. She stopped, noticing Jana for the first time.

Jana shook her head disbelievingly, throwing a glance at Kristof.

"You son of a bitch."

Cass frowned, throwing Jana a mock scowl. "Hey, I'll have you know that *that* was completely my idea."

Kristof shrugged. "It was."

Cass glanced around the crowded landing platform, stepping aside as a trolley full of bags rumbled past.

"Shall we get to it? The shuttle leaves in a couple of hours. And *you*..." she glanced at Jana "...probably shouldn't be standing around in the open in the first place, now that I think about it."

As they walked back along the platform towards the Siren, Cass chattered continuously with Kristof. Jana, however, barely heard a word. She was staring at the horizon where, far in the distance, the lights of Verkat filled the sky with a ruddy orange glow. Her house was out there. Her home. What little family she still had.

She looked around, watching as Kristof reached down from the skimmer's side door, pulling Cass up into the skimmer's hold. He met her eye.

"Want a hand?"

She nodded, reaching out. She gave Verkat a final look as Kristof pulled her on board.

Cass smiled at the group.

"Hi everyone. Had a little trouble, did we?"

"You could say that." said Nadir. Jana could feel his eyes on her, even though her back was to him.

"I've got your idents for you. Should get you on the shuttle to Ashka, but we'll have to get new ones for the way back."

Cass pulled a stack of thin red booklets out of her bag.

"We're not all related again this time, are we?" rumbled the man in the greatcoat from the rear of the group.

Nadir grinned. "I don't know, I quite enjoyed having a big brother for a week."

"Don't worry about it," said Cass, handing the booklets around the group. "No-one's related to anyone this time, I made sure of it." She narrowed her eyes at Kristof. "Especially after you gave me such a hard time about the last batch."

Kristof glanced at Nadir. "Well, nice to have some good news for a change." He opened his ident, and his eyes narrowed as he skimmed the text inside.

"Johan Strohm. That's a name I can live with." he muttered, smiling to himself.

Cass smiled as she handed Jana a booklet. "Congratulations, by the way."

Jana flicked the ident open, skimming the lines of text and the silvery code stamps beside them.

"Thanks, I guess. What for?"

"On your marriage." Cass winked at Kristof.

"Ah." he said, opening his booklet again and peering inside. He glanced at Jana's.

"How romantic." he added, drily.

Jana watched the group sullenly. She was confused, she was scared, these people were taking this *far* too lightly…

"I think you owe me an explanation." she muttered, staring at the group with all the defiance she could muster.

Kristof paused, glancing over his shoulder at the others briefly, before looking back to Jana. He smiled disarmingly, in that annoying way he seemed to have.

"I suppose we do owe you that. What do you want to know?"

"Why me? Why now? Why is the most famous inquisitor in the fucking universe after you?" she paused, trying to stem the flood of questions, and failing. "Who *are* you people?!"

Kristof paused, glancing up at the ceiling and pursing his lips in an overly theatrical display of thought.

"Well, we…"

Another voice sounded, low and gravelly, lent a metallic echo by the confines of the skimmer.

"Kristof, let me explain."

Both Kristof and Jana turned as the man in the faded greatcoat stepped forwards, tucking one of the booklets into his pocket as he did so.

"You sure?" Kristof said, a faint look of surprise flashing across his features.

"Someone has to talk straight around here." the man muttered, before turning to Jana.

"I don't think we've been introduced." he said, his voice deep, his tone level but not unfriendly. He reached out with his hand, extending it towards Jana.

"Wulfe. Pleasure."

Jana felt herself taking a step back.

"No." she said muttered, her voice echoing her disbelief. "You are lying to me."

"I was?"

"Bastian Wulfe? *Captain* Bastian Wulfe? Of Carth? Hero of… There's a street named after you in the…" Jana paused, trying to collect her thoughts.

"I don't believe you." she stated, finally.

Wulfe shrugged.

"Suit yourself."

"And *you*!" Jana spun about, pointing a shaking finger at Kristof, who gave her an apologetic wave. "I remember you. Its not *just* Kristof, is it? It was…" she waved a hand vaguely, mentally begging the childhood memories to return. "Sergeant… Legionary… Kristof… or something. I remember you from the stories. You worked for *him*!"

She shook her head. "You son of a bitch." she muttered again, glaring at him.

Nadir spoke from behind her.

"If I could get a comment in…"

Jana spun around.

"And who are you two then? Councillor Kelreen? One of the bloody Scribes? Any more war heroes want to make themselves known?!"

Nadir grinned in response to her accusations.

"I'm just me. Boring, I know. And her?" he gestured to Cass. "She's boring too. Trust me, you'll find that out sooner or later."

Cass punched him in the arm.

Jana sat down on one of the benches, sinking her head into her hands.

"Who *are* you people? What are you doing here?"

Kristof shrugged. "Working. Trying not to starve to death, I guess."

"What the fuck does 'working' mean?"

"Doing jobs."

"Illegal ones?"

"Not always."

"That's not a no."

"No, it isn't."

Jana heard a metallic scrape as Kristof sank into one of the chairs opposite her, swinging his booted feet up onto the remaining one. As he met her gaze he shrugged, a small smile still playing about his features.

"Did that answer your questions?"

Jana fixed him with a glare. "Not even close." she growled, her confusion and fear now slowly turning to a simmering anger, despite her tiredness. "And don't think I've forgiven you for mixing me up in all this in the first place. I *liked* that job."

Kristof looked up, seemingly genuinely surprised.

"You did?!"

Jana paused. "Well maybe *like* is a strong word but…"

"I knew it." Kristof grinned. "Now you have a second chance to do something new with your life."

He seemed to think for a moment, staring vacantly at the table beside him. When he continued his voice bore a much more sombre tone. "For what it's worth, I am sorry. Didn't mean for anyone to get caught up in… well… *that*."

Nadir spoke up again.

"Maybe we could have this conversation later? I'm sure these two are just *fascinating* but I would really rather leave before that Inquisitor finds us again."

Chapter 6

"So what do you think of her, if you don't mind me asking, Captain? I've never met an inquisitor before." the young soldier beside him asked quietly.

"Better not let her hear you call her that." Captain Wulfe muttered, stirring the contents of his mug with a thoughtful expression. "I don't know. They could have brought us anything on that ship, and they sent us fifty men and a... and a killer."

"Are you still gonna be in charge, Captain?"

"You're asking a lot of questions, Kristof. Try to work on that."

In its 135th year, the Ashkan Union now encompassed all twelve of the habitable worlds in the triad solar systems. It had been generations since the collapse of the Varian hegemony, and the Union expanded rapidly over the war-torn remnants of their brutal rule. Some of the isloated peoples of the Twelve came easily back into the fold, seduced with promises of wealth, technology or stability, whilst those most cruelly treated by the previous regime had descended into near barbarism, and were often coerced through military force.

The nature of space lent itself to dominion. The Ashkans maintained their grip on the Twelve through three primary means: The military might of the Ashkan Legions, The intellectual power of the Commissary, and the logistical might provided to them by the two vast interplanetary transports that had traversed the depths of space between the worlds of the Twelve for almost a century.

She used to watch them when she was a girl. An indistinct shape, hanging high in the sky, the *Pioneer* and the *Imperious* would pause in their travel, falling down into low orbit around the planet. Shuttles would be ejected from the main ship, making their way towards critical points on the surface, before returning to the main ship with a new clutch of hopeful travellers. They were vast. Unimaginably so, really. They were like floating cities, eternally forging a path between the triad's systems.

As a young child Jana had been awestruck, staring open-mouthed as the sky filled with ships, like flocks of birds as they spread out across the planet.

Current Jana folded her arms defensively, watching as the ships flocked back to their nest: the indistinct shape of the *Pioneer* hanging low on the horizon. She swallowed nervously, glancing up at the crowds that surrounded her.

"What do I do?" she asked, in hushed tones.

"Look scared, nervous and a little bit excited, like its your first time in a shuttle." Kristof glanced down at her briefly, treating her to a brief smile before straightening up to peer over the heads of the crowd.

"I'm not an actor, Kristof. What if they..."

"You're doing a marvellous job already." the soldier murmured. "Just keep it up."

"Thanks." Jana replied acridly, swallowing her nerves for a moment. "And the skimmer?"

"Trust Nadir, he knows who to pay to get it on-board." Kristof replied, taking a look around before glancing down at Jana. "I'm going to split off a little. Relax, you'll be fine!" he said, before vanishing into the masses.

Nadir and Cass had disappeared into the crowds a while back, but Wulfe had stayed with them, following closely. Without even looking, Jana knew he was behind them; feeling the heavy tread of his booted feet through the stonework or hearing the occasional muffled grunt as he adjusted the load of the heavy equipment bag he carried over his shoulder. She glanced back briefly, and treated him to a quick smile. He had become, if anything, more subdued as they began to approach the shuttle. His eyes were constantly in motion, flickering across the crowds. His posture had become hunched, defensive, the collar of the legionary greatcoat he wore turned up against the cold.

"Do you do this a lot?" she asked as his gaze finally met hers.

Wulfe sighed.

"Too often." he looked up and nodded over the heads of the crowds around them. "We're moving."

Jana stepped forwards as the crowd around them shuffled into motion, forcing herself to be calm as she stepped towards the shuttle's main doors. The crowd was dense, packing in closer and closer as they pressed towards the entrance to the small shuttle.

Suddenly an arm extended in front of her, wearing the greyish armoured gauntlets of the Legions. She glanced nervously up at the figure who had appeared out of the crowds beside her, a thousand excuses already beginning to form in her mind...

"Wait here, please." the legionary commanded, tersely.

Jana pushed her hands into her pockets to stop them from shaking, and glanced past the soldier. The crowds thinned beyond the barrier, with individuals being moved for inspection.

"Station one, on the right." said the legionary, stepping aside.

 Her heart caught in her throat. She stepped towards the registrars, holding out the small leather booklet Cass had given her like a shield.

This isn't going to work.

The registrar smiled disinterestedly at her, throwing a short glance at the ident. Jana flashed a carefree smile in return, hoping desperately that it didn't look *too* much like the manic grin it felt like.

I'm going to die.

She threw a sidelong glance at the legionaries that flanked the station. Despite the bitter wind, she felt herself beginning to sweat.

I am going to die.

The registrar looked up, handing the booklet back to her.

Jana took it from him, resisting the urge to snatch the booklet and run with an iron will. She stepped aside and walked into the shuttle, staring fixedly ahead of her, expecting at any moment for a cry of alarm or for a heavy hand to fall on her shoulder.

A hand fell on her shoulder.

"Told you we'd be fine." Kristof grinned.

Jana gave him a cold look. She took a deep breath to steady herself, glancing over her shoulder at the gate, then up at the vast spacecraft that loomed above them.

"Do we wait for the others?" she asked, glancing over her shoulder at the teeming crowds beyond the gate.

"We'll find somewhere to hunker down, I reckon. Wulfe usually has some issues with his uniform. Legionaries always seem to want to talk to him."

"Wouldn't it be easier to take it off?"

"Do you want to tell him that?"

"I guess not."

They stepped aboard the shuttle together, Jana following Kristof almost blindly through the crowds that now packed the narrow corridors of the craft.

"Was it true what you told me back there? About him being… *him?*" she muttered, falling in beside him again as they made their way deeper into the ship. Kristof clicked his tongue almost reproachfully, glancing up at one of the garishly lit overhead signs for a moment as he pondered an intersection.

"Will me saying yes make much of a difference to what you believe?"

"Probably not." Jana muttered as she was swept off down one of the corridors.

"Tell you what, think about it like this: I'm a good liar. If I was going to lie to you, don't you think I'd have picked a better lie?"

Jana shrugged. She couldn't deny that that made at least *some* kind of sense.

Kristof turned to one of the doors beside them, tapping at the operation panel with one hand as he squinted in through the misted glass of the window.

"We're still having that talk, you know?" she added.

With a sibilant hiss of inrushing air, the door cracked open.

"I can't wait." Kristof responded drily.

Chapter 7

Post Contact Report - 19th Ledas, 2067.34 Core Time

Rioting at the South Harbour Emergency Distribution Checkpoint. Elements of 11th Legion headed by Capt. Wulfe dispatched to assist local forces in defence of civilian assets. Upon arrival, shots were fired from within the crowd, injuring A.Tars, T.Morikov and V.Urva. The riot had clearly been instigated as a trap for the reinforcing troops.

Attacking forces were eventually driven back and riot suppressed.

Report compiled: Sergeant Kristof Richter

The Union could simply not exist without the *Pioneer* and *Imperious*. The twin ships were the lifeblood of the collective, allowing for transit and transport between the disparate worlds of The Twelve. They ran in constant circuits, travelling from one world to the next on a timeframe so closely choreographed that it was said only the Ashkan Council itself had any true influence over it. Due to this cycle, any Union citizen travelling this way was likely in it for the long haul.

A journey from Valmeer to Ashka took 9 hours. A return trip took four months.

Jana spent most of this time asleep. When she wasn't asleep, she worried. Nothing added up, nothing made sense.

And she didn't buy this "Wolf of Carth" thing for a second.

It didn't seem real. It couldn't be real. The Wolf of Carth was a hero. He was one of the most famous men in Union history. He wasn't… that.

The doors of the shuttle opened, and the masses within poured forth onto the streets of Ashka, the heart of the Union. Jana barely had time to think as the herd swept her with it, and before she knew it she had set foot on the soil of another planet.

Jana stumbled through the busy streets of Ashka, senses swimming in the sights and smells of the city. She hadn't thought there could be this many people in the whole universe. Shopfronts were lit up with digital displays, their contents flickering and changing in a dazzling display of colours. Skimmers and drones roared overhead, filling the air with the constant hum of traffic.

They were all here too, the people of the Union. She'd heard all about them, but she'd never seen them like this. Together. Amongst the crowds of Ashkans she spotted the tall, slender builds of the Varians, the flame-red hair of the Celthari. She heard snippets of familiar conversation as two Bolvar strode past, arguing intensely about the price of a coat.

The size of the city was staggering, like someone had taken the Union spire from Verkat and multiplied it a hundredfold. When Jana was small, she and the other Envoy kids had played in the ravines and gullies that tore up the landscape outside of Verkat. This city made her feel like a child again, the walls of stone and glass rising for thousands upon thousands of meters above her, the soft morning sunlight filtering down through the clouds.

She staggered, buffeted by the crowds like a leaf on the wind, struggling to keep the heavy equipment bag slung over her shoulder. The damn thing was heavier than it looked, and it looked bloody heavy. Offering to help Wulfe carry it had been a split-second decision that she was now beginning to regret.

With a final heave she managed to tug the bag back into position just as she caught up to where the others had stopped. Jana had begun to discover what a wonderful beacon Wulfe made, his powerful form meaning he always stood at least a foot above the crowds around him. As she darted between two other pedestrians, the sound of Kristof's voice caught her ears.

"Are you sure you know where you're going, Cass?"

"Kristof, the only mistake I've ever made is deciding to lug you around with me." The young girl glanced around for a moment, before pushing her slate into Jana's hands. "Hold this a sec."

Jana fumbled with the bag and slate for a moment, feeling the rough strap of the satchel slip off her shoulder. She lunged to catch it, and came up short as she almost stumbled into the satchel as it hung from Kristof's hand just a few feet off the ground. He winked as she straightened up sheepishly.

"You focus on keeping hold of the Slate." he said. "She'll have the skin off my back if I let you drop it."

The soldier grimaced as he shouldered the satchel. "This thing is heavier than it looks, isn't it?"

Jana nodded earnestly. "It is. What do you keep in it?"

"Well, most things…" Kristof paused, narrowing his eyes. Jana faltered for a second, before she realised that he was looking past her. She turned to see Cass scrambling up the base of the statue, traversing the smooth stone with surprising athleticism.

"…Is she supposed to be doing that?" she heard Kristof murmur.

"Are you going to stop her?" Wulfe remarked, also having turned.

"No. Are you?"

Wulfe shook his head.

Kristof shrugged. "That settles that then."

They watched together as the young girl stared out across the heads of the crowd, her brow furrowing in thought. She pursed her lips for a moment and, clearly having come to a decision, leapt from the statue's raised plinth, disappearing into the crowds below once more.

"Looks like someone's in her element." Jana said with a smile.

Kristof nodded silently, the same smile playing about his lips.

"Careful there!"

Jana felt a tug at the collar of her jacket, causing her to stagger backwards. She spun around to see that a rift had opened in the crowds where she had been standing, as people drew back from the hulking trio that trudged down the street towards them.

"Wouldn't want to get trodden on on your first day on the job, would you?" said Kristof with a smile.

The figures were huge, towering over the crowds they strode through, standing over seven foot tall. Humanoid in shape, the figures were covered head to foot in thick metallic plates. The heavy thudding of their footsteps was accompanied by a whining of servos as the powered frames worked to support the weight of the armour bolted to them.

"Fantastic, aren't they?"

Jana glanced sideways at Nadir, who was staring intently at the colossal figures as they passed by.

"Centurion suits. Highest of the high-tech. Those things could lift a skimmer in one hand." he muttered, eyes alight. "Watertight. Airtight. They can regulate their internal temperature, too, to operate in hostile environments. Bulletproof too. Impractical as hell when you get right down to it, but still…" The little man had a wide smile on his face.

"Waste of money." muttered Kristof under his breath, folding his arms as he watched the troops pass.

Nadir stayed silent, chewing absently on his lower lip as he stared, hungrily almost, at the passing soldiers.

"You done?" said Wulfe as he walked by. Nadir shrugged turning to follow.

"You know, I almost joined the legions to pilot one of those." he said to Jana, staring over his shoulder at the retreating figures. "They get all the nice toys."

"Why didn't you?" said Jana.

"Too Varian." Nadir grimaced. "Back then we weren't allowed in the Legions, at least not in significant roles. You'd almost think our council representatives being backstabbing scum reflected badly on the rest of us! Anyway," he paused, and his usual grin returned. "You have to be built like a gorilla to be able to support one. I never had that kind of build. ...Wulfe could do it, I reckon."

Wulfe half turned, fixing the man with a long, hard stare.

"Watch it." he muttered.

Nadir grinned.

The buildings were set close and tall here, only a thin sliver of sunlight breaking through the gap between the rooftops and piercing the gloom of the alleys below. The walls of the houses were plastered with graffiti and grime, and the air was warm and stagnant, not a breath of wind disturbing it in this twisting labyrinth. The crowds had faded, although the hum of the city still surrounded them.

The Waterfront, she'd heard the others call it. Well, it had been a waterfront once, but the city of Ashka had sprawled so far these days that you could travel for hours and not hit the sea. The area wasn't entirely dry, however. The streets of the Waterfront were crisscrossed with a thousand tiny canals that threaded their way around, through and below the city blocks that towered overhead. Jana wasn't used to seeing this much water. It was beginning to grow on her.

She stopped next to Cass, glancing up at the strip of sky far above them. She was used to being able to see the sky most of the time, and being this isolated made her uncomfortable. At home, if you weren't in sunlight, you were usually freezing. She'd decided that tall buildings *really* weren't her thing.

"Where are we now?" muttered Wulfe, his voice strained with frustration. He turned to Kristof as the man stepped up beside him. "And where are we going, come to that?"

Kristof looked around, eyes narrowing as he squinted down the length of the alley. He shrugged.

"Should be here."

"Well it's not." Wulfe growled.

"I noticed." Kristof retorted drily, still glancing around, clearly trying to get his bearings in the twisting maze of streets and alleys.

"Let's try the end of the street." he muttered, seemingly to himself. He glanced at Nadir.

"You can wait here, we'll give you a shout if we find it."

"Best plan you've had all day." said Nadir, ambling over to the side of the alley and seating himself precariously on a small outcropping with a contented sigh. He looked up at Kristof and Wulfe, leaning back and placing his feet on an old discarded waste container.

"Well, off you go then!" he said to the other two men, with a sarcastic snap of his fingers. "You've got work to do."

The two soldiers exchanged a glance, before turning away and walking down the alley.

Jana, already exhausted from the bustle of the city, leant against the wall across from Nadir, crossing her arms as she stared after Kristof and Wulfe. She still wasn't sure if she believed anything about them, yet. They didn't look like she'd imagined them. Wulfe was imposing, but…

She shook her head. It might help if she thought of them as people instead of characters from a story.

"You don't need to watch them, I'm sure they can take care of themselves." said Cass.

"What?" said Jana, drawn abruptly from her musings.

"I said you don't need to…" Cass paused, and shook her head. "Nevermind. What were you thinking about?"

"I wasn't…"

"You were staring, Jana."

"Just… its strange. Everything."

"What, them?" Cass said, giving Jana a quizzical look.

"You don't think it's strange? Not at all?" Jana replied, perplexed by the girl's lack of interest. "They're famous! I used to have a poster of *him* on my wall!" she added, pointing towards Wulfe's retreating form.

"I could ask him to sign something for you, if you want." said Cass with a smirk. "I'm sure he'd love to hear from a fan."

"He really wouldn't." said Nadir drily, from his seated position against the wall of the alley. "And honestly, Jana? Don't ask. Wulfe won't talk about it, and Kristof will lie about it."

The Varian sat back and closed his eyes, resting his head against the wall as he bathed in the tiny sliver of sunlight that made its way into the narrow alley from above.

"He must have been so young." Jana murmured half to herself, watching as the two soldiers disappeared around the bend in the alley. "He's barely older than me. And Wulfe seems so... withdrawn."

One of the Varian's dark eyes snapped open, focussing on Jana.

"You said you knew the story, didn't you?"

"You don't?"

"I didn't have much time for reading when I was young. And no time for watching or listening. Too busy making poor choices and paying for them." The man smiled ruefully.

"You've not changed much, it seems." said Jana, slightly more acridly than she intended.

"Well..." Nadir hesitated. "No, you're right. It's not bad though. Outdoor work. No uniforms. Anyway... stories, Jana! Tell us all about their scandalous pasts."

Jana frowned, reaching back for those faded memories.

"There was a revolution in a small city called Carth. They were led by a man called... well the stories just called him 'The Butcher of Carth', but he probably had an actual name too. And he fought against Commissary Atesca and Captain Wulfe. They had all kinds of adventures together, stopping his schemes..."

She paused, blushing slightly as she caught Nadir's raised eyebrow out of the corner of her eye.

"Hey, I was ten. I wasn't exactly reading the press reports." she protested.

Nadir grinned at her. She scowled at him, folding her arms defensively.

"Do you want to hear this or not?" she said, the embarrassment lending a sharpness to her words.

"Alright, alright!" Nadir laughed. "Carry on. Ignore me."

"That's really all it was." Jana continued, treating Nadir to a hard look as she did so. "They travelled around together and fought against the Butcher of Carth. The first book was called 'The Wolf, the Hawk and the Butcher', I remember that."

"Which one was Wulfe?"

Jana glared.

The Red Ivy Cafe was a nondescript little coffee shop, nestled at the base of one of the large tower blocks that made up the bulk of the Waterfront. It was a cozy, up-and-coming social spot at the heart of downtown Ashka, according to its owner. According to everybody else, it was a front for information trading.

Kristof pushed the door open slowly, glancing up as a little bell above his head gave off a quick trill. The room was deserted, the only sounds the faint hiss of the coffee machine behind the counter and the low sounds of a radio wafting in from one of the back rooms.

Large windows. whispered a soft voice at the back of Kristof's mind. *Good sightlines of the main approaches. Defensible interior. Solid concrete.*

Kristof shook his head, trying to ignore the voice as he and Wulfe settled into an alcove by the front window. He couldn't ignore it, not really. It was a part of him. It was always there. Observing. *Analysing.*

He shifted uncomfortably on the leather seat-cover...

faux-leather

He shifted uncomfortably on the faux-leather seat-cover, eyes drinking in every detail of the shop's interior as he glanced about curiously. Beneath the thin veneer of normality, he could feel there was something off about the place. It was too clean, too organised, lacking any of the bumps, scrapes and other imperfections of life. It felt like he was sitting in a cheap film set.

One of the two doors behind the counter swung open,revealing a short, blonde-haired woman, each hand holding a pair of battered porcelain mugs.

"Hey you two! I'll be there in a minute, I'm sorry." she said with a broad smile, placing the mugs down on the counter and ducking back through the closing door.

Kristof smiled back, watching carefully as the woman disappeared from view once more.

Investigating the noise of the bell. She wanted a look at you.

"She just..." he began, before Wulfe cut him off.

"...wanted to know what she was dealing with, I know." the soldier rumbled quietly. He paused, catching Kristof's expression. "What, you think you're the only one who pays attention?"

Kristof smiled sheepishly.

The two of them looked up sharply again as the door swung open, this time revealing a short, burly man in his late forties. He hurried over to the table where they sat, a calloused hand rubbing nervously at his unshaven cheek.

"Wiktor Kozlov." he said quietly, leaning over the table as his eyes scanned the street outside through the windows. "I heard there'd be four of you."

Bolvar accent. Trace.

"Five now." said Kristof, trying his best to shut out the voice.

The waiter shrugged. "Makes no odds to me. You get paid the same regardless." He stood up, stroking his beard thoughtfully for a second.

"I suppose you had better come to the back. Are the others on their way?"

"I'll get them." rumbled Wulfe, squeezing out of the small gap between table and wall. "We had a hell of a time finding this place."

Kozlov chuckled wryly. "I would hope so too. I put a lot of effort into making it that way."

He extended a hand as Wulfe passed, giving a broad, toothy grin to the two men. "Before you go, I'd better know who I'm dealing with."

Kristof rose to his feet, taking the man's hand in his own. "Kristof Richter. That's Wulfe."

The broad grin remained fixed on Kozlov's face, but all mirth vanished from the man's eyes.

Ex-military.

"Sure you are." the waiter muttered flatly, releasing Kristof's hand and turning away. He stepped back towards the rear of the cafe, weaving between the tables as he went with a practiced step. As he reached the rear doors, he turned briefly.

"What are you waiting for? Get the others, I've not got all day."

Jana wasn't sure what she had expected. Secret doors, perhaps. Dimly lit, smoke-filled rooms. Henchmen.

She wasn't expecting the obvious, which was a kitchen. A kitchen strewn with papers and charts, stacks of books, dossiers and folders occupying almost every available surface. The floor was bare concrete, as was the ceiling, the exposed piping that ran along it creaking and rattling ominously as the party trooped inside.

It was dimly lit, at least. She was going to count that as a win.

She quietly shuffled some papers aside and leant against the rim of a stained, heat-cracked sink at the back of the room, folding her arms as she settled down to watch the proceedings.

Kozlov grumbled quietly to himself as he sifted through the piles of paper, eventually gathering up an armful and turning back to the group.

"This is a strange one, I'll warn you." he muttered, dropping the stack of paper onto the table in front of him. "Take a look if you want."

Oddly, Cass was the one who went for the papers. The other three continued their conversation.

"So what are we doing and how much are we making?" Nadir said, glancing around the kitchen with a certain air of distaste.

"The deal is 1200¥." Kozlov replied.

"Each?" the Varian replied hopefully.

"You wish. As for what you're doing: There's a laboratory complex. And old one, probably pre-union or close thereabouts. The client wants whatever you can drag out of it: Test data. Prototypes. Documentation. The lot. They want it done quietly and they…"

He was interrupted by a gasp from Cass, who had been poring over the papers on the table in front of them.

"How did you find out about this place? I mean this is…" she looked up, pausing as she leafed through the papers to glance at the others.

Kozlov paused. "I can't tell you that." he said flatly.

"What's wrong, Cass?" Kristof said quietly, turning to the girl from across the table. He could see she was worried

"This is *serious*, Kristof. I think they'd shoot us just for knowing about what's written here. Look!" she leant across the table, shuffling through the papers and thrusting one of them at Kristof.

"You see that? That's a Commission stamp. Inquisition. And this…" the paper shuffled again, and another document was pushed at him. "That's a high-level administrative document. Councillors might get to see these. *Might*. If they ask really, really nicely."

She turned to Kozlov, waving the papers at him.

"Where did you get these?!"

The man folded his arms, glancing past Cass towards the rest of the group.

"How does a young girl know so much about the administration?"

"Just answer her question." said Wulfe, watching the man intently.

Kozlov sighed.

"Those were sent to me. I can't tell you who by, because I don't know."

"Someone you trust?"

"As much as I trust anyone I don't know, yes."

"This isn't right though." Cass continued, seemingly half to herself. "These lines don't match up. Not on any of them. It looks like they've been... reassembled. Salvaged, somehow." She looked up at Kozlov sharply. "These were deleted, weren't they? Someone deleted them, and you dug up whatever splinters you could and stuck them back together. Why?"

Kozlov shrugged, still looking at the young girl in bewilderment at the interrogation he was receiving.

"No good asking me. Like I said, I wasn't the one to do the digging."

Cass opened her mouth, a sharp retort clearly already on the tip of her tongue as Kristof cut in.

"What *are* they, Cass? What did someone go to this much trouble to dig up?"

"These are..." she stopped, and her brow furrowed as she re-read a line on the document. "Construction reports. Orbital scans. They used them for deep-earth mapping, like when they were dealing with the Warrens."

Cass thumbed through the documents, eyes intent on the pictures in front of her. Wulfe reached down, picking up one of the discarded sheets and glancing at it curiously.

"Looks like someone's been busy." he muttered. "There's a whole complex down there, it looks like. Miles of the stuff."

Cass was digging through the paper stack almost frantically now.

"This is..." Her lips moved silently for a moment as she read. "This is dangerous, Kristof. Everything about it. I know I'm not usually the cautious one, but..."

Her words trailed off as she stared up at the others, worry creasing her features.

"What is it?" Jana said, the urgency of Cass' reaction having drawn her back in.

"Look." Cass held the paper up for her to see. The image was a mess, with seemingly hundreds upon hundreds of smaller frames overlaid, one atop the last. He could make out the rough shape of Ashka in the bottom corner

"I don't know what I'm looking at, Cass."

"It's a map. There's an old… thing in the hills outside the city, near the old refineries."

Cass threw a glance across the blank faces of the group, and swiped another one of the frankenstein documents off the table.

"Do you know what this is?" the girl asked insistently, holding it up for the rest of them to see.

Kristof looked at the document. He knew. And he knew Wulfe knew too. He opened his mouth to speak.

"No, what is it?" Jana cut in.

"It's a Commission Order of Silence. Or what's left of it, anyway. What it means is that people have probably died for this. Lots of them. To keep whatever *that* is hidden."

"Well I can't speak for all of you, but that sounds like a good reason to stay away from something." Jana replied.

"Cass is overstating things." Kristof shrugged. "Those things get handed out like free drinks at a fancy party by the Inquisitors."

"Kristof, they built something in the mountains, threw away the key and buried it. You don't think it might be something they don't want found?"

Kozlov spoke up again. "I am prepared to offer another 600¥ on top of the initial fee if that will sway you my way. I've been speaking to some friends on Valmeer, and you seem like a good fit for this. I like working with a professional crew."

"1800¥?" Nadir murmured, hissing through his teeth. "Now this is getting a little harder to turn down."

Kristof nodded quietly in agreement, before glancing back at Cass.

"See? I'm not suggesting we go down there to sate our personal curiosity, Cass. We're getting paid."

Cass glared at him, before shaking her head.

"I don't like it." she muttered again, turning and stalking out of the kitchen. Nadir caught Kristof's eye, shrugged, and turned to follow, following the girl out of the room.

Kristof stayed behind as, one by one, the others filed out of the dingy kitchen. He stood silently for a moment, his eyes focussed on the papers in front of him. He reached out, turning a page carefully, the paper rustling gently in the now-silent room.

"I know what you're doing, Kristof." Wulfe's voice rumbled in the darkness behind him.

Bastard can move quietly when he wants to.

Kristof turned, raising an inquisitive eyebrow at the old soldier.

"I'm doing something? That's news to…"

"'We're not going down there to sate our own personal curiosity', are we?" The soldier shook his head grimly. "I'm not sure I believe it. I think you'd love to find something down there."

Kristof straightened up a little, staring levelly back at Wulfe.

"And why would I want that?"

Wulfe shrugged.

"It would make you right."

He stepped forwards, placing a hand on Kristof's shoulder.

"Let it go. What's done is done. I understand, but don't risk what you have for something that could be. Not again."

"I have no idea what you're talking about." Kristof replied, smiling disarmingly.

Wulfe shook his head and stalked out of the room, muttering a few choice curse words under his breath as the door slammed shut behind him.

Chapter 8

3rd Frejas, 2067.86 Core Time

Casualty Report – Carth Conflict – Combined 12th and PDA, Month 7

Union Casualties: 12 killed, 23 wounded

Civilian Casualties: 16 killed, 44 wounded

Estimated Rebel Casualties: 16 killed, 38 wounded

Confirmed Rebel Casualties: 5 killed

Cpt.Bastian Wulfe Commanding

Jana climbed the stairs of the hangar-column slowly, deep in thought, her ears filled with the sounds of mechanical labour as she toiled up the seemingly endless flights of stairs. Even the sight of a Sparrowhawk Heavy Carrier, its hangar-spanning wings crawling with personnel failed to pull her out of her reverie. Any other day that would have been an event worthy of a diary entry.

She pushed aside the door of hangar 27, and walked back towards where she had left the Siren; huddled in its designated corner of the hangar, in the shadow of the much larger Tetrax V that dominated the central space of the chamber.

As she approached a noise pulled her from her thoughts. The noise of scraping, of metal on metal. She looked up sharply, and with surprise noted that the utility panel under the left wing had been unscrewed and left hanging open. She shook her head with exasperation as she made out the figure of Nadir, lying across the skimmer's leftmost floor runner, his hands busily working at the undercarriage of the Siren.

"What are you doing here?! And how did you get here before me?"

"I ran." the Varian's voice rang out from beneath the skimmer's hull. "You mentioned something about them tracking you back there at the Waterfront, and the idea of flying around with a beacon hanging off our backside isn't an appealing one to me. Speaking of which, how do I get into this bloody thing?"

"Three screws on the left." Jana recited from memory, almost automatically. "They're inset so they're hard to spot."

"Ah, I see them. Thanks." The sound of metallic scraping resumed. "What brings you back here? I thought people were staying at the Red Ivy?"

"I thought I might sleep here, if I'm honest. Give you people some space."

"I guarantee you..." There was a muffled grunt from beneath the skimmer. "I guarantee you that Wulfe will have had the same idea. He likes his space, that man."

Silence fell across the two of them like a shroud.

"You could just leave, you know? If you want to." Nadir said quietly.

The phrase that had been echoing through Jana's mind now hung in the air, seeming to swell to fill the entirety of the silent hangar.

Jana squatted down beside the prone man, placing a forearm against the skimmer's battered aluminium plating for balance. She drew a thoughtful breath, listening to the sound of metal scratching on metal for a moment before she replied.

"And do what?"

"I don't know. What would you want to do?"

"Can't say I thought about it much. I thought I'd be stuck on that rock for the rest of my life." Jana said. "I suppose I'd like to see the sights, you know." she added, speaking slowly, thoughtfully, almost to herself. "Varia. Ashka. Cethar... Carth."

"You're welcome." muttered Nadir, through what sounded like gritted teeth. "That's one out of four off the list alrea..."

There was a muffled clank from beneath the skimmer, and a string of sharp, staccato curses in the Varian tongue.

"Everything alright?" Jana said, chuckling quietly to herself.

"...dropped a plate on myself." Nadir muttered. "*Sacra miet,* those things are heavy!"

Jana gripped the aluminium plate, and with some exertion managed to drag it out from beneath the skimmer and lean it against the vehicle's dipped wing tip. She looked around the empty hangar, her gaze sweeping past the garishly-coloured warning barriers and over the city beyond.

The sun had begun to set over Ashka, its rays scattering into a thousand shards of red, auburn and gold as they struck the atmosphere above the city. Arcs of light flashed between the vast hab-columns, the very buildings themselves beginning to glow from within as the day's light began to dim outside.

It was stupid, Jana knew. Every neuron in her brain flared with the correct answer. She had skills, she had talents, and thanks to the ident she was once again anonymous. She could be anything, so why be a fugitive and a thief?

Because it isn't a job. whispered a voice at the back of her mind. *Because it isn't flying the same route twice a day, every day, for seven years at the behest of a group of stuck-up bureaucrats who will never even remember your name.*

Because you're afraid. You're scared out of your mind that they might catch you again.

Because it's the first time in twenty years that you've felt alive.

She hunkered down again quickly, leaning against the Siren's hull.

"So, hypothetically, if I were to stay... what's my part in this?" she almost whispered.

"Say what?" said Nadir, his voice muffled as he lay half concealed by the Skimmer's hull plating.

"What do I do? I don't know how to raid Vaults."

"But you know how to fly this, right?" replied Nadir, poking his head out from under the Skimmer.

Jana nodded wordlessly.

Nadir pursed his lips. "I'd stick with that then. Know your strengths!" He flashed her a quick grin and disappeared back under the skimmer. Jana rolled her eyes, drumming her fingers nervously on the hull of the craft.

"Seriously though," the Varian continued, his voice echoing out from behind the aluminium plating. "It'll be nice to have you along. Usually we have to run away from these things, which works about as well as you'd imagine it would."

There was a scraping sound from behind the plating, and a grunt of exertion from Nadir. Moments later, he pulled himself out from under the skimmer, holding a small cylindrical coil, with a weave of broken wires hanging off it.

"Now either this is the beacon or I've just broken something important."

He grinned, and tossed the coil into the corner of the room.

"Well, only one way to find out. Want to give it a try?"

Despite herself, Jana smiled.

Within seconds the engines of the Siren began to give off a faint hum as they wound themselves into motion. Jana, having completed a quick pre-flight walkaround, clambered back aboard the skimmer, aided by a helping hand from Nadir.

"Everything to your satisfaction?"

"I've seen her in worse states." Jana said, smiling. She saw the Varian's eyes flicker over her shoulder and she turned, following his gaze to where Cass stood in the doorway to the stairwell.

"What the hell are you two playing at?" the girl shouted over the roar of the engines, clutching at her hair as it thrashed and flailed in the rising winds.

"Jana was about to take her first un-monitored flight!" Nadir's voice sounded back. "Fancy tagging along?"

"What kind of question is that?!" the girl grinned.

Jana laughed as she ducked under the skimmer's low doorframe, swinging herself into the cockpit and settling herself behind the steering column.

She felt a hand on her shoulder, and heard the Varian's voice beside her ear.

"Remember, pass on the left, fly high, and make the most of the time we have." he said.

Jana smiled broadly as the Siren roared to life once more.

Contrary to Nadir's worries, the Siren ran like a dream. Or as much like a dream as usual. She had a little trouble adjusting to the crowded sky above Ashka; you couldn't fly too high or too low, you couldn't turn too fast, you could only get so close to buildings... The list was long, but with Nadir whispering instructions into her ear she settled in fast, and almost began to enjoy the leisurely pace of urban flight.

The sun had dipped below the horizon as they turned the skimmer back around to make for home. Nadir stepped back into the hold after a while, leaving Jana and Cass alone in the cockpit, staring down at the city below them.

"I never get tired of seeing it like this." the girl sighed, pressing her forehead against the screen as she strained to get a clearer view of the streets below. "It looks *so* much worse up close, you wouldn't believe it."

Jana smiled, leaning forwards to get a better look. She had to admit, it was... majestic. Even now the streets were crowded with people, a river of colour, light and movement that flowed sluggishly through the spaces between the vast spires that towered over them. As Jana watched, the road they were following reached its end, opening out into a vast square filled with the bright light and constant movement of thousands of people.

She glanced back up, keeping a cautious eye on the skies.

"What's down there?" she asked Cass, not looking back.

Cass raised an eyebrow. "You don't…" she laughed. "Sometimes I forget what kind of backwater planet you're from. You do a good job of hiding it."

"Backwater?!" said Jana, slightly offended.

"Well, compared to where I'm from, anyway. Three people tried to sell me horses while we were there, Jana. One tried to buy me *for* a horse. We were only there a week!"

Jana chuckled. "Alright, I'll give you that. The Bolvar can be a bit stuck in their ways. We're still working on them."

A thought occurred, and she cast a sidelong glance at Cass.

"Where are you from? You don't look like a Varian, and you haven't got the hair to be Celthari…"

A small smirk crept across Cass' face.

"I'll tell you, but if you breathe a word to the others I'll push you out of the Skimmer." She pulled on Jana's sleeve, leaning down over her shoulde so they were at the same eye-level, and pointed out across the city.

"About half a mile that way."

Jana could feel the surprise showing on her face.

"You're from here?"

Cass nodded. "Native Ashkan. Lived here my whole life, until I picked up the others."

"Kristof said they picked you up."

"Well he would say that, wouldn't he?" the girl smirked. "Now pay attention, you're flying an aircraft."

The streets of Ashka were never empty. Jana had noticed that by now. But the wall of sights and sounds that hit her as they coasted out over the square still managed to leave her speechless for a few moments. Even above the hum of the engines the muted roar of thousands of voices that rose up from the square below could still clearly be heard. The square below them was a riot of colours, of flashing lights and roaring fires, the drone of electrical announcements and the excited chatter of the people of the Ashkan Union all blending together into an experience to dazzle the senses.

In front of them, almost buried from sight beneath the teeming crowds, the ground took on a slight gradient, sweeping downwards into a gentle slope across the entire length of the square. Like the dunes on Valmeer, Jana thought, but formed of steel and concrete instead of ice and sand. The familiar banners of the Ashkan Union hung over the crowds, fluttering gently at the slightest breath of the wind. At the far end of the square, three vast archways loomed above the crowds like the maw of some vast beast. It was here that the crowds pressed closest, funnelled inwards by the arches, jostling and pushing for position as they passed through.

And just like that they were past it again, drawn by the flow of traffic back into the now comparatively lifeless side streets of Ashka.

A half-forgotten memory surfaced somewhere in the back of Jana's mind.

"Those are the Warrens?" Jana asked.

She saw Cass lean forwards beside her, craning her neck to see downwards through the slanted windshield.

"Yeah." the girl said. "Well, that's the entrance. Askanzi Square on the surface and Tulharden Square down below. There's five or six of them scattered around the city."

"Can we have a look later?"

"Maybe." Cass pursed her lips. "Well, no, not really. You wouldn't want to. You get some shady types down there, so maybe it'd be better if you took one of the others. I think Nadir had some business down there. I'm really not dressed for brawling with murderers right now."

"Its that bad, really? They let a place like that exist right here in the capital?"

"There's nearly a two million people down there Jana. What are you going to do, force them out?"

"But this?"

"Well..." the girl said, gesturing vaguely. "Its all got messy recently. People started digging themselves basements because it was cheaper than building up. And then they just sort of kept going. So these days you've got a chaotic mess of tunnels that go nowhere and everywhere all at once, where no-one legally owns anything, and any attempt to regulate the place sends the whole thing up in flames."

"You'd think they'd want some regulation if its as bad as it sounds."

Cass shrugged.

"That's what happens when you let the paranoid cheapskates dig their own city. They breed and multiply and you end up with super paranoid-cheapskate hybrids. Who knows, maybe they enjoy the chaos?"

A half-hour later, the skimmer touched back down on the concrete-tiled floor of hangar 27. Jana fumbled with her belt a little, slinging it back over the seat as she clambered back into the Siren's hold. Nadir sat on one of the benches, staring curiously at the contents of the skimmer's toolbox.

"Enjoying the view, Nadir?" Cass said with a smirk, almost skipping up next to the Varian. "I bet you didn't even look up once."

"After looking at this kit I'm not surprised this thing is in such a state." Nadir replied, picking up one of the screwdrivers and holding it up with a critical eye. "How do you even turn a screw with this? The corners have all rubbed off!"

"A lot of time, effort and frustration, that's how." Jana said, plucking the tool out of his hand and dropping it back in the case.

"So, Nadir?" Cass said. "Jana wanted to take a look at the warrens. Are you still heading down there?"

The Varian looked up, still smiling, but with a faint flash of suspicion in his dark eyes.

"You do?" he said, raising a cynical eyebrow. "Why is that?"

"I've heard a lot about them." Jana shrugged, still a little taken aback that Cass had broached the subject so quickly. "And you can't build downwards in my part of Verkat. Its sand all the way down."

"There are a lot of things you could see up here, and with a lot less danger." Nadir glanced down at the girl that stood between them. "And I'm sure our walking tourist brochure here could give you some pointers if she wanted to."

Cass scowled at him. "We've got plenty of time for that after the... *thing*. Come on Nadir, when did you get boring?!"

The varian sighed theatrically. "*Mone discar.*" he murmured under his breath. "Hunted by the most famous inquisitor of the Ashkan Union and here I am getting pushed around by a... how old are you now? Nineteen?"

He met Cass' glare for a second, before grinning and turning to Jana.

"Listen" he said, his tone a little more serious. "You're here, so I know you're bad at staying out of trouble. Do you know what the Varian Syndicate is?"

Jana shook her head silently.

"Underbelly of the Varian Free Trade Conglomerate." Nadir said, waving a hand dismissively. "Anyway, they are not nice people, in a not nice place, and I am going there to buy something especially nasty off them. You can have a look around, but try not to stray too far. Its easy to get lost down there. You got that, *telva?*"

Jana nodded.

"Sure, I can do that."

Nadir laughed.

"Hah! Look at that, Cass, she's a good liar too! Look at all these useful skills we're uncovering." he grinned, and treated Jana to a wink as he hopped out of the skimmer and made his way across the hangar.

"Meet you downstairs in two hours!" he called back.

Whilst Ashkanzi Square and the entrance to The Warrens below looked imposing from above, nothing had prepared Jana for the sheer scale of the structures from the ground. Ashkanzi square was vast, near-featureless plain of smooth concrete that gently inclined towards the towering metal gates that formed the entrance to the warrens below. Every inch of the square, however, was packed with life. Rugged market stalls had been constructed in loose rows or circles, interspersed with more refined, commercial stands and displays. Rows upon rows of banners and pendants fluttered in the breeze, all bearing the interlinked rings of the Ashkan Union.

The gates themselves were a claustrophobic press, as thousands upon thousands of Ashkan citizens flowed back and forth between the city above and the city below. Despite that, however, Jana was surprised at how spacious the Warrens seemed at first. Tulharden Square, the subterranean counterpart to Ashkanzi Square, was still almost of equal size despite the dozen or so vast stone columns that lined the square breaking up the view.

As they descended, however, Jana found the passageways and tunnels becoming narrower and more winding. The slick corporate storefronts and polished outlets of the upper Warrens gave way to a claustrophobic tangle of concrete maintenance passages, interspersed with larger chambers that were still just as packed with people as the upper levels. The whole place reminded Jana of a sewer. Or a tomb.

Nadir, however, looked entirely at peace. He navigated the narrow passages at a casual pace, a confidence to his gait that Jana felt unable to match.

He paused, catching Jana's gaze as he turned to glance back.

"Nervous?" he said, with a smile that was only slightly mocking.

"Sure. A bit." Jana replied a little defensively. "How far underground are we?"

"Ah." the Varian chuckled softly to himself. "Claustrophobia hadn't occurred to me as a problem. Try not to think about it."

"Alright. I'll see what I can do." Jana nodded, trying to keep her gaze down so as not to look at the ceiling above her. "So what are you looking for down here?"

The Varian hesitated for a moment, glancing about the deserted corridors quickly before responding.

"A neural relay. Its a little something we use for, well, for breaking electrical systems." he glanced about again. "Come on, I don't want to be late."

"And why is it a *neural* relay?" Jana asked as they hurried through the narrow passageways.

Nadir grimaced. "They're a Quin design, with all the mystical baggage that entails. Digital and Serial relays are for people who know what they're doing, but they take time and... well, did you have pesh on Valmeer?"

"Pesh? No."

"Nasty stuff. Quin again. You'll begin to notice a pattern here." Nadir grinned as he ushered Jana into an open room with a dozen intersecting passageways, before heading slowly towards a door that was inset against the far wall. "They use the stuff to generate hallucinations. Imagine taking some of that and then wiring your brain into a computer. That's a neural relay. Anyway..."

He stopped beside the door.

"Just try to stick to the background once we're in there. I don't know how they'll react to a... a not-Varian in there." he grinned again as he swung the door slowly open. "I'm sorry, there's a word for it in our language."

The room they entered was eerily quiet, a feeling of claustrophobic closeness striking Jana almost as soon as she stepped across the threshold. The air itself was thick with some kind of sweet-smelling mist; cloying, and dense enough to lend the room an almost ghostly atmosphere. The walls and ceiling were covered in drapes of brightly-coloured cloth, in a half-hearted attempt to conceal the bare concrete beneath.

Figures lay sprawled about the room, lying in makeshift beds and chairs, their ragged breathing the only disturbance amidst the still air. Jana took a hesitant step forwards, eyes straying over one of the sprawled figures as she did so. The man was young, almost Jana's age, in fact. His mouth hung open slightly, a thin line of drool making its way slowly out of the corner of his mouth. His face and limbs twitched occasionally, like a child dreaming.

Nadir held out a cautioning hand towards Jana.

"Wait here." he murmured, before stepping forwards a little. "Vishkar?" he called out, his voice shockingly loud in the silent room.

A figure stepped out from the doorway at the rear of the chamber, a tall man, slender almost to the point of being gangly. From the eyes downwards his face was a mess of tattoos and modifications, looking to Jana more like some kind of horrific injury than an artist's work in the darkened room. His skin had an unhealthy pallor to it, what seemed to have once been the smooth olive tones of the Varians leeching away, leaving a strange mottled texture, like a moulting snake. He paused as his gaze fell upon Nadir, and he raised a slender finger to his lips.

"Den ha are marchis?" Nadir said, his voice dropping smoothly into the drawling Varian tongue. *"Aen Nadir."*

The strange Varian, who Jana assumed to be called Vishkar, seemed to consider for a moment before giving Nadir a quick nod. *"Dae vaan."* he murmured, beckoning the Varian into the rear chambers.

Jana backed up to the wall as she listened to the voices drift in from the far room. She felt like she needed her back to something. Her eyes stayed locked on the sleeping figures, as if at any moment they might make a lunge for her.

This whole place made her skin crawl.

It was only minutes later that Nadir re-emerged, though it felt like a century. Jana was all too happy to leave, hurrying behind him as they strode from the choking confines of the drug den to the, by comparison, warm and welcoming streets of the lower Warrens.

"Did you find what you wanted?" she asked, eyeing the cheap cloth sling bag that Nadir now carried over his shoulder.

The Varian nodded. "Got it. Vishkar is a snake, but at least he's a competent one."

"What does he do?"

"He finds things." Nadir paused. "And sells drugs. Mainly drugs, if I'm honest."

Jana looked about. Maybe the den had skewed her perspective, but it was feeling a lot cozier down here now. She heard scraps of music filtering down one of the side corridors as they passed by, accompanied by roaring laughter and the chatter of a dozen voices. It was only just beginning to strike her that some people really lived in a place like this. A whole lot of people, in fact.

"You know, you're really not doing the Varian reputation for being thieves and murderers any favours like this." she joked, giving Nadir a nudge as they walked. "And I thought you were so innocent when we first met!"

The Varian looked back for a moment.

"That's how we get you. And if you think you can find better company than myself then I wish you the best of luck, because you're going to need it." he replied with a wink.

Chapter 9

40th Frejas, 2067.54 Core Time – Electronic Messaging Certificate – Confidential

Preliminary investigations into the 'Butcher' of Carth have yielded results. Current evaluation of witness accounts and combat structure analysis suggest a high standard of analytical skills in a logistical and tactical sense to an almost 1st-class degree. Recommend that further resources be deployed to Carth to ensure stability whilst investigations continue.

Forward as one,

Atesca Seratov, Commissary 1st Class

A few hundred years ago, when the Ashkan Union was really beginning to gather steam, that's when progress had been made. Interplanetary travel. Artificial Intelligences. A whole new realm of exploration and expansion had begun to open up.

But these things were never perfect. As the fledgling Union expanded, it began to envelop the scattered remnants of humanity that lived across the surviving worlds of the Twelve. As the population swelled, the Ashkan's taste for progress began to sour. Why build an automated factory when there were a thousand workers willing to work twelve-hour shifts to cover the deficit? Why invest in administrative AI when a hundred clerks will do the same work for far less investment?

And as with all things, what was once belief became culture, what was culture became tradition, what was tradition became law. Now the Union had begun to stagnate, its lands scattered with reminders of what once could have been.

Kristof Richter stood quietly, gazing thoughtfully down at one such reminder as his eyes roved across the floor plans that lay strewn across the table in front of him.

It should be simple. A quick in-and-out job. Deployment records suggested that there weren't even any guards. The complex was all but abandoned.

Nothing is ever simple.

Jana was a problem. If only because she was another mouth to feed. She wasn't built for this.

Kristof chewed on his lip thoughtfully.

She'll make mistakes. She'll draw heat.

Letting her go would draw heat too. In Ashka? It would be like dropping a gazelle into a lion enclosure. She'd be dead in weeks, or captured in days.

Kristof shook his head. There wasn't a choice. Not really.

There's always a choice.

There was always more to consider. Legion redeployments. Excavation works. Work routines of the local workers. Weather. Season. Even the phase of the god damn moons changed what light they would have to work with...

The door to the kitchen creaked slightly.

Kristof looked up sharply. Kozlov stood in the doorway, framed by the faint light that sifted in from the room beyond. The fixer looked as surprised as he did, taking a moment for his eyes to adjust to the gloom of the ill-lit kitchen.

"I'm sorry, I didn't think anyone would be up."

Kristof shrugged non-committally.

"I couldn't sleep."

"Can I get you something? Coffee?"

"So you actually make coffee in this place?"

"It would be a lousy cover if I didn't, wouldn't it?"

Kristof smiled wearily. "Sure, I'll try some."

"Varian or Corinthian? The Corinthian is a little richer, but the Varian has some pep to it. Its cheaper, too, if that helps."

"Honestly wouldn't know the difference. Corinthian? Whichever is the richer one."

He glanced back down at the table as the fixer began to bustle around the room, the sound of clattering crockery and boiling steam now filling the silence that previously had been so prevalent.

400¥ from the Valmeer Job, plus 275Л from Sihyld, minus 120¥ for Liszter's lot...

"What's this?"

A Varian ฿ is about 1.2¥, so...

"Hey."

Equals... 320¥. Enough for a very cheap shuttle trip.

Kristof looked up.

"Hmm?"

Kozlov had paused on the far side of the table, a pair of mugs hanging from his fingers as he picked a piece of paper off the table. Kristof leant forwards to get a closer look.

"A shopping list." he murmured, furrowing his brow as he scribbled down a final note before placing his paper on top of the others. "Have a look in that pile, see if you can find where they sourced the doors from. If we get an idea of the thickness we know how much spice we need to get through them."

Kozlov shifted the cups to one hand and began rifling through the papers with the other.

"Says here... Trivoli MK3 Sliding... 47 purchases. Does that sound right?"

Ashkan make. 2-inch honeycomb steel alloy.

"Shit." Kristof muttered, half to himself.

"Not what you were looking for or not what you wanted to hear?" said Kozlov.

"The latter."

"Shame." The man shrugged and offered Kristof a mug, before leaning himself against the far wall. There was a moment of comfortable silence as both men took a sip.

Varian spice, hissed the voice sharply. Kristof shook his head.

"You alright?" Kozlov said. "It must do your head in working on this stuff so late. Are the others not going to help?"

Kristof grinned sheepishly. "They do what they can. Honestly, I'm happier working on these things alone. It gives me space to think."

Kozlov nodded sympathetically. "Makes sense."

Silence blossomed once more.

"So..." the fixer said quietly, taking another sip of his drink. "What's your deal, if you don't mind me asking? I see a lot of... *men for hire* in this line of work, and honestly you people don't strike me as the type." He paused for a moment, thinking. "Apart from the Varian, perhaps, but maybe that's because I don't usually work with 'em. Varians around these parts tend to fall in with their own kind, and however legal the Syndicate claims to be I try to keep them at arms length."

Kristof smiled disarmingly.

"Well its nice to meet a fixer with standards for once. The last one we tried to work with threatened to break my legs within five minutes of meeting me."

"Was that Drago? From Verkat?" Kozlov grimaced, nodding sympathetically. "Yeah, nasty customer."

There was a short silence as both men collected their thoughts.

"So what *do* I strike you as?" Kristof said, running a thumb across the mug's stained surface.

He paused for a moment as the fixer stared at him intently.

"You're calculating." Kozlov muttered. "You've got an eye for detail, I can see that. People seem to do what you say because they like you. To my mind that puts you in one of two categories."

"Which are?"

"Bureaucrat or serial killer."

Smile.

Kristof grinned. "Well I haven't killed anyone today so it looks like I've got a promotion on the way."

Kozlov smiled, his eyes still fixed on Kristof. They narrowed slightly.

"Ever been in the Legions, Kristof? The names that the two of you are using mean quite a lot to some of us soldiers."

"I have. Four years and I hated every second of it, does that help?"

"What rank?"

"Sergeant."

The fixer chuckled. "Really playing into that story, aren't you? You don't strike me as a sergeant. The one I had in the Medicae was a real bastard."

"You're telling me I'm too friendly to be a sergeant?" Kristof said, raising an eyebrow.

"I'm saying you're too friendly to be a sergeant for long." Kozlov shook his head, as if trying to dislodge the smile that still clung to the corners of his mouth. "Sorry pal, not buying it. The other guy pulls it off well but you two need to get together and work on your cover story."

Kristof laughed, giving the man a sidelong glance. "You seem awfully sure of yourself."

"The Bolvar have a saying, I don't know if you know it: You can put a blanket over a donkey, but that doesn't make it a stallion. People have... *shapes*. They tend to show through."

Kristof shrugged.

"And here I was just looking forward to my new job..."

Days passed.

Jana sat alone in the back of the skimmer.

The planning bored her, and it didn't seem like they had much need for her help anyway. She felt like a charity case. But, she had to admit, they had saved her... from trouble *they* had got her mixed up in.

She still wasn't sure how she should feel about all that.

She slumped onto one of the seats, leaning back and placing her feet on the bench opposite. It was strange, she mused, only a week ago she would have thrown a fit if she'd seen one of her passengers doing this, and yet here she was. Funny how your priorities changed, really.

Wulfe was... Interesting. They hadn't spoken much. In fact, Jana wasn't sure if she could remember a time when they'd really said more than a couple of words to each other. He seemed the quiet sort. Not unfriendly, but withdrawn. Nothing like the way she'd always imagined him. The small part of her childhood self that still lived in the back of her mind urged her on, to go and ask him about... well, everything. But there had never really been the time to ask.

She liked Nadir. He was funny. Knew a damn sight more about skimmers than she did too, which Jana felt slightly irritated by. She'd only been flying the things her whole bloody life. And that was only the first thing on a whole list of irritating qualities the roguish little man possessed. But he was refreshing to be around, she couldn't deny that.

Cass was Cass. She was a strange girl. She should, by rights, be as out of her element as Jana was. When Jana was that age, she'd been... what? Just started commercial theory training? Cadets? And here Cass was, flitting around the Union with a some of its greatest heroes paying her for the privilege. On top of all that, she seemed to cope extremely well. Jana found it all hugely unfair.

She'd barely seen Kristof the last few days. He was always there somewhere, but never quite in a position to speak to properly. The man had a talent for slipping away the moment she decided to confront him as to what exactly was going on. Like Wulfe, she had a list of questions for him that was three miles long, and was growing by the day. That being said, she didn't feel like he was avoiding her. Just busy. Or naturally evasive, she wasn't sure.

Something on the seat-back behind her was digging uncomfortably into her spine. She shuffled to one side, lying down on the bench as she fished behind her head for the irritating object. Drawing it forward, her brow furrowed as she stared at the faded, grey-green legionary greatcoat she now held in her hands. Bastian Wulfe's coat. The usually deep green of the coat had given way to a sickly grey-brown, and now she looked closely she could see several locations that had been patched or recently repaired, judging by the colour of the material.

She ran her hand over the series of badges and ribbons that adorned the right breast of the coat. She was no expert in military decorations, and the strange symbols that had been roughly stitched to the coat were like an alien language to her.

"Go on, put it on and give us a damn twirl while you're at it."

Jana almost fell off the bench, the coat falling from her hands as she scrambled to her feet.

Wulfe stood in the doorway, bag slung over one shoulder. He winced as the coat hit the ground with a dull thump.

"And don't bloody drop it, either. I've only got the one."

Jana quickly knelt, picking it back up and folding it carefully over the side of the bench once more.

"Sorry," she stammered. "I just… I was just looking. It's not often you get to see one up close." She paused for a second, and decided to go on the offensive.

"What are you doing here?"

Wulfe grunted. "Bringing you some food. It was getting cold." He held out a hand, offering Jana a dish of what seemed, with a little imagination, to be edible.

Jana took the dish, only now realising how distinctly not-hungry she was as she stared at the watery soup that pooled at the bottom of the dish.

Wulfe caught her expression.

"Don't blame you." he muttered, settling himself onto a neighbouring bench with a low sigh.

Jana sat too, sensing that this, at last, could be a chance to actually *talk* to the man. She threw him a cheery smile.

"Mum always taught me not to waste food, and I'm not about to start now." she said, realising the awkwardness of the sentence and forcing herself to plough on regardless.

 Wulfe closed his eyes, leaning his head back against the interior wall of the skimmer.

"Good for you." he muttered.

Jana cursed inwardly. There it was again. That attitude. It wasn't standoffish, or hostile, just… disinterested. Placid. It killed any conversation before it even began.

She raised the bowl to her lips, taking a quick sip of the soup to cover the silence. It technically qualified as soup. It was watery and had bits in it, she thought as she looked down at the bowl. That made it soup, right?

She paused, looking back up at the soldier who sat, seemingly dozing, against the far wall. She found herself staring, and took another sip of the soup, using the tilt of the bowl to somewhat hide her prying gaze.

Not much was left of the man she'd read about as a child. A face which once could have been almost considered handsome had become weathered, the cheeks sagging, the eyes growing sad as age took its inevitable toll. His hair now streaked with silver, his clothes ragged and drained of colour. Jana wasn't sure if what she remembered of the Hero of Carth was right, but it was definitely more than this.

One eye opened, squinting at Jana.

Wulfe shifted in his chair a little, folding his arms as his eyes closed once more.

"If you've got something to ask, ask it."

Jana hesitated. "I wouldn't want to annoy…"

Both eyes opened this time.

"We're way past that, Jana. Get it over with."

Jana paused, thinking over the hundreds of things she had wanted to ask, and trying desperately to think of a way of saying them that didn't sound *completely* insane.

"Are you really him?" she asked eventually, her voice quieter than she intended.

"Am I really me?"

"You know what I mean."

"Yes, I am." the soldier said flatly.

"What are you doing here?" Jana asked. "Why?"

"Where else would I be?"

"I don't know… in the Legions, fighting to defend humanity?"

"Defend it from what?"

Jana hesitated. "…what?"

Wulfe sighed, a low growl in the silent hold.

"Never mind."

With a low groan he leant forwards, pulling himself to his feet. He looked down at Jana, and his stern expression softened slightly. He stepped forwards and sat down beside her on the bench.

"I'm not what you expected, am I?" he asked, not unkindly.

"I mean I didn't expect to see you at all. You're…" Jana stopped herself. "No." she concluded.

Wulfe chuckled ruefully. "I'm not what I expected to be either, if it helps."

There was a moment of silence. Jana sat, desperately searching her mind for something to say, to keep this brief spark of conversation alive.

Say something. Say anything!

"I used to have a poster of you on my wall, you know?"

Not that!

There was no response. She didn't even dare to look at the man across from her.

"Mum brought it back when she was home on leave." Jana said, forging on despite the silence. "She was with you on Carth for a while. She was the one who used to tell me all the stories."

Wulfe shifted slightly.

"What's her name?"

"Schleifer. Same as me."

"First name, I meant."

"It was Anna."

There was a moment of silence. Jana could see that the man was thinking intently. Eventually he shook his head.

"Sorry."

Jana smiled.

"Don't worry about it. Can't expect you to remember everyone."

"You remembered us though. Me and… Kristof."

"To be honest, I'd almost completely forgotten about you until about two weeks back. If I introduced you to nine-year old Jana though…" Jana chuckled quietly to herself. "You'd never get rid of her."

She threw him a sidelong glance.

"Although Atesca was always her favourite character." she said, determined to push her luck.

She sensed the atmosphere shift almost immediately. The air temperature in the hold seemed to drop by several degrees.

Wulfe sighed, and stood up slowly.

"Got somewhere to be?" Jana asked nonchalantly, cursing herself for doing whatever it was she had done.

The soldier rumbled something that might have been a "Yes", and stamped off down the exit ramp of the skimmer.

And just like that, they had run out of time. Jana stood in the Siren's passenger bay, trying to focus her thoughts over the deafening roar as the engines of the old craft ran through their warmup cycle. She looked out through the open doors of the hangar block, the vista of the High City of Ashka sprawling out across the horizon, the cloudy sky set aglow by its myriad lights.

She wasn't even sure that she could put into words what preparation had been done, only that there had been a lot of it. It almost felt as though the deed itself was more of a technicality than anything else.

She was going to do it though. Commit a crime. A big one too, by the sounds of it.

Well, there was no way out now. In for a penny in for a pound. There wasn't really much she had left to lose, and as nice as the others were she didn't expect for them to put up with her forever without something in return.

And, of course, there was Atesca. Jana had not been able to shake her from her memory. Even thinking about it now tied a sick knot in her stomach, bringing the terror of that evening flooding back. But even stranger and more unsettling was the lingering pleasant thoughts that accompanied it. She found herself *missing* the inquisitor; wanting to hear her voice again, just to be in her presence and...

"Miss Schleifer?!" a voice called above the rumble of the engines.

Jana flinched, torn from her reverie, and focused her gaze on the windswept form of Wiktor Kozlov as he hurried across the concrete floor of the hangar bay. She hopped down, giving a quick wave of reassurance to the others as she hurried to meet him, thrusting her hands into the pockets of her jacket to stop them flapping in the strong air currents whipped up by the skimmer.

The fixer looked nervous as the two of them met, clearly uncomfortable out of his domain. He looked at Jana, eyes narrowed against the wind, and pressed a plain white envelope into her hand.

"Just got this, by courier if you'll believe it!" he called. "The client asks you to read it after you're finished!"

Jana smiled, and hurriedly stuffed the letter into her pocket before the wind could tear it away. Behind her, she heard the howl of the engines dim a little as the engines switched to standby, and the noise dropped to more tolerable levels. Kozlov breathed an audible sigh of relief, and straightened his clothing a little as the winds subsided.

"I don't know how the lot of you aren't deaf yet." he muttered, glancing over her shoulder at the full skimmer. Jana looked back, and saw Kristof drop out of the bay doors and stride across the concrete to join them.

"I suppose this is it then." Kozlov said. "If I can hazard a guess as to the contents of that letter, I won't be seeing you again."

He stuck out a hand, which Jana took.

"Best of luck." the fixer murmured, before taking a step back and waving to Kristof as the man approached. "Miss Schliefer has everything you need to know!"

He turned, and without a backwards glance, strode out of the hangar. Jana turned, walking back across the landing area towards the skimmer. Kristof fell in beside her as she reached him.

"Anything new?" he asked as the two of them clambered aboard. "He left in a hurry."

"I don't think he likes being out of his cafe." Jana said. "He said this was from the client."

She held out the letter, which was promptly snatched from her fingertips by Cass.

"He said it was for *afterwards*, Cass!" she complained as the girl started picking at the corners of the paper. Kristof reached out and put a hand on her shoulder.

"Leave it for now. We need to go or we'll miss our slot." he said. "Jana, are we ready to go?"

Jana nodded. "Ready as I'll ever be."

"Well then." Kristof smiled. "Get us in the air, Miss Schleifer."

Chapter 10

41ˢᵗ Frejas, 2067.54 Core Time

Casualty Report – Carth Conflict – Combined 12ᵗʰ and PDA, Month 8

Union Casualties: 3 killed, 8 wounded

Civilian Casualties: 4 killed, 5 wounded

Estimated Rebel Casualties: 13 killed, 7 wounded

Confirmed Rebel Casualties: 13 killed

Cpt.Bastian Wulfe Commanding, Com. Atesca Seratov Advising.

Kristof dropped out of the skimmer. His boots hit the Ashkan soil with a dull thump, sending up a spattering of mud and water as the waterlogged ground gave a little under his weight.

The skimmer had landed in amongst the vast forests that made up the southern end of the Ashka-City sector. The trees towered overhead here, forming a near-impenetrable canopy broken only in a few areas of rough or rocky ground. It had been a hell of a job getting it down, but it had worked. They had made it, and they were all but invisible from the air.

As the engines wound down and the forest grew quiet once more, the dry voice welled once more in the back of his mind.

Sixty-two percent humidity. Two hours until sundown. Three hours until darkness.

He looked up, brushing a few errant drops of rain from his shoulder. The famed Ashkan rainfall hadn't hit yet, but if the forecast had been correct a class 4 rainstorm should be on them before nightfall.

Light wind, mist, and heavy rain. Perfect cover.

He was almost smiling to himself as he stepped over to the cockpit, glancing up at where Cass and Jana watched from behind the reinforced glasswork, now starting to slick with rain and moisture.

"You sure you two know what you're doing?" he called out softly, making sure he could be heard through the glass.

"I thought we were just supposed to stay here, out of the way." Jana asked, an expression of confusion plain on her features.

"Exactly right. Just double-checking." Kristof grinned and stepped briskly out of sight around the skimmer before the pilot could think of a retort.

Wulfe stood apart from the skimmer, shaking an old-fashioned compass that he held in one gloved hand. He looked up as Kristof approached.

"Up that hill, I think." he said, giving the implement another shake. "Bastard thing isn't working properly."

38 ° from sundown, 3 miles

"Sounds like a plan." Kristof said quietly. "Get moving, we'll be right behind you."

Wulfe nodded, slinging the black canvas bag higher over his shoulder and turning to forge a path up the forested hillside.

Kristof turned. Nadir was arm-deep in the skimmer's maintenance tool compartment, an expression of deep concentration on the man's face as he felt around the inset toolbox.

"Nadir!" Kristof exclaimed as he jogged up. "This isn't the time to be messing around."

"Two seconds, that's all I need." the Varian muttered, his face still a picture of concentration.

"Anything you could possibly need is in Wulfe's bag. I didn't spend three straight nights planning this to forget basic tools."

"I know you didn't. You spent three nights planning this because..." Nadir gave a sharp tug and withdrew his arm, a small, triangular-headed blade now clutched in the tattooed fingers of his right hand.

"Look at that!" he said, happily. "A type four. Can't buy these things anywhere these days."

They hurried up the hill after Wulfe, catching him as he paused near its crest. Nadir looked around, staring between the trees, confusion written plain on his face.

"Is this it?" he said. "There's nothing here!"

Wulfe scowled, glancing at the compass.

"Ought to be." he muttered. "Lets have a look around and see what we can see."

Kristof stood silently as the two scattered, trying to keep the pair of them in vision. He wasn't used to forests. Compared to the deafening sounds of Ashka this place was a grave.

His radio crackled, and Wulfe's voice sounded sharply in his ear.

"Nothing here."

"Or here." Nadir said. *"Kristof, are you sure this was right? There ought to be a sign somewhere, right?"*

"I don't know." Kristof said. "Keep looking, the entrance has... has..."

Soft loam

Kristof looked down. Small rivulets and pools of water had begun to well up as the rain started to intensify. He dug a foot into the earth, kicking up a spray of the loose dirt and mud that pattered down across the clearing.

This much rain should sink right in

He frowned, squatting down in the mud to get a better look.

"Kristof?" Nadir's voice came through again. *"What's up?"*

"It's here." Kristof muttered slowly. "Look at how the water is pooling. Its flowing over something solid close under the surface."

"Son of a bitch, I should have spotted that." Wulfe said, his voice tinny and faint now. *"How do we get in?"*

Two FreeTech Hangar Doors, Version 2x

"We need to head down. Look for a cliff or a steep slope. This mud might have covered it." Kristof muttered, following the rivulets with his eyes. He stood up, walking cautiously across the clearing and into the woods beyond, watching as the narrow flow of water danced and weaved its way between rock and root.

Small trees here. No room to set down root.

He accelerated his pace, breaking into a light jog as he darted between the trees.

Splashing water. Lots of it. Listen.

And then Kristof stopped.

The ground fell away in front of him, an almost vertical cliff overhung with grass, foliage and slipped earth. It ran for dozens of metres, sweeping away from where he stood in a long, lazy arc, its precipice broken at intervals where a thin rivulet of water broke through and tumbled almost a dozen metres into the dirt below.

But it wasn't just the cliff that had stopped Kristof in his tracks. It was the faint glint of worked metal that shone through the mud almost five metres below him.

"I found it." he whispered into the radio.

Minutes later, the three men stood at the base of the cliff. Traversing the overhang had been difficult, and they had eventually been forced to slide down the steeply inclined slope, stumbling to a halt in the ankle-high stream that had formed at the base of the gulley. Now they stood together, gazing up at the large steel doors that blocked their path. From down here it seemed obvious, but from outside of the gulley this structure was nearly invisible.

"*Mieda*." cursed Nadir under his breath. "This place is bigger than I thought."

Kristof glanced behind him, almost involuntarily. He was getting jumpy, he could feel it.

"Can you open them?"

"If the mechanism is what I suspect it is…" he muttered, screwing one eye shut as he squinted up into the gap where the door disappeared into its frame, itself embedded deep in the concrete walls that lay half-obscured beneath the mud and grime. He frowned for a moment, his lips moving almost silently as he sized up the structure before him.

"…call it three… five mil for the shaft radius, that has to be at least a metre long, two locking wheels of half a metre each, both working their way down to *there*. Structure this old probably has an in-line gearing system, so add another half-metre… so by all accounts… aha!" He brushed at the surface of the metal. Beneath the dust and weathering Kristof could barely make out a thin, hairline crack, becoming clearer by the second as Nadir began to work a thin, razor-sharp blade around its perimeter. The tools dug in one by one, until the edges of the now-defined plate seemed almost to bulge out of the wall itself.

With a final breath, Nadir tapped a knuckle against right-most blade. With a sharp crack the plate sprung free, falling into his lap in a shower of grey dust and a metallic tinkling as a dozen paper-thin blades hit the ground around him.

"If you people paid me what I'm worth, you'd be bankrupt." he commented flippantly as he placed the metal sheet carefully down beside him.

"Nadir, we *are* bankrupt, that's why we're here. Now get on with it." Kristof muttered, glancing around nervously.

The little man shrugged, and turned back to his work with a smile still playing about his lips.

"Would you look at that." He said, squinting into the half-darkness of the hatchway. "I can tell you one thing, Kristof. No-one has opened this thing in quite some time. Those two…" he gestured with the torch. "…have almost rusted into each other they've been like that so long."

Kristof and Wulfe leant in, following the light of the torch as it played across the mechanical relay of neatly aligned gears, the rust-specked surfaces lending the torchlight a strange glint in the darkness.

"Shouldn't be too hard." Muttered Wulfe, reaching out towards the nearest of the gears. "Looks like most of it will brush right off, its so dry in…"

Nadir's hand shot up, grasping Wulfe by the forearm as the soldier reached past.

"*Please*…." Nadir said sharply, with an exaggeratedly pained expression playing across his features. "…don't try to help. These systems are balanced on a razor's edge a lot of the time. You drop something in there and you could jam the whole system up. At least if I do it we all know who to blame, right?"

Wulfe stood back, glancing at Kristof with a shrug.

It took three more minutes as the two of them watched the small Varian man wrestling with the machinery, filling the air with muttered curses in his strange, soft-spoken language. Three minutes which Kristof spent nervously pacing, the voice in his mind pointing out every minute detail of the surrounding area in that dry, analytical, *irritating* way that it had. It always did this. Maybe one day he'd work out how to put a stop to it.

Wulfe, however, seemed characteristically relaxed. He stood with his back to Nadir, hands in the pockets of his worn Legionary greatcoat, his collar turned up against the drifting rain, and simply waited, a font of calm against Kristof's rising paranoia.

Keeping watch. Kristof felt the voice mutter. It seemed old habits died hard for some, he reflected as he turned and paced anxiously back across the hillside.

"Looks like rain." muttered Wulfe, inclining his head towards a bank of black cloud that boiled above the Ashkan Gulf to the west. Kristof nodded. The voice had pointed it out to him three times already.

They both turned towards Nadir as the wiry little thief sat back on his heels, brushing the errant strands of black hair out of his face with the back of his hand. Faintly, barely at the edge of hearing, Kristof could make out a faint hum emitting from the gap in the panelling, rising in pitch and volume with each instant.

"That ought to do." Nadir muttered, brushing at the dust that now clung stubbornly to the front of his shirt with a mock frown. "I should be able to get you in the door now, at the very least. I'll work on the systems while you're inside, see if I can find you some lights."

"You're too kind." said Kristof drily, as the man scrambled to his feet.

As the hum reached its crescendo, Nadir flashed him a grin.

With a shriek of tortured metal and the grating protest of grinding gears, the vast metal doors began to slide slowly aside. Plumes of mud and dirt fell from above, loosed by the shuddering grind of metal against metal.

As the noise subsided, Nadir stepped up beside the narrow gap that had been opened up between the two doors, throwing a practiced glance around the inside of the frame before stepping aside with a mocking bow.

"*Dae Vaan.*" he smirked. "It's all yours."

Kristof grimaced, unable even at a time like this to stop himself smiling at his friend's antics.

"Keep an eye out. Tell us if anything happens. And let Cass know where we are."

He glanced at Wulfe, gave an encouraging grin, and stepped into the darkness.

Chapter 11

The chamber was large. Vast, even. It looked like a hangar of some kind, with vast steel support structures clinging from the walls at regular intervals, running up from the polished stone floor towards the lightly domed ceiling that curved overhead in the darkness above. Moisture ran down the walls, forming shallow, fetid pools around the perimeter of the hall. Footsteps echoed around the hall as the two soldiers advanced slowly,

Kristof whistled through his teeth.

"This place is old." he muttered. "50 or 60 years at least, to get in this state."

"Watch it." murmured Wulfe, playing his torch across the far wall.

Kristof grinned.

"Looks like Cass was right about the destruction being a cover then, doesn't it?" he said quietly. "Place seems in relatively good condition from what I can see."

"Too good for my liking."

"What's that?"

Wulfe shook his head, eyes fixed on the circle of torchlight as it panned across the far wall.

"I've been in places like this. They're a mess. This one has been cleared out."

Three exits whispered the voice gently in the back of Kristof's mind. He tapped Wulfe on the shoulder, gesturing with his torch beam.

"Go have a look at that door, see if you can get it open. I'll see how Nadir is getting on with the power."

As Wulfe rumbled his assent, Kristof cracked on his radio.

"Any chance of some lights Nadir?" he said quietly, almost unconsciously hushing his voice to match the silence of the hall.

"I'm about fifty metres behind you." came Nadir's voice in a distorted crackle. *"You couldn't come and ask me in person?"*

"Just testing the radio signal."

"Well I wouldn't count on it working any further in. You can get a signal like this through perhaps one foot of stone, but not much more. As far as lights are concerned, I'll need more time than that. I've got to get the second panel open, find the primary connections, serial codes, get the slate adjusted... And that's assuming there is even enough power to this place..."

"Well, where are you up to so far?"

"It's been two minutes. I've got the panel open."

"Alright. Keep us updated."

"Absolutely. And if you have any more helpful advice don't hesitate to let me know."

In the darkness of the vault, Kristof rolled his eyes.

"You know how much I enjoy our little chats." Nadir added.

The line clicked, then went dead.

Kristof sighed. "Forget I asked."

He looked up at Wulfe's silhouette, glad that the darkness concealed the small smile that he couldn't quite shake.

"Looks like we're in the dark for now."

The soldier nodded grimly, seemingly too preoccupied to reply. He was standing by one of the depressions in the hangar's side wall, thoughtfully sizing up the door that sat nestled within it. As Kristof stepped up beside him, he saw what had caught the man's attention.

It wasn't much, a single battered LED sputtering with a faint crimson light, its irregular flickering casting strange shapes across the panel's warped surface.

"You see it?" Wulfe muttered quietly. "Place is still powered."

"Can we do anything with it?"

"Don't know. Nadir might want to know." Wulfe placed a calloused hand against the door's surface, giving it an experimental push. "I think I can do something with this."

"You get on it then, I'll let Nadir know about the power."

Wulfe nodded silently.

"Nadir?" Kristof said, flicking the switch on his radio again.

"*What's up?*" the feed was patchy, but recognisable. Kristof could faintly make out the scrape and scratch of Nadir's tools in the background.

"The place is powered. We've found…"

"*Yeah I noticed. Thanks.*"

"Made any progress?"

"*Nothing yet. The place has power, I can see that. I just need to…*" the voice paused for a moment, the sentence fragmented by a grunt of irritation. "*I just need to get the damn thing to let me access it. Its fighting me a little.*"

"Ok. We'll check in again when we can."

"*Mhm.*"

Kristof gazed out towards the main doors as the line cut out. He could still make out the thin column of light that managed to pierce the gap between the doors before being swallowed by the darkness of the hall's interior. His gaze swept the hall itself, across the bare concrete floors, the dilapidated support structures that hung from the walls and ceilings like the remnants of some monstrous web.

He spun around as a sharp crack sounded from behind him.

Wulfe dropped the crowbar, digging his hands into the door's cracked surface at around waist-height. His whole body tensed, his powerful build turning for a moment with singular purpose as, punctuated by the sharp cracks of snapping metal, he pried the door apart. With a final rending *crack* the door was flung aside, hanging limply in its bearings.

The man groaned, standing back and rolling his shoulders a little, grimacing as he did so.

"Son of a bitch that hurt." He groaned again as he leaned down to retrieve the crowbar. "Next door is your problem." he muttered as he stowed it in the black cloth bag that he had hung over his shoulder.

They stepped forwards together, crossing the threshold torch-first, quickly sweeping the room as they entered.

"Office compound." Wulfe muttered, glancing over the arrays of desks.

Smell of copper. Or blood. Faint.

"Looks like it." Kristof stopped, closing his eyes for a moment as the stale air washed over him.

Stale air.

"I'll take a look at this bank. See if you can get any data cells out of that set over there."

The two men split, and the air soon filled with the soft clanks of metal on metal as the panelling on the computer banks were pulled away.

Stale air.

Kristof stared blankly at the wall of cables in front of him for a moment.

Air.

How is the air still breathable this far down?

He frowned, reaching into the bank and tugging at the cells hidden between the web of cables. Flicking the catches quickly, he withdrew the small rectangular chip and held it up, squinting at it in the light of his torch, turning it back and forth.

C60x Titanium. Pristine.

A used cell would have a darkened area around its base, where it slotted into the main relay. This one was almost new.

He moved along the row, pulling the plate free with a little more force than necessary.

Pristine.

"Shit." he muttered. "Anything on your end?" he called out, wincing as his voice echoed around the silent halls.

"Nothing." came the reply. "Most of these don't even have datachips."

Kristof stood up, shining his torch across Wulfe's hunched form, watching as the old soldier wrestled with a new panel.

"Do you mind?" Wulfe muttered, taking a hold of the panel rim. "I can't see a thing like..."

The flash lit the room for a moment, searing a line of neon colours into Kristof irises. The sound followed a fraction of a second later, the sharp, whiplike crack of discharging electricity. Wulfe staggered back clutching at his hand, raising his singed digits to his lips as he stared at the panelling in shock.

"Bastard thing almost got me." he hissed, treating the cold metal to a withering glare before glancing at Kristof.

"Must be a short underneath the panelling." Kristof muttered, stepping closer to the centre of the room.

"Or Nadir's messing with the systems is causing surges." Wulfe growled.

"Or that. I'll head out and let him know." Kristof turned, shrugging the bag off his shoulder and propping it against the doorframe. "Keep an eye on that for me. And try not to touch anything."

"I'll try to contain my curiosity." growled Wulfe, throwing a sullen glance at the panelling.

Kristof stepped back out of the room and into the main hall, his footsteps suddenly sounding very loud in the still air.

"Nadir, whatever you're doing is surging the power like crazy." he said, staring across the hall towards the faint shaft of light that broke through the cracked door from the outside world. "You almost torched Wulfe back there!"

"Sorry to disappoint you, Savri, but I've not touched a thing. The damn thing backlashed and fried my slate to a crisp. Completely bricked. So unless I accidentally lashed it right back its going to be running whatever routines it damn well pleases until I can get hold of another slate from somewhere."

"Pretty sure there are a few on the skimmer. Cass has one, definitely. See if you can raise Jana on the radio, maybe she can help you out."

"I'll see what I can do."

Kristof spun around as a dull clank sounded from behind him. The room was silent and still.

"Was that you?" said Wulfe, glancing up sharply from the wiring he was working on.

"No. Was it you?"

"No."

Kistof's torch traced the far wall, his senses straining against the darkness as he grasped in vain for the slightest movement, the slightest sound in the stale, musty air of the vault.

Behind him, he heard a deep chuckle from Wulfe.

"The bag fell over." the soldier muttered, gesturing vaguely towards the door with a fistful of cables.

The black cloth bag lay flat in the doorway. Kristof grinned, and chuckled nervously.

"Bunch of schoolgirls, we are." he muttered.

Metal on stone

Kristof stopped, his ears suddenly straining for any sound amidst the silent halls.

Metal grating on stone

Slowly, Kristof's gaze moved to the floor. He dropped to his hands and knees, then his stomach, pressing an ear against the smooth cold stone.

"What the hell are you..."

"Shhhh!" Kristof hissed. He heard it again, clearly now. A horrible, dry grating sound, echoing up through the stone.

With a grunt of effort, he pushed himself back up onto his knees, pausing once more to listen for the sound. He reached out silently for the fallen bag at his side, eyes closed as he immersed himself in the silence of the halls.

His hand hit the bag clumsily, shifting it on the stone and waking him from his near-trance.

It moved.

Kristof looked at the bag, and his heart froze.

Moving with glacial slowness, inch by grinding inch, the thick steel door was closing. It moved implacably, driving the heavy bag in front of it without slowing as it ground its way across the frame.

"Wulfe?!"

He heard footsteps, and a muttered curse.

"Probably Nadir's idea of a joke." the soldier muttered. He didn't sound like he believed it.

Kristof shook his head. "He got backlash from the system. He's locked out until he can get a slate off the other two."

"Shit." whispered Wulfe.

"Was there anything else in there?" Kristof ventured, realising that the two of them had started whispering at some point.

Wulfe shook his head solemnly. "Not a thing. This place has been cleared out."

The silence blossomed once again. Kristof glanced back at the door by which they had entered.

"This place has been dead for years. The machines are dry and dusty. Old, too." Wulfe said, speaking in low, hushed tones. "That door shouldn't have moved. Nothing in here has moved for years. I…"

He paused, looking at Kristof.

"You feel it too, don't you?"

Kristof nodded wordlessly, staring into the darkness that surrounded them, prickling ice beginning to crawl up his spine.

"It feels like something *really* doesn't want us here."

"*Jana?*"

Commercial Skimmer Pilot Schleifer leant forwards, picking the headset off the dashboard in front of her and holding one of the headphones to her ear.

"Go ahead, Nadir." she responded, leaning back in her seat and placing her feet on the steering column in front of her.

The voice crackled again, muted and dim. Jana leant forward and fiddled idly with the transmission settings as she listened.

"*Do you have a slate on that aircraft of yours?*"

"I've got mine. I think Cass has one too, but I also know you've got one of your own. What's up?"

"*This thing is… interesting. There are a few pieces here that don't match the plans. Someone's been tinkering with the design, I think. Its… complicated. There's software here I've never seen before. Its all moving. Every time I change something it reroutes somewhere else. Its like dynamic, self-repairing… Its fascinating, Jana. So, in the interests of scientific advancement, I've decided to break it. And in doing so, of course, see how it works.*"

"And you need my slate for that?"

"*Well, you see, it's already fried mine…*"

"You're not selling this terribly well."

"*I'll buy you another one. Hell, for something like this I'll buy you two. I don't think I can adequately explain to you how interesting this is.*"

Jana frowned thoughtfully. "Fine. I guess so. As long as you try your best not to break it. It'll take us time to get there though, will Kristof and Wulfe be alright in the meantime?"

"*Take your time. I want to take a look at the electrical side of things first before I really dig into the software, and if Kristof and Wulfe get into trouble I've got my neural relay as a backup.*"

"Neural what?"

There was a brief pause from the end of the line. "*Neural relay. Its an exceptionally quick and exceptionally dirty way to work through a system. Probably the most illegal thing I own.*"

"Is that safe?"

"Absolutely not, but I want it here just as a backup. Sometimes being quick is what you need."

"Alright. Try not to use it. We'll hurry over and get the slate to you as soon as we can." Jana said hesitantly. "I'll send Cass over with it as soon as I can. Shouldn't be more than a few..."

"Jana? *Jana!*"

She looked up fast as Cass' cry echoed in from outside, shrill, the note of terror in her voice carrying on the wind. She scrambled to her feet, throwing her headphones aside as she rushed for the cockpit door. Something caught her eye, something half-glimpsed on the forested hillside above her.

A figure, rifle in hand.

She threw herself to the ground, screaming as the cockpit exploded around her.

Chapter 12

"Strength is nothing without belief. Without the spark, the fire cannot burn."

– Bastian Wulfe, The Saviour of the Union.

Kristof and Wulfe looked up together as a series of distant snapping noises drifted gently through the still air of the tunnels. However much they sounded like a child's firecrackers from this distance, they both knew the sound all too well.

Gunfire.

Outside.

Wordlessly Kristof spun about, dashing back the way they had come towards the source of the sound. He heard a clatter behind him as Wulfe dropped his bag and took off in pursuit, his heavy form thundering through the narrow corridors behind Kristof.

"AC20's…" Wulfe called out. "Those are Legion guns!"

"Nadir?! Can you hear me?" Kristof shouted, thumbing the switch on his radio as he ran.

"Kristof? Faen! Fuck!" The sound of gunfire crackled over the connection, a hollow mimicry of the sound echoing through the halls a moment later.

"There's Legionaries here. Dozens of them!" Nadir's voice hissed breathlessly.

"Hold tight! We're coming!"

Jana lay on her side, huddled under the console, her breath running ragged as the final fragments of broken glass settled like fresh snow on the floor around her. A deep silence washed over her, seeming to smother all other sound as the ringing in her ears began to recede.

"Cass?!" she hissed, rolling gingerly onto her hands and knees and craning her neck as far out as she dared to see into the main cargo bay.

For a moment she saw nothing, before a flash of colour caught her eye. Cass had squeezed herself into the gap between the sliding bay doors and the wall. Even from where she lay, Jana could see that she wasn't well hidden. The space was tight, the gap between the wall and the door barely enough for the girl to squeeze into. Anyone entering the skimmer would spot her in seconds.

Gently, cautiously, Jana eased herself back beneath the console. She reached up, slowly placing a hand on the top of the console, fingers feeling for her headset. Her hand shook as it explored the smooth metal, slowly working its way along as she wracked her memory, trying desperately to remember where the equipment had landed. She shuddered slightly, stifling a whimper, expecting at any moment to hear another thunderous detonation from the cliffside above.

Her questing fingers closed around the rough plastic of the mic, and she grabbed it frantically, dragging it down and holding it close as she thumbed the transmission switch.

"Nadir?!" she whispered, as loudly as she would dare. "There's someone outside. They're shooting at us!"

She paused for a moment, trying to quieten her breathing as she listened intently for a response.

"Nadir? Anyone?!"

"*Jana?!*" Kristof's voice seemed distant, the connection fraying and rebinding second by second.

"Kristof?! What's happening?" she hissed breathlessly, feeling a surge of elation as she heard his voice.

"*I don't know. We were...*"

Jana froze as a sound reached her ears. The soft crunch of footsteps on shale. The slow, implacable footsteps of booted feet from outside the aircraft.

"There's someone coming." she whispered frantically, dropping the headset and leaning back around the doorframe into the hold.

Outside. She mouthed, gesturing as best she could from her prone position. *Hide.*

Cass nodded, shuffling herself deeper into the shadow of the doorframe, her face white with fear. Jana could see it was hopeless. The Siren wasn't a large craft. There was nowhere better to hide.

A voice sounded outside, the words muffled, but their tone distinct. Short, staccato. *Orders.* She swung back around the corner as she caught a flash of green from the doorway.

Legionaries. Unmistakeable. Jana flattened herself against the doorframe, slowing her frantic breathing lest it give her away.

The footsteps traced into the hold slowly, deliberately. Jana listened, heart in her mouth, pressing herself as far into the corner of the cockpit as she could, away from the doorway.

Then came the voice again, distorted and alien through the legionary's visor as the automated systems scrambled his voice into tac-speech. The footsteps sounded, two steps, towards the cockpit. It spoke again. It paused, seeming to listen for a moment. Jana heard a faint metallic snap as the Legionary removed his visor. The voice sounded again, the distortion vanished from its voice.

"You're kidding me." the soldier whispered, his voice filled with exasperation and disbelief. "We've got bodies down in two sectors! You can't just pull us..." it stopped sharply, catching itself mid-sentence. "Yes, captain. Immediately. Permission to confirm bodies down before departure?"

There was a second sharp snap as the Legionary's visor clicked back into place. Another bout of metallic squawking filled the inside of the Siren's hold as he spoke once more, the sophisticated equipment masking his speech.

Jana's eyes roved franticly around the cockpit, looking for a way out, a weapon, anything.

The footsteps sounded again, one, two... a pause, followed by the wet splash of boots hitting mud.

Silence fell once more as the legionary faded back into the mist that spawned him.

Kristof wrenched open the door, flinging it aside as he charged out into the main hall. He felt Wulfe's hand grab hold of his shoulder, bringing him up short.

Silence filled the hall. Deep, oppressive silence. Their footsteps echoed hollowly around the Vault's cavernous interior.

Kristof looked back in confusion, before casting a cautious look around the hall. It stood as they had left it. Silent. Imposing. Empty. A faint shaft of light piercing the darkness from the far end of the chamber, playing across the ground by Kristof's feet.

"Nadir?" he said quietly, eyes still scanning the chamber suspiciously as the two of them advanced across it, side by side.

The line remained silent.

"What the fuck is going on?" he muttered under his breath as he and Wulfe stepped forwards, a sick fear beginning to build in his stomach.

"I don't know." replied Wulfe, the concern plain in his voice. "Did they find us?"

"They couldn't." Kristof whispered to himself. "I..."

A million-to-one-chance.

Kristof took a deep breath, hurrying forwards towards the light. He could feel Wulfe at his shoulder, their echoing footsteps mingling as the pair advanced up the short slope towards the outside world.

But still a chance.

Kristof slowed as they approached, quieting his footsteps as he padded towards the opening.

Something has changed.

Kristof felt his heart drop. He glanced back at Wulfe.

"The opening isn't as wide..."

He stopped as the old soldier raised a finger to his lips. Though he gestured forwards, his eyes spoke volumes about what he was seeing.

Rain. Wet leaves. Mould.

The sky outside had darkened, and Kristof could smell the fresh scent of coming rain drifting on the breeze as it pressed its way into the vault's darkened interior.

Another scent rode on the tails of the wind, however. One that set Kristof's heart racing as he reached the crack in the Vault door.

Blood.

Without pausing, Kristof stepped out of the vault. Even the dim light of this rain-spattered gulley seemed blinding compared to the blackness of the interior he had left behind, and he was forced to stare blindly for a moment, willing his eyes to adjust to their surroundings.

The forest was still and silent. The rain pattered gently down around Kristof, the gentle breeze tugged at his clothing, and the soft chirping of the woodland birds hung in the air around him.

However, one sound rose above all others, setting Kristof's heart racing once more: The soft sound of a shuddering breath. Kristof turned, and even as his vision began to settle his heart dropped as he laid eyes on the source of the sound.

Nadir sat against the door's frame, head resting gently back against the side access panel that he had opened. His tanned, olive skin was drenched in rain and sweat, his hair hanging down his head in lank strands. His eyes stared at Kristof, his usual bright smile now a rictus grin of terror, adrenaline and desperation.

Nadir's arm was thrust, shoulder-deep, into the access panel. Trails of blood had begun to soak up the arm of his jacket, spreading across his chest and side from where the limb had become tangled in the mechanism, ground mercilessly between the two locking wheels. His other hand pressed firmly down on the neural relay, his knuckles white, the force enough to draw blood from the thousands of tiny needles that now pierced the soft flesh of his palm.

“Nadir?! You…”

The man gave a soft chuckle, the sound broken as he drew in another shuddering breath, his eyes becoming misty and unfocussed for a moment. He blinked, glancing at Kristof as he knelt down beside him, and hissed through gritted teeth.

“…told you I'd keep it open, didn't I?” he said, the ever-present smile still hovering about his lips.

“What happened?” said Kristof, staring in horror. He needed to act. He knew it. But his mind only gave him more questions that needed answering. “Wulfe, quickly, get…”

Nadir’s eyes began to lose focus again, drifting away from Kristof’s face even as the soldier knelt down beside the two of them.

“*Antaek a vari, dellim aess... aess...*” the Varian slurred, his lips barely moving as he spoke. “*dellim aess kantash sin melhelsh..*”

I see about me a realm of blackness, of death, and fear I will never return

“What? No. No, Nadir?! Look at me. *Kaess’avren*, come on!”

And above them the heavens opened, drowning the silent forest in sheets of driving rain.

Chapter 13

"He is *dying*, Kristof!"

Wulfe's voice echoed around the still confines of the skimmer's hold.

"I've seen wounds like this before and I know damn well you have too. He has hours at most."

Kristof paced the width of the hold like a caged animal. His eyes were wild, almost unseeing as he strode back and forth, caught up in the agony of indecision.

Help him.

"The first thing they'll want is identification. If they find out who he is, they'll kill him." he whispered frantically, almost to himself.

"If you keep him here, *you'll* kill him! We have to do *something*." Wulfe snarled.

Why did it still have power? Help him. Why did the legionaries leave?

Kristof shook his head sharply, trying desperately to clear his thoughts.

I told you I'd keep it open, right?

The soldier paused, seeing Kristof's distress. His tone softened slightly.

"I know you don't trust them. I know. I understand. But if he doesn't get help, he will be dead in hours. We have to get him to a Medical, and soon."

"We can't take him. If we take him in, they'll want names. They'll want explanations."

"So what do we do?"

Help him.

Kristof paused, staring down at the Varian's still form. With a defeated sigh, he sank down against the wall in a sitting position, burying his face in his hands.

"I don't know."

Help.

From the back corner of the skimmer a voice spoke up, quietly, yet with a budding determination to its tone.

"I know something." Jana said, eyeing the group cautiously as she spoke, as if she expected them to turn on her at any moment.

"There's an emergency line for courier pilots. Its only for use in life-threatening circumstances. You're supposed to land immediately, call it, and wait for pickup."

Jana paused, hesitating as the gazes of everyone in the skimmer fell on her.

"We can leave him somewhere they'll find him. Find an empty platform, arrange for an emergency pickup, and leave before anyone arrives to ask us questions."

Silence fell. In briefest moment of hesitation, Kristof and Wulfe's gazes met.

"Do it. Quick as you can, Jana." Kristof said, without looking round.

Jana turned and darted through the doorway into the skimmer's cockpit.

"It's the best we can do." Wulfe muttered quietly.

I told you I'd keep it open, right?

"I know." Kristof said. "It doesn't make it feel any better."

Why did the Legion leave?

"Guys…" Cass' voice was quiet. Hesitant, almost.

Where did they go?

Kristof shook his head.

What is going on?

"Doesn't feel right, just leaving…"

"Kristof. Wulfe." Cass cut in again, insistently.

“What?”

Cass stood against the far wall.

In one hand she held five small, red booklets. Idents. Her other held a small sheet of creased white paper.

“They said to read it if something went wrong!” she said, defensively, catching the surprised looks the two men threw at her. “This is wrong! Everything has gone wrong!”

Wulfe opened his mouth, then paused as the girl raised the paper and began to read from it, her voice still trembling from stress and exhaustion.

“‘Take these. With your existing idents, arrange for two trips on the *Pioneer* and two rooms in the *Excelsior*, Sector 2, Ashka.’ Meet us in Cothiq at 17:78 in three days, on the Walkway between sections 27 and 37, floor 20. We will help you.’”

“I…”

Cass cut in. “There’s more.”

She continued.

“Stay off the network. Tell no-one where you are going. Stay off the network. Do not return to the Waterfront. Stay off the network.”

Jana leapt into her seat, working through the launch procedure with one shaking hand, even as the other reached for the comms.

“Flight control, we have a severe injury on board. Requesting emergency pickup at…” her hands traced the local chart on the screen beside her. “…platform 321C.”

“Confirmed, Siren-class. We’ll have them there in 10 minutes. Good luck.”

Jana hauled the skimmer into the air. 321C was only a few minutes away. They would have time. They could make it. Nadir was going to be ok.

The next few minutes were the longest she had experienced in her life. Rain spattered against the glass in front of her, a faint, cold mist pressing through the narrow slits cut by the legionary’s bullets mere hours earlier. She was beginning to find things hard to process. Too many things had happened. She had known that today was going to be difficult. Dangerous, even. But things had gone more wrong than anyone could have imagined. Why couldn’t things just *work*? Why did nothing ever just…

She brought the skimmer down onto the concrete landing platform. Rain, whisked up into a fine mist by the force of the engines, spattered against the hull as Jana reached for the comms again.

"Go, quickly!" she yelled over her shoulder, her voice barely audible over the sound of the engines as the hull doors on the skimmer's flanks were pulled aside.

"Flight control, we have arrived. Is there medical staff on-site?"

"Negative, Siren-class. Incoming in four minutes. Will you require remote medical assistance while you hold?"

Jana watched as Kristof and Wulfe staggered through the rain outside, the injured Varian carried between them. Workers stopped and stared as they rushed past, ghosts in the mist, pressing on through the driving rain towards the Control Office.

"Negative, Control. Will hold and await further instructions."

The rain drummed against the glass. She sat there in tense silence as she watched the two men lay Nadir's body down in the cover of the Control Office's outer canopy. They paused for a moment, before hurrying back across the landing ground.

She heard the flank doors slide open, heard the damp thudding of boots on the skimmer's hull.

"Clear, Jana!" came the call from behind her. She didn't need telling twice.

Jana hauled back on the control column, lifting the skimmer into the air. As she swung the craft around, she could still make out a faint form below the canopy of the Control Office, shrouded by the mist and rainfall.

As the airfield disappeared below them, she cast a glance over her shoulder. Wulfe sat beside Cass, his back to the wall, one hand idly stroking her hair as she buried her face in his shoulder, her body wracked with grief. The man stared silently at the ground by his feet.

The flank doors had been left open a crack. Rain gusted in, churned to a fine mist by the skimmer's engines. A faint ray of light shone into the bay from outside, thin, almost invisible amidst the rain and mist.

Kristof stood outlined in the faint light of the rain-soaked moon, bracing himself in the doorway as he stared out at the airfield below them. The wind whipped at his clothes, his hair already drenched by the mist, his head bowed against the lashing rain as the skimmer picked up speed, drawing ever further away from platform 321C, and away from Nadir's broken form beneath the control-centre's awning.

Chapter 14

33rd Sihyl, 2094.55 Core Time – Electronic Messaging Certificate

URGENT

Commander Adran,

With all due respect, I must enquire as to your motives when it came to cutting our supply. In one move you have changed the course of this war. The Commissary and I could have had the Butcher's forces dismantled within the month; now we are on the back foot again.

Cpt. Wulfe

The rain beat down on the hull of the skimmer, running across the metal in a thousand tiny rivulets. To Jana, however, it promised safety, warmth, and somewhere dry. She hurried towards it, holding her jacket over her head in one arm to ward off the worst of the weather.

She looked around as she hauled herself on board, shivering as a few droplets of rain from the top of the bay doors managed to find their way down the back of her neck.

They had landed the skimmer… somewhere. She wasn't even sure if she remembered the name of the district anymore. It wasn't at all like she had imagined Ashka to be as a girl. The buildings were squat and grey, the streets were largely deserted. What people she had seen hurried by with barely a glance. There was no bustle. No vibrancy. Things were just grey.

She shifted the bundle that she held under her arm. Bread. She was starting to like bread, as a concept. It was reliable. Wherever you went, bread would always be there for you. Especially if you were hungry, which she very much was.

Wulfe and Cass sat side-by-side in the skimmer's hold. The old soldier was half-sitting, half lying against one of the support beams, his head resting on his shoulder as he dozed. His hand rested in his lap, a dog-eared set of cards held loosely in them.

The remaining cards were held by Cass, who sat beside the sleeping man, still diligently playing their game. She was clearly deep in thought, brow furrowed, the tip of her tongue sticking out of the corner of her mouth as she stared thoughtfully at the cards arrayed on the hold floor in front of her. She caught Jana's gaze, cast a sidelong glance at Wulfe, and shrugged.

Jana grinned, tossing the girl one of the small paper packages.

"Kristof?" she mouthed.

The girl pointed a hand towards the cockpit, before going back about the task of winning the one-sided game. Jana smiled to herself and went in search of the second hero of Carth, hoping he'd be more awake than the first.

Kristof sat in the pilot's seat, feet kicked up onto the dashboard as he stared out at the rain. He glanced back as Jana leant through the hatchway behind him, and hurriedly pulled his feet down with an embarrassed cough.

"Sorry." he muttered.

"Don't worry about it." Jana smiled, tossing him one of the paper parcels. "I do it all the time."

Kristof caught the bag, unwrapped it, and tore into its contents with a savagery that only the starving could muster. Jana laughed.

"Hungry?" she asked, taking a bite of her own.

"Incredibly." Kristof murmured through a mouthful of bread. "After yesterday, I needed this."

He looked up, suddenly serious.

"Cass told me what happened. I'm glad you're both alright."

"So am I." Jana smiled. "I'm sorry about Nadir."

Kristof nodded grimly. Wordlessly.

"I'm sure he'll be fine." Jana said, in what she hoped were encouraging tones. "It's just an arm, right? He's still got one left."

"He's fine. Or he will be." Kristof smiled, glancing back out at the rain for a moment. "Things could have been much worse."

Jana nodded, sadly. She was still impressed that they had all made it out alive. She felt like she had been through far more than any 4th Class Skimmer Cargo and Personnel Pilot deserved to survive, and it had only been… what? Four days? It was a surprise that any of them were still standing.

"How did you know him?" she asked, hesitantly. "Nadir, I mean? If it's not… you know…"

Kristof looked up, surprised. "No, no. It's fine. We picked him up …Me and Wulfe, this was before Cass' time… we picked him up after Carth. He… well, he helped us leave."

"Why would he do that?"

"We paid him." Kristof chuckled. "A lot."

Silence blossomed in the cabin for a moment as they both paused, listening to the rain pattering against the hastily patched glass. Jana watched thoughtfully as a bead of moisture slowly coalesced along the bottom of one of the patch panels.

"You never did tell me, by the way." she said.

Kristof looked up.

"Tell you what?"

"Why you left Carth. You know, why you're *here*? I thought you were heroes. I've been hearing stories about you since I was seven, and now I run into you… doing what? Petty theft?"

"I'd argue that this is some pretty major theft."

Jana chuckled. "Alright. Fair enough. No changing the subject though: Why did you leave?"

"Wulfe decided the Union wasn't for him anymore."

"And you?"

"Wasn't for me either."

"Why not?"

Kristof sighed melodramatically. Jana smiled. She could see he was deflecting. There was no way she was about the get the whole story.

"You don't want to get me started on politics, do you?" he said with a grin.

"Kristof, I am literally asking for it. I spent my whole childhood hearing about you. About Captain Bastian Wulfe, the hero of Carth. The Wolf, the Hawk and the Butcher. You don't expect me to be even the least bit curious? What happened to you? You were heroes. People looked up to you. *I* looked up to you. You stood for everything the Union said mankind could be!"

"Did we? Who told you that?"

"I've told you before, I used to read the releases about the war as they came in from the…"

"And who wrote them?"

Jana was silent for a moment. Kristof grimaced, and looked back out towards the rain.

"I did warn you not to get me started." he muttered. "For what it's worth, its not all lies. Even a stopped clock is right twice a day."

"What bits were true?"

"Wulfe. If anyone deserves to be called a hero, its him."

Silence filled the cockpit for a moment. Jana took another mouthful of bread, watching as rain slowly began to drip from behind the rough repair work on the main screen. She was about to leave when Kristof spoke again.

"Have you wondered why we didn't change our names?" he asked, quietly.

"I did." she conceded.

"Might want to ask Wulfe about that."

"Ask me what?" a new voice rumbled behind them.

Jana glanced back, startled. The soldier could move worryingly quietly when he wanted to, it turned out.

Kristof leant his head back, throwing Wulfe a broad smile over the back of the seat.

"I thought you were asleep." he commented, his voice returned to normal.

"I was. Thought it might serve as a pick-me-up."

"Did it?"

"Take a wild guess."

Kristof grinned.

"So…" Cass said, looking around at the group. "Are we doing this?"

"Doing what?" Wulfe said, glancing back.

"*This*, Wulfe." she flapped the paper in his face for a moment, and then read from it again.

"*…meet us in Cothiq at 17:78 in three days, on the Walkway between sections 27 and 37, floor 20…*"

"I don't see why." the soldier rumbled. "Pick another city. Keep moving. With luck we'll never hear about this ever again."

"It's nice to dream, Wulfe, but that felt like sticky trouble to me." Kristof said, not turning around. "The kind of trouble you can't get rid of by just running away.

"You're saying we should do what it says?" Wulfe said. "These are the same people that got us into this mess in the first place, mind."

"They said they can help, Wulfe." Cass said, gesturing at him with the crumpled scrap of paper.

Wulfe scoffed. "Well they would say that, wouldn't they?"

"We should tell someone." Jana said, quietly. "Whatever happened down there could be dangerous. The Council could…"

"Whatever that place was existed within the full knowledge of the Ashkan government, Jana." Kristof cut in. "Their stamp was on the documents we used to find it. Odds are they built it, whatever *it* is."

"You don't know that." Jana said, almost defensively. "Cass said the files had been deleted."

"They must know." Kristof said. "The Legionaries that fired at you must have been responding to the site somehow. It's the only explanation. As to why they left I..."

He sighed. "I don't know. And I hate not knowing. That piece of paper that Cass is holding may just have the answers. If we don't like them, *then* we run. But we need to know what we're dealing with."

A brief silence settled across the cockpit, before Cass' voice broke it.

"That's settled then. How far is it?"

Jana took off her cap, running a hand through her hair as she stared thoughtfully up at the ceiling of the skimmer's hold.

"If I'm remembering my Ashkan geography from school right it must be at least a couple of days flight. We should have the fuel for it, on the bright side."

Cass grinned.

"No sense in rushing then. Come on, I'll show you how to play Trips."

Jana treated the two soldiers to a shrug, screwed on her cap once more and allowed herself to be guided off into the hangar by the young woman. Kristof smiled to himself, settling back in the chair as he watched the rain running down the screens in front of him. He had always liked rain. Especially from indoors. There was something soothing about knowing that if you didn't have this shelter, things would be just that little bit worse.

It rained like this on the day of the White Harbour massacre.

Kristof blinked.

Blood in the rain.

I told you I'd keep it open, didn't I?

Above the patter of the rain, Kristof heard a slight creak as Wulfe shifted where he stood.

"I told you we should walk away." The man murmured, his voice barely audible above the rain. "That we should just stop."

"I know." Kristof said.

"You haven't stopped, though."

"I know."

"I hoped you'd left that stubbornness behind." Wulfe rumbled, his voice like distant thunder. Slowly, quietly, he knelt down, bringing him level with Kristof as they gazed out at the rain together.

"No more. I've had my share of fighting and bloodshed, I can tolerate it. But Jana and Cass are innocent in all this, and I won't put them in harms way. Nadir knew the risks when he signed up, I told him myself. He had his choice. They didn't."

Chapter 15

34th Sihyl, 2094.74 Core Time – Electronic Messaging Certificate

Captain Wulfe,

I am afraid the information you are requesting is under strict control by the Commission, and can therefore not share our "motives" with a legionary Captain, no matter how prestigious. Simply have faith, and be sure in the knowledge that what we did is the correct move to further the interests of the wider Union.

Incidentally, I have left instructions with some of the local administrative sections for you to participate in some form of interview or media appearance. My colleagues in the Commission have informed me that this will likely be beneficial for both civilian and legion morale, and I am inclined to agree with them.

Forward as one,

Adran Massri, Commissary (2nd Class), Ashkan High Command.

It was midday the following day before Jana got the chance to ask Wulfe the question that had been burning in the back of her mind.

The sun was high in the sky as they streaked along the coast of the Ashkan gulf. The vast ocean spread out to her left, the land below her stacked high with buildings, the industrial heart of the Union spilling out into the sea beyond. Jana found the ships below fascinating, always keeping one eye on the ocean below as she guided the skimmer along the coast.

She started as she heard a gruff cough behind her. Wulfe stood in the hold doorway, holding one of the white paper packages from the day before out to her.

"We were going to finish them. I thought you should have the last one, as you fetched them for us and all."

"Very thoughtful of you." Jana smiled, reaching a hand back for the package as she balanced the controls carefully in neutral.

"Given the choice between feeding two children and the pilot, I'll feed the one who's keeping me two thousand metres up in the air." the man replied drily.

Jana was surprised. That had almost sounded like a joke.

"What are they up to?" she asked.

"Arguing." Wulfe shrugged. "They seem to enjoy it though, so I left them to it."

He turned, as if to leave. Jana sprang into action.

"Wulfe?" she said, placing the package aside for a moment.

Wulfe turned back, his brows furrowing as he stared at her.

"What?"

"While we're here, can I ask you something?"

"I get the feeling that you're going to anyway." he muttered.

There was a moment of silence.

"That was supposed to be a yes." Wulfe added, slowly.

"Why didn't you change your name? If you're on the run?"

There was a pause. Jana glanced back, and saw that the soldier was, himself, staring over his shoulder into the hold behind him. He looked back, catching her gaze.

"Because it's *my* name."

"But…"

Wulfe sighed.

"Describe the Wolf of Carth to me."

"Well, he was tall. Black hair…"

Wulfe cut in again, his voice a low rumble almost lost against the muted roar of the engines.

"You're describing me. Describe *him*."

"You say that like there's a difference."

"There is. You said yourself that I'm not what you expected. You talked about the stories, the tales you've heard, right? Tell me about *him*." Wulfe said quietly, a trace of bitterness clear in his voice as he spoke the words. "Tell me about the *Wolf of Carth*."

Jana paused, then began to speak slowly, her words gaining confidence as she found her verbal footing.

"He was a hero. We always heard, growing up, about how the Union protected us. Even though we were millions of miles from Ashka, it watched over us. We knew that it protected our way of life, kept us fed and sheltered. We knew what it stood for, and what it stood against on our behalf. The Wolf was all those things. Every battle he fought, every word he spoke, it was… it was right. It was the right thing to do, and he did it *because* it was the right thing."

Jana was a child again. She could feel the icy winds of Valmeer on her skin, hear the coarse chatter of the Bolvar children as they rushed past her, see the faint speck that was the Pioneer slipping below the far horizon, wreathed in a cloud of grey-white mist.

"There was war everywhere. It felt like the world was falling down around us. Mum tried to keep it from me, but... I knew. I wasn't stupid. Kids are very quick to notice when an adult is worried. Then stories of The Wolf began surfacing, and... it gave us something to cling to."

She felt the warm embrace again. That final, lingering embrace, the kind that both sides hope never ends. She felt the hands drawing away, saw the soft smile again. *Be good* whispered a voice somewhere in the darkness.

"I was small. My mum was away, for years sometimes, fighting a war somewhere that I barely knew the name of, and… and the idea that there was some great hero out there with her was…"

She looked up again, staring out of the front window, away from Wulfe. She had gone misty-eyed, and she hated it.

A comforting hand rested on her shoulder, and she glanced up hesitantly, her cheeks flushing with shame.

Wulfe stared out of the front window, averting his gaze from hers as he felt her move.

"They tell a good story, I'll credit them with that." he said, not unkindly.

He paused for a moment in quiet reflection.

"A damn good story." he muttered again, shaking his head. "They created something on Carth. It had my face, it had my name, but it wasn't me. I'm not the man you heard about as a child."

He turned, and Jana felt the hand slip from her shoulder.

"I'm sorry if that is hard for you to hear." The Wolf murmured as he stepped out through the hatchway.

They didn't even find a port on the evening of the second day. They sat together under the wing of the Siren, staring out at the crimson dusk as the sun sunk below the Ashkan gulf.

Only now had it begun to strike Jana just where she was. A different *planet*. Over the last two days she had watched the landscape shift below her; towering cityscapes giving way to dense farmland, the patterned rows of trees and bushes divided by vast, sweeping rivers that coiled across the countryside, threading their way between the few scattered settlements that occupied the higher grounds.

"That's a lot of water." she murmured, half to herself.

"Don't you have oceans on Valmeer?" Cass said, looking up from her slate, which she had been using to sketch a rough imitation of the crimson sky.

"There's two, and they're tiny." Jana responded. "Nothing like this."

"At least it doesn't bloody rain all the time." Wulfe muttered.

"You're underestimating sand, Wulfe." Jana said. "Rain dries up eventually. Sand scratches the paintwork, it gets in the electronics, clogs up the moving parts, it even works its way into the ventilation. You have no idea how many hours I spent digging sand out of this girl's heating ducts." She patted the hull of the skimmer affectionately. "A life well spent if you ask me."

Wulfe grunted non-committally.

"It'll do you good, Wulfe." Cass said, giving the soldier a nudge in the ribs. "The rain is giving your coat its second wash this year."

She grinned.

"If it gets washed too often it'll wear out." Wulfe muttered defensively.

"Wouldn't be a problem if you didn't wear it every day."

"Its comfy. I've worn these things for forty years now. You get used to them."

"Maybe we should get Kristof one so the two of you match." Cass said with a smirk.

"I'll pass, thanks." the other man muttered, looking up from his cards for a moment.

"You don't think they're comfy?" the girl pressed.

Kristof shifted a few cards about in his hand, before adding two to the pile between them. The smile fell from Cass' face, and she glared suspiciously up at the soldier.

"Not my style. Sergeants had their own uniform." he murmured, clearly pretending not to notice.

Jana looked over. "Huh, I thought the coats were universal. Mum had one, I think."

Kristof shrugged.

"I'll take a hat like Jana's."

"You'll look ridiculous." Cass muttered only slightly under her breath.

"Hey, that's *my* hat you're on about!" Jana said, turning on the girl.

Kristof glanced at Jana and grinned.

"There's just no pleasing some people." he said with a shrug.

"Focus, Kristof!" Cass hissed, extending a leg and giving the man a nudge with her foot to get his attention. "You can't play two cards there, you know that."

Kristof's eyes narrowed, and for a moment he sat silently, his gaze flickering between his hands and the pile. After a moment, Cass cut in again.

"Two things: A, You're a terrible actor. B, I know I've won. You play *that*," she gestured at one of the cards in the pile. "I play *this*. Then there's nothing you can do except fold."

Kristof grimaced for a moment. "Well you've seen cards you shouldn't have been able to, how about we call it a draw?" he asked with a grin.

Cass laughed. "Not a chance. You're a terrible loser, you know that?"

Kristof shrugged.

"Nobody's perfect."

The third day dawned.

Kristof sat in the corner of the skimmer, trying to ignore the roar of the engines, a sound that had been his near-constant companion over the past three days. It was beginning to grate.

He brushed aside the half-finished game of cards lay on the seat beside him, a remnant of the games he and Cass had been playing before they had both got bored and agreed to call it a draw. Throwing a furtive glance at the doorway he reached back with his foot and slid Wulfe's black canvas bag out from under the bench on which he sat. His eyes roved around the room, falling across the soldier's sleeping form nestled comfortably on one of the corner benches, greatcoat wrapped tightly against the drafty interior of the aircraft.

Silently he reached down, and drew forth two pieces of finished metal.

Perfwedd .05. Legion Issue Sidearm. Robust and almost impossible to jam. Holds 14.

He cracked the piece open.

Still loaded.

Snapping the weapon back together, he placed it quietly back in the bag.

Trest Atreus .07. Outdated self-defence sidearm once issued to envoy families on Celthar. Powerful, but prone to backfiring.

Taking a handful of rounds, Kristof began methodically re-arming the weapon.

Holds five.

"You think that's going to be necessary?" Wulfe's voice sounded, barely audible above the drone of the engines.

Kristof looked up. The soldier hadn't moved from his corner, but his eyes had opened, and were now fixed on the weapon in Kristof's hands.

"I'm not taking any chances." he replied.

"Do you have a plan?" Wulfe shook his head. "Who am I kidding, I know that mind of yours. Do you have a good plan?"

"No. We don't have anything to go on." Kistof said, slotting another round into the weapon and prying the mechanism into line with a practiced hand. "I'm working on it though. I can take the meeting, but I need you find something to keep those two out of the firing line if things go south."

The soldier nodded again, then paused.

"Do you think they will?"

"What?"

"Go south."

"With our luck? Almost definitely." Kristof shrugged, flicking the slide back into position. The weapon primed with an audible hiss. He sighed, and glanced sidelong at Wulfe.

"I don't see what other choice we have, though. After… whatever that was, I think we could do with a friend or two."

"You think they're friends, the people we're going to meet?"

"I think that *they* think that. That's something. And I can't honestly think of any reason to invite us here otherwise."

Wulfe pulled a face.

"Maybe they'll just help us, and ask nothing in return." he muttered.

Kristof chuckled, rising to his feet and tucking the weapon into his belt.

"Now that sounds more like the Wulfe that I've heard so much abou…"

He bit down on the words as Cass lunged back through the cockpit door, pushing past him and plastering herself against the small window in the craft's flank doors, seemingly oblivious to the two men's presence. Jana's voice sounded from just behind Kristof's head with a burst of static, making him jump.

"You might all want to hold on to something for a few minutes." The pilot's voice crackled over the intercom. *"The local flight control is talking me through it, but I've never flown over something like this before. We might hit some turbulence."*

"Kristof, look!" hissed Cass. She reached down, eyes still fixed on whatever it was outside the window, and tugged at his shirt. Kristof pulled himself to his feet with a sigh and glanced down over her shoulder.

The grey-green waters of the Ashkan gulf fell away below them. They churned and writhed as they were dragged over the cliffs, the entire ocean seeming to simply drop away into a haze of mist-wreathed spires of grey oceanic rock. The gorge ran from horizon to horizon, as far as the eye could see, the low evening sun glinting off the mists that were being churned up by the spectacle, turning the entire valley into a burning fissure of dancing shadows and glinting starlight.

On the horizon, Cothiq hoved into view. The city clung almost precariously to the edge of the gorge, huddled into one of the thousands of crevasses that pocked its surface. The city had a silvery sheen to it, sheathed in the very same oceanic rock that had formed the gorge that surrounded it.

It was a striking sight, even Kristof had to admit.

The skimmer shuddered briefly, caught for a moment in one of the seams of twisting air that writhed up out of the mists below. Kristof, who had heeded Jana's warning, caught Cass by the back of her shirt as she stumbled past him. The girl flashed him a brief smile, seeming to barely register him as she pressed herself back up against the window, eyes wide as she stared down into the gorge below them.

"Well, that wasn't too bad, was it?" came the voice again. Kristof smiled to himself. It was good to hear Jana in her element again. It was strange how much people changed when they were on their home turf.

Cass reached out slowly, eyes never leaving the scene below them, and lifted the intercom microphone out of its wall socket.

"Jana, can you see that?" she whispered, her voice hushed with awe.

"Cass, I'm flying the skimmer. You'd better hope I can see it." crackled the response.

Jana wrestled with the elements as the skimmer descended towards the city. There was a port below her that she could make out without the aid of Control, and she brought the skimmer down through the whirling mists towards it.

The air around her was thick with the sound of engines, from smaller single-man transportation units to the hulking, quad-engined freight skimmers that loomed like the shadows of vast birds of prey in the sky above her.

"Control, this is a Siren-class transport, requesting a spot to land on the south-west platform." she said, kicking the altitude into neutral and bringing the skimmer to a near-standstill in the air.

"Stand by, Siren-class. We will have a spot for you in a few moments."

The city was beautiful, really. She found herself lost, staring out over the white stone of the rooftops that almost seemed to glitter in the morning sunlight. It was a far sight from the grey stone of Ashka's tower blocks or the dust-riddled catastrophes that were the Bolvar market towns.

Jana smiled to herself, flicking the transmission switch on the dashboard in front of her to internal broadcast.

"You people really do take me to the nicest places." she said, hearing her voice amplified back in the hold behind her.

She reversed the switch again to external, and paused as her fingers momentarily traced one of the shallow scars the Legionary's rounds had left on the console's rim. That had been nearly three days ago now.

Jana shivered slightly, shifting uncomfortably in her seat at the memory.

She had felt helpless. In all honesty, she had been helpless, and that's what made it even worse. You always imagined yourself as a hero in these situations, that you'd come up with some genius plan and save the day.

But she hadn't. She'd hid under a console and screamed as the glass rained down around her. They had survived only because... well, they didn't even know that. They just had.

Jana blinked, and shook her head. She really had to stop daydreaming behind the wheel of a three-tonne flying machine.

"Still waiting for that landing spot, Control." she muttered under her breath, making a point of not pressing the transmit button. "Sometime this century if you can squeeze us in would be ideal." she added sardonically. She leant back in her seat, tugging her cap down a little to cover her eyes from the streaming sunlight that turned the mist around her to a glittering sea of diamond.

And in seconds, the spell was shattered.

Out of the boiling sea of mist in front of her swept a freight skimmer, its engines on full and turned to maximum thrust, fifteen tonnes of thundering metallic fury scything through the air at breakneck speed. It barrelled towards Jana and the Siren, making no signs of halting or slowing, the roar of its engines growing louder by the moment.

Jana had barely seconds to react. Instinctively, she kicked down with her right boot, bringing the altitude out of neutral and sending the skimmer plummeting downwards as the engines locked up tight. She felt her stomach rise as gravity took hold, tugging the aircraft down moments before the hulking freighter roared mere inches overhead. She heard Cass scream in the hold behind her, heard the shrill wail of the stall alarm, heard the shrill whistle of air through the bullet holes in the glass beside her, the sounds mingling in her mind as the skimmer tumbled towards the gorge below.

She thrust the control column forwards with one hand, mashing the auto-restart button with her other as the craft tilted forwards. She felt the airflow catch the engines, and as the drone of the engines rose she eased back on the column, bringing the craft back into a stable airspace.

Almost as fast as it began, it was over. Jana sat in her chair, heart racing, hands gripping the column so tight it felt like they might leave a mark in the polished metal.

Chapter 16

Media Release Extract – Ashkan Union Data Archives – Broadcast 32.44.2033, Recorded 31.44.2033

INTERVIEWER – "…And Captain, perhaps you could elaborate for us: Months ago we were being informed that the war was almost over, that the last remnants of the Butcher's forces were being surrounded and destroyed. Now we are being told that the war has begun to blossom from occasional insurgencies into a full-blown insurrection, with armed pockets of rebels taking and holding portions of the city. Could you shed any light on this for us?"

CPT.WULFE – "We… we were close. But in war things can happen. No matter the cause, mistakes can be made…

COM.ATESCA – "I think what the captain is trying to say is that despite his admittedly valiant efforts at securing the city, the rebels are tenacious willing to sacrifice both their own lives and the civilian population for their victory. Against such a brutal enemy, progress will always be slow. In this time more than any other, it is important for us to stand as one, and to present a united front to the forces that wish to tear our beloved Union apart."

CPT.WULFE NODS, BUT OFFERS NO FURTHER COMMENT.

"Someone tried to kill us." Wulfe muttered.

"You're sure it wasn't an accident?" Kristof said to Jana earnestly. "We're new here, are you sure you weren't just in the way?"

"I don't know." Jana said. Despite landing safely on the south-western platform of Cothiq, she still hadn't been able to drag herself out of her seat. The adrenaline crash had hit her hard, and she felt like she wanted to sleep, vomit and cry all at the same time. "I... I don't know. Those things shouldn't be flying that fast around landing areas. There are rules about it back home. Some of the automated ones even have limiters. Control said it shouldn't have happened, there wasn't even a departure scheduled."

"Doesn't sound like an accident to me." Wulfe rumbled. "Who was it?"

"I don't know anyone who kills you with heavyweight transports." Kristof muttered. "Anyone upset any trade companies lately? Fallen foul of the Var... Varian..."

He paused, his brow furrowing as he stared blankly into space, almost as if listening.

"Kristof?" said Cass from the ground beside Jana's chair.

The man's lips moved for a moment, almost silently.

"Talk to us, Kristof." the girl repeated.

"Some of the automated ones have limiters." Kristof whispered, almost to himself. He looked up at Wulfe, and for a moment Jana almost thought she saw fear in his eyes.

"Someone tried to shock you in the Vault, Wulfe. Someone tried to shut us in. Now someone drops a skimmer on us." he said, staring the soldier directly in the eyes, his voice gaining in confidence as he spoke. "That's all... computers. Electrics."

"There's no way." Wulfe muttered. "How would they know where we are?"

"I gave the skimmer class to Control." Jana said quietly. "There can't be many Sirens on Ashka. Its a desert-specific variant of the sparrowhawk transport."

"And how would they know we're in a Siren transport?"

Silence fell for a moment.

"The Legions would." Jana said.

"Not possible." Cass piped up. "You would need some insane processing power to break into a Legion system. Their databases are monstrously encrypted. Thousands of people work on it every day. Millions, maybe."

"But what if someone found a way?"

"Its not possible, Jana. That isn't how the system works. Just trust me." The girl repeated.

"So the attacks came from someone with high levels of Ashkan central system access." Kristof said, his eyes never having left Wulfe's. "A name springs to mind, Wulfe. Someone who very much wants us dead."

There was a pause for a moment, then the soldier's eyes widened in recognition.

"No." he said flatly. "She wouldn't do that."

"Are you sure, Wulfe." Kristof said slowly, his voice sinking to a growl. "Are you sure you know what she would and wouldn't do?"

Wulfe's weathered features seemed to tremble for a moment as a myriad of emotions played across them. He stared almost defiantly at the other man for a moment, straightening up slightly, his powerful frame dwarfing that of Kristof.

"I know, and she wouldn't."

Silence fell for a moment.

"Stop it you two." Cass snapped, her voice breaking the stalemate. "We need to do something. We can't just sit in this bloody skimmer all week." She reached into her pocket and pulled out the crumpled, dog-eared piece of paper.

"This meeting is in an hour. Do we go, or do we get the hell out of here?"

"We have to go." Kristof said. "I can't not know what's going on."

"This could be another trap." Wulfe murmured.

"Within half an hour we could have all the answers we need!"

"Or we could be bleeding to death in an alley. It's not like you to be this blindly trusting, Kristof. Stop, take a deep breath, and think things through."

"We can't run forever, Wulfe." Jana said. "We need answers. If that happens again I can't promise I'll be quick enough."

There was another moment's silence as Wulfe stared about the confines of the group.

"Alright." he muttered. "You're right. Lets get it over with."

The air of Cothiq was damp, saturated with an ever-present moisture that seeped up from the gorge beyond the city. Jana had decided that she wasn't a fan of the damp. Within minutes her hair had begun to curl, and her clothes had turned clammy. A slick sheen of liquid covered the waterproof fabric of her flight jacket, pooling in the wrinkles of her sleeves and running down over her hands whenever she moved. She tossed her head, trying fruitlessly to clear the loose strands of damp hair from her vision. She'd take the cold winters of Verkat over this any day.

"Glad I'm not a pilot in these parts. Must be a nightmare to keep things from rusting around here." She muttered to Cass, before realising that the girl clearly wasn't listening, all of her attention focussed on the city above.

They climbed slowly up from the port, leaving the twin roars of skimmer engines and rushing water behind them as they ascended the narrow, white-paved streets towards the city above. What people Jana could see were hurried, spending as little time as possible outside as they darted furtively from building to building, the hoods of their clothing pulled up against the drifting mist.

The city rose in front of them, built into the very cliffs of the canyon itself. Smaller buildings stood between the vast walls, crisscrossed by thousands of tiny walkways. The walls of the buildings themselves were ornately engraved, detailed with tiny, intricate murals, picked out in darkened stone. Jana felt her mind shudder at the thought of how long it must have taken to detail the city like this. Hundreds of years, surely.

Almost instinctively, she looked down at Cass. The girl's eyes were wide, her mouth *almost* hanging open as she stared up at the city in front of her, awestruck. Jana grinned.

"Watch it Cass, you'll catch flies." she said.

The girl shot her a glance of pure venom before turning her attention back to the vision of shining marble that towered above them.

Even Kristof whistled through his teeth as he looked around.

"Imposing." he muttered.

They ascended into the city proper. It felt empty to Jana, the streets tidy and clean, free of the teeming crowds of Ashka or the chaos of the Bolvar markets she once called home.

There were soldiers too, interspersed amongst the crowds. She could tell that Kristof was doing his best to avoid them as they moved further into the city, turning several sharp corners to avoid direct confrontation when the streets cleared momentarily. The legionaries paid them no heed, much to Jana's relief.

However, as they approached the centre of the city, Jana began to notice a change. The soldiers they passed were no longer legionaries. Their attire was more outlandish, with long skirts and sashes that to Jana seemed more suited to a summertime in Valmeer than a mist-soaked city by the ocean. Their heads were clean-shaven, and they all had their right arms bared to the elements, their intricate Quin tattoos seeming almost to writhe as they ran the full span from fingertip to shoulder.

There were other, larger figures amongst them too. Centurions towered over their fellow soldiers like vast statues, implacable and terrifying in their stature. She watched them curiously as they walked by. These looked different to the ones Nadir had showed her on Ashka. They seemed taller, somehow, and bulkier, the reddish-brown tinge to their armour causing them to glow oddly in the dim light that filtered down from the distant sky.

One of them turned its head to watch them as they passed, the pilot's face unreadable behind the thick armoured visor. Jana looked away hurriedly, but she could feel its steady gaze on her as she carried on up the street.

"We stick out like sore thumbs around here. I don't like the idea of splitting up." Wulfe rumbled.

Kristof nodded, glancing around the small side street they had paused in. The voice in the back of his mind was jumping at him at every opportunity now. It was in a new environment, and it had found a lot to catalogue.

"We do. This place isn't what I expected." He shook his head. "We need something to go on, though. If all of you stick together you should be safe enough. Just... stay inconspicuous if you can. Keep out of sight."

"I'd still like to know more about this place." Wulfe said. "Call me paranoid, but with our recent luck knowing the fastest ways to get around the city could come in handy."

Brushing some loose water off her sleeve, Jana glanced back the way they had come. "I'd like to have a look around the port, if that's alright. I can have a talk with the air control and find out what's going on in these parts."

"Are you just trying to get back to the skimmer?" Cass said.

Jana grinned. "Alright, you got me. She was making some strange noises on the way here, and I thought I should give her a look over while we have the chance."

"Really Jana? Now?"

"Better now than later, when you need it." the pilot shrugged. "Listen, Cass, that skimmer is one of the few things in this... escapade of yours that I understand. Just take my word on this."

Kristof frowned, but nodded.

"Go on then. But be careful."

"You too." Jana said, turning away and hurrying back down the street.

Kristof stared after her for a moment, unsure if he had made the right decision.

She's out of the way. She's safe.

"Kristof?" Cass' voice cut through his musings.

"What's up?"

"I wanted to come to the meet too."

"Why?"

"I found it. I arranged it. I want to help."

"The best way for you to help is to keep somewhere safe so we don't need to worry about you." Wulfe said quietly.

"Wulfe, I want to *help*. My neck is just as much on the line as yours is."

"We made a deal, remember. You can come along as long as you stay out of trouble."

Kristof winced, stepping forwards as the girl turned on Wulfe, her eyes suddenly aflame.

"No, the deal I remember making is that I would get you two out of the disaster you had got yourselves in on my doorstep, and in return…"

Feelings of inadequacy and helplessness. She feels pressured and on the defensive. the voice hissed in the back of his mind.

"Cass." Kristof said quietly, calmingly. "Cass, listen to me. I know you want to help. I would too, right?"

Build background and form a bond.

"…And you can. We…" Kristof said, gesturing at Wulfe , himself and finally towards Cass herself. "We all do have our ways to help. Look at Jana. She doesn't talk the talk, she can't fight, she doesn't speak Quin, so what does she do? She sticks to what she knows. *Skimmers*. She'll get better with time, but for now? She does what she does best."

Provide assurance and confidence.

"You, Cass, you know what you do best? *Places*. I need someone who knows Cothiq like the back of their hand, and I'll need them soon."

Gently request aid.

"Can you do that for me, Cass?" he said, placing a hand on her shoulder.

Cass was fighting herself, chewing thoughtfully on her lower lip as she stared thoughtfully at the leather ident booklet in her hands.

"I know you're trying to distract me, Kristof." she muttered, without looking up.

"It's working though, isn't it?"

"Don't push your luck." she said, treating him to one of her most withering scowls as she turned away.

Kristof straightened up, flashing a quick smile at Wulfe over the girl's head.

"See how I did that?" he said, shooting the soldier a quick wink as he darted in through the open doorway, sliding it shut behind him with the hiss of compressed air.

Jana made her way along the streets of Cothiq. She glanced up at the sky as she walked, more out of force of habit than anything else. It was an impressive sight, and she found herself slowing, gazing at the alien city that surrounded her. The main street rose steadily as it ran along the ravine's floor, and in the far distance Jana could make out a large structure looming above the rest of the city. The ravine's walls were a mess of doors, windows and walkways, which crisscrossed the sky above her. She felt like a fly in a web.

She also realised, as she walked, that she had forgotten about the dampness of the air around the port. Why on earth had she insisted on coming back here again? Verkat, for all its many faults, was at least dry.

The platform was strangely empty as Jana made her way across it, her feet splashing across the stonework as she hurried towards what she assumed to be the control centre. She ducked inside as the glass doors swung open automatically for her, and breathed a sigh of relief as she brushed some of the loose water from her sleeves. She took her hat off, shaking out her hair a little as she approached the front desk.

"Hey." she started. "I was wondering if..."

"Ident."

The gaunt-faced young man leant back in his chair, eyes fixed on the slate that he held in his slender fingers, barely registering Jana's presence beyond the single word. Jana reached into her flight-jacket, producing the slim leather booklet and holding it out to the man.

She was treated to a look of such withering scorn that she withdrew the book again. The man looked at her over the top of his slate, before staring pointedly at a small, grey capture scanner that lay on the desk to Jana's left. Jana obliged, placing the document on the scanner.

"You've come a long way." the man commented, glancing at the screen for a moment as Jana laid the ident on the scanner.

"Yep." Jana nodded.

"The capital." she clarified after a while, when further conversation didn't seem to be forthcoming.

This didn't have the reinvigorating effect on the conversation she had hoped. The man had turned back to his screens, the soft blue text sparkling in his eyes as they processed the document. Jana waited for a few seconds before folding her arms on the desk in front of her and leaning in to wait.

"So I was hoping you would have some spare maintenance kits lying around. My old flightpath used to give them out for free if they were out of date or damaged, and I could really... really..."

She trailed off. The colour had drained from the man's face, and the expression of vapid boredom had given way to a frown of concern.

"Is everything alright?" she said, a shiver of fear running down her spine. They hadn't tried the idents since they had booked those rooms at the *Excelsior*. What if something had gone wrong? What if their identities had been blown? What if..."

The man rose hurriedly to his feet, a nervous smile flitting across his features.

"I'm so sorry Mrs.Karikova." he said, taking the ident out of the scanner and handing it back to Jana.

Jana took the ident from the man's shaking hand and pocketed it quickly, trying carefully to mask her confusion.

"Your craft was unusual, I didn't recognise you." the attendant continued. "Most of the Councillor's entourage use the MKIV, not..." he leaned to look through the curved glass windows and across the concrete towards where the Siren stood. "...not one of those."

Councillor's entourage? Of the Ashkan Council? Does this place have a city council? Or is 'The Councillor' a title?

"So what did you think I looked like?" Jana asked, careful to keep her tone level.

"I didn't..." the man hesitated nervously. "You didn't look like..."

"I didn't look like a diplomat?" Jana took a leap of faith. "Well, I'm not. Not really. I just fly them around, you see, but they think it makes my job easier if they load me with all these fancy titles."

She leant over the desk, exaggerating a conspiratorial whisper.

"It really doesn't."

The man smiled, clearly relieved. She felt like she was getting better at this whole lying business. It seemed that practice did, after all, make perfect.

"Well, I'm sorry for the confusion. What can I do for you?"

"Do you keep any tools on-hand here? I was worried that the fuel-coupling was going to shake right off for a few minutes on the way over."

"Ah, right. Maintenance kits." The man vanished below the desk for a moment, before re-emerging and pushing a metallic blue case into her hands.

"That ought to have everything you need."

Jana beamed, relieved that she had managed to allay the man's suspicions, but more than that she was simply pleased to see another friendly face. She hadn't realised how long it had been.

"Thanks!" she said. She turned to leave, and paused, before turning back slowly towards the desk.

"So do the other diplomats land around here? Seems a little wet to be bringing dignitaries through all the time." she said conversationally, flipping the kit open in her hands. Might as well dig for some information while she was here, she thought. The others might appreciate it.

"Oh no, if they're going to speak with the Councillor then they will land up at the embassy. Did they not tell you where to go?"

Jana shrugged, and flashed a nervous smile. "New on the job. The induction training wasn't exactly informative."

The clerk grimaced. "Well I hope you're not in trouble. They can be a touchy lot, and you seem... seem like..."

Jana realised that the man's gaze had shifted, and that he was staring over her shoulder once more out through the glass doors.

She turned as they slid aside, and two figures stepped into the room. They were tall and powerfully built, and beside the beautiful orange sashes they wore about their waists Jana could make out the cold metal of handguns.

They were the Quin guards she had seen near Cothiq's centre. One of them looked up, running a hand across his bald scalp to brush away the errant drops of moisture that still clung to it. His eyes were not unkind, but cold in that piercing way that soldiers often had.

The clerk stood up.

"Can I help you, gentlemen?"

The soldier raised a gloved hand.

"Please take a seat, this is not an Ashkan matter." he stepped forwards, leaning in closely to whisper to Jana.

"Miss Schleifer, I would ask you to come with us. Please do not make a scene."

Chapter 17

The hearty laughter of the Legionaries drifted across the grim stillness of the rest of the camp.

"You are joking." Captain Wulfe rumbled. "Give me that." he said, reaching for the small book that his fellow soldier held.

"Dead serious, Captain, says it right here, look." The legionary cleared his throat. "'The Wolf of Carth: An Untold Story'"

Sgt.Richter grinned. "It describes you as valiant, stoic, and a shield to the weak and helpless. Are you feeling particularly valiant or stoic at the moment, Captain?"

"It's been a long day, Kristof." The Wolf of Carth muttered, staring down at the release with troubled eyes.

Kristof climbed the stairs slowly, ears alert for the slightest sound.

The Walkway between sections 27 and 37, floor 20.

As he climbed, he drew the pistol from his hip, counting the remaining shells quietly under his breath. He glanced up at the floor counter as he reached the next landing.

Floor 17.

He climbed further, closing the weapon with a near-silent click. 5 shots. More than enough.
If he needed more than five he was dead anyway.

Floor 18.

He paused for a moment, listening intently, counting the seconds under his breath. 14 beats later, he stepped abruptly around the corner into the next stairwell.

Empty. Silent.

He climbed onwards.

Floor 19.

Kristof stopped again, pausing on the landing. He reached out, sliding the exterior door aside and stepped out onto the walkway of floor 19. His eyes moved quickly, scanning the surrounding buildings and walkways.

Curse this city, he thought, struggling to make out details amidst the stylised architecture and tangled web of walkways that surrounded him.

He turned around, glancing up at the bridge directly overhead, already mentally drawing out sightlines to the doorway he would be stepping out of in a few seconds time.

The walkways around him seemed empty. The buildings too, their windows covered with heavy shutters, blocking any view inside or out. The walkways were open from either end, with nothing in the way of cover. The structures themselves were solid rock, however, with the balustrades providing plenty of cover from the neighbouring walkways. Kristof nodded quietly to himself. It could be worse. He'd had worse.

Kristof stepped back, pulling the door shut behind him quietly. With a final breath, he stepped onto the stairs.

Floor 20.

Kristof stepped out onto the walkway between sections 27 and 37, floor 20.

A single figure stood near the far end of the bridge. One boot was up on the balustrade, bracing as the man leant forwards, the cloud of acrid smoke he blew from his mouth whirling about him as he stared down into the void below.

Ashkan, with a touch of Quin.

The man dressed like a soldier. He wore a rough uniform in orange and black, although not one that Kristof could put a name to. His skin was pale, his hair and beard coarse, black and short.

The man didn't look up as Kristof approached, instead idly shifting his weight as he crushed the end of the cigarette against the stonework beside him.

He knows you're here.

Kristof glanced around again, eyes scanning the maze of walkways above and around him one last time as he stepped forward.

"You dropped this on your way up." he lied, holding out the ident pass. The man glanced down at the small leather booklet, before reaching out with his left to take it.

Ambidextrous. Smokes with his right, favours his left.

"I thought you'd never show up." the man murmured, flicking open the book with one hand to stare at its contents.

"We had a long way to come."

The soldier chuckled.

"I know." with a slow and deliberate motion he folded back the covers of the booklet and tore the pages from its interior, folding the two pieces together before pocketing them.

Strong. hissed the voice in Kristof's mind.

The soldier extended a hand, turning to face Kristof at last.

"Kyran Aurelien." he said.

Kristof took the man's hand. "Kristof Richter."

Very strong.

Kristof glanced over the edge of the walkway, his gaze sweeping the spot where he had stood minutes before. Kyran chuckled softly.

"I'm not going to hurt you, no need to be jumping at shadows."

"Who are you?"

"Come with me and find out." Kyran said, beginning to turn towards the far end of the walkway.

Kristof remained motionless.

"No." he stated flatly. "Who are you?"

Kyran paused. Without turning around, he spoke, his voice quiet and level.

"Jana's ident was used two minutes ago at the gorge-side landing port. Cassandra and Bastian are on their way to the Administration Centre on the central parade ground as we speak. They should be crossing the main avenue about now, I believe. Follow me to my employer, and they will join us on the way."

Kristof could hear the smile in the man's voice.

"If I wanted to hurt you it would already have happened, Mr.Richter. Come with me."

The Cothiq embassy stood at the centre of the city, its central spire surrounded by smaller wings that radiated gently outwards like the petals of a vast flower. Much like the rest of the city, a web of elegant walkways lay draped across these structures, criss-crossing, merging and un-merging, cutting the weak evening sunlight to ribbons before it could even touch the soft grasses and white stone that lay beneath.

Kristof watched as the others approached, each under a light escort. Wulfe bristled visibly, a towering and foreboding presence that made even the soldiers attempting to guide him keep their distance. Cass and Jana seemed relaxed, but Kristof could feel their eyes on him and knew that their response would be the same as his own.

Kyran glanced around the group before stepping aside and gesturing to the path ahead.

"Shall we?"

They trooped silently across the grounds, the embassy's central spire looming higher and higher above them as they approached it.

Kristof felt Cass tugging at his sleeve. He glanced down, trying to silence the voice that sat in the back of his mind. Watching. Calculating.

They're no legionaries. Not local guard, they're too well equipped. Too formal to be Mercs.

"Kristof, I think… those documents…"

Ambassadorial Troops.

Kristof nodded silently, watching the men around him intently.

"I'm stupid. I should have known." Cass continued, speaking in a tense whisper. "They had the stamps and everything. I even *said…*"

 "I know, Cass. It's ok." he murmured, placing a hand on her shoulder.

They were led into a sumptuously decorated foyer. The architecture was clean-cut, with an almost sterile aesthetic. The walls of the semi-circular chamber were draped with long reels of cloth, each decorated with strings of florid embroidery so vivid that they almost seemed to dance in the light that drifted down from the domed ceiling above.

Approaching the centre of the room, Kyran brought the party to a half.

"We'll wait here."

"…for the ambassador." Kristof finished the sentence.

Kyran chuckled quietly to himself.

"No, Mr. Richter, I *am* the ambassador."

Kristof paused, watching the man carefully.

"And your employer?"

"Who employs ambassadors, Mr. Richter? My patron is Councillor Song, Quin representative of the Union world of Cothiq alongside the associated cultural territories, and 11th Member of the Ashkan Council."

They all turned as the doors behind them slid quietly open. A solitary figure emerged, carrying itself with such grace that it seemed to almost glide across the floor. Her long, black hair had an unnatural tinge to it, a turquoise, almost metallic sheen, like the back of a magpie's wing. The black dress she wore left her right arm bared to the shoulder, displaying the intricate web of Quin ancestral tattoos that wound their way across her otherwise flawless skin up towards the shoulder before continuing down the back of the dress, the pattern picked out in fine silvered thread, to where its hem gently caressed the ground behind her as she walked. Though her skin was pale, her features were Quin: Sharp and angular, high, elegant cheekbones crested by a pair of silvery blue eyes, calm and clear as a mountain lake.

And just as cold.

The figure turned to Kristof, smiling gently, and extended a pale, delicate hand.

"It is a pleasure to finally meet you, Sergeant Richter. My name is Councillor Song."

Chapter 18

"What is this, Atesca?"

"It appears that one of the interviewers last week took a shine to you, Captain. And I can't say I blame them."

"This isn't... I didn't say a word of this! They've made it up wholesale."

"And is that a problem, Captain? These are troubled times, I imagine a few stories like this would be good for morale."

"It isn't right. Men have died for these lies."

"Think of it like this, Captain. That story is a small piece of the pillar that holds the Ashkan Union aloft in the public's collective minds. Alone it may not seem like much, but a hundred such stories may prevent another conflict like this one from occurring. You save lives every day, Captain. This may help you save a few more."

"I saw that one of the identification cards was checked into a medical bay in southern Ashka. Might I enquire as to what happened to him?" the Councillor asked gently as they followed her along one of the sunlit corridors that swept the edge of the embassy's main spire.

"He was injured when the job went sideways." Kristof explained.

"I am so sorry, all of you." Song said, pausing in her step for a moment. "This was never my intent."

"We still don't know what your intent *was*." Wulfe rumbled.

"All in due time, Captain." the councillor said. "Whilst you are here, you are safe. We will have time to talk everything over to your heart's content."

Jana watched the Councillor carefully as they walked through the long, white-tiled corridors of the complex. There was a perfection to Song that unsettled her. Her skin was flawless, not a single blemish to be seen. Her eyes were a strange shade of blue, almost crystalline, like a layer of ice over a deep ocean. Her features weren't Imperial, or Varian, or Quinn, or any other that Jana could bring to mind.

They stepped out into a wider corridor. Light streamed into the hallway from the vast glass wall that stretched along its left-most side. What lay beyond the glass, however, removed all thoughts of the councillor from Jana's mind.

The gentle mists from the Ashkan gorge drifted down onto a forest, richer than any Jana had ever imagined. Dew clung to the leaves, sparkling in the golden evening sunlight that shone down through the canopy above. Small, brightly-coloured birds fluttered through the trees, a riot of colour and song, dancing and weaving amidst the sun-dappled greenery. Jana fancied she could hear their song, crisp and melodious as she had ever imagined. She found herself slowing. She'd never seen this much green before.

There was a tugging on her sleeve. Cass had stopped beside her, staring out through the glass in wordless awe.

"Jana…" she whispered.

Jana laughed. "I know…" she looked back at the garden for a second. "We don't have anything like this where I'm from."

"I don't think they have anything like this anywhere."

"Follow Councillor Song, please." Ambassador Aurelien's voice sounded quietly from behind them, as he stepped past in pursuit of the group.

"Please." he repeated gently as they both turned to face him, startled slightly at his silent approach.

The embassy felt more like a palace, something Jana would have read about in books as a child, something even the most decadent of Varian noble families had abandoned centuries ago. It felt ostentatious, but not in the swaggering, arrogant, overblown way that the Bolvar were. Much like Song herself, the decorations radiated a quiet confidence, a sense that this was how things *should* be.

Within minutes, she had found herself seated on a large, delightfully soft divan, a drink being pressed into her hand by an earnest young Quin. It felt like a dream. Not a pleasant dream, but not an unpleasant one either. She felt like she had just woken up from a long nap and had forgotten where she was.

Not all members of the group were taking things as well, however. Jana was shaken out of her reverie as she watched Wulfe turn on a man who had attempted to guide him towards a seat. Like a striking snake the old soldier's hand whipped out, catching the man by the orange sash that he bore from shoulder to waist.

"Keep your hands off me." Wulfe snarled, gently but firmly pushing the man back to an arm's-length away.

From behind the low oaken table that occupied the centre of the room, Councillor Song raised a placating hand.

"Please. Is there anything I can have brought for you, Captain?"

The soldier looked up sharply, and visibly took a deep breath.

"Wulfe." he said flatly. "I think we want an explanation."

Song gave a soft laugh, and waved away the attendant with a delicate hand.

"I see the brusque demeanour of the Wolf of Carth was not an exaggeration."

"Hmm." grunted the Wolf of Carth, his eyes not leaving the Councillor as she swept around to the far end of the table.

Jana watched the three carefully. Kristof had already begun leafing through some of the papers piled on the table, eyes scanning quickly through their contents before he set them aside.

"And what would you like to know first, Wolf?"

"What was that place you sent us?"

"You saw for yourself. A myth. A rumour. A digital ghost in the systems of the Union."

"Mhm." Wulfe nodded. "And what was it really?"

"That I wasn't sure about. I knew that someone had spent a lot of effort removing any written trace of it from existence, and that intrigued me. So, as an experienced thorn in the Union's side, I did what I do best: I pried."

She paused, and raised a gentle hand to usher the remaining servants out of the room. As the doors slid shut, she leant forwards over the table, resting her chin on delicate fingers.

"Three days ago a routine patrol in southern Ashka was diverted from its usual route along the Lenzbeyer river by an urgent order from Legion High Command. They rushed to a small forested area to the south of Ashka, where they fired upon a Siren-class skimmer that had landed in the exclusion zone. One of the men also reported seeing a strange metallic structure in a gully with a man standing beside it. Seconds after engaging, the patrol was called off, again by an order directly from High Command."

The two crystalline eyes lingered on Jana for a moment, the Councillor's face an unreadable mask.

"I think you already knew that part of the story, no? But do you know what happened to this patrol next?

Kristof shook his head. "Something happened to them?"

"Two days later they boarded a skimmer to take them on a different patrol route around northern Ashka. A little airborne rapid response force for any serious criminal activity." she glanced at Kristof. "Gangs, murders, terrorist attacks and so forth. Unfortunately, one of the service drones had fuelled the skimmer with Kerosene-based D12."

"D12?" Jana said quietly. "That's for combat interceptors, not the transport classes. That would..."

"Precisely." Song replied with an almost imperceptible smile. "D12 burns hot and fast, so the resultant fire was easily contained. Sadly all three occupants were dead within seconds."

Cass gasped, covering her mouth with her hands in horror. Kristof grimaced, shaking his head slightly as he did so.

"I take it that they are not trying to cover our tracks for us."

"I am afraid not. Your narrow shave a few hours ago more than confirms that for me." she sat up, noticing Jana's expression of surprise. "This is my city, Miss Schleifer. Very little happens here that I don't hear about."

"So someone is trying to kill us."

"They are finding ways to have you die." the ambassador said. "Usually that would be pedantry, in this case it is an important distinction. Simply put, they want it to look like an accident."

"And you don't know who it is?"

"No."

A silence fell, long and uncomfortable. Kristof appeared to be deep in thought, whilst Wulfe smouldered with barely-concealed resentment. Cass was silent, huddling close to Jana on the luxurious divan. It was Song who drew Jana's attention the most; her body relaxed and standing with the same ethereal grace as before, a creature of almost effortless poise and elegance. Her eyes, however, were focussed and unwavering, their almost predatory fixation on the two soldiers not faltering even for a moment.

Eventually, Wulfe spoke.

"And why are we here?"

Song shrugged simply. "You are an invaluable man, Bastian. Regardless of your current status under Union law, I felt like it would pay to have a friend like yourself in the long term. I was very excited when I discovered that the name that you gave was not, in fact, false."

"So you want something in return, is that it?" Wulfe almost growled.

"Nothing at all. Consider it a favour. And as much as I would like to continue working with all of you, there will be plenty of time to discuss that in the coming days. You are welcome to stay here at the embassy for as long as you wish. You will have food, clothes, anything you require. This place is a safe haven against our common foe; electrically and digitally isolated from the outside world by some of the finest network design in the Ashkan Union. Whilst you are here, I guarantee your safety."

"And if we leave?"

"Then," Song replied, the smile on her lips as warm as her gaze was cold. "I am afraid there are no guarantees, Bastian Wulfe."

Her gaze softened, and she looked to the ambassador.

"Ambassador Aurelien, could you have them shown to their rooms?"

As they began to file out of the meeting room, Song's soft voice rang out again.

"May I speak with you a moment, Sergeant Richter?"

Kristof paused in the doorway. He looked up, and noticed that Wulfe had stopped beside him.

"Don't." the old soldier cautioned quietly.

"It's ok." Kristof muttered. "Stay with them." he added, gesturing to Jana and Cass as they followed Ambassador Aurelien down the white halls of the Cothiq Embassy.

As Wulfe stepped out through the ornate archway, Kristof turned back towards the Councillor, smiling disarmingly.

"Of course, Councillor. Or may I call you Song?"

The Quin smiled.

"Certainly, sergeant. In fact I insist upon it."

She sat down at the table, gesturing with an intricately tattooed hand to the chair opposite.

"Please, sit with me." she said. As Kristof complied, she raised a delicate finger to her lips for a moment, as if indecisive, before beginning to speak once more.

"I know a lot about you, Kristof Richter. More than you would like, I imagine." she said slowly, thoughtfully, each word falling carefully into place like pieces in a puzzle. "And I can give you my word that your secret has not, and will not leave this room."

Kristof sat silently for a moment, forcing himself to show no emotion.

"Well we appreciate that." he said, holding Song's gaze impassively.

"I am no friend to the Union. I make no secret of that. The way they bow to the fears of the masses hurts more than it could possibly heal. This suspicion of technology, of progress. The glorification of 'humanity' and 'unity', these amorphous, evasive words, their meaning changing with the winds and tides."

She paused, then smiled softly.

"I am a Councillor, Kristof, and a leader. I know that the Union's internal politics are not an exact science, much to my disappointment. Alliances are made and broken in the same instant. Brotherhoods are forged in fire, before turning brittle shattering in the heat. The landscape is ever-changing. It is a great part of what makes it exciting for me."

"All empires fall, Kristof. Three hundred years ago my people brought life to the twelve, now we occupy one planet and a handful of offworld cultural enclaves. The Varians took what was left with fire and sword, and collapsed to infighting in less than a century." She shook her head almost sadly. "It is an inevitability. An empire will form cracks in its shell, these cracks widen and widen until the divide is so great that the structure collapses in on itself. The Celthari partisan cells have taken to their forests and mountains once again, the Quin and the Bolvar are squabbling over contested territory, Varia is in the midst of a dynastic meltdown of near-cataclysmic proportions..."

She looked up and, catching Kristof's suspicious glare, smiled disarmingly.

"Please, Kristof. A professional troublemaker like myself has to keep up with *all* the latest disruptances."

She paused for a moment before continuing.

"And yet, somehow it still holds, despite all my efforts. Vital messages go undelivered. Phantom votes plague the council sessions. Communication disruptions strike at the most inopportune time. Ashkan politics is never clean, but this is something else, Kristof. It is as if the very network itself is fighting against me.!

Kristof sat back in his chair, staring thoughtfully at the Councillor.

"You think our mutual friend is sabotaging you?"

"I know it. Something is fighting me, Kristof. It is fighting *us*."

"I wasn't aware there was an *us* yet."

"I know all about you, *Kristof Richter*. If there is no *us*, then you stand alone, and no one man can stand against the Union. Whatever this entity is, it will destroy you."

"Why would it do that?"

"Because you know of its nature. The attack outside the Vault proved that it was willing to defend itself, but the killing of the Legionaries? It is willing to strike out against its enemies. The attack bore all its hallmarks: Brutal and efficient, but subtle in its own way."

"Subtle?" Kristof spat, in a harsher tone than he intended. The conversation had him on edge. "Setting a freight plane alight is hardly subtle."

"Oh, but it is, Kristof. Who would possibly think what happened above the docks just now was in any way intended? A machine error, of course. You know what those pesky machines can be like, don't you? So unreliable, so prone to faults and failures. Much wiser to trust in a human being with thoughts and feelings." Song's gentle smile turned almost mischievous for a moment. "At least, that's what the Commission tells us. And, incidentally, what the Ashkan media is undoubtedly reporting as we speak."

"So, whoever it is, they are trying to kill us. But why the subtlety? Why the smoke and mirrors? No-one would look twice at a group of small-time smugglers that got smoked outside Ashka. There's no need for it."

Song laughed softly, the sound ringing in the room around Kristof.

"Why indeed, *Sergeant Kristof Richter?* What is it about you that could provoke such a strange response?"

"Wulfe? Me? Nothing that would keep us alive in that situation. We're just people now. Two amongst billions."

Song cut in, her voice gentle, her steely-blue eyes locked on Kristof.

"I recognised you, Kristof." she smiled. "You may think that people have begun to forget about Carth. And maybe they have. It was such a long time ago, and so very, very far away for most people. But the knowledge is there. A generation has been raised on the tales of The Wolf. The Legions still draw lessons from Carth to this day. Warped lessons, twisted beyond recognition for those who fought in the conflict, but lessons nonetheless. The Council holds thousands upon thousands of files on you, Kristof Richter. You will never, ever be truly forgotten, even in death."

Song fell silent, letting the final sentence hang in the air between them.

"That still doesn't explain why it let us escape."

"Perhaps it realised that your deaths would have wider consequences." the Councillor said, her voice almost a whisper now.

"There's no-one in Ashka who would even recognise us. Not the real *us*. And when…"

He stopped, the pieces beginning to click into place in his mind.

"Atesca." he muttered quietly to himself.

"Precisely. She stepped off a Legion shuttle nearly a week ago. A mere two days before your assault on the Vault." Song smiled softly. "Tell me, Kristof, what would the Hawk of Carth do if she caught the scent of this elusive entity?"

"Is it human?"

Song shrugged her shoulders gently, running a finger around the rim of the decanter as she stared thoughtfully at him.

Kristof could see her in his mind. Atesca Seratov, the Hawk of Carth. The woman who had waded through a sea of corpses to run down one man.

"She'd kill it." he said with absolute certainty.

"And there you have your answer. The legions were an instinctive reaction to a threat, like a turtle withdrawing into its shell. But even as it lashed out, the gears behind the scenes had begun turning. Once it realised the potential consequences of its move, the entity withdrew, seeking to cover its tracks until a better opportunity presented itself to dispose you, and the danger you brought with you."

She placed the decanter down on the table carefully, and Kristof felt the full intensity of that crystalline gaze turned upon himself.

"I know more about what you face than anyone. I can help you escape it, if you help me find it. Whoever …or whatever… this entity is, it hates us both with an equal passion. And I am sure that the Ashkan Union sees neither of us as loyal subjects any more, does it Sergeant?"

"And you think I could help?"

"*Side vremen ande tirche, nellen af vearet,* Kristof." the Councillor intoned in the fluid sibilance of the Quin tongue. "It is an old Quin phrase. It means… 'Keep your friends close, and your enemies… confused? Off balance, perhaps. There is no easy translation.' "

"Very poetic. What exactly are you proposing?"

"Kristof, my dear, I am a Quin. Poetry is in our blood. We can't all be dry, analytical Ashkans, can we?"

"I'm no Ashkan."

"Believe me s*ergeant,* I am under no illusions as to what *you* are."

Chapter 19

Kristof stepped into the sumptuously decorated chamber slowly, his head spinning with a myriad of thoughts. He could see Wulfe through the open door, the old soldier silhouetted against the light of the late afternoon sun.

As he walked across the room, his eyes moved carefully, checking the walls, the corners, the dark spaces of the room where anything could be easily hidden. Looking up, he met the old soldier's gaze as the man turned about.

Wulfe chuckled quietly, shaking his head.

"Its ok, I've checked. No-ones listening to us."

The two of them lent on the balustrade together for a few minutes, soaking in the silence of the sun-dappled city below them. Eventually Wulfe broke the silence, speaking in low tones.

"She wants you, doesn't she?"

Kristof nodded, silently.

"Doesn't take a genius to work that out." Wulfe muttered, a note of sympathy entering his voice. He pulled a wry face, drumming his fingertips thoughtfully against the stonework. "Was it tempting?"

Kristof nodded silently again, chewing thoughtfully on his lower lip.

"I hope you told her where she could stick it."

The tension broke as Kristof chuckled to himself.

"You're not worried I sold you all out for a shiny new uniform?" he said.

Wulfe shook his head. "If I thought you were like that you wouldn't be here. Betrayal isn't your style."

"Well you were right this time, at least. Still..." Kristof paused, resting his chin in the palm of his hand. "...if not here, then where? And what? I can't imagine we'll ever get a better ally than this. It could solve... everything."

"And what's the price for solving everything?"

"Whatever it is that Councillor Song wants me for."

"So where do you draw the line? A few million crowns-worth of property damage? A dozen or so lives? A few hundred? A few thousand?" Wulfe waved a hand dismissively and turned to Kristof, his imposing form hunching over as he prodded him in the chest. "I'll tell you where that line is, Kristof. One. One life. Yours. Do what you will with it, but the moment that martyr complex of yours pushes you into harming others, you'd better take a damn good look at what side you're on."

Silence fell for a moment. Wulfe held Kristof's gaze for a moment, before his almost aggressive posture softened and a sheepish smile flickered across his features.

"One thing at a time." he said, stony-faced once more. "We get out, then we worry about where to. Do you think she will let us leave?"

"You heard the way she speaks, this isn't an act of charity." Kristof said, shaking his head. "I doubt it. If we're very lucky we'd get outside the compound before she had us quietly killed. This is her city. Every single person in this compound works for her in some capacity, and the ones in the city itself serve Ashka. Who's going to stop her?"

Wulfe sighed deeply. "I think I knew that already."

For a moment silence reigned, before the old soldier spoke up once more.

"I wish things were easy. Just once, like in fairytales, or even in Jana's bloody stories. I'd even settle for things being clear, you know? Just an obvious right and wrong, a chance to do the right thing without toppling a thousand other dominoes in the process."

Kristof threw the old soldier a sidelong glance. Despite his stony expression, the man's eyes danced in the sunlight, bright with pain.

"One day, maybe." he murmured.

The silence sank in once again as both men reflected quietly to themselves.

"We'll need to keep an eye on the other two." Wulfe ventured after a while, his voice having returned to its usual growl. "They're not used to this. They'll let their guard down in time."

Kristof's eyes swept the city as he nodded thoughtfully.

"We don't have long." he said. "So how do we do it?"

"Beats me. Escaping from places has always been your department."

Wulfe straightened up, patting Kristof roughly on the shoulder as he did so.

"Think it over. For all my talk of vigilance, I need some sleep."

"Sleep well."

"We'll see."

Kristof stood quietly as the door clicked shut.

The dry, sibilant voice crept back into his mind, as if it had never left.

It was a tempting offer, though.

It was.

A man could do a lot, with an ally like that. Quin representative of the Union world of Cothiq alongside the associated cultural territories, and 11th Member of the Ashkan Council.

Cassandra could have her adventures, free of danger, free to come and go as she pleases.

Wulfe could find his peace, somewhere that no-one would ever find him again.

Jana could go home, as if you had never entered her life in the first place.

She could set them free.

You could set them free.

Set them free, and then help to tear the world down around them. Kristof shuddered. He had had enough war for one lifetime.

Did you decide that, or did Wulfe?

He watched the city thoughtfully for a moment. Watched the last rays of sunlight as they played across the rooftops, filtering gently down into the streets before being cut to ribbons by the maze of walkways that covered every inch of the city's paths. The lights of the port glinted in the far distance, flickering and dancing as the mists consumed them.

Cothiq was dead. He could taste it in the air. The streets were empty, the houses cold, the heart of the city motionless in the moonlight. The roar of the Ashkan gorge skirted around at the edge of hearing, the whirling mists that it flung up causing the moonlight to warp and twist as it played across Kristof's features.

Above it all stood the shuttle docks. The three vast, box-like shuttles sat at its heart. Ashkan dominion. Even a Councillor couldn't stop the Pioneer unilaterally.

Eight idents, thirteen small calibre shells, and a skimmer we can't reach.

And time to plan.

It just wasn't enough.

More than enough.

Moments passed. Kristof's eyes flickered almost unseeing across the rooftops of Cothiq, his lips moving soundlessly in the pale moonlight.

You have something. Something that hates her as much as it hates you.

Kristof paused.

It could be done. Song said that it was always listening, always watching. Perhaps…

It hates us. It would try to destroy us the first chance it gets.

Do not give it the chance.

What could we offer it? You can't bargain with an empty hand.

You can offer it her.

It has no reason to listen, let alone trust me. It hates us.

The enemy of my enemy

It wants us dead.

Doesn't everyone?

It would be a risk.

It always is.

Kristof turned and stood silently for a few moments, staring unseeing at the smooth stone-sheathed wall of his room. A close observer would be able to make out minute movements in his features, movements of a man deep in thought, caught in the agony of indecision. His lips moved soundlessly, his eyes flitting from side to side, as if reading from a text only he could see.

Minutes later, the door to Kristof's room opened slowly, soundlessly, before gently clicking shut once more.

Chapter 20

Post Contact Report, White Harbour Incident - 22nd Corin, 2076.32 Core Time

Detonation at White Harbour entrenchment. Possible presence of Butcher suspected, leading to Cpt.Wulfe and Com.Seratov leading elements of the 12th to support. Rebels eventually driven back after heavy fighting.

5 Legionaries and 12 Civilians killed in the initial Detonation, with a further 3 Legionaries and 7 Civilians killed in the firefight.

Cpt.Bastian Wulfe wounded in the fighting.

The bird reared back, its silky white feathers ruffling as Jana approached. It trilled sharply at her, before strutting pompously away across the grass.

Jana knelt in the middle of the clearing, watching the strange creatures intently. She had laughed at Cass for being so easily awed by things which, to Jana at least, seemed almost mundane. But now she understood. There was something about the birds, something about this place, that made her keep coming back. They had been in the embassy for almost 3 days now, and she must have come to see them dozens of times.

One of the birds strutted closer, cocking its head aside to stare curiously at Jana. She extended a hand towards it, cursing quietly as the creature scuttled back out of reach, before stopping to preen itself once more.

"Fascinating, aren't they?"

Song stood behind her, watching the birds with a bemused expression on her face. She stood radiant as ever, the soft crème gown complimenting the harsher blacks and browns of her ancestral tattoos, her long, dark hair contrasting sharply with her snow-white skin. As Jana looked up in surprise, the Councillor smiled almost encouragingly.

"I've never seen anything like this before." Jana said, hesitantly. This was the first time she had seen the Councillor in the three days since they first arrived, and it was definitely her first time being alone in her presence.

"I would be very disappointed if you had. These were very expensive."

"Where are they from? Ashka? Celthar?"

"These don't exist anywhere in their natural form. Not anymore. My father was an avid historian, and he used to show me records of creatures like this whenever I gave him the chance. Driven to extinction, usually."

She smiled. Jana hated it when Song smiled. It was beautiful, but it felt... *artificial.* Something primal in Jana raised its hackles every time.

"I decided to make some. Just for myself." Song continued, looking down as one of the creatures brushed against her dress.

"So, they're not real?" Jana said, unable to hide the disappointment in her voice.

Song gave a short, bell-like peal of laughter.

"*That* depends entirely on what you define as real, Jana. They aren't natural, no. But they're as real as you or I."

"So they're... machines?"

"In a sense, I suppose. Part organic, part machine." Song chuckled to herself again. "If I remember correctly, their beaks are derived from your common harrier. You have a few of them on Valmeer, if I am not mistaken?"

It was phrased as a question, but Jana could tell that the Councillor already knew the answer.

"Yeah, I... Yeah." Jana paused, before a thought struck her. "Isn't this illegal?"

"Extremely."

"Oh."

There was a moment of silence. One of the birds brushed against Song's leg again, cocking its head to stare inquisitively up at the Councillor. Song, however, was watching Jana closely. Jana could feel her eyes on the back of her neck as she looked out across the garden.

"You don't like it." Song commented, her voice perfectly level.

Jana sighed.

"No. It doesn't *feel* right, I guess. I don't feel like we should meddle with living things. They're special."

She looked up at Song, and hesitated.

"It just bothers me a little, that's all."

"It shouldn't bother you, Jana. My birds are very happy the way they are."

"But they didn't choose to be like this."

"Did you choose to be the way you are?"

Jana shut her mouth, feeling like she had just walked into a trap. She looked up at Song and hesitated, trying to find a way to express her slight distaste at the concept.

Song raised a placating hand.

"I understand, Jana. The Union is very firm in these matters. You must have been told, hundreds upon hundreds of times. Humans are *natural*. Nature is *real*. Everything else is just hollow mimicry."

Song looked around, gesturing to one of the larger, white specimens that perched on a nearby rock, preening its feathers furiously.

"But what do you do if the mimicry surpasses the real thing? Did you know that the common harrier never stops growing? A normal harrier will die within a few thousand days of its birth, when it gets too large for its light bone structure to support it properly. My birds do not have this problem, and thanks to my 'meddling' they will live far, far longer and more fulfilled lives. Do they therefore have less right to live? Are they less *real*?"

There was a moment of silence as Jana felt herself lost for words. Song paused for a moment, regaining her composure a little as she turned back to Jana.

"Councillor?" a familiar voice rang out across the gardens. Song turned almost abruptly, but Jana continued to stare, the councillor's outburst still fresh in her mind. Kristof stood in one of the doorways that led into the domed habitat, propping the automated system open with one hand.

He grinned, disarmingly.

"I hope I'm not interrupting anything?"

Song smiled softly in return. "Of course not, Kristof. I do apologise for being so unavailable in recent days, but a Councillor's life is a busy one, as I'm sure you can understand."

"No problem." The soldier waved a dismissive hand. "I just wanted the opportunity to pry Jana from your grasp for a few moments." he added with another grin.

"Only on the condition that I can pry you from hers shortly afterwards." Song countered with a laugh. "We have barely talked since you arrived, and as I recall we still had much left open for discussion."

"Of course, Councillor." Kristof said, giving a short bow. Song beamed as he stepped forwards and guided Jana gently into the deeper forest. The moment they were safely out of earshot, Jana felt the soldier's demeanor change sharply. The smile leeched from his face, and he spoke to her in a harsh whisper.

"I need you to do something for me, Jana."

"I don't like the sound of that. What are you doing, Kristof?"

Kristof smiled fondly, but Jana could see the hard look in his eyes as he stared straight out across the woodland. She glanced up, following his gaze, and caught a glimpse of Song's reflection in the polished glass, waiting patiently by the habitat's entrance. Kristof was watching her like a hawk, and she them.

"Smile. Laugh. Just pretend we're talking about the birds." he muttered.

Jana gritted her teeth and smiled.

"What are you doing, Kristof?" she whispered back.

"I'm finding us a way out of here. Now listen..."

Minutes later the habitat doors slid shut behind Kristof, as he and Song walked slowly back through the embassy's winding corridors towards his quarters.

"How is everyone recovering, Kristof? I gather from the others that you have had quite the ordeal in recent weeks."

Kristof, glancing back at the closed doors, looked up hurriedly.

"Yes. Yeah. Great." he shook his head and collected himself a little. "Everyone is doing fine, thank you."

Song smiled gently at his agitation. "I trust the quarters are for your liking? The stewards were very excited to use them, they are usually reserved for other Councillors visiting the embassy, and since I am something of a pariah in council circles I rarely get an opportunity to air them out."

"They're very nice. More than nice, I've not been in quarters like that... well... ever. Can't say I've even slept in a proper bed in years." Kristof said, choosing his words carefully.

"Since Carth, I would imagine." the Councillor commented gently.

Kristof paused. "Yeah... since then." he responded suspiciously.

"You may not know this, Kristof." the Councillor said, ignoring or not registering Kristof's changed tone. "But at the time I actually placed my vote against significant Union intervention in the conflict."

Kristof threw her a questioning glance. Song smiled.

"Are you at all familiar with the Quin, Kristof? The Story of the First Cycle? The Solar Philosophies? I apologise, I never asked."

Kristof shrugged, shaking his head.

"I'm sorry, the life I've led hasn't leant itself to book learning." he muttered.

"Nothing to apologise for, I understand fully. How to begin..." the councillor pondered for a second, before continuing.

"Setune sits, in stellar terms, in a strange place in the triumvriate of stars we inhabit. It recieves light from both its home star, Tenov, as well as its two siblings Sihyld and Olara. At different intervals and intensities of course..." She waved a hand dismissively. "Those born under Sihyld's light are raised from birth to be our leaders, our warriors, our guardians. I, for example, was one such child. We are, by virtue of Setune's orbit, also very rare, perhaps one or two in a hundred. The Quin take these responsibilities very seriously, and we have done so for generations. Even in ancient times, tribes would equip their *Sihyldan,* as we call them, for war, and the few chosen would fight for the sake of the many. Many of our most treasured stories concern members of the caste doing their duty to the tribe despite unimaginable odds. The tradition has kept into the modern day, and though we have traded spears and shields for guns and tanks, the duty of a Sihyldan to their people has etched itself into our collective psyche."

They turned a corner, walking down the long curving corridor that ran along the edge of the forest habitat.

"So you can imagine that the image of a lone man fighting for his home at any cost was received quite differently amongst my people. The Butcher is perhaps not a liked figure amongst the Quin, but he is a respected one. They believe he died doing his duty to his home, rather than as the coward and murderer he is often portrayed as elsewhere."

Kristof shrugged, non-committally.

"Everyone's got their own version of the truth. Who am I to tell them otherwise?"

"You are being uncharacteristically quiet on this matter, Kristof."

"We don't talk about it." Kristof muttered. "There's not much to say any more."

"Do the others know your story?" Song enquired gently.

"We don't talk about it."

Song paused, turning her piercing blue eyes on Kristof.

"Why not? If there is any story worth telling, it is yours. If the story remains untold, then the Commission wins once again."

"We're done. Finished." Kristof murmured, shaking his head. "We fought our battles and paid dearly for fighting them at all. Wulfe deserves his peace."

Song nodded sombrely, making no further comment. They left the habitat's edge, and soon found themselves skirting the outside of the embassy tower, strolling along one of the many extended balconies that encircled the structure. Kristof walked silently, his eyes on the white stonework in front of him, his mind elsewhere.

"My offer still stands, Kristof." the Councillor said suddenly, turning to face him. "Work with me, and perhaps together we can make the Ashkans pay for what they took from you. I hold the resources of an entire peoples at my disposal. I speak with the weight of almost a billion souls, and can gather to my side almost a billion more. I can help you in an unimaginable number of ways. Allow me to."

Chapter 21

INTERVIEWER – "And do you follow the releases yourself, Captain?"

CPT.WULFE – "On occasion."

INTERVIEWER – "How do you feel about them? Personally I adored reading about your heroic response to the White Harbour Incident."

CPT.WULFE – "There was nothing heroic about White Harbour."

INTERVIEWER – "But Captain, of course it was! The way that you…"

CPT.WULFE – "Enough! People died there. Real human beings, with families and feelings. Dying for a war that should have been ended months ago!"

- RECORDING STOPPED-

Jana stepped through the embassy gates. She walked calmly out, giving a wave of acknowledgement to the two guards as she stepped through the doorway into the city beyond.

Four days. It had taken her four days to get to this point. Every day, walking out of the gate with the same bag, walking the same route down to the skimmer port, through the soaking mists, through the near-deserted streets of Cothiq. The first time had been difficult. The guards had searched her, radioed command, called for the ambassador's approval; in short, they had put up one hell of a fight. But she'd done it. Keep telling a lie for long enough and people began to believe it, just as Kristof had said. By now, they seemed largely unconcerned.

It was growing dark as Jana pulled herself on-board the Siren once more.

"Do you still have the Union tracking beacon that Nadir pulled out of the Siren?"

"Possibly. I don't remember throwing it out."

"Do you think you could fix it?"

She unscrewed the maintenance tool storage panel, and reached inside, one hand groping blindly as she stretched as far as she could into the darkness. They always built these bastard things too *high* she thought as she scrambled up the hull a short way, digging the toes of her boots into the gaps in the support struts. Who in the twelve bloody dominions designed…

Her hand closed around the beacon in the darkness. She drew it out, glancing back over her shoulder as she leapt down off the skimmer's bodywork. The door was closed. She was safe.

She sat down against the wall, legs crossed as she examined the object in front of her closely, one hand reaching into the bag at her side for her slate.

How hard could it be?

Nightmarish, as it turned out. The wires were thin and fiddly, the diagrams unclear, and the device had a nasty tendency to just fall apart. Despite all that, she did get it back into one piece. She held it up to the light, feeling unreasonably proud of herself.

"Don't turn it on. Just fix it."

She stopped. Almost reluctantly, she placed the beacon in the bag by her side.

"Nadir left his Array Sequencer in one of the lockers. I put the Neural Relay with it."

The locker door clanged open.

"The Mag-Strips were in Wulfe's bag under the rear seating."

Minutes later, Jana stepped out of the Skimmer, dropping to the concrete slightly unsteadily as the weight of the bag tugged at her.

"Find the shuttle port."

It didn't take a lot of finding. She could see the shuttles from where she stood. Vast, rectangular structures, towering above the buildings around them. They lay still, inert, like the carcasses of some vast sea creature, the mist pooling and condensing on the dull metal, to run down its flanks in a thousand tiny rivulets.

Jana glanced up at them as she approached, reaching up to brush a strand of sodden hair out of her face. The shuttle port was as deserted as the streets around it. She rushed up below the arched entryway, staring through the glass at the displays beyond.

Two days. 13:34 to 14:26.

She knew what Kristof was planning now. Most of it, anyway. Jana had the sinking feeling that the Siren wasn't making it out of Cothiq, even if they did. The Shuttles waited for no man, that much was known. The launch had such precise timing that delays were simply not possible. They would leave come rain or shine.

Fugitives or no.

That was their window. Under one hour.

"Find a route back. Keep it short. Keep out of sight."

She walked quietly through the near-deserted streets, padding down the back roads cautiously, eyes watching the buildings around her for any trace of movement. She was painfully aware of the bag at her side, its weight beginning to cut into her shoulder after carrying it for such a long way.

Cothiq had no shortage of back streets, and within a half-hour she could see the white spire of the embassy building breaking the skyline ahead of her.

"Walk it twice. Make sure you know it by heart. You'll have to lead the others."

She walked it three times, just to be sure.

"The others?"

"Just trust me."

"Are you sure about this, Kristof?"

"You can do it. I know you can."

Jana still wasn't sure about that last bit.

But she would try.

Shouldering the equipment bag, she turned back towards the embassy gates.

Chapter 22

"I understand, Bastian."

"I know you do. It just felt so hollow. I can't lie to people about what's happening here. I won't!"

"Don't think of them as lies. You are an ideal to them, to us, a shining symbol of what the Ashkan Union represents and the good it brings to people's lives. You are not lying to them, Bastian. You are inspiring them."

When you get the chance, run for the Pioneer.

That was all the instruction that he had been able to give them. They knew where to go, and they knew that they had to stay together. If they could make it on to a shuttle, they would be safe. Telling them anything else only put them more at risk. Wulfe would know what to do.

They aren't safe.

In the dim light of his quarters, Kristof grimaced to himself. They were safe. As safe as he could make them.

And yet...

Kristof shook his head. He had to focus. He would only get one chance at this, and should he fail they would all be far from safe.

He checked the bag one final time. Jana had done well. He had everything he needed. He was as ready as could be.

Given the circumstances.

He cast a final glance around the room, shrugged the bag over his shoulder, and stepped out into the corridor. As the door slid shut with a steely hiss the automated caretaker system kicked in, killing the lights and plunging the room into darkness.

Darkness, except for the faint flashing light of the tracking beacon of the Valmeer Industrial 'Siren' Transport that lay on its side by the door, hooked up to the embassy's power grid.

Jana stood with her back to the room, leaning gently on the windowsill as she gazed out over the city beyond. It was a nice day. Beautiful, really. The sun had finally managed to break through the grey haze that seemed to perpetually blanket the Askhan sky, and rays of sunlight were now striking the city itself, setting the mist sent up by the Ashkan gorge aglitter.

She heard a cough behind her, and made space for Wulfe as he stepped up beside her.

"Hey." she said, quietly. It seemed like the time to talk in hushed tones, for some reason.

Wulfe flashed the ghost of a smile in response, his eyes never leaving the window.

"Did he tell you the plan?"

"I think he told me what I needed to know."

Wulfe nodded thoughtfully, but said nothing. Eventually Jana cracked.

"Why, do you think something is wrong?" she asked.

"If anyone can do it, he can. But no-one's perfect. I just…" Wulfe sighed. "I like to know what I am getting into."

They were silent for a moment, watching the sunlight dance amidst the mists.

"He gave me a gun." Jana whispered, feeling its weight in her inside pocket. "That's not a good sign, is it?"

"He's just trying to keep you safe. That's what all of this is for."

"Then he should tell us what's going on."

"He can't do that." Wulfe muttered sourly. "We might try to help."

Silence fell for a moment. Jana shrugged her shoulders experimentally, feeling the weight of the gun in her pocket once more.

"Any tips for using it?" she said to Wulfe, attempting a smile.

"Don't." he scowled. "Damn things aren't worth the effort."

"I'm serious, Wulfe. My life might depend on it."

"So am I. Listen," the soldier reached out, drawing Jana and Cass in close. "When whatever happens happens, we stick together. We move quietly and stay out of sight. If we get caught and bogged down, we're done."

"What about Kristof?" Cass whispered.

"He's on his own." Wulfe snapped. "We're getting out. He'll find a way."

"But…" Cass stammered.

"Cass, it's okay." Jana said gently, placing a hand on the girl's shoulder. "I'm sure he's been through worse."

They sprung apart as the door to the chamber clicked. An embassy attendant stood in the doorway, hands clasped behind his back, his face carefully neutral as he peered into the room.

"Ms. Schleifer?"

"Yeah?" Jana said, looking cautiously at the man, trying to gauge how much the man had overheard.

"The Councillor wishes for you to join her in the gardens, if you would be so kind." the attendant intoned levelly.

Jana felt her heart sink in her chest. "I…" she glanced at Wulfe and Cass for a moment, then made up her mind. "Sure!" she said with a smile, ruffling the girl's hair fondly as she stepped past. "I had been meaning to stretch my legs anyway."

The attendant bowed his head briefly and stepped aside, allowing Jana to cast one final glance over her shoulder before she left. Cass was staring at Wulfe helplessly, the rising fear plain on her face. The soldier had a stronger grip, and treated Jana to a grim nod as she filed out of the room after the servant.

No plan survives contact with the enemy.

The crowbar bit deeply into the door's frame as Kristof pressed his weight against it. The metal yielded slowly and silently, before the lock snapped with an audible *crack*!

Kristof heard a hollow clank from inside the door itself.

Deadlocked.

"Shit." he muttered. They had to know something was up by now. There wasn't much time left.

He dropped the bag to the ground with a muffled clatter. It only took him seconds to apply the two remaining mag-strips to the door's frame, his heart hammering in his ears all the while. With a final glance up and down the empty corridor he ripped away the firing tape and turned his back.

The mag-strip flared with a blinding light. Even with his back turned, the reflections from the white-concrete walls was enough to set afterimages dancing in Kristof's eyes for a few seconds.

The door to Server Core #3, however, was a ruined mess. It rolled aside easily as Kristof pushed at it, the two semi-molten halves of the deadlock bar clanking to the ground as he stepped inside.

The room was vast, far larger than he could have imagined. Racks upon racks of data processing terminals lined the walls, ranging from floor to ceiling in vast columns, stretching for almost fifty metres down the length of the room. The air was cold and dry, with a strange coppery taste to it.

This was Core #3. This place has at least two more of these.

Kristof was no expert in the world of technology, but even he knew this was too much computational power for a single embassy.

Personal projects.

Within minutes, Kristof was sat amidst a tangled web of wires and cabling. Nadir's slate lay on the ground in front of him, beside his own, both screens bathing Kristof's corner of the Processor Core in a cold blue light. With shaking hands, Kristof laid out Nadir's Neural Relay in front of him, the roll of copper-riddled fabric glinting in the faint light of the screens. He chewed on his lip apprehensively as he stared at the thousands of thousands of tiny, needle-like micro-injectors that seemed to weave and dart like the tendrils of some kind of venomous sea creature, each and every one filled with a tiny dose of Pesh.

Simple, fast, and incredibly dangerous.

He placed a hand on the cloth, wincing as the tiny, needle-like fibres pierced his skin in a thousand different places at once.

Quick and dirty.

He drew a deep breath. He had seen it done a dozen times. How hard could it be?

His other hand touched the fabric, but his senses were already numbing. He barely felt the pain as, with a sickening twist, the world seemed to spring to life around him.

The sensation was almost overwhelming.

He could feel it now, the confines of this world, the embassy's isolated network. Colour flooded his vision, and he felt himself swaying as if in a drunken haze. He could feel numbers. He could taste data. It wasn't real, his rational mind screamed. The Neural Relay merely acted as an interpreter between him and the machine world. It wasn't real.

He drew in a shuddering breath, trying hard to focus, ignoring the flood of information that felt like it was coursing through his very veins.

Problem was, right now it felt very real indeed.

The embassy was an island, he could feel that. Running almost entirely on its own internal networks, a thousand rings of interconnected systems, a nigh impenetrable fortress with its gates barred to the outside world.

Kristof's eyes burned. He screwed them shut for a moment, his body wracked with coughing as his dry throat managed to pierce the wall of sight and sound that assailed him. He felt drunk. His mind refused to focus, the edges of its attention frayed by the myriad of colours.

The slates in front of him were not a part of the fortress. They were almost glowing, in constant motion, data feeding in and out faster than Kristof's mind could process.

There was a screeching now. A wailing, toneless scream that seemed to be building at the very edge of his hearing, gnawing away at the back of his mind.

With a shudder, Kristof reached out, heart thundering in his ears. Tears rolled down his cheeks. His whole body felt like it was tearing itself apart, wrenching itself inside out as the dataflow around the slates and the embassy network began to intertwine, weaving ever tighter together into an embrace that threatened to smother Kristof with its intensity.

It was then that he felt it. A presence, almost, like watching a silhouette shift beneath the waves. A shifting, looming presence that wound its way almost sinuously amidst the crushing embrace of the dataflow. Kristof's mind shuddered, all sense of scale falling away as the blackened tendrils coiled about him and around him, pressing their way into the chamber. Riotous colours turned to black, smothered by the cloying darkness. The scratching turned to screeching, the blackness around the corners of his vision turning to crushing pressure. Even as he watched the sinuous threads coil about him and press into the chamber, Kristof felt his throat constrict, the hammering of his heart drowning out even the hideous wailing at the heart of the storm.

For what seemed like minutes he floundered helplessly amidst the waves, unable to breathe, unable to move, unable to feel as he was dragged under.

He felt his body pitch backwards, his hands detaching from the neural relay with a sickening tearing noise. He struck the ground with a sharp crack, and lay shuddering on the cold stone floor as the rush withdrew and reality came crashing in again once more. His whole body shook, although whether from exhaustion or the chill air of the maintenance room he could not tell.

As he lay there gasping for breath, sweat drenching his body despite the cold air of the processor chamber, his mind was filled with only one thought. Whatever had pursued them since the Ashkan Vault was now here. He had opened the floodgates; wall had been breached. The entity that tried to kill Nadir was in the embassy.

And in his final moments on the network, it had tried to kill him too.

"…of course, my interactions with the Bolvar have always been somewhat strained." Song said. She and Jana strolled through the gardens at a leisurely pace, the afternoon sunlight filtering through the leaves above setting the "Councillor Ostroy of Valmeer was quite possibly the single most pig-headed man that I have ever had the displeasure of negotiating with." She laughed, catching Jana's sceptical expression.

"Please, Jana. It is quite possible to disapprove of the actions of the Union, possibly its very existence, and still want the best for your people. Or *all* people, for that matter. The Councillor was sitting on some extremely lucrative resources and was unwilling to capitalise on them."

"Why was that?"

"The people, Jana. I'm sure you understand how touchy the Bolvar can be, and dear Ostroy was doing his very best to avoid antagonising them more than he already had. The poor man has to represent almost two billion Bolvar, five million Ashkans, and a handful of Celthari without any one group walking away from the table. My people are almost docile by comparison."

"I don't mean to be rude, but I thought you wanted the best for *all* people? Surely the Bolvar should be included in that?"

"What do you think it is that the Ashkan Union sent your family to Valmeer for, Jana? Was it the best for them individually, or was it part of a move to civilise and enlighten the warlike Bolvar and ultimately improve life for all the people of The Twelve?" Song smiled lightly. "We have a metaphor about making small sacrifices for the greater whole in the Quinn tongue, but I don't think it translates well."

"Can't make an omelette without breaking a few eggs?"

Song laughed then, bright and bell-like.

"I adore how simple and straight-forward the Ashkan language can be." she paused, taking a breath as she turned her crystalline eyes out across the gardens.

"Do you know what it is your Union runs on, Jana? The single resource without which it could not exist in its current form?"

Jana frowned, her lips moving silently for a moment. "Humanity." she eventually said, a little uncertainly. "Hope, maybe?"

Song cocked her head a little, straightening a few errant strands of hair as she watched the light glittering across the domed roof of the habitat above.

"Interesting. Very poetic. I could certainly see how an argument could be made for either of those. I, however, believe it is much of the opposite. *Fear* is what truly runs the Ashkan Union. Not in a dramatic, oppressive sense, although that is certainly a part of it, but a mundane, day-to-day fear of the future, of the unknown. Undesirables threaten my home, so they must be pacified. Other beliefs threaten our stability, so they must be suppressed. The march of technological progress threatens my job, so it must be curtailed... you see the pattern. We are no longer reaching outwards towards the stars, climbing the stairway toward a greater goal, we are reaching downwards to make sure no-one threatens our rightful position on the stairs. We are stagnating in ignorance and distrust."

"I think they have good intentions." Jana replied slowly, thoughtfully. "Without the founding principles I wouldn't have had a job. Hell, I probably wouldn't have been on Valmeer. Envoy families are sent as a gesture of goodwill, I don't imagine it's the most efficient way of doing things. Without the Humanitarian principle, I..."

"*Humanity First.*" Song almost spat the words. Jana looked up in surprise, but the Councillor's face was still as serene as ever, not a trace of the frustration that had laced her words present in her flawless features. "Why combat the spreading forests of Celthar when for every settler claimed two new ones arrive on the next transport? Why develop new methods of automated freighting when five hundred Ashkan families will take on the job for almost nothing? Why innovate new, sustainable sources of transport when a dozen Bolvar can cross the freezing desert on their flea-riddled mares without issue? Why evolve when any issue can be solved with enough human sacrifice?"

"Well what's the alternative? Let them starve?"

"The alternative, Jana, is not to create a pan-solar union that falters under its own bureaucratic weight in the first place."

They walked on through the gardens in silence for a while. Jana watched the roof of the dome above them, eyeing the sky nervously. Something was going to happen. And when it did she didn't know what to do.

Song spoke again, her voice returned to its usual silken tone.

"As I was saying earlier, I have always intended on visiting Valmeer. I hear the northern winters can be spectacular in certain regions."

Jana nodded, her mind elsewhere as her mouth ran on autopilot.

"Yeah, the dust devils throw up snow and sand. I've heard its quite nice."

"You have never been yourself?" Song enquired earnestly. "I don't think I would be able to resist. It sounds absolutely fascinating, both from an aesthetic and a scientific perspective."

"I always meant to go. Never had the time."

Song nodded understandingly. "If you would like to I am certain I could arrange it for you. There will be plenty of time for you to see to other things once... once we..."

She faltered almost mid-sentence, her gaze going distant for a moment. She seemed to look almost through Jana, those pale, crystalline blue eyes staring, unseeing, into the middle distance.

"What *are* you doing?" she murmured softly, thoughtfully almost, her tone one of mild bemusement.

"The Councillor, what was he…" Jana faltered, taking a step back as she attempted to ignore the hideous sinking feeling in the pit of her stomach.

The councillor blinked, and this time Jana felt the full force of that icy gaze as the Councillor turned to face her, the curious smile melting from her perfect features.

"What is Kristof doing, Jana?"

Chapter 23

27ᵗʰ Sihyl, 2094.69 Core Time – Electronic Messaging Certificate – Confidential

Atesca Seratov, Commissary 1ˢᵗ Class

You are to inform Captain Bastian that further interviews for media releases have been delayed due to budgetary issues.

I can only trust that you are keeping in close contact the Captain, and that any indication that he is unable to adequately perform his duties will be passed to the relevant authorities immediately upon recognition.

"You should not be down here, Mr. Richter."

Kristof froze as he stepped out into the corridor once more.

Ambassador Kyran stood in the centre of the passageway, flanked by members of the embassy guard. To his right stood the hulking form of one of the Centurions, all the more intimidating for its unmoving, unflinching stature.

Kristof turned slowly, watching the guard's tracer light playing across his chest. His vision was still swimming slightly. He felt drained. Drunk. He raised his hands, palms flecked with pinpricks of his own blood.

"I got lost."

The Ambassador shook his head, almost in disappointment.

"What a curious choice of last words. What were you doing?"

Time. They need time.

"Exploring."

The ambassador sighed, and gestured the soldier beside him forward.

"I won't waste time asking again. You, keep him covered."

He stepped back, turning to the Centurion that loomed in the darkness behind him.

"Break his legs."

Kristof backed away warily as the soldiers advanced, trying to keep both in his field of vision as they moved to encircle him. Two versus one.

Bad odds

With a hiss of decompressing hydraulics and the whirr of activating servo engines, the centurion took a step forwards, shaking the very ground beneath Kristof's feet.

Very bad odds

The corridor lighting flickered spasmodically for a moment, creating an odd strobing effect as the two guards advanced, weapons raised. A dull cracking began to filter down from the end of the corridor, like the snap and crackle of damp firewood.

Gunfire. Small calibre.

"Don't move!" ordered the guard as he approached, levelling his rifle to almost poke at Kristof's chest.

Too close for his own good. the voice whispered seductively at the back of his mind.

With a crackling hiss the corridor lights went out, plunging them into pitch darkness.

Perfect

"Kristof?" Jana stammered, her heart dropping into her stomach. "I... I don't know. Where is..."

She stopped. Song had fallen silent, her eyes staring into the middle distance, her entire body almost statuesque in its stillness.

Jana made to step away, but her gaze was drawn to one of the beautiful harriers that stood nearby. The bird's head cocked to one side, twitching spasmodically as it stared at Jana. One wing extended, lightning fast, trembling in the cool air. It lowered its head slowly, almost toppling over, and began to brush it gently across the grass in front of it, softly at first, but getting harder and harder until its beak was leaving visible marks in the dirt beneath. Its beak opened, emitting an unnatural, keening whine. It toppled sideways, writhing across the ground, the keening rising in pitch as its whole body began to convulse, shuddering, shaking, talons tearing helplessly at the earth in its agony.

Jana stepped back in horror, revulsion gripping her as she watched the creature's death-throes in hideous fascination, unable to tear her eyes away.

She jumped as, with a sickening crack of breaking bone, another bird hit the ground beside her, a bundle of bloodied feathers and bone that shivered and writhed on the damp earth. Another struck the ground, and another.

In eerie silence, Jana watched as the white-plumed forms began to rain from the trees above her, filling the air with the soft, sickening crunch of breaking bones.

Song stood silently, unmoving in the centre of the clearing, oblivious to the carnage that surrounded her. Her hand pressed delicately to her forehead and temple, her gentle features locked into an expression of mild discomfort. Her lips parted, and she spoke in a soft whisper.

"No."

Her form seemed to tremble for a moment, her hand shaking almost imperceptibly as, with glacial slowness, she lowered it to her side.

"Get. Out." she hissed, each syllable as soft as snow, but hard as ice.

Jana glanced around, her gaze sweeping the clearing of writhing, convulsing forms, the discordant chorus of agonised keening ringing in her ears. She stepped back.

Song's hand lashed out, catching Jana's wrist in a grip of iron. Jana froze, staring back at the councillor.

"Out." The voice whispered again, this time carrying a steely note of finality.

Song's eyes opened. She blinked once, slowly, lethargically, her gaze running briefly around the clearing before the two piercing blue eyes came to rest on Jana.

"Do you understand what you have done?!" she hissed, her voice as sharp as a steel blade. "Can you even comprehend the damage you have inflicted?! Decades of work! You…"

She stopped. Jana floundered as she stared into those twin pools of silvery darkness. She tried to step back, to draw away, but the Councillor's grip was like iron.

"You don't understand, do you?" Song whispered, quietly.

Jana felt Song shudder again, the Councillor's grip wavering for a fraction of a second. The councillor's eyelids seemed to almost flutter for a moment, the faintest trace of a snarl warping her perfect features. For the briefest of moments, Jana felt the ground tremble slightly beneath her feet.

Then the eyes flashed open again. Cold, steely blue eyes, like the calm before the storm.

"He didn't tell you a thing, did he? This is what he does. This is who he is. He cannot create, he cannot cooperate, and he cannot learn. All he can do is burn, and kill, and destroy that which others have wrought. He tosses his friends and allies aside like a child its toys, leaving them broken and discarded by the wayside when he has no further use for them."

Suddenly the air was filled with glass as the windows of the habitat shattered inwards. Jana shrieked, covering her face with her hands as the fragments rained down around the pair of them.

"I can see what you are thinking, Jana." the Councillor continued, swaying slightly as she stared down at the creature she held in her talons. "*He wouldn't leave me. He's not like that.*" Song smiled. "I can see it in your face. You are doubting him. You are doubting yourself. Well let me tell you something, Jana Schleifer."

She drew Jana in close, her grip like steel as her perfect features twisted into a sneering smile of pure malice.

"That is exactly the man that your Kristof Richter always has been."

A voice rang out across the clearing. A voice Jana knew well.

"*Song!*"

Wulfe stood in the habitat's entrance.

The soldiers were fast, but Kristof was faster. He threw himself backwards as a hail of blindfire ripped through the darkness above him. In the brief, strobe-like flash of the muzzle flare he saw a single figure outlined against the blackness.

Weight placed on his right leg

He kicked out, sending the soldier sprawling to the ground beside him with a startled cry.

Loose grip on the weapon

With a practiced twist he wrapped his arms around the rifle and rolled sideways, prying it out of the man's weak grip, rose up onto one knee…

Easy kill shot

And froze as the corridor was suddenly filled with a dazzling blue light.

The headlights of the Centurion suit flared to life, blinding Kristof as the vast construct took a step forwards, swinging its heavy battle cannon around to face him.

Dead to rights

The headlights flickered for a moment.

The Centurion's arm flung outwards, catching the other guard as he staggered to his feet and crushing him against the concrete wall with a hideous cracking noise. The arm bent further, wrenching itself backwards as it smeared what was left of the poor soldier across the wall beside it, the plated gauntlet tearing chunks out of the solid concrete structure as it did so. The construct staggered as if drunk for a moment, its lights flickering again as it struggled to right itself.

It stood there for a second, frozen like some hideously bizarre statue, its gauntleted arm dripping with viscera and gore, the corridor filled with the tortured whirring as its servo-supported joints tensed.

A new sound reached Kristof's ears. A voice, muted through layers and layers of reinforced steel and ceramic plating. Screaming.

An arm began to move, rising with glacial slowness as its servos fought for control. The muffled screams ceased as, with a grinding crack and the wet splatter of viscera and hydraulic fluid, the Centurion tore its own head from its body.

Kristof took a step back, trying to still his heavy breathing as he stared intently into the blackness ahead of him. The corridor was dark, a thick, all-consuming blackness, illuminated only by the occasional spastic flickering of the light from the centurion's ruined visor and the thin, tenuous strands of daylight that filtered around the corner behind him.

Footsteps sounded in the darkness to his left.

Favours his right.

Kristof felt the blow take him in the chest, the force of it almost knocking him off his feet as he reeled backwards. His back hit the smooth stonework of the corridor wall and, his vision still blurred from the brutal impact, he instinctively threw himself sideways into the darkness. He felt the second blow whip past his ear and heard a sharp crack as it splintered the laminar wall beside his head.

Stronger than you.

He never even saw the third blow. It took him in the face, spinning him around and sending him sprawling across the cold stone floor.

Faster than you.

He could taste blood on his tongue. His vision was shaken, the soft patterns on the stonework in front of him refusing to focus. Footsteps sounded behind him, and he stumbled unsteadily to his feet, turning around to face Kyran, watching the silhouette approach in the flickering half-light that consumed the passageway.

He lunged forwards, darting to one side and driving his fist into the soldier's flank with all his might.

The blow felt like it struck rock. Kristof winced at the unexpected pain, and the momentary hesitation was all that Kyran needed. He caught Kristof's arm in his own, wrenching it around and pulling the man off-balance.

Kristof felt a booted foot stamp down on his knee as he stumbled sideways, buckling it under him with a sickening crunch. He crumpled to the ground with an agonised cry as he felt Kyran release his arm, letting him fall.

Time. They need time.

He rolled aside and scrambled to his feet, staggering briefly as his leg gave under him.

Wrenched knee. Likely fractured.

One hand extended, his fingertips brushing against the wall beside him as he moved, he began to retreat cautiously down the corridor. Every step brought a fresh stab of agony to his knee, and he was forced to lean harder and harder on the wall as he progressed.

In the faint half-light that streamed around the corner in front of him he could make out a faint outline. A pair of dark eyes glinted in the darkness as Kyran padded slowly along the corridor after him, feet hitting the ground almost soundlessly as he stalked towards Kristof.

"Once a traitor, always a traitor." the words crawled forth, dripping with venom. "Was *this* a part of your plan, *Kristof Richter*? Dying like some cornered animal?"

Kristof stepped back into the light of the long, narrow corridor. Stone walls gave way to glass, and he could faintly make out the city sprawling away to his right as he backed away from the advancing soldier. His whole body shook from the exertion of walking, each step sending flashes of hot lead through his leg. The taste of blood stuck to his tongue, filling his nose and mouth with the coppery scent of death.

Time.

And through it all, Kristof smiled.

Some things are worth dying for

Song stared up into the light, her smile only broadening as her eyes fell on the figure standing there.

"Is this how you express your thanks, Captain? For sheltering you?"

"Sheltering us from the evil you led us into, Song."

"A deed of which I am not the sole performer, Captain. I am sure Jana could think of a few examples."

Jana tugged at song's arm. There was something hideously unnatural about Song's grip. Song was far stronger than her slender, delicate figure made her out to be. Far, far stronger. Something was wrong.

She stumbled as she was spun about, her feet dragging across the floor until she stood between Song and Wulfe.

"Wulfe?!" she whispered, suddenly terrified. "Just go…"

The sentence ended in a scream as Song's hand tightened like a coiling serpent about her own, pressing inwards with a force unimaginable. She felt the bones in her hand crack and splinter, her knees buckling beneath her as for a moment all light seemed to drain from the world.

"Song!"

The pressure released, if only slightly. Jana looked up, through eyes blurred with tears.

Wulfe had drawn something from the inside of his coat. The short, snub-nosed side-loader Jana had seen before. He raised it towards Song, sighting carefully along the barrel.

"Let her go, Song. We'll leave. We can all walk away from this."

Jana swung out, catching the councillor in the stomach with a fist. It was like striking iron.

The pressure on her hand intensified again, and the world dimmed for a moment as the world filled with agony. Jana could barely see now, the voices around her muted by unending pain.

"Strange." Song mused, her serpent-calm gaze resting coolly on Wulfe. "In this moment above all others, I finally understand you, Captain. Perhaps once you were a good man. You had values, and principles, and the iron will to carry them to their end. But now? You are broken. I can see it in your face every time she screams. You just want it to end. You just want everyone to stop fighting."

Jana looked up from where she knelt, huddled around her shattered hand, still helpless in Song's vice-like grip.

"Just run, Wulfe." she whispered.

"Is that why you did it, Captain? Was it fear? Or are you simply afraid of what fighting will do to those around you?"

"I did the right thing." Wulfe snarled. "Now let her go."

"Or what, Captain?" Song said, quite levelly. "I don't believe for one moment that you would shoot me. And even if you did, to what end? I am your only friend in this world. I can give you the peace that you have spent years seeking."

Through eyes that almost refused to focus, Jana saw Wulfe's gun dip ever so slightly. She reached out to him in the darkness, calling out in a voice that seemed barely her own.

"Don't you dare, Wul…"

Song tightened her grip. The world dimmed again. Somewhere in the darkness, Jana could hear own voice descending into anguished whimpering.

"I promise you, Captain, that if you drop your weapon she will not be harmed any further."

Silence fell, the distant, ghostly sound of gunfire echoing around the ruined habitat from the embassy beyond. Jana knelt in the darkness, her world a world of agony. Her breaths came quickly, a panicked and shallow, providing nothing in the way of respite from the sea of pain she found herself in.

Amidst the thundering of her heart and the distant roar of her breathing, she heard the faint clatter of metal on stone as Wulfe's gun struck the ground.

She could feel it. The weight of the weapon Kristof had given her, nestled softly in her inside pocket.

Fighting the fog of agony and despair, she raised a hand shaking with exertion. With a strangled snarl of defiance she drew the weapon and brought it up, pointing it directly between the Councillor's eyes. Time seemed to slow as Song looked down, and for a moment Jana quailed under the piercing stare gaze those two soft pools of crystalline blue.

With a final, shuddering breath, she shut her eyes and pulled the trigger.

Kristof staggered backwards into the sun-dappled hallway, his hand leaving a bloody smear on the polished glasswork as he struggled to remain upright. His gait was unsteady, heavily favouring his left leg as he pushed himself off the glass, only to slump against the far wall in agony as his leg gave beneath him.

"I warned the Councillor against consorting with you." a voice sounded behind him, as Kyran stepped out into the hallway. "I told her that you do nothing but sow chaos. She thought better of you. I told her that you can't use a rabid dog to guard your home. She thought better of you."

The diplomat advanced slowly as Kristof retreated. Calm. Predatory.

Time.

"Somehow I expected more from a man of your reputation. This…" Kyran smiled cruelly. "This just tastes of desperation."

Kristof paused, resting his forearm heavily on the glass as he turned to face Kyran for the last time.

"I must be getting old."

Kristof felt the punch as it snapped his head back. He toppled to his knees, watching with bemused detachment as blood spattered across the ground in front of him. Sounds became distant, muted, seeming to come from everywhere and nowhere at once.

Stand up.

A voice spoke to him, low and guttural. The sound of blood rushing in his ears drowned it out. A hand gripped the front of his shirt.

Fight back.

Impact. The shattering of glass. The feeling of cold, fresh air against skin.

Save them.

A single gunshot sounded, somewhere in the darkness.

Chapter 24

Sergeant Kristof Richter rested a hand gently on his Captain's shoulder.

"I liked what you said in there, Captain. Even if it never sees the light of day, I'm glad someone said it." he said, a fond smile playing about his lips. "And if you get kickback from the commission or the council, then at least you know you went out doing the right thing. That's more than a lot of people get to do."

Jana scrambled backwards, the sound of the gunshot still ringing in her ears. She felt Wulfe's hand take her by the shoulder and haul her unsteadily to her feet. The pain from her shattered hand sliced through her mind with every movement, her eyes blurring with tears, her whole body trembling with the exertion of suppressing the agony. She looked up, blinking away the tears as she stared at what she had done.

Song stood in the centre of the room, unmoving. Her head was kicked back, her back arched impossibly from the raw impact of the bullet.

But, somehow, she did not fall. Her body remained rigid, motionless, a horrifying statue amidst the carnage around her. Lost feathers drifted in the gentle breeze, the same breeze that had once carried the distant sound of gunfire and chaos, now eerily silent.

Slowly, with hideous grace, Song straightened up.

The councillor's face had split around the shell, like a piece of fine porcelain. A fine, hairline crack crossed her features from jaw to eyeline, running across her flawless skin like a river across a silver plain. The eye itself lay in ruins, a sick, black, oily substance leaking from the ruined socket, glinting in the weak light that filtered down from above. It pooled briefly between the socket and Song's high, elegant cheek-bones, before creeping slowly down her cheek in a rivulet of blackness. As Jana watched, a droplet began to form, running along Song's jaw before dropping silently down to her collar, where it meshed slowly with the rich fabric.

The councillor raised a hand, slowly, unsteadily to her ruined features, moving almost as if in a trance, her single remaining eye watching almost curiously at the viscous oil that now darkened the skin of her delicate fingertips.

Suddenly a voice cut through the silence.

"Jana, back. Now." Wulfe growled, not waiting for approval as he thrust her towards the open door.

"I didn't... What..."

"Now!"

Jana stumbled back towards the doorway, allowing Wulfe's hand to guide her. She clutched her hand to her chest, her eyes never once leaving Song as they backed out of the gardens.

The councillor of Cothiq paid them no heed as they retreated. A hundred white-feathered corpses surrounded her, writhing and twisting on the soft, dew-specked grass of the clearing, their voices raised in a discordant hymn of agony. Song's remaining ice-blue eye stared in detached bemusement at the viscous, dark liquid that streaked her fingertips. Tears of blackness rolled down from the crack in her cheek, drawing ragged black scars across those pale, delicate features.

As Jana felt herself half-dragged, half-carried around the corner, she saw a new expression creep across the councillor's ruined features, inch by hideous inch.

Alone in the forest, amidst the keening, anguished cries of a hundred tortured souls, her blackened lifeblood seeping forth to crawl with glacial slowness down her once-perfect features…

Song smiled.

Kristof collapsed to the floor as the force holding him in place suddenly vanished. He rolled onto his side, drawing in a shuddering breath and immediately coughing it back up as the coppery taste of blood burned in his throat.

He felt hands on his shoulder. On his face. There was light again.

"Kristof!?"

He struggled to his hands and knees, ignoring the flash of pain from his knee as he did so, and stared downwards into the face of Ambassador Kyran Aurelien. The man lay on his back, his torso matted with blood from the heavy-calibre rifle round that had shattered his ribcage.

Fractured knee. Mild concussion. Hyperextension on right shoulder.

He moved to kneel up, and immediately doubled over, retching over the corpse of the ambassador, watching as droplets of his own blood spattered across the man's face.

Mild concussion the voice at the back of his mind repeated, insistently.

He felt a cool hand against his cheek, before moving to guide his shoulder as he slowly knelt upright, blinking the blood and sweat from his vision.

"Kri... Are you... ...do I do?" a voice seemed to say, distant and muted by the insistent ringing that smothered all hearing.

"Cass?" he coughed, wiping a smear of crimson from his cheek. Everything hurt. "You shouldn't... I... Where's Wulfe?"

"I... He..." Cass stammered, staring down at the body by her feet. The rifle clattered to the ground, falling from her shaking hand as the enormity of what she had done seemed to strike her. "He was going to kill you, Kristof. I couldn't..."

Kristof staggered upright, pulling himself up against an unbroken section of the glass. He stepped forwards, unsteadily, kneeling in front of Cass as he placed a hand on each of her shoulders.

"Cass. It's ok. It's ok." He smiled weakly as the girl's eyes focussed on him, tearing themselves away from Kyran's still form.

Cass nodded mutely, visibly taking a breath to steady herself. "Are we gonna run?"

"Where's Wulfe?"

"He went to find Jana. I came to find you... I didn't want to..." she paused. "They know what to do."

Kristof smiled, grimly, testing his weight on his wounded knee.

"Then it's just us." he said. "Come on, let's go before they send more men."

"Can you run?" the girl asked, suspiciously.

No

"I can try. Come on."

The two of them set off through the embassy, running as fast as Kristof could bear.

The Cothiq embassy had fallen silent. Its corridors had never been busy over the time they had spent there, but they at least felt occupied, like they were to some extent lived-in. Now they were dead, filled only with a hideous, oppressive silence that bore down on Jana and Wulfe as they hurried through the complexes winding passageways.

Jana moved as quietly as she could, the initial fog of agony lifting as she grew at least somewhat used to the pain. Her hand still hurt. She hadn't even dared to look at it yet, but she could feel the wetness of blood on her skin as she clutched it to her chest. She felt a new kind of emotion now. She felt charged, almost electric, riding on the crest of a wave of adrenaline and fear. Her hands shook, her whole body shook as the two of them darted through the silent corridors.

"Wulfe? What happened?"

"I don't know."

"What was she?"

"I don't know."

"Where are the others?"

"I don't…" Wulfe paused, gently pressing Jana against the wall with one hand as he peered around the next corner. He ducked back, and threw a hunted glance back the way they had come. "Are you alright?"

"No, but I can walk."

"Mhm. Good." he glanced back again, stumbling over his words. "Yeah. You did good." he added, nodding hesitantly, before stepping out into the corridor beyond.

"Do you think she'll follow us?" Jana hissed as they hurried towards the next intersection. She was starting to recognise this place now. The great stairway through which they had originally entered the complex, and through which Jana had left it only twelve hours ago.

Wulfe paused, staring out into the room beyond. "I think she has bigger problems."

The entrance hall was a smoking ruin. The chamber had been plunged into darkness, a flickering half-light from a single source on the high ceiling the only source of illumination for the grisly scene inside. The scent of blood, iron, and the acrid tang of gun smoke hung like a fog in the air as Jana and Wulfe entered.

The two centurion gate guards lay in crumpled heaps beside the door they had been guarding. Three of the Quin guardsmen lay strewn about the ruins of the central table, their bodies broken and torn, huge chunks of flesh ripped from their bodies by the fire of the centurion assault weaponry. One was still moving, lying on his back in a pool of his own gore, lips twitching soundlessly as he struggled to scream through blood-choked lungs.

Jana's step faltered, recoiling in horror at the scene that surrounded her.

She felt Wulfe's arm take her around the shoulders, guiding her gently towards the two ornate doors that lead to the city beyond.

"Don't look, just keep moving." he muttered grimly, eyes fixed firmly on the door ahead.

They passed by one of the Centurion suits, cold and silent as some kind of hideous statue, its autocannon still levelled at the far end of the room, its joints seeming to have locked up in some grim parody of rigor mortis. Jana could smell the smoke more clearly now, the sharp acidic scent becoming thicker in the air as they approached, along with... Bolvar Herdmeat. Cooked... Cooked meat...

They can regulate their internal temperature, too. Highest of the high-tech.

"Wulfe..." she began, before words left her and she had to fight the urge to retch.

Wulfe grimaced wordlessly.

"Did we do this?" she stammered, covering her mouth and nose with her hands as sickness lapped at her. "Did Kristof do this?"

"I don't know." Wulfe shook his head, eyes playing across the room around them for a moment, before snapping back towards the door. "I really don't."

He stepped forwards, bracing a shoulder against the door as he levered it open with a grunt of effort.

And the two of them stepped out into the streets of Cothiq.

The main embassy building stood at the heart of an ever-expanding spiral of smaller structures that arced out across the white stone plazas of the embassy grounds until they melded almost seamlessly with the city proper. As with much of the city, the embassy grounds were crisscrossed with dozens of walkways and elevated paths that provided easy access between the administrative outbuildings and the main structure itself.

The endless mists swirled around Cass and Kristof as they dropped through the shattered window onto the rooftops of the exterior buildings. They ran together, sticking close to each other, and within moments they had cut across the spiral outbuildings and were looking down a short slope towards the rooftops of Cothiq beyond. The roof plating was smooth and slick with moisture, the tiles inclined to give a smooth path for the surface runoff, and Kristof found himself sliding downwards at a frightening rate before he crashed onto the rooftops with a grunt of discomfort.

They were free of the embassy.

That was the easy bit.

On a normal evening, the mist above Cothiq was white and red, glittering with the scattered rays of the low sunset. Tonight, it had been turned black with smoke. They wouldn't be the only ones heading for an escape from the city, that much was clear.

He turned, hurrying into the mist's after Cass' retreating silhouette, slipping and sliding across the slick ceramic tiles of Couloin's rooftops, painfully aware of the hundred-metre drop into the white-paved streets below that awaited him if he should step too far astray.

Kristof cursed under his breath as his foot slipped on one of the tiles, twisting his leg painfully as he stumbled to right himself. Cass turned, pausing as she crouched by the drop to the next rooftop.

"I'm fine. Keep going!" Kristof called over the rising roar of the gorge. They were getting closer now. He could see the port in the distance, the roar of falling water growing louder and louder with every step they advanced.

Look back. the voice at the back of his mind prompted, quietly.

Two figures were picking their way across the rooftops behind them. Slowed by the mist and the poor footing, but closing ground.

200 metres to effective range, at most.

Kristof picked up his pace, staggering across the rooftops in pursuit of Cass. They had to keep moving. Keep that distance open. They could outrun them.

Not with a fractured knee.

Not forever.

Not for long.

Chapter 25

34ᵗʰ Sihyl, 2094.74 Core Time – Electronic Messaging Certificate – Confidential

Commissary Atesca Seratov, Commissary 1ˢᵗ Class

You are hereby ordered to cease all individual pursuit of the individual known as "The Butcher of Carth", Target 337. You will remain on assignment providing logistical support to deployed legions, and are permitted to take whatever steps you feel adequate to ensure that the conflict remains stable and contained. These orders are, of course, highly confidential.

The port was packed. The ragged crowds that had gathered outside the doors of the vast shuttles were tense and frightened. Jana could taste it in the air. The smell of fear, that primal, animalistic sense that lurked just behind the eyes, the tiny fragment of remaining lizard brain that could just *feel* when something was off. Families huddled together, children clung to parents, the whirling mists of the gulf flowing over them as they sheltered each other from the worst of its effects. In the dying light of the day they pressed together, escape the only thing on their minds.

And Jana could see why. As she glanced back over her shoulder, she could see almost directly up the main thoroughfare across the city as it curved gently upwards towards the base of the embassy. The lights were out, the building seeming empty and deserted. Several thin, ominous trails of black smoke rose almost lazily from within, curling like snakes in the eddying breeze that swept the city's rooftops.

"One's already gone." Wulfe remarked, glancing at the assembled shuttles as they hurried forwards. Jana could see he was right. The closest of the port fields was deserted, the vast, claw-like landing structures hanging empty amidst the whirling mists.

Jana stopped halfway down the short flight of steps leading down to the port basin, her eyes scanning the crowds busily. They would be here.

"See anyone?" Wulfe muttered, pausing beside her.

"No." said Jana, feeling her heart sink in her chest as if somehow the admission had made it true. The two of them hurried down the slick stone steps, stepping towards the group of armed Legionaries that had formed a line between the huddled crowd and the safety of the shuttle's interior.

"What was the plan Wulfe? Should they be here?"

"No. But I hoped they might be."

She felt the soldier's arm fall about her shoulders, pulling her deeper into the crowd. She allowed herself to be guided, clutching her broken hand close to her chest for protection as they stepped in amongst the press of bodies.

The next few minutes seemed to pass in a haze. Afterwards, she found she could barely remember a thing. The press of bodies. The warmth of Wulfe's arm about her, shielding her from the rain and shifting crowds. The worried chatter of hundreds of voices as the crowd surged forwards. The dull, endless, throbbing pain from her shattered hand. The sharp, staccato snap of orders from the Legionaries as they ushered the crowd into the cramped confines of the shuttle. Wulfe's haggard, rain-soaked features as he searched the crowd with worried eyes.

And the deep, rumbling roar as the second shuttle's engines fired up.

"There's people behind us."

"I know." Kristof muttered through gritted teeth. Every step was agony. His foot slipped on the slick tiling and he stumbled for a moment, letting out a muffled cry as pain shot through his leg. In a moment, Cass was at his side, her arm supporting his.

"Here…"

"No, go ahead." Kristof grunted, stumbling to his feet once more. "We need to get down to street level, somewhere out of their sight."

"I can help you."

"No. Just…" he forced a smile. "Scout ahead. Find a route. I'm ok."

"Alright. But you shout if you're in trouble." Cass replied hesitantly, stepping away before taking off across the rooftops at a run, disappearing into the haze within seconds.

Wearily, Kristof pressed on into the mists.

A deep rumbling caught his ear, a low thrum that seemed to shake the very building on which he stood.

The second shuttle.

Looking up was useless. He could barely make out the roof opposite, let alone the sky.

Not much time left.

He stumbled to a halt as a silhouette emerged from the mist ahead of him.

"Down here, Kristof!" the figure called in Cass' voice. "There's a walkway!"

It was then that he heard the sound that he had been dreading. A low, sharp crack echoed through the air behind him, followed by the scrape of tearing air as the bullet ripped past him in the darkness.

"Go, Cass!" he called, stumbling slightly as he reached for the pistol in his belt.

Too dark, too far away.

He snarled in frustration, plunging the weapon into his pocket as he lunged forwards, dashing across the rooftops towards where Cass had been standing.

Where Cass was still standing, frozen in the agony of indecision.

Waiting for you.

"Go!" he roared.

He saw the girl's expression harden, and with a brief nod she vaulted the parapet and disappeared over the edge into the streets below.

She won't go far.

Kristof grunted in pain as his foot came down poorly. He staggered doggedly on through the swirling mists, the water soaking him to the skin, the cold wind of the Ashkan sea biting at his face and hands, wincing as bullets ripped past him in the darkness.

Neither will you.

With a final surge of effort he collapsed against the parapet, staring down into the street below. The walkway was only metres below, crossing between the two upper floors of the buildings. An easy jump, in normal circumstances. He could see where Cass crouched, huddled in the small overhang at the far end of the walkway as bullets from surrounding rooftops splintered the stonework around her.

He glanced back. He could see the figures around him now, fleeting ghosts amidst the glittering mist. He could hear their shouts and cries, orders relayed back and forth in the oddly musical dialect. He with a grunt of effort, propping himself up on one arm as he slowly unslung the rifle from his shoulder.

Three in the mist to your left, two at the parapet to the right. Poor visibility for them. Just enough for you.

"Come on!"

Cass' voice pulled him back. He spun, rolling over the parapet even as the rooftop behind him exploded in a hail of fire and steel.

He landed with an anguished cry, his injured leg collapsing under his weight with a jagged flash of pain and sending him sprawling on the rough concrete walkway.

Bullets splintered and cracked the walkway around him, showering him with shards of granite and dust as he flattened himself against the ground.

A terrified scream cut through the cacophony.

"Kristof!"

Looking up, Kristof saw Cass break from the shelter of the far building, dashing towards him across the walkway. Bullets tore through the air around her, sending up clouds of dust and shrapnel as she rushed out onto the bridge.

Kristof scrambled to his feet, terror lending new strength to his limbs as he broke into a staggering run across the walkway towards Cass. His leg and ribs screamed with pain, the sound of his footsteps thundering in his ears as he dashed towards her.

He collided with her, hearing a faint gasp as the impact drove the air from her lungs. His weight drove her back, sending them tumbling back through the doorway into the room beyond in a tangle of limbs.

The world fell silent as the doors slammed shut behind them. Kristof lay still for a second, his heart still hammering in his chest. He coughed, sending up a mist of the white masonry dust that covered his body. Gathering all the strength he had left, he rolled onto his side with an agonised groan. His whole body felt bruised, his leg and ribs sending bright flashes of pain through his mind with every movement. He could feel fresh cuts on his face and hands, where the shards of stone had done their grizzly work.

Move. They're coming.

He pulled himself up on one elbow, feeling every inch of his body strain with the effort. With a strangled grunt of exertion, he planted his palm against the cold stonework and rose unsteadily up onto one knee.

Two minutes.

He straightened up, drawing in a shuddering breath as he flexed his aching shoulders. Forcing a weak smile, he glanced over towards Cass.

"Still in one piece?"

The smile fell from his face as he saw the pain in her eyes.

Cass hadn't moved. She lay on her back, where she had fallen. Her face was pale and drawn, her whole body seeming to shake as she stared up at the ceiling, eyes bright with fear.

"Cass?"

He scrambled to her side, kneeling over her, his hands falling to her shoulders. He felt one of her shaking hands lock around his forearm, her nails biting deep into his skin with the strength of the grip. Her eyes stared up at him, searching, almost, her gaze skittering restlessly across his features

He didn't look down. The dark crimson that stained her tongue told him everything he didn't want to know.

Internal haemorrhaging. hissed the voice again, creeping in unbidden.

"Hey. It's ok, Cass. It's ok." he whispered, wishing it was true.

Cass' eyes met his for one fleeting moment.

"'s ok." she slurred, an expression of almost mild bemusement crossing her features as her fingers brushed against his collar.

Shock.

Her whole body seemed to shudder for a moment. Pain flashed in her eyes, her lips moving soundlessly, her hand tightening its grip around Kristof's forearm.

Seizing.

"It is, Cass. You're going to be fine."

Cass was silent now, her gaze beginning to drift. Her face was serene, her expression placid.

Catalysis.

"I promise." Kristof whispered, uselessly.

Death.

Chapter 26

"And how am I going to tell my men that they've got to survive against the Butcher's rebels with thirty rounds per man?" Sergeant Richter asked.

Captain Wulfe grimaced. "I've got no choice. With no supply we can't risk pushing."

For a moment Kristof seemed about to speak further, before sighing and sinking down into the seat beside him.

"Son of a bitch. Half the time it feels like they don't even want us to win this war."

Wulfe said nothing.

Jana staggered out of the shuttle, jostled and shoved as the crowds poured forth into the bowels of the Pioneer. Wulfe strode down beside her, hand on her shoulder as he guided her towards the far end of the vast hangar.

The chamber was thronging with people. Hundreds upon hundreds were pouring out of the shuttled and milling about in the staging areas. What few legion personnel she could see called desperately for order, medical orderlies dashing amongst the crowds tending to the injured.

One of them approached Jana, his eyes fixing on her injured hand. She waved him away as he approached.

"Just give me the things. I can sort myself out, I think. There are people who need you more."

The medical nodded silently, thrusting a small pouch into her hand before moving along to the next huddle of civilians.

Jana pushed the bag into her pocket, craning her neck to see above the thronging crowds that filled the hangar as the shuttles disembarked. She clutched her hand protectively to her chest as she was jostled from side to side. She glanced up at Wulfe helplessly. The man towered above the crowd, eyes flickering around the busy hall, his face locked into a worried frown.

"Anything?" Jana asked.

Wulfe shook his head, his eyes still roving across the crowd. Jana watched him intently. She tasted fabric in her mouth, and realised she had begun chewing on her sleeve again out of nervousness.

Wulfe glanced down briefly, and caught her worried gaze. His expression softened slightly.

"They'll make it. Kristof always makes it." He looked back up, gazing across the crowds. "There's still a shuttle to come in."

He took her by the shoulder, guiding her gently towards one of the hangar's walls.

"Have a sit down." he said, quietly. "You've taken a beating, you've earned it."

"But what if they come?"

Wulfe shrugged. "When he comes we'll find them, or they'll find us. No sense in tiring ourselves out any more than we have to."

Jana paused for a second, then reluctantly sat, nestling herself in a corner beside one of the huge steel columns that lined the edge of the hangar. She sat there silently for a time, staring up at the passing crowds, listening to the chatter, the crying children, the roar of dying engines, the screams of the injured. She huddled closer, drawing her knees up to her chest and wrapped herself in her jacket. She rubbed her eyes wearily.

"You really think they'll make it?"

Wulfe looked down at her from where he stood, staring out over the crowds. He nodded.

"Yeah."

"But what if they don't?"

Wulfe paused, then sighed. He knelt down beside Jana, and with a muffled grunt sank into a seated position against the wall.

"I wish you wouldn't ask things like that." he muttered.

Jana fidgeted with her broken digits, trying idly to wrap them in the hem of her jacket. She knew she shouldn't, the 'Health & Personal Preservation Stage I' skimmer pilot training course had been very firm about it. She gasped as a tremor of pain shot up her arm, and decided to stop. She let out a deep sigh, resting her head back against the hangar wall with a dull clank.

"Are you ok?" Wulfe said, glancing over. "They'll have a medical officer somewhere, I can go and take a look."

Jana held out a hand, stopping the man as he made to rise.

"I'm fine as long as I don't move." she said with a smile. "Stay here. Please."

The soldier looked surprised, but made no objection as he settled back down beside her.

"You think they're just going to come walking out of one of these shuttles?" she said eventually, as the two of them watched the crowds go by.

"He always had a knack for that ...Kristof did. He's done it before. I've seen him in firefights, bombings, riots... Dozens of times where I thought it was all over. Then there'd he'd be, walking out without a scratch on him. Don't know how he did it. He always came back." He stopped, and shook his head. "*Came* back. See, you've got me doing it now. He'll be here. I know it." He stood up again, eyes moving restlessly as they scanned the ever-shifting crowds.

"He always liked you, you know that?" Jana said, quietly. Somewhere inside her she knew she shouldn't say these things, that they were secrets, told in confidence. Right now, though, she found it hard to care.

"He said you were the best man he had ever known. That every single thing they said about you was true."

Wulfe snorted derisively, watching the crowds with concern etched plainly on his features.

"Kristof says a lot of things."

"I felt like he meant it though."

"Maybe he did."

Jana could sense him locking up, the familiar deadpan tone entering his voice. She wasn't in the mood to pursue it right now, anyway.

Wulfe stood a little taller, craning his neck to see over the crowds. Jana looked up at him inquisitively.

"Looks like there's one coming in at the far end." he muttered. Jana reached out with her good hand, and Wulfe hauled her upright.

"Go check." Wulfe added, giving her a gentle push. Jana nodded, threading her way through the mass of people as the sound of engines filled the hangar once more. "I'll be right behind you."

She watched as the doors slid open, the sudden inrush of air sending her jacket and hair fluttering gaily in the breeze. She stood as tall as she could, peering over the heads of the crowd, her eyes scanning the faces that emerged from the compartment.

Kristof was a tall man. Not as tall as Wulfe, but enough to stand out from a crowd. Jana's heart leapt as she recognised him amidst the thronging masses.

"Kristof! Cass!"

She began to push her way through the crowds towards him, ducking and weaving through the mass of people. She could hear Wulfe behind her, boots thudding heavily across the metal floor. Her broken fingers brushed past someone, sending a sharp jolt of pain up her arm, but she didn't care, darting through the crowd towards the shuttle doors.

Then he stood in front of her, and her heart sank like a stone.

Cass lay cradled in Kristof's arms. Her eyes were closed, her face serene, her head lolling limply with Kristof's every step.

"Cass." Jana gasped, rushing forwards. She reached out for Cass' hand, holding in tight in her own, staring hopelessly at the girl's placid expression. She stopped, staring at the red smear across her palm. Looking up, she met Kristof's gaze.

"She's fine."

Jana reached out once more, tenderly reaching for the girl's wrist. Her heart fell once more as she felt the coolness of Cass' skin against her own. She looked up at Kristof again, staring searchingly into those blank, dead eyes.

"She's fine." The words were little more than a whisper this time.

Jana had had a friend when she was a girl. Another envoy child, called Jakob, a young boy from Taynia, Ashka's second moon. He was brash and boisterous, as young boys often were, but he was fun, and genuine, and exciting to be around.

She broke his arm once. They were wrestling by the side of one of the Bolvar cattle pit, playing without a thought to their surroundings as children do. A single shove was all it took, a little harder than intended, but a shove nonetheless, and her friend lay sprawling at the bottom of the six-foot hole in the sandstone. She remembered being ushered back to the spire, the rush and bustle of the medical orderlies, the rattle of the cart they carried him in on, the click and chatter of machinery around them as she clung to her friend's side.

It never quite settled in for six-year-old Jana. The whole thing felt like a dream. Not a nightmare, that implied some kind of genuine attachment and understanding of what was going on around her, just... detached. Isolated. Like she was viewing events through the body of another, her thoughts and feelings barely her own.

Jana felt that same dream-like suspension now. Hours passed as if in a blur. She could remember sitting by Cass' body as the orderlies bustled around her. She remembered the weight of Cass' shoulder bag as one of the Legionaries solemnly pressed it into her hands. She remembered them speaking to her, earnestly and genuinely, their words lost in the haze. She remembered feeling the comforting weight of Wulfe's hand on her shoulder, and seeing the bleakness in his face as he stood beside her.

She didn't remember seeing Kristof leave. No-one did. It took her hours to find him, sitting alone amidst the twisting bowels of the Pioneer, head bowed in quiet contemplation.

She knelt beside him in the silent hallway, the dim, blue-tinged light from the emergency illumination casting strange, shifting shadows over the pair of them.

"You're hurt." she said, deciding to get straight to the point.

"It's nothing."

Jana paused. "Didn't look like nothing out there. Still doesn't."

"I'm fine."

The words had a trace of finality about them. Jana sighed, then turned, dropping into a seated position beside Kristof.

They sat there for a time, she had no idea how long, listening to the faint clamour of voices, the low thrum of the engines and the hiss and whine of the lights as they flickered spasmodically on and off.

Jana pulled out the small cloth pouch that the medical orderlies had given her. A white cross had been stamped onto the side, the dye already fading in places. She opened the bag, pulling out a thin roll of plastic-gauze. The dim, low-power lighting of the hall was barely enough to see by and she had to raise her hand, resting it on her knee as she prised the injured digits into position.

"You're hurt?"

Jana looked up, meeting Kristof's eyes briefly. He watched her intently as she began to wrap the gauze around her fingers, binding them in place. She smiled at him, giving what she hoped was an impish grin.

"It's nothing."

She held up her hand, wiggling her fingers by way of demonstration. She immediately regretted that, gasping as another white hot flash of pain shot through her hand.

She clutched it to her chest again, grinning sheepishly up at Kristof.

He glanced over at her, and for a brief moment she saw life return to his eyes as a low chuckle broke the silence.

"Take care of yourself, alright? Just… be careful." The voice was quiet, but as Jana looked up once more she felt a genuine note of compassion in the words.

She smiled. "Only if you do the same."

Kristof grimaced, and shook his head sadly.

"No promises at this point."

They sat together in silence for a while. Eventually Jana slipped the shoulder satchel onto the floor beside them, and nudged it towards Kristof with her foot.

"What's that?" he asked.

"It's her slate. Wulfe said you'd want it."

Kristof reached out, slowly drawing the device from the bag. He turned it over and over in his hands, idly watching as the screen, detecting the motion, sprung to life. Kristof stared at the device in his hands, raising a shaking hand to tap slowly at the display. He paused, and Jana saw his brow furrow slightly as he stared at the symbols that flashed up on the screen.

Kristof, I told you to stay out of my things

Even in the semi-darkness of the Pioneer's interior, Jana saw a flood of emotions cross the man's features, slowly subsiding into a weary, fond smile. He reached into the bag, drawing out a pair of red ident booklets, and stared at them thoughtfully for a moment.

"These were the reason I brought her along in the first place, you know? I didn't want to, but…" he shook his head with a wry smile. "They're are just so *damn* useful."

"Wulfe told me not to. Nadir didn't like it either." he continued. "But I knew best."

He raised the slate, and Jana caught a short glimpse of the thin, silvery lines of text across the screen. "I wanted to get my hands on this for so long. I never thought that this would be how I'd get it."

Jana saw his grip on the slate tighten. "I killed her." he muttered, half to himself. "For this. I dragged her into this, and now she's dead."

Jana reached out, hesitantly, placing her hand on his shoulder. She felt him draw back, shrugging his shoulder away from the contact.

"She loved it, Kristof, she really did. Back in Ashka, she told me how much she enjoyed it. I could see it in her eyes. You didn't force her to do anything. It was her choice. She chose to come with you."

"I shouldn't have given her the choice."

"But you did. That's all that matters. How many of us get to choose how our lives go? I didn't. Wulfe didn't. I don't know about you, but I'm sure you've had choices made for you in the past. Things you had no say over. Life is all about making choices. You just gave her another one."

"You're right." Kristof sighed quietly. "I know you're right."

He stopped. The corridor fell silent once more.

"Now what?" he asked quietly. Jana looked up, unsure if he was talking to her.

"What do you want?" she asked, quietly.

The soldier remained silent for a moment, turning the booklets over and over in his hands.

"I don't..." he shook his head. "I want it to stop. I just want to be free again."

"Well, lets do it then." Jana said.

She hesitated as Kristof's bleak gaze raised to meet hers for a moment. This time, however, she pushed through.

"I'm serious! It'll be simple. If we get a shuttle back down to Ashka, we can find Cass' contact. They can get us the idents we need to get to Verkat. I know the place, there's companies that'll give you work without an ident, plenty of them." She smiled at him encouragingly. "You can put all this behind you. Isn't that what you're always saying? About second chances?"

"I'm not sure I deserve another one."

"Everyone deserves one. That's what you said to me, first time I met you. I don't see what's changed. There's Bolvar tribes out there that have never seen a legionary before and don't speak a single word of Ashkan. If you want to be alone it's the place to be."

"She'll see that coming." Kristof muttered. "She'll find us. She always does, eventually."

"Celthar then." Jana said, wracking her brains as she dug through the scattered memories of geography lessons in the Spire of Valmeer. "Or Gaia. Plenty of uncharted territory there. We had a few Celthari bards that used to stop by Verkat periodically, they always talked about how beautiful it was. Or Varia?" She added, hitting her stride. "They'll do anything for money, I'm sure we can get someone to cover our tracks."

She stopped, noticing the lack of response.

"My point being, Kristof." she said, a little more gently. "We can do it. We can make it happen, all of us, if that's what you really want."

He looked up at her then, catching her gaze in the half-light of the Pioneer's hallway. She could see the conflict in his eyes, as if some vast battle was being fought just beyond her sight.

"Where's Wulfe?" he asked, seeming to suddenly realise that the soldier wasn't present.

"Probably looking for you." Jana said. As the two of them rose, she touched Kristof gently on the arm to get his attention.

"I mean it, though. Lets get back down to Ashka, then we can talk about it. We'll need those idents one way or the other."

Chapter 27

"In many ways, Ashka and its Union owes its existence to the Wolf of Carth. The war for the white city was, simply put, a power play, to demonstrate the might of the Ashkan Union and its willingness to ensure its own integrity. A failure at this stage could have meant disaster for the Union, but a success, especially in a war of this scale, raised the population's confidence in this new political union immeasurably."

- Bantaric Vess, War for the White City

For a city so full of life, nothing in Ashka seemed to change an awful lot. The streets still thronged with people, the skies filled with the roar and whine of skimmer engines as they tore through the dark clouds that hugged the rooftops of the capital.

It had been a rough night, spent huddled in the cold and uncomfortable underbelly of the Pioneer. This morning one of the late shuttles was being sent down to the planet for refuelling, and they had been able to hitch a lift down to the city itself. Getting on the Pioneer was usually the hard part. They couldn't wait to get you off it.

As always, it was raining. Jana watched the raindrops as they pattered down around her feet, the overhang of the market stall she stood beside shielding her from the worst the weather had to offer. The Bolvar running his little stall had been wary at first, but after hearing Jana's attempt at the traditional greeting in his home tongue had gladly beckoned the three of them under his shelter.

Jana sighed, rubbing her eyes for a moment. She was hungry and tired, and while the acrid smell of the charring Bolvar herdmeat did help a little with the latter, it exacerbated the former to an almost unbearable degree.

She needed a shower. And a change of clothes. And about three day's sleep.

Glancing up at Wulfe she could see he felt the same. The giant man had huddled into his greatcoat, its collar turned up against the wind, his hands dug deep into its pockets, the scowl that perpetually adorned his features deepening as he glanced around at the crowds that thronged the narrow market streets around them.

"How much money do we have?"

"You're eating the last of it." Kristof said with a weak smile. Jana could see he was struggling, although he tried hard to show it. His words lacked the energy they used to, his jokes had lost their edge, and he frequently lapsed into long periods of silence. Jana hoped it was just the exhaustion and hunger, but she suspected... well she suspected it was something more.

"How are you doing?" she asked quietly as Wulfe turned away, grumbling to himself under his breath as he scanned the crowds that surrounded them.

Kristof glanced up, and gave a wry chuckle.

"I'll be the first to admit I've been better."

Jana grinned. "I'll second that."

She paused, staring glumly out at the crowds for a moment.

"So what do we do now?" said Wulfe quietly.

They paused for a moment as a skimmer roared overhead, the sound of its engines deafening in the narrow confines of the street market.

"Can we check in on Nadir?" Jana said, hopefully.

"How? 'Hello, we're the people who left him in the rain in critical condition with a mangled arm, can we see him?'" Kristof said, bitterly. "Atesca would be on us in seconds, even if she hasn't… even if she hasn't got to him already."

"Best thing we can do for him is stay away." Wulfe nodded.

"Seems like that would be the best thing for a lot of people." Kristof murmured, almost under his breath. He shook his head, and turned back towards them with a fresh energy to his movement.

"Look," he said "if we want to go somewhere new we need clean idents. That means either tracking down Cass' contact or looking for a few of our own. The Warrens are bound to be home to a few good counterfeiters, if we can scrape some money together…" Kristof paused, and sighed. "But we don't have any money, do we."

He fell silent, staring out into the rain silently for a moment.

Jana stepped forwards. "Kristof…"

Wulfe placed a hand on her shoulder, shaking his head silently. Jana stopped. The man was right, best not to push too hard.

As they stared out at the rain together, she reached into Cass' satchel-bag that she carried over her shoulder now. Cass' slate was light and slender, unlike the weighty, angular unit Jana had managed to purchase on her pilot's wage back on Valmeer. Jana drew it out of the bag, looking at it curiously as if for the first time. There had to be a way in somehow.

"There's nothing on there. I've checked a hundred times in the past." Kristof muttered acridly, seeming to have sensed her movement without even looking around.

In the silence that followed, Jana turned away, covering the screen from the rain with the hem of her jacket as she powered it up. The slate lit up with a faint silver light.

Password.

Jana pressed a few keys at random, more out of idle curiosity than any hope of progress.

Password Incorrect

As expected. She tapped a few more times. 1234... Password... Admin...

Password Incorrect

Just call me the master codebreaker she thought bitterly.

However, as she went to put the slate away she noticed something. The device had not reset. The failure prompt faded slowly, to be replaced with a few lines of plain white text.

Kristof, I'm going to assume something horrible has happened. If it hasn't, put my slate down and walk away because you just can't comprehend the hell I will inflict on you if I find you with it.

Ashka, Sivren Block, Floor 6, Door 216. He'll help you out.

"Kristof?" she said, quietly.

The two men paused in their conversation. Kristof frowned as he turned to see Jana holding the slate.

"I think she knew you'd stopped looking." Jana said, passing it to him with a gentle smile.

He hid it well, but there was no disguising the flash of pain in his eyes as he read the message. His hand dropped to his side, and he glanced out into the rain again.

"Always one step ahead." he muttered, the faintest trace of a fond smile crossing his features. Then his expression turned sour again, and with a grimace he handed the slate back to Jana.

"Well, we're one step closer to those idents." he said.

They both looked around as Wulfe spoke up.

"So where do we go when we have them?" he said. "Ultimately, I mean."

"Ultimately…" Jana hesitated, then glanced across at Kristof. "You didn't tell him?"

Kristof shrugged. "Hadn't found the right time yet."

"Well someone better tell me." muttered Wulfe irritably, glancing between the two of them. "I take it the two of you made plans?"

"We were thinking Verkat." Jana said.

"We?" Wulfe said.

"All of us. There are tribes out there that get by with minimal Union contact, Wulfe." Jana said, placing a hand on his arm to get his attention. "And they won't gossip with outsiders, not even with an inquisitor. We'd be safe if we can persuade one of them to take us in. We could lose Atesca there. For good."

Wulfe looked at Kristof. "Do you really believe that?"

The man shrugged. "I'd like to believe in something. What do we have to lose?"

Within an hour they were there. Jana walked through the wide avenues of central Ashka quietly, a bittersweet sadness in her heart as she once again walked the pathways that she and Cass had walked together only weeks earlier.

"That…" Kristof glanced around, then up at the building in front of him, a short laugh passing his lips. "This is where we first met. Right here. She arranged a meeting right outside her own house." The smile fell a little. "She really had no idea what she was doing."

Jana started slightly as a face appeared behind the metal gate. It was old, wrinkled, its skin seeming to almost hang off the skull that it surrounded. He looked like the physical incarnation of not getting enough sun.

"What is it?" he called out, in a shrill, rasping voice. "I've told you before, I…" He paused, and his eyes narrowed, staring intently past Jana at the looming figures of Wulfe and Kristof behind her.

"Bastian Wulfe and Kristof Richter. I remember you." The narrowed eyes swivelled towards Jana. "That would make you… Jana Schleifer, correct? You don't look at all like your picture. Terrible lighting."

Jana put on what she hoped was a disarming smile. "Hi. We just wanted to stop by and pick up a few things. Cass sent us…"

"Sandra?!" The man's eyes widened slightly. "Is she here?" He pushed forwards a little, pressing his face up close to the iron gate as he strained to see out past Kristof and Wulfe.

Out of the corner of her eye, Jana saw Kristof's fists clench. She shifted sideways a little, placing herself between him and the strange old man, who was still pressed up close to the gate.

"She's a little busy at the moment. She just sent us to pick up a few things."

The man frowned, his worn face wrinkling as his brow furrowed. "Never tells me anything, that girl."

Jana hesitated, her mind racing as she tried to keep up with this new development. "She said she would stop by the next time she could though." she said, immediately regretting it.

The man's eyes darted upwards to meet hers, bright with excitement. "Oh? And when will that be?"

Jana hesitated. "Soon. Probably. Things are a little up in the air at the moment."

"Well, I suppose that will have to do." said the man with a short sigh. "Come in, come in."

He raised his hand to a weatherworn metallic keypad that jutted out of the wall beside the gate, and slowly and deliberately pushed a few keys.

They followed the man carefully as he stumbled up a perilous flight of metal steps that wound their way up the outside of the building, waiting as he paused after each landing to take a single deep gulp of air before continuing.

Jana watched the man curiously every time they paused to wait. The deep green colour of his eyes as they narrowed against the glare of the hall's lighting. The way his expression changed when he spoke, as if to emphasise every spoken syllable. The barely contained energy in his every step. The way that his hair curled and, despite its whitening, still contained strands as dark as the darkest night.

Just like Cass.

"Do you mind if I ask your name?" Jana asked as the old man turned on one of the landings, fiddling with a small keypad on the wall.

"Ah!" he said, looking up at her quickly. "Hm, well don't spread it around too much, but its Eder."

The keypad beeped gently, and Eder pulled open the steel grate that covered the door, before reaching for a ring of keys to unlock the door itself. Catching Jana's gaze, he smiled nervously.

"Can't be too careful." he murmured.

The room was dark, illuminated by a single light embedded in the ceiling and the combined glow of several large, high-resolution monitors set against the far wall. Jana recognised the layout of the room well. They had the same design in the Ashkan spire in Verkat. Compact, energy efficient, and dirt cheap to build. The Union constructors could churn out hundreds of these in a day.

"So, what was so dreadfully important that that my little girl couldn't come and ask me for it herself?" the old man asked, gathering up an armful of loose stationary from his desk and offloading it into a small, already overfilled filing cabinet before turning to face them. "Would you like anything? I have some coffee hidden around here somewhere..."

He began to bustle off in the direction of what Jana already knew was the kitchen. She spoke up quickly.

"No thanks, we're fine. Don't want to take up any more of your time than we have to, you know? We were wondering if you couldn't... obtain some passes for us to get to Valmeer. Verkat, specifically."

"...Obtain? Strange choice of wording. What *has* that girl been telling you about me?"

"Not much, really."

"Good! Doing as she's told for once." Eder murmured, then spoke a little more clearly. "I can have those registered for you right away. Should take an hour or two at most."

Jana found herself smiling. There was a certain charm to the old man's demeanour.

"Do you need anything? We can take some pictures, if you need them."

"Oh, no need, no need. I think I still have the hard copies lying around from the last time. They'll just need a tiny bit of modification so they don't double up in the database."

Eder jumped down from his chair and began to scramble through the cluttered desk, shuffling aside paper and electrical scraps as he went.

"So that's... four of you to Verkat... *this* circuit? Next one should be in around two months, unless you can think up an excuse for me to get you a Legion carrier." He leant forwards and peered closely at Jana over the top of his glasses. "That was a *joke*." he winked. "I'm not a miracle worker."

"Four of us will do fine." Wulfe rumbled from beside Jana. She could see a faint smile playing around his lips even in the half-darkness of the apartment.

"Fine, fine." Eder muttered, turning back to his search. "Have a seat. Kitchen is down the corridor, Bathroom is out the back. Oh, and if you're picking things up for Sandra her room is on the right."

As he turned away, Jana frowned. She had really set herself up for that.

It was OK. She would just look.

Taking a deep breath Jana stepped forwards into the room. It was just a room. The kind Jana herself had had when she was younger. A single low bed sat against the far wall, strewn with blankets and cushions. The walls were covered in an array of maps and drawings, pictures of cities, deserts, oceans strewn across the walls. The images were old and dog-eared, many of them bearing annotations and notes.

Jana made out a familiar image amongst the mess, and pulled it free from its pin with the quiet sound of tearing paper. The red tundra of Verkat stared back at her, the crests and furrows in the landscape dusted with a light frost, glinting in the orange light as the sun rose over the mountains behind them. To the right of the picture stood a city, Jana couldn't make out which, illuminated by the soft blue glow of a million lights. Specks of light spread outwards from the city, each one a single skimmer winding its way across the tundra. Jana stared down at the image, and found herself cracking a fond smile.

She glanced up at the hundreds of pictures that covered the span of the wall almost from doorframe to window, each one taped neatly into place. She saw the Ashkan Council Halls. The white fields of Dhaka.

On the far wall hung a single large piece of fabric, a huge cloth map of the Union. Jana reached out and brushed at its surface with her fingertips. It must have been expensive. Especially for a young girl. The kind of thing you would have to save up for years for.

Her fingers traced across the map, brushing across Ashka, Verkat and the inner circle, out across the endless void of space towards Sihyld and Cothiq and beyond. So much to see. Too much for one person. More than enough to fill the dreams of one young girl.

She froze as she heard the sound of footsteps behind her. She turned, watching as Kristof stepped slowly into the room, eyes roving about, taking in every detail. She felt her heart grow heavy as she once again saw the pain well in his eyes.

"Kristof…"

He turned and, without a backwards glance, left the room.

Jana re-emerged into the sitting room, her head abuzz with frustration. What was she thinking, bringing him here? Of course it was going to hurt. She was barely keeping her composure herself, she couldn't imagine what he must be going through.

Eder was chatting animatedly with Wulfe as she entered, although admittedly the conversation was largely one-sided. The soldier threw a concerned glance at Kristof, before turning to Jana and raising an eyebrow.

"…I have a printing system rigged up in the basement. I'll set this off and take a walk down there to see if I can get it warmed up for you." He glanced at Jana. "You did want physical copies, didn't you?"

"Mhm. Physical." Wulfe rumbled, nodding.

"'Yeah, definitely." Jana said, the horrors of the Cothiq embassy still fresh in her mind. "Mind if I come with you?" she added, suddenly. She found something strangely endearing about this old man.

Eder grinned and beckoned her forwards, and shuffled off towards the door. He swung the protective grate shut behind them, and began to descend the metal stairwell that clung precariously to the outside of the building.

"Sandra has rubbed off on you, I can see. Always preferred the physical to the digital, that girl."

Jana followed the man as he shuffled his way down the narrow stairway. Quietly, she followed him the nearly eight floors down to street level, and then down another stairway that curved beneath the deep foundations of the vast spire. They entered a small room together, barely more than a cupboard, the space taken up by an arcane array of wiring and whirring spindles. Eder squeezed himself onto a small seat somewhere in the depths of the machine, and began tapping away at a screen in front of him.

Jana hesitated, choosing her words carefully.

"Can I ask you a question?"

"Mhm." the man nodded his assent. "Ask away."

"Are you alright here on your own? Without Cassandra, I mean."

"What? Yes! Fine." said the man, not looking back from his work. "As long as I have this little thing and the power to sustain it," he tapped the computer fondly. "I can do anything. That's what Sandra never understood, you know? I showed her the universe from here, but she never *believed* it was there. She had to see everything with her own eyes."

Jana stayed quiet. She regretted asking the question.

The old man had fallen silent too, the only sound in the room the creak of his chair as he shifted occasionally in his seat.

"Still, I suppose she's having fun at least." he murmured quietly, as he began tapping away at the keys in front of him.

The room was silent for a while, filled with the sound of clacking keys and the whirr of the press. Eventually Jana broke the silence.

"So how does this work, getting all these idents? Or is it top secret?"

"Sandra never explained it to you?"

Jana grimaced to herself. *Get the idents. Just get your hands on them, then you can explain everything.*

"She liked her secrets." she said, as nonchalantly as she could manage.

Eder frowned, and turned back to the screen. The printer had begun to grind and whirr, a series of short, staccato cracking noises echoing out from the bowels of the hulking structure.

"Well, I like to use their systems to do it, you see. Built in a few little loopholes for myself to use, back when I was junior back office transport administrator. Awful title. Such a mouthful, I always thought. But then again, we Ashkans like our long, complicated titles, don't we?"

Jana grinned. "You can say that again. It took them seven words and an acronym to call me 'pilot' usually."

Eder nodded, his aging features bathed in the greyish light that emanated from the screen before him. Numbers scrolled past him. Numbers, and names. Authority Codes. Segment Codes. Residence Lists. For a moment he seemed to get lost in the endless data, his eyes flickering from point to point, his posture hunched, every fibre of his being seeming to be working towards the same goal.

Then he looked up, and smiled as a familiar picture of Wulfe's grizzled features materialised on the screen in front of him.

"Anyway, I find someone in the database who won't travel much. Some Bolvar herdsman, or maybe a Varian ganger or two. Or just some low authority Ashkan, if need be. One who won't travel much. Then I stick your picture over theirs, replace a little of the personal information to make sure it matches, and done! Well, apart from a few cases, of course, but... Did I say something wrong?"

Something was wrong. Jana froze, her mind filling with the voice of Councillor Song as the words dredged themselves back up from her memory.

...its reach is vast. There is no system in the Union that it cannot touch...

"You upload them somewhere?"

"Well I do but... Oh, don't you worry about that. It's all perfectly safe. I've been doing this for twenty-two years and they haven't caught a breath of me yet."

"Is the database official? Is it..." Jana struggled to find the words. "Is it Union?"

"As official as it gets, my dear. It's a part of what we used to call 'the core systems", meaning..."

...its power is unlike anything I have ever seen...

"Can you stop it? Right now?"

"What? Why? I've had them processing since nearly the moment you walked in here. They'll be long done by now."

...and, right now, it wishes every last one of you dead.

Jana hit the door at a run, tearing off up the stairs, the icy fist of terror seizing her heart once more.

"Kristof!"

Chapter 28

"How are you faring?"

"I've been better."

"Is there something I can help you with?"

"I didn't think you cared."

"Come, Bastian, a commissary should feel at least a little responsible for the captain she reports to, don't you think?"

Kristof heard the cry, heard the footsteps approaching

"Eder has been uploading the pictures." she hissed breathlessly, her shaking hands fumbling with the grate. "They're the same ones we used after the Vault! The thing Song mentioned, it's going to notice!"

"Uploading where, Jana?!" Wulfe said, casting a concerned glance at Kristof.

The Ashkan Central Database

"The Union has a database. They've got names, photos..."

And then they heard it. A faint, but unmistakeable sound amidst the dull pattering of rain on the metal staircase.

The discordant squawk of tac-speech, echoing up from the streets below them.

Legionaries

Jana spun about, leaning out over the rusted iron rail that ran the length of the stairway as she stared down into the streets below. She jerked backwards, lurching back away from the edge as she turned back to face him.

"They're here already, below us!" she whispered, her voice trembling with faint notes of panic. She grabbed the gate again, shaking it once before the dull rattling noise forced her to stop. "Bastard thing is self-locking. Where's..."

"Where's Eder?" Wulfe said, suddenly.

Jana looked up.

"He's..." She stopped, and a look of horror passed across her features, and she spun about to stare back down the side of the winding stairway below her. "I can see him, I think. If I can..." She turned back, desperately fiddling with the lock on the grating. "...if I can just get this..."

Wulfe reached out, grabbing Jana by her sleeve and pulling her in close to the bars, speaking in a desperate growl.

"Go help him, Jana. Get him somewhere safe. You can't do anything here."

"I can't just…"

"Yes, you can. Run, run as far away from here as you can. Find somewhere safe, and we'll find you."

"You'll die. Both of you. I won't…" she stammered, her eyes flickering between the two of them.

"We'll find a way, trust me."

He released her, pushing her back towards the stairwell.

"Trust us, Jana."

And with a final, hesitant look back over her shoulder, she did. Wulfe paused for a moment, listening to the metallic clanging of her footsteps on the stairs as she descended them two at a time.

Kristof had fallen silent. His mind raced. The voice was usually a whisper, but it was shouting now.

Ashkan mass produce apartment complex.

He met Wulfe's gaze as the man turned away from the doorway.

One entrance, for security purposes. Self-locking with a passcode. One narrow window over a sheer drop.

"Any ideas?" Wulfe muttered, striding across the room and casting a worried look out of the window. He ducked back in quickly. "Shit, Jana was right. Looks like just the local units have responded so far, but there'll be more on the way."

Kristof's fists clenched and unclenched impulsively as he wracked his brains for a solution. He stared about the cramped apartment feverishly. There had to be a way out. There always was.

Optimised for space, cost effectiveness, external insulation, and... and the terror in Cass' eyes as shock set in.

He shook his head, trying to quell his anger. It was immature and illogical. Cool heads needed to prevail.

Cost effectiveness. Blood welling in Cass' throat as she gasped for breath. External insulation.

"The kitchen." he hissed from between gritted teeth, his eyes screwed shut. "The walls will be thin."

"I'll go check." he heard Wulfe's heavy footfalls as the man hurried past him into the kitchen.

The Legionaries were drawing closer now. He could hear them outside, the strange squawking of their scrambled transmissions sounding almost like the clamour of birdsong as they climbed the stairs towards him.

It had found them again. Three times now it had tried to kill them. First at the Vault, then outside Cothiq, now here.

"I told you I'd keep it open for you" Nadir whispered, his eyes bright with pain.

Deep inside Kristof, something snapped. He stepped towards the computer, hammering on the keys as he rushed to open up a comms channel. Within seconds, the system sprung to life.

"You can hear me. I know you can." he hissed, his voice surprisingly calm despite the rage seething in his veins.

He took a deep breath. The channel sputtered and crackled. Silence.

"What the fuck are you doing?!" Wulfe said, appearing in the doorway.

"Interior wall, Wulfe. I know what I'm doing." Kristof heard his own voice say, levelly.

For a moment the soldier seemed torn, wracked with indecision. Then with a muttered curse he took off down the corridor.

Kristof leant forwards, placing a hand on the table as he stared intently at the screen in front of him.

"If they catch us, everything is out. You won't have a secret left in the world anymore."

Silence.

"I don't know who you are. I don't know *what* you are. But I know who *she* is. The one out there. And if she finds me, I will hand you to her on a silver platter. There won't be anywhere for you to hide."

The channel clicked once. Then silence.

"You think they won't believe us." Kristof said, thoughtfully.

The distorted hiss seemed to intensify for a moment. Voices echoed up from outside, distant, but approaching with every passing second.

"Maybe you're right."

Silence.

With a snarl of barely contained rage, Kristof brought a fist down on the desk in front of him.

"Damnit, talk to me! I know you can!"

There was a crash from the room beside him, and Wulfe's voice echoed through the apartment.

"It's done, Kristof! Get moving."

Kristof could hear footsteps on the stairwell now, the rapid pounding of boots against grated metal as the legionaries ascended the stairs. He placed both hands over the table, eyes fixed on the screen in front of him. He wasn't leaving now. Not without a last word.

"Fine." he hissed. "No more pleas. No more games. No more begging. I am coming for you, I will find you, and you are going to pay for every single last drop of blood you have spilt."

He paused for a moment, breathing heavily. Engines roared outside, the sound of distorted voices and footsteps echoing through the building. The sound of gunfire echoed up from the lower floors, from where he had sent Jana. Kristof raised the microphone one more time, snarling through clenched teeth.

"Every single one."

The lights flickered.

The screen in front of him sparked briefly, springing to life. Sigils flashed, bathing Kristof in an almost pleasant blue glow as he stepped back in surprise.

The single word that now stood at the bottom of the screen was far from pleasant, however. Despite his rage, Kristof felt a shudder run down his spine.

Likewise

Jana tore down the staircase, taking them three at a time as she clung to the guard-rail for balance. The metal was slick with the rain that had started to fall, and she could barely make out the steps in front of her except by the faint star-lit reflection they cast.

She didn't see Eder until she almost cannoned into him. The old man climbed the stairs as fast as he was able, his breath already unsteady from the exertion. Jana stopped herself at the last second, grabbing the man by his shoulders as she focused her panicked gaze on him.

"Where do we go?! Eder, you know this place. Please, where can we go?!"

"What's happening? Is it the Watch?"

"It's A… It's an inquisitor. They've sent an Inquisitor after us."

Eder blanched, one of his hands beginning to visibly shake before he plunged it into a pocket. His voice trembled as he spoke.

"Is this about the Identity Certificates? I... I can explain it to them? Maybe they'll..."

Jana grabbed the man by his shoulders, watching as his expression calmed slightly. Her fingers dug in deep, and she realised how frail the man was. His whole body shook, with exhilaration or fear she couldn't tell.

"They won't listen, I promise. Eder, please. There must be somewhere to hide. Think!"

She watched his eyes narrow in thought.

"Down. If we can find our way out of the building, the Port is only a few streets away. Yes." he murmured, before stopping, his eyes going wide. "Sandra! Is she…"

In the corner of her vision, Jana caught a single errant flash of light from the far intersection of the corridor.

"*Hide!*" she hissed, pushing him back into the doorway as she darted back across the corridor, nestling herself in a recessed wiring vent on the far side.

The corridor flooded with bright white light for a moment. Footsteps sounded, seemingly far off, but approaching rapidly. Figures rushed past, one, two… six, in total. Jana could see the deep green hue of the Ashkan Legions in their coats as they filed past, torches sweeping for targets, the corridor echoing with swift squawks of tac-speech. She heard the clank of boots on metal as they found the stairs and began to climb.

Eder stepped cautiously out from his hiding place and began to scuttle down the corridor, beckoning to Jana as he went.

"We can get out the same door they came in." he muttered as Jana caught up with him.

The building was alive now. The sound of skimmer engines blasted in from outside, the sound of footsteps, tac-speech and cries of terror echoed throughout the building as the residents began to take notice of the uproar occurring in their midst.

A dozen floors above, Kristof and Wulfe hurried through the corridors as fast as they were able, dodging amongst the confused occupants of Sivren Block as they emerged from their apartments to investigate the commotion outside.

"Get back inside!" Wulfe called loudly as he pushed his way gently but firmly through the crowds. "It isn't safe out here!"

Kristof darted through the hallways as fast as he dared, his mind afire with a thousand unhelpful queues.

"Now what?" Wulfe muttered as they cleared the worst of the block's occupants, and found themselves ducking into a maintenance corridor.

"Stairwell." Kristof said curtly. "They know we were with Eder, they'll assume we're in his apartment, which has no access to these corridors..."

Right.

He flung himself sideways, hitting the stairwell door with his shoulder. "We need to get as close to ground level as we can before they realise their mistake." he murmured as the two of them descended into the darkness.

As they rushed down the stairs, taking them a flight at a time in some cases, Kristof's mind still raced. The dry whispering voice was almost screaming at him now, its judgements and advice seeming to overlay and overlap more and more as he descended.

Go back. Help her.

He couldn't. As much as he wanted to he couldn't. She was smart. She'd make it.

Criminal response protocol dictates all entrances should be covered within four minutes of the alert being raised.

One minute left.

Kristof rounded another corner, almost slipping on a discarded bottle that lay sideways on one of the steps. He cursed under his breath.

It can talk.

It has a sense of self.

It can threaten.

These legionaries were slower. More methodical. Jana could hear them approaching at a walk, their torches flickering across the hallway as they searched every nook and cranny.

They hadn't made it far. They had managed to descend a couple of floors through strange little maintenance corridors and fire escapes, but now they were getting bogged down. The patrols were more cautious now, and more frequent. The Legionaries knew they had escaped. They were on alert now.

Jana backed up, nestling herself deeper into the tangle of rogue wiring that flowed like webbing from wall to wall of the narrow maintenance alcove. She was hidden, but not well. If the lighting in this place had been any better they would have been spotted a dozen times over by now.

The first Legionary stepped past, then the second. Jana stood motionless, not daring to breathe as the light played across her hiding place for a fraction of a second.

Then it was done. It was over. The legionaries advanced further up the corridor, plunging Jana and Eder into blackness once more. Silently, Jana breathed a sigh of relief.

"Junior Administrator Eder Descar."

They both froze as a voice washed across them. Jana felt a shiver of terror creep down her spine as the familiar voice echoed down the corridors of Sivren Block, punctuated by the squawk and hiss of broadcast feedback.

"My name is Atesca Seratov, Commissary First Class in Service of the Ashkan Union."

The footsteps from down the corridor had paused. A discussion seemed to be taking place, judging by the eerie shrieking of the voice-masking devices the Legionaries used. Jana shrunk deeper into the alcove as the torchlight flashed mere inches from where she stood. She glanced at Eder, who had dug himself into the mirror alcove in the far wall of the corridor. She was still looking at him when the next words made her heart stop.

"We have your daughter, Mr.Descar. Give yourself up, and she will not be harmed."

In seconds, she watched Eder crumble. The terror that gripped him had been good, the kind that kept you quick, kept you alive. This new kind brought only death.

How did she know?!

Jana froze.

4 idents left. 3 returned. It knew. She knew.

Eder had gone silent. Jana could see his eyes in the darkness, wide with terror as they glinted in the flickering light of the hallway.

No! she mouthed, desperately.

"Think of your daughter, Mr.Descar."

Jana snarled in frustration, gesturing furiously at the man across the hallway from her. *Stop.* she mouthed, trying to force his terrified gaze to rest on her. *She's lying.*

She wasn't getting through to him, she could see that.

Look at me, damnit.

Jana froze as she heard footsteps approaching down the corridor. Two pairs. Two pairs of heavy, booted feet. Torchlight danced across the corridor around them, plunging the two of them deeper into the shadows.

Nestled in her corner, barely hidden amidst the crumbling plaster and exposed wiring she stared at Eder in a desperate attempt to convey meaning without words.

Finally, he met her gaze.

And shook his head, silently.

Even as she opened her mouth to protest, to say anything that would stop him, some small part of her had been ready. It knew she wouldn't be able to change his mind. As Eder rose to his feet, raising his hands above his head as he stepped out into the corridor she moved, darting across the passageway towards the stairwell beyond.

She felt a light fall across her.

There was a squawk of tac-speech from the Legionaries, its unnatural, high-pitched tones echoing around the corridors around them. Eder cried out, the dull crunch of a Lexan-reinforced gauntlet impacting flesh falling on Jana's ears as she hit the far door, driving it open with her shoulder as she sprawled into the stairway beyond. Ignoring the bright flash of agony as she caught herself on her injured hand, she rolled over and aimed a savage kick at the base of the door, slamming it shut even as the Legionary rounded the corner beyond.

Jana abandoned any pretence at stealth, scrambling up the stairs two at a time and lunging through the first open door to her left. Even as she dived, the stairwell behind her filled with a blinding flash of light as a burst of automatic fire stitched along the wall where she had stood only seconds before. She threw herself backwards, slamming herself against the door and plunging the room into a grey, inky blackness for a moment before the lights sprung to life automatically.

The room was empty. A small pile of discarded packing material lay in the corner, beside the window. A table. A single chair. Nowhere to hide.

She stared frantically about the room once more, eyes searching for any path of escape. She could hear footsteps behind the door, thudding across the rough stonework. Mingling amongst them she could hear the faint, shrill sound of Eder's voice, although she couldn't determine the words.

She couldn't let them…

She screwed her eyes shut, forcing the thought from her mind. He'd made his choice. There wasn't anything she could do. Not now.

Without a second thought she ran towards the window, placed a foot on the sill and swung outwards into the night. The night was dark, the air filled with a drifting rain that covered the smooth concrete of the building's front in a slick layer water. Jana hesitated, testing the balustrade with her foot even as her eyes searched the wall above her for any kind of handhold.

She paused, drawing in a deep breath. This had been a mistake. She could feel her heart pounding in her chest once more as she desperately tried to stop her gaze wandering downwards towards the darkness below.

She failed. The rain fell away into the streets below her, striking a set of lower rooftops further down before finally sliding off them into the narrow alley below. *We're on floor 15. If you fall, you are dead.* She drew back, flattening her back against the wall behind her and screwing her eyes shut. *You're a pilot, you've been higher than this.* It wasn't as comforting a thought as she had hoped.

She began to edge along the platform, shuffling her feet slowly, carefully along the ledge, one hand cradled close to her chest, the other reaching, still desperately questing for any kind of handhold on the wall's surface. *Find another window and you can get back inside.* She looked ahead, narrowing her eyes against the rain, shaking her head in an attempt to dislodge the strands of damp hair that now clung to her face. She drew in another deep breath, forcing herself to be calm. The rain and the cold were doing their work, and she shrugged her jacket tighter around her shoulders with her injured hand, her numb fingers questing across the smooth concrete wall for a handhold.

Suddenly, a voice broke the silence. The tac-speech rang out, barely audible above the sound of the rain dashing itself across the stonework.

Jana turned, fast as she dared, and stared back the way she had come.

A figure watched her from the window that she had emerged from. A legionary, silhouetted against the light beyond. Watching.

Jana accelerated her movement, her heart sinking in her chest. She felt it, deep in her stomach, an almost indescribable feeling of sheer dread. For a moment she paused, staring back at the figure in the window who watched her impassively, unmoving, silhouetted against the light from the room.

No way back now.

The rain plunged into the dark abyss below her, forming into small rivulets that wound their way down the side of the building. It was slick, but as long as she had something to hold on to… Maybe she could climb down. Or along, maybe. There could be another window, somewhere to get back inside.

She was going to die out here. She knew it, deep in her heart.

No way back.

Jana gritted her teeth, forcing her body into action once more, shuffling towards the corner of the building, half-blinded by the rain.

She lunged forwards, a hand wrapping around the metal strut that protruded from the building's corner. She rested her weight on it, choking down a sob of relief. Even with her new handhold though, she was no safer. She had to continuously re-adjust her footing on the smooth stonework to prevent her feet from slipping out from beneath her. She shuffled back against the wall, pressing her back to it as she stared into the void below her.

And Atesca stared back.

Engines flared with a deafening howl as the skimmer rose up out of the night, its searchlights blinding Jana as she clutched desperately to the face of the building. Jana stared back, with all the defiance she could muster, instinctively clutching tighter to the metal struts as her foot slipped on the smooth, damp stonework.

The inquisitor stood silently, watching Jana, as a cat would watch a mouse in its claws. The flank doors of the skimmer had been flung open, the dull red glow of the interior lighting illuminating the inquisitor as she stood there, one hand grasping the support rail, the other dug deep into the folds of the greatcoat. The wind whipped at her figure, causing the waterlogged material to flap soddenly. There was no urgency in that stance. No fear, no sense of danger. Just a mild curiosity that needed to be sated.

"Why are you fighting us, Miss Schleifer?" The inquisitor called over the deafening roar of the engines. "We are simply doing what is right. What we are ordered to do." The inquisitor cocked her head to one side slightly, an expression of almost mild confusion crossing her features. "I know you are not one of them. Not truly. Help us stop them. Help *me* stop them."

She leant forwards slightly, hanging out of the craft by one hand, extending the other towards Jana.

"We do not want to hurt you, Miss Schleifer."

Jana felt it again, the feeling creeping in. Despite what she knew, despite everything, Atesca's words rang true. The Inquisitor could help her. The Inquisitor was right…

Jana gave a brief shriek as her foot slipped again, her hand closing around an outcropping of stone in the building's surface at the last possible moment. The rain ran down her face, mixing with the blazing glare from the skimmer's spotlights, almost blinding her. She raised her broken hand, pawing at her face with the sodden bandage, willing her eyes to focus on the inquisitor.

"You don't understand!" she called out, her voice shaking. "There's…"

"I am not here to understand." Atesca responded. "I am here to do my duty. There is no reason to fight me, Miss Schleifer. You owe these people nothing, and they owe you nothing. You are throwing your life away."

The Inquisitor was right. She knew it in her heart of hearts. There was no reason to fight anymore, not for Kristof, not for Wulfe, not for anyone. She was throwing her life away.

"I am here to help you, Miss Schleifer."

Jana felt her foot slip from under her. Her hand scrabbled for purchase on the slick stonework, but found none. She looked up at Atesca, a final, despairing scream tearing from her throat as she felt the world fall out from beneath her feet.

And the darkness of the streets rushed up to consume her.

Chapter 29

"So, Captain, any plans once this is over?" the sergeant asked, stirring the contents of his tin mug with a battered old aluminium spoon.

"Right now I'm more concerned with making it through the week, Richter. Don't have a lot of time to dream about the future."

"Best time for it in my opinion, Captain." Kristof sighed, sitting back against the rubble and taking a sip from his mug. "I was thinking I might try my luck on one of the envoy planets. Celthar, maybe. Or Valmeer. Somewhere with a lot of nature and not a lot of people." He looked around, and shuddered.

"Feel like I've had enough of people to last me a lifetime."

"Junior Administrator Eder Descar. My name is Atesca Seratov, Commissary First Class in Service of the Ashkan Union. We have your daughter, Mr.Descar. Give yourself up, and she will not be harmed."

For a moment, all Kristof saw was red. He gritted his teeth, his hands clenching into fists as he fought the urge to do something impulsively stupid.

"That smart little..." he paused, lost for words as he shook his head. They were at the base of the block now. They had moved as fast as they were able, skirting the blockades even as they were being put up. Now they were only inches away from escape.

"Son of a bitch!" Kristof snarled again. "He'll fall for it, too."

Jana won't.

He looked at Wulfe. The soldier had paused at the sound of the voice, a strangely reverent look in his eyes as he gazed upwards at the ceiling; towards the source of the voice.

She still has him.

"Wulfe!" Kristof hissed. "Pay attention! This isn't the time."

The man shook his head as he emerged from his reverie, his eyes turning to Kristof once more.

"Sorry. I just..." he shook his head again. "Forget it. Come on."

They hurried through the maze of corridors towards the building's outskirts, moving as silently and as quickly as they could. The patrols were thin here; the base of the building barely seemed occupied.

They're stretched thin.

They could hear it now, the faint patter of rain. Kristof could feel the stale air of the block shift against his skin for a moment. They pushed on, towards the source of the sound, an almost animalistic instinct pressing them faster and faster as they rushed towards freedom.

...and into the forms of a pair of unsuspecting Ashkan Legionaries.

Kristof lashed out with a fist instinctively. The legionary reeled back from the kinetic force of the impact, his eyes temporarily glazing over as his world filled with stars.

Unarmoured at the neck, side, and groin.

He barely felt his knee come up, and the legionary doubled over, the wind crushed from his lungs.

Panic response: A wild, uncontrolled blow at the opponent's face with an improvised weapon.

Kristof ducked, feeling the gun whistle over his head as the Legionary swung it like a club in a wide arc. He reached up, grabbing the hand almost without thinking.

Twist and break.

With a practiced twist he wrenched the man around, bringing the soldier stumbling off-balance as he crushed the man's weapon-hand against the concrete wall of the passageway, his scream of agony emerging as a strangled squawk as his visor transmitter scrambled the sound.

Cass, choking on her own blood.

With a sharp jerk Kristof wrenched the weapon from the man's grasp. The world had gone... fuzzy. He could hear shouts. Shouting. He lashed out with a kick, numbly watching as the Legionary stumbled backwards, clutching at his broken hand in agony as he collapsed to his knees.

You can put all this behind you.

Kristof raised the rifle.

He felt a hand grab his collar and he was hauled bodily backwards, wincing slightly as his injured knee buckled beneath a heavy footfall. He fell in behind Wulfe as they stumbled out into the rain-soaked streets of Ashka. He felt the rifle clatter from his hands as they ran, his world still a blur, its colours muted as they emerged back onto one of the main thoroughfares of the city. They stopped amidst

the crowds, and Kristof felt himself breathe a sigh of relief almost immediately.
They were safe, for now.

"They won't be far behind us." he muttered, turning to Wulfe. The soldier stood
silently amidst the crowds, staring back at Sivren block as it towered above them.
Skimmers circled around the tower like huge birds, their silhouettes looming and
ominous in the night sky above them.

"She's smart." Kristof murmured. "She had a head start on them. She'll make it."
he added, half to convince himself.

"We could go back." Wulfe said quietly, eyes still fixed on the tower above.
"Maybe she'll listen."

Kristof frowned, realising that he had misread the man's intent. "She... she won't.
We need to go. Now, Wulfe."

With a visible effort, the man tore his gaze away from the tower and turned to
Kristof, eyes filled with despair.

"Where to?" he asked.

"I have an idea."

Jana's scream was cut short as she hit the outcropping rooftop with a sickening
crack. She felt a flash of white-hot pain in her side as she half slid, half bounced
off the edge before landing with a damp thud on the streets below. She lay there
for a time, her body wracked with pain, feeling the rain on her face, the water from
the street's surface soaking slowly into her clothes. She could taste blood in her
mouth. Her right arm lay flung out by her side, fingers still numb with the cold.
She could barely feel her left, only a faint throbbing pain managing to force its
way into her mind.

She blinked as her vision began to clear. Colours melded together, images
stitching themselves slowly back together. The rush of blood in her ears slowly
withdrew, giving way to the deep, throaty roar of engines.

She rolled over onto her side, pulling her hand out from underneath her and
planting in on the ground, gritting her teeth against the pain as she pulled herself
shakily to her feet. She staggered sideways, slamming against the wall beside her.
She pulled herself forwards, resting on its surface for support, breaking into a
tottering run along the street.

Voices called out around her as she ran, still half stunned, her vision blurred, her
whole body in agony. She barely knew where she was headed now, running half-
blinded through the dark streets, navigating purely by instinct. She stumbled as she

heard the skimmer roar overhead once more, its spotlight drawing a brief arc of light across the alley ahead of her before it passed on, the roar of its engines receding into a distant hum as it swung around for another pass.

She heard the sound of footsteps from ahead of her, and she turned left into another road, her feet splashing across the asphalt as she dashed for the cover of the opposite alley.

There was nowhere to run. She could hear them in the buildings around her, the squawk and shriek of their words like the cries of circling vultures in her ears. Skimmers roared overhead, kept at a distance only by the narrow confines of the alley that Jana was stumbling down. They would find her eventually.

Her head swam. She felt sick. She tottered sideways a little, stumbling against an overfilled waste-bin that stood against the left side of the alley. She leant against it for a moment, begging her vision to come back into focus.

There had to be somewhere to run. There had to be. Somewhere they couldn't follow.

"a chaotic mess of tunnels that go nowhere and everywhere all at once" Cass said

Somewhere they...

"where no-one legally owns anything, and any attempt to regulate the place sends the whole thing up in flames"

...couldn't follow.

She straightened up. She knew where to go.

How long she ran for she didn't know. Every muscle in her body screamed at her to stop. Her hand was in agony. The left side of her torso and body were battered almost to the point of breakage. She fought the urge to vomit with every step, the rain from the cloud-filled sky soaking her to the skin.

Suddenly, there it was before her. The port, an almost blinding array of lights and sounds, its roads and pathways filled with traffic. Skimmers roared overhead, swinging around to land amidst the thronging crowds of people that threaded their way amongst the market stalls that were opened even at this late hour.

She ducked out into the street, lowering her gaze as she hurried through the crowds that surrounded the port. She could feel people's stares as the bedraggled figure pushed past them, limping visibly, one hand clutched to its chest. She forced herself to straighten up, to walk normally despite the waves of agony that tore at her.

Heavy footfalls rang out behind her as two armed legionaries hurried past, their eyes and lights scanning across the crowd as they ran. Jana raised her pace a little, stepping behind one of the port workers as the two soldiers hurried past.

Now walking was becoming easier. There was a crowd to follow. All she had to do was keep pace. Glancing up, she saw the mouth of the warrens looming over her, the three vast tunnel-like structures through which the crowd was funnelling.

She glanced back as she stepped into the darkness, peering as best she could over the heads of the crowd for any sign of Kristof and Wulfe. She knew it was hopeless deep down, but she felt she owed them that much.

Chapter 30

25ᵗʰ Sihyl, 2094.23 Core Time – Electronic Messaging Certificate – Confidential

Commissary Atesca Seratov, Commissary 1ˢᵗ Class

You are to assume direct control over the operations in Carth. Cpt.Bastian Wulfe is to maintain his rank, and is by all accounts to appear as heading the conflict as far as public and press are concerned. The Commission has deemed this conflict as sufficiently vital to Union integrity to take a direct hand in matters.

The tunnels of the deep warrens were a maze. Built over centuries, without oversight or guidance, they were little more than a web of interconnecting passages and rooms, twisting over, into and around each other, extending for miles beneath the planet's surface. Most Union officials had long since given up any attempt at imposing order on the chaos, most sectors simply ignoring the titanic task that any such imposition would be. For a system already floundering under the heavy bureaucracy, the civilisation of the warrens was something the Union could barely afford and had little appetite for.

The air was thick and acrid, clouding some lower tunnels in a perpetual grey haze as smoke and fumes battled with whatever basic ventilation system the inhabitants of that section had been able to install.

A lone figure walked these passageways, a coarse woollen blanket wrapped about its shoulders and head, despite the muggy heat of the tunnels. The figure moved carefully, shrugging the blanket tighter about itself as it ducked through an archway, bowing its head to avoid the hanging wires that trailed across the ceilings of the tunnels.

A hand, wrapped in a stained, battered grey bandage reached out, fumbling almost clumsily at the door's handle. The figure muttered a few choice curse words, reaching forwards with its other hand and pressing the door open with its shoulder. The ancient metal structure swung inwards, the rusted hinges screaming in protest as they were once again forced into motion.

Jana lowered her makeshift hood slowly, her gaze sweeping the room as she did so. It had been four days since her flight from Atesca, and they had hit her hard. Blood still stained the sleeve and hem of her flight jacket, and though the deep cuts and abrasions had for the most begun to scab over, the left side of her body was a riot of purple-hued bruising and torn skin. Her eyes were tired and sleepless, the result of a series of uncomfortable nights, waking at every sound, fearing that the legionaries had finally tracked her down. Not that there were many, this deep down. It seemed like the folk living this far from civilisation liked to be left to their own devices, judging by the hostile glares the soldiers received whenever they passed through.

The gates of the warrens had been closed. They had claimed it was a safety measure, but Jana knew the truth. The voice that had crackled around the upper levels of the vault had been eerily familiar. It was terrifying to be trapped down here, but in a way Jana found it comforting. She didn't believe for a second that Atesca would lock down a million people just for her. The others had to be down here too. They just had to be.

If they weren't she was in real trouble.

The Pesh den was almost exactly the way she remembered it. The scented mist still hung heavy in the air, sickly and cloying, though less sweet than Jana recalled. The gaudy cloth hangings barely obscured the rough, brutal concrete structures beneath, and the furniture was battered and stained in a thousand different ways.

Unlike the previous time, the couches were unoccupied. The den, which had previously been filled with the gentle breathing of a dozen unconscious figures, was now deathly silent.

Jana turned slightly, swinging the heavy metal door slowly shut behind her. She patted her pockets nervously as she waited, their emptiness still seeming strange to her. Most of her possessions were gone now, everything but her slate and Kristof's gun traded away for enough food and drink to last a few days.

She rolled her shoulders slowly, feeling the weight of the gun in the inside pocket of her jacket. It had three bullets in it. She didn't know why she'd kept it, really, it just felt like the kind of thing a fugitive should have. It wasn't like she knew how to use it, and it certainly wouldn't help her if the Legions caught up with her.

You could sell it, at the very least. For someone without a single coin to their name, trapped dozens of miles underground, that was definitely something.

As the door clanged shut, Jana heard movement in the room behind her. The faint shuffle of a footstep on concrete. She spun about, and stared into the eyes of the same grey-skinned Varian that Nadir had come to meet almost a month ago.

The man stood hunched, his posture coiled and defensive. His skin seemed, if anything, more mottled than when Jana had last seen him, the unhealthy pallor having only deepened in the intervening weeks.

"*Pescha?*" he said in Varian, though Jana felt she could interpret the simple one-word question given her circumstances.

"You're Vishkar, right?" she replied, keeping her voice low, forcing herself to meet the man's gaze. Kristof had been right, there was a knack to acting tough. She wasn't sure if she had it yet, but she could feel that there was one.

The Varian paused for a moment, his eyes locked with Jana's.

"Who told you my name?" he said quietly, his whole stance screaming wariness.

"I got a recommendation."

Vishkar's eyes narrowed slightly.

"Back here. Away from the door." he whispered.

He stepped back through the doorway, sweeping aside the thin curtains that covered it. Jana followed carefully, alert for any sign of danger. Everything about this place unsettled her, from the comatose figures that littered the room, to the strangely sweet-smelling air that dulled the senses and robbed her focus. It put her teeth on edge.

She stuck her head through the curtains, ready to withdraw at a moment's notice, quickly scanning the room. Vishkar stood alone in its centre, arms folded, a featureless grey table between him and Jana. The walls of this room were bare concrete. In fact, most of the room was bare, in stark contrast to the lavishly decorated room she had just left.

The man caught her gaze, and a small smile flickered briefly across his features.

"Don't worry, this is where all my guests come to discuss payment."

The smile vanished.

"Now, what is it?"

"Business doesn't seem to be going well." Jana said. Hopefully it would help to put him on the back foot.

"Maybe." The Varian swayed a little from side to side as he spoke. "What do you want?" he restated quietly.

"I'm looking for someone. Two people, actually." Jana reached out, placing two dog-eared pieces of paper down on the table. Wulfe and Kristof stared accusingly up at her from the idents.

Vishkar picked up the booklets with one hand, glancing briefly at them before his gaze flicked back towards Jana.

"Just… found?"

"What? God, yes!" Jana nodded hurriedly. "Describe me to them. They'll know who I am."

The man nodded slowly, eyes fixed thoughtfully on Jana as he did so.

"These things can be expensive…" he began.

Jana reached into her pocket, tossing her slate onto the table with a clatter. "Find them and its yours."

A hand darted out, snapping the device up. Vishkar held it up to the light, turning it over and over in his hands. He waved a hand across its surface, blinking as the bright light washed across his face.

"You haven't been taking good care of this thing, have you?" he mused, seemingly to himself, eyes scanning the device's surface intently. He reached out, placing it gently back on the table in front of Jana.

"I'll see what I can do." he said, slowly. One eye twitched slightly as he regarded Jana closely. "And how should I contact you if I get them?"

"You shouldn't. I'll be back tomorrow. Or the day after. Every day for as long as it takes."

The man's lips moved slowly for a moment, before a small smile crawled across his features. "Yes. That will do." He glanced down at the pictures again before cramming them into a pocket.

"Now unless you want to partake I'll have to ask you to leave, I have sleepers to wake up."

Jana nodded, retrieving her slate from the table and stepping back through the curtains. She kept her breathing shallow as she walked back through the far room, listening to Vishkar's footsteps as the man padded along behind her. The place still sent shivers down her spine.

She paused in the doorway, glancing back over her shoulder. Vishkar had stopped, and was bending over the comatose figure of a young woman who lay half in, half out of a small, cushioned alcove in the wall.

"Where Cass took you. Midday. No names." he said, without looking up, eyes still fixed on the woman's face. "I have not forgotten." A slender hand reached out, gently brushing aside a stray strand of hair from the woman's face. The figure shivered, giving out a faint sigh as she shifted slightly in her sleep.

Jana shuddered, stepping out through the archway and swinging the heavy iron door shut behind her.

She headed back through the tunnels of the deep warrens, mind wandering as a hundred thoughts fought for her attention. She had to believe they were still alive. Both of them. Without them she was probably dead anyway, she couldn't keep selling her possessions off for favours forever, and she didn't have the knowledge to survive in this new, hostile environment she found herself in. Even hearing about Vishkar had been more luck than judgement, a scrap of whispered conversation that she caught whilst dozing uncomfortably against a support pillar.

She flattened herself against a wall as a pair of figures stalked past, their faces partially obscured in the gloom. The warrens were a hostile place, as she had found out, and it was probably best to avoid confrontation if at all possible.

Stepping out into a familiar cavern, she paused for a moment, glancing around to get her bearings. It was getting late. *Probably. Probably getting late.* She still hadn't got the hang of the time down here. People seemed to manage it somehow, she thought, looking around. But she was tired, and that was probably all that mattered.

She still missed being able to see the sky.

Three days she had been here now, alone in the warrens. It had also been three days since the vast steel doors that made up the entrance to the warrens had been slammed shut, sealing the network off from the outside world. Quarantine, they had claimed. Disease control. But Jana knew better.

There was a strange kind of camaraderie in this place, despite the squalor and poverty. The lights around the cavern had been lit, flooding the chamber in a soft yellow glow. Jana nodded in acknowledgement to a few people as she passed; a few faces were beginning to become familiar.

She settled herself against one of the walls, shifting as she sought a more comfortable position on the bare stonework. Her bruised ribs sent occasional flashes of pain through her mind as she moved, but all in all she thought she was doing quite well. She could certainly be worse. Even her broken hand hurt less now that she had had time to properly support and splint it. It wasn't going to heal well, but if she was lucky it would at least heal.

"How were the Varians, little dove?" called a jovial voice. Jana looked up at the man who had spoken; a thickset Bolvar dressed in a motley collection of Ashkan-styled clothing. He had turned around from the group with which he sat, leaning back on one elbow to grin expectantly at her.

She smiled back at him. "He said he'd help!" she called back haltingly in her best Bolvar.

The man laughed uproariously, drawing curious glances from his fellows; A gaunt-faced Celthari and an Ashkan dressed in a battered robe.

"Good for you!" he replied. "Don't lower your guard around that snake!"

Jana grinned as the man turned back to his friends. The people down here were a strange breed, but they were helpful.

She rolled over onto her uninjured side, and nestled herself in the room's corner, letting the clamour of voices wash over her. Ashkan. Varian. Bolvar. Even a little Quin. She thought about Nadir then. She wondered what he was up to. It had been nearly a month now, even the most grievous of injuries didn't render you bedridden for that long.

If he was still alive, of course.

If any of them were still alive.

For now, all she could do was wait. Bathed in the dim glow of the lamplight and surrounded by the clamour of a dozen low voices, Jana rolled herself in her flight jacket and closed her eyes.

Chapter 31

27th Sihyl, 2094.69 Core Time – Electronic Messaging Certificate – Confidential

Commissary Atesca Seratov, Commissary 1st Class

Due to the high emphasis placed on Captain Wulfe in the most recent releases, his stability and survival are now of utmost importance. You are to keep him under close observation and report any anomalies in his behaviour immediately.

"Well?" Jana asked archly.

"Well?" Vishkar whispered, aping her tone as he stooped over another prone figure. His thin, reedy fingers reached out and gently peeled back the man's eyelid, and he gazed seemingly in fascination for a moment at the eyeball beneath. The comatose man shuddered a little, and Vishkar straightened up.

"Well, I have good news for you." he said, giving the man a sharp jab with his foot. "Up! Now!" he turned to face Jana as the other man spluttered to life at his feet.

"The two you are looking for, we have found them." he said, leading her back towards the far room where they had conversed the day before.

Jana's heart leapt. They had made it. They were here.

"Where are they?" she asked, the excitement plain in her voice.

Vishkar smiled weakly. "Before I tell you that, I feel we should discuss the matter of payment."

The slate clattered as Jana threw it down on the table.

"It's yours. Where are they?"

The two snakelike eyes remained fixed on hers as the fixer reached out and took the slate off the table.

"They were very difficult to find..." he said, letting the sentence hang there.

So that's how it is. Jana thought, watching the man carefully.

"I'm sure it was." she responded, flatly.

"Perhaps this is no longer enough."

"Then perhaps you give it back and we go our separate ways." Jana said.

 The man shook his head slowly.

"I..." Jana felt the taste of triumph turn to ash in her mouth. "I don't have anything else. Please..."

"Find something." Vishkar hissed.

"I don't have anything..." Jana said, almost pleading.

But she did. Jana's expression turned cold. No fear. No anxiety. She'd seen too much to be pushed around by this... this gutter rat!

She reached up, and slowly drew Kristof's pistol from her jacket pocket, savouring the expression of surprise that flitted across Vishkar's mottled features. Within milliseconds the bravado had returned, but the moment had been there, and Jana would not forget it. She paused, staring at the man levelly.

"Do you know what my people will do if you harm me?" he said, almost pleasantly.

"I don't care."

"There will be a lot of blood."

"And you'll still be dead. Information or the slate, your choice."

There was a long moment of silence. A long, lingering moment. She almost, almost wished he would do something stupid. Almost.

"They'll be there." he spat.

"Thanks." Jana muttered, turning abruptly and stalking towards the doorway. "Pleasure doing business with you."

The upper levels of the warrens were much less lawless, much more refined, like the city above. The caverns were more spacious, the air fresher. The structures here felt more like a spacious hangar or foundation cellar, rather than the kind of claustrophobic rats nest that you found yourself in if you descended. It was no less busy, however, and the tunnels were packed with figures as Jana pushed her way through the crowds.

Jana made her way towards the crowds, pushing her way towards the Tulharden square, the primary branching point of the warrens where the city above met the city below. She hadn't been this close to the surface since she had first escaped into the warrens, and her nerves were beginning to get the better of her again. She stood out up here. Her threadbare clothes were still stained by dirt and blood, although the stains were easy to conceal. The rips, tears and abrasions were less simple, and she simply had to resign herself to a few strange looks as she shuffled through the streets, averting her eyes from the curious gazes. The only consolation was that she was far from the strangest figure walking the streets of the warrens.

Minutes later, after a seemingly endless series of twists and turns, the passageway opened up, and Jana emerged blinking into the bright lights of Tulharden square. Figures swarmed across the floor of the vast cavern, hundreds pouring in-and-out of the three towering archways that made up the mouth of the warrens. The buildings around the square themselves were cut into the rock and dirt, much like the rest of the warrens. These, however, had a polished sheen to them, a certain sleekness to their design that was lacking in the depths below.

Jana walked slowly through the crowds, eyes scanning them for any sign of Kristof or Wulfe. The centre of the cavern was supported by a single vast support pillar, and Jana headed towards it, hoping against hope that the others might think the same way. She was beginning to regret her decision to meet here, she had forgotten quite how busy, how huge the square was.

She turned abruptly sideways as she heard the tramp of boots on stone ahead of her in the crowd, pretending to investigate a nearby shop display as the group of legionaries marched past her. As they disappeared into the crowds, she turned to watch them once more. They moved like sharks amidst a school of fish, the crowds parting to allow them access, but never drawing entirely away. She could see the venom in people's stares. She certainly wasn't alone in fearing the Legions down here, especially with the quarantine in progress. People were getting jumpy.

Jana spun around as a figure cannoned into her, wrapping its arms around her and pulling her into a tight hug.

Kristof's face was haggard and worn. His face was unshaven, his hair hanging down past his face in an unkempt mass. He looked, if anything, worse than Jana did.

"You stupid, beautiful, clever little… you…" he released her, dropping her on her feet, one arm still hung affectionately around her shoulders.

"Wulfe, if I ever underestimate this lady again…" he stopped, grinning breathlessly at her. "I don't even know. Don't ever stop surprising me, Jana."

"As lovely as it is to have her back, we probably don't want to stay here too long." said Wulfe, eyes roving across the crowds suspiciously as he spoke, although the corners of his mouth still bore a small smile.

"Lovely to see you again too, Wulfe." muttered Jana as she stepped up beside him.

"Mhm." he murmured, staring into the distance. "Glad you made it too."

"No need to get so emotional about it." Jana said with a smirk. "What happened to you two? How did you make it out?"

Wulfe looked around. "Later. This place doesn't feel right for a chitchat."

"Go on then, I'm right behind you. You're not losing me that easily again." Jana said, giving him an encouraging pat on the shoulder.

She turned, and saw Kristof. The man stood silently at the base of the statue, staring out towards the vast, imposing doors that sealed the entrance to the warrens. A crowd had gathered at its base, a milling, restless crowd. Some threw rocks and bottles which clanked harmlessly off the door's enamelled surface, others simply shouted, some had set fires, filling the air with the greasy taste of burning debris.

"We should go." he muttered, his voice barely audible above the rising noise from the crowd. "This is going to get nasty."

 "Kristof, they've been there for days. They're just restless…"

"Trust me. They're frightened. Alone. Isolated. People get like that, they'll lash out. Two words from the right source and we'll have a mob on our hands."

They hurried out of the square together, skirting the areas where the crowd was thickest, and headed back the way Jana had come. They walked onwards, the streets growing narrower, the air heavier, and the lights dimmer as they descended into the labyrinthine warrens once more.

Jana couldn't help but chatter excitedly as they moved. She was still riding the high of having found them again. Having them back was nice, but the fact that she had managed to track them down even in such a hostile environment as this was really the icing on the cake.

"There's no way this quarantine is real, right?" she said to Kristof as they walked. "I wasn't there to see the doors come down, but I didn't... I've heard those doors haven't shut in twenty years. There's no way."

"Hell of a coincidence if it was. I think our old friend is playing games again." He shook his head. "It's clear it's got feelers in every damn system out there, I'd imagine it must be a small thing to put up an alert like this. Then the whole system grinds into motion before anyone notices something's wrong. It's almost clever in its own way."

"So what does it do now?"

"It's locked us in. I don't think it knows how to deal with us yet, but it has us cornered." Kristof muttered, scowling to himself. "It's not right. Song said it was smart. She said it was subtle. This is neither. It pulled out of attacking us at the Vault because it noticed Atesca was after us, and yet... this time that didn't stop it. Either its getting desperate, or its found a way to hide its trail better."

He grimaced.

"I don't know what it'll do next. But we're not staying here long enough to find out. There's no way that those doors are the only way out. Not in a place like this. We just need to find it."

"Who's going to let us out?" Wulfe said, lowering his voice as they passed a group of Varians who were loitering in an alcove off the side of the passageway they were on. "What do we have to offer them? Carving your own paths to the surface is illegal and difficult, not just anyone has access to something like that."

"There's a Varian Syndicate outlet up there, I'm sure. They'd have the money, will and resources to pull something like that off. Assuming they're not Dusk Cabal of course."

"We can't deal with those cutthroats." Wulfe said. "I could throw them further than we could trust them."

"Is there a better idea? Asking around after smuggling rings is a good way to get yourself quietly disposed of down here."

Jana suddenly spoke up as an idea struck her.

"I know someone. The one I paid to find you." She rushed on, seeing Wulfe's frown. "He runs one of those sleeper dens in the deep warrens."

Kristof looked at Wulfe, and shrugged. "Someone running a place like that has to have connections. You don't make it there without making enemies, and then you need friends to watch your back. Those friends are usually pretty heavyweight, especially in the deep warrens."

Wulfe nodded slowly. "Seems like our best chance right now. Let's go."

Chapter 32

"The ending of the Carth revolt was unexpected for many. Within a single night the rebels resolve seemed to crumble, and the Commissary and the Captain seized this opportunity to end the war once and for all, cornering the Butcher of Carth in his hideout. He was reported dead less than an hour later."

-     *Sari Veth, "The War for the White City", 2084.72.*

"Down here?" Kristof said quietly as they walked down the narrow passageway towards Vishkar's den.

"Yeah, just around the next corner." Jana responded.

"Alright, let me take a look. We want to be sure he's not taken on any extra security after your last conversation with him."

"Can we stick together, Kristof? It'll be…"

"Two minutes." he smiled. "Promise."

Wulfe sighed as the other man disappeared around the corner.

"He's not right." he muttered, seemingly half to himself.

"What's up?" said Jana, looking up from rewrapping her bandage. The cloth she had used was getting ragged and moth-eaten at this point, but it was better than nothing.

Wulfe shook his head. "He's different. I think… I think what happened at the embassy broke him a bit."

"Wulfe, you're overreacting. He's fine." Jana smiled. "Tired, see? Like the rest of us."

"Hm." Wulfe grunted. "You didn't see how we got here."

"So, what happened?"

"We cut through the building and found a maintenance stairway. Managed to make our way down to ground level almost without issue. Then we got cut off. Two of the perimeter guards got in our way."

"And..?"

"Kristof tried to kill them. I barely managed to stop him."

Jana blanched, stifling a gasp.

"That has to happen, right?" she said. "You were running for your lives."

"I've seen a lot of people die, Jana. Seen a lot of people kill too."

"So?"

"Usually they hesitate first. There's a moment of pause while they think 'do I really want to do this?'." Wulfe paused, staring down the corridor with a troubled expression painted across his features. "Kristof didn't hesitate for a second."

Minutes later, they approached Vishkar's den together. Both Kristof and Wulfe gave quiet exclamations of surprise as they passed through the doorway into the sleeping chamber beyond.

"Keep an eye on the door." Kristof said to Wulfe. "Let's not scare him more than we need to."

Wulfe nodded silently, turning back into the room.

"Fuck this place." he muttered, staring out across the still forms that lay draped across the furniture.

Together, Kristof and Jana swept aside the curtain that led to Vishkar's back room.

"Vishkar, isn't it?" Kristof said, almost brightly.

The Varian, who had been sitting back in his seat with boots rested on the table in front of him, nearly fell out of his chair. He stood up hurriedly, the chair scraping back across the concrete.

"What do you want?" he muttered as he sized up Kristof. His eyes fell on Jana and there was a moment of recognition before they narrowed once more in suspicion.

"We were looking for a crook, and my friend here remembered your name."

"I run a legitimate business…"

"Sure you do. And several illegitimate ones as well, I'd imagine." Kristof said, leaning on the table beside him with an almost casual air.

The Varian paused in his retreat momentarily.

"Selling things. Buying things." Kristof continued. "Things that the Union may or may not want you to be buying and selling."

Vishkar's snakelike eyes were fixed on Kristof now, unblinking.

"And to do that," the soldier continued. "you would need a route to the outside world. A way of bringing in said goods without attracting too much unwanted attention. Or, at the very least, a friend who might bring things in for you."

Kristof leant forwards tapping his knuckles on the tabletop as he levelly met the man's unwavering gaze.

"Are you following where I'm heading with this, Vishkar?" he asked, a little too brightly.

The Varian's eyes flickered around the room, and met Jana's for a moment. His gaze filled with malice, his pale lips twitching momentarily into the shape of a snarl.

Kristof stepped forwards, causing the Varian to flinch back.

"*I'm* talking to you, Vishkar. Look at me." he said sharply.

The cold, grey eyes flicked back.

"No. I can't do it."

"We can pay."

"Not enough." Vishkar murmured.

"Well what can we do, Vishkar?" Kristof said, almost amicably. "Just introduce us to your friends and we'll give you something in return. Is that so hard?"

The man hesitated, frozen in place, eyes darting about the room as he searched it for some form of rescue. Then he stopped, his gaze meeting Jana's once more.

"They won't like this." his voice was low, a sibilant hiss in the silent room. "Do you know what they do to people who ask too many questions?" The man's tongue crept out, running across his cracked lips, his eyes fixed unblinkingly on Jana. "So much blood. It takes forever. They have people who can break every bone in your body, one at a time, a hundred times over. Sometimes they skin them. Sometimes they let me have the skin."

Jana recoiled, taking a hesitant step away from the man's snakelike stare. Even as she did so, she saw Kristof lunge forwards. Bringing both hands up he slammed into the smaller man, driving him back against the wall, fingers hooking into the man's clothing as he did so. Jana winced as Vishkar's head cracked off the concrete wall, his eyes glazing over briefly with the impact.

She watched, half relieved that the strange man had stopped his threats, the fight seeming already won as Vishkar was pinned against the wall by the front of his shirt, struggling helplessly against Kristof's iron grip.

But Kristof wasn't finished.

Jana felt her heart drop as Kristof tugged the man forwards, sending him slamming down against the rough concrete floor with an audible crack.

"Kristof?" she said, starting forwards.

The smuggler knelt over the fallen man, eyes filled with rage and hatred and anger, his lips pulled back into a savage snarl as he drove his fist into Vishkar's face.

"You are talking to *me*!" he hissed.

Jana stepped forwards now, watching in horror as the merchant struggled in Kristof's grip, blood oozing from the deep cuts in his face.

"Kristof, stop! You'll kill him!"

She reached for his arm as Kristof raised it for another swing, but Kristof shook her loose and brought a clenched fist swinging down again, slamming into Vishkar's jaw. The smaller man was almost incoherent now, his face a mess of blood and split flesh, bloody froth bursting from his lips as the blow struck home.

Jana took a step back, terrified now. She stumbled backwards towards the door, eyes still locked on the grisly spectacle.

"Wulfe?!" she called.

She turned, dashing from the room.

"Wulfe! Help!"

She turned a corner as the soldier cannoned past her, the tacky bead curtains torn aside as he forced his way into the room. She turned to follow, almost frantic now as she rushed back into the room.

The low growl of Kristof's voice cut through her horror.

"You. Stay. Away. From. Them!" each word punctuated with a sickening crunch as another blow fell

Wulfe's hand closed around Kristof's shoulder, lifting him almost effortlessly and sending him reeling back across the room, away from Vishkar's ruined form.

"What in god's name are you doing?" he roared, turning about, placing himself between the two of them, back towards the fallen man. "You could have killed him! We needed his help and you do... this?! You of all people should know that this isn't how we do things!"

Kristof scrambled to his feet unsteadily, leaning heavily on the wall as he rose, supporting the weight of his bad knee. His breathing was ragged but his pose was defensive, and Jana could already see that the madness had left his eyes.

He stared blankly for a moment as a myriad of conflicting emotions crossed his features. Shock. Fear. Loathing. Revulsion. Then, wordlessly, he stumbled out of the room.

Wulfe and Jana stood silently for a moment, their heavy breathing and the faint whimpering of Vishkar the only sounds that permeated the silence. Eventually the soldier looked away from the doorway through which Kristof had disappeared, and quickly took stock of the situation. Jana saw him visibly steady himself, an iron will driving the confusion and worry from his features.

"Shit." he murmured, looking down at Vishkar's now-silent form. "Can you do anything for him?"

"No… I…" Jana stopped. "I don't know. I can try."

"Fuck." Wulfe muttered again. He cast around for a second, before stalking across the room and casting a discarded shirt off a nearby shelf towards Jana.

"Do what you can. I…" He glanced over his shoulder towards the doorway. "I should… I knew there was something wrong with him! Why didn't he fucking tell anyone, the stupid…" He looked down at Jana again. "Do your best. I'm going after him."

He left, the tattered bead curtain clattering as he shouldered his way through it. Jana paused, staring down at the man in front of her.

Vishkar was a mess. His lips were cut and bruised, a faint trickle of blood oozing from the corner of his mouth where he had bitten through them. One of his eyes was swollen, the eyeball clouded so badly Jana couldn't tell if the organ itself was even intact anymore. His bald head bore several deep cuts and abrasions from the impacts with the concrete.

She reached out gingerly, and rolled the man onto his back. As she did so, a gout of air burst from his lungs and he coughed weakly. She could see a faint bubbling in the red spittle around the corners of his mouth as the shallow breaths forced their way in and out.

He was breathing. That was… something.

She did what she could, wiping away the blood with the hem of the shirt, doing her best to check for broken bones and more serious injuries. 2nd level flight-pilot medical training hadn't prepared her for this, she thought wryly as she worked, her ears listening intently to the voices that filtered in through the archway behind her.

"He threatened Jana." a familiar voice echoed through the concrete bunker. The tone of voice was

"So what, you crack his skull open? What, you think she's in less danger now? You think any of us are in less danger?"

"I was protecting us."

A wry laugh echoed around the bunker.

"Protecting us from the man who's head you caved in with your bare hands, right."

There was a pause; a long, stony silence, only broken by Vishkar's laboured breathing. Jana stopped, her hand falling to her side as she listened intently.

A voice broke the silence.

"You're right. I'm sorry. It's just with… It's just reminding me, you know? It's all coming back."

"Listen, there's a time and a place. I know it's hard, I've dealt with it myself. But for now, do what you can to keep it out of your head." Wulfe placed a comforting hand on the smuggler's shoulder. "For now, all you have to do is remember one thing. You are Kristof Richter, and you are better than… *that*."

The conversation continued for a while, in muted tones. Jana turned back to her task, although it was becoming clear that the Varian's wounds weren't fatal. None of the wounds were more than skin deep, and beyond the shock and some nasty bruising he'd probably recover in time.

Eventually she straightened up. The room was a mess. Blood was spattered across most of the far wall and the central table. There were all kinds of things there: Money, strange cartridges filled with a transparent liquid, a sheaf of disordered papers, a bottle of water... all now flecked with crimson. She reached out gingerly with her bloodstained hands and picked up the bottle, using its contents to rinse off the worst of the stains. Her slate was on the table too, hidden beneath the sheaf of papers. She'd recognise that battered piece of crap anywhere.

She hesitated a moment, before reaching out and pocketing the computer. He *had* threatened to kill her.

But she *was* stealing from an unconscious man.

Jana shook her head. They needed it. She would pay him back one day if they made it out of here.

It took about fifteen minutes before the two soldiers returned. Vishkar was conscious once more, albeit barely, propped up against the same wall that was still stained red with his blood. As his swollen, blood-reddened eyes settled on Kristof once more he let out an involuntary shriek, spattering Jana with flecks of crimson.

"No no no please!" the Varian begged, his words slurred and halting even in his terror as he scrambled clumsily back across the room away from them. He cowered against the far wall, hands curled protectively around his head and face.

"No more." he whispered.

Kristof looked at Wulfe, who nodded gravely. He took a few steps forwards, dropping onto one knee beside the man he had been savaging only minutes before. Vishkar whimpered as he saw the motion, pressing himself closer to the wall.

Jana turned her back. This didn't feel right, even after all they had been through, even with everything at stake. This was a side to Kristof she hadn't seen before.

She glanced over at Wulfe. The old soldier watched sullenly, a look of grim resignation on his face. It was clear he wasn't enjoying it any more than she was. He caught her glance, and shook his head slowly.

Jana felt a tingle on the back of her neck as a low, threatening voice rang out behind her.

"Now are we going to keep this civil, Vishkar?"

There was a shuffling noise, and a faint whimpering from the smaller man.

"You do have friends, don't you Vishkar? All we want is to talk to them." Kristof's voice was menacing, monotone, a low hiss in the silent room.

"I don't know anyone!" Vishkar hissed, backing away as far as the wall would allow. "I'll find something though! I promise! I just need time!"

"How long?"

"Three days."

"Make it two. We'll be back."

As they left the den, Jana looked at the two men who accompanied her. Wulfe strode wordlessly ahead, his expression and demeanour as black and imposing as an Ashkan Thundercloud. Kristof was subdued, seemingly deep in thought, his usually attentive attitude pushed aside by what had transpired minutes ago. Eventually, Jana spoke.

"It's alright." she said, placing a hand on his arm. "It's ok."

Kristof closed his eyes and drew in a deep breath. When he opened them again, a little of their usual light had returned. A little.

"I'm sorry." he murmured.

"Talk to me, Kristof. Talk to us." Jana said earnestly. "We're in this together."

"Sometimes I really wish we weren't." he muttered. "It's just more to worry about. More to lose."

That hurt a little.

"You don't have to tackle everything on your own." she responded. "...and definitely not like that." she added, the words slipping out before she could stop them.

Kristof shook his head.

"Always had a problem with bullies." he murmured. "I know it was wrong, but..."

"You nearly killed him."

"No I didn't." Kristof countered flatly.

Jana paused for a moment, dumbfounded as no further explanation came forth. Kristof paused in his stride, and turned to face her with a final glance up the corridor towards where the old soldier strode ahead of them.

"Wulfe is all I have left, Jana. I lost a lot on Carth. Lost everything. Wulfe was the one who kept me going, brought me back."

He frowned, and turned towards Jana, placing his hands on her shoulders. Jana met his gaze, feeling those piercing blue eyes bore into her.

"I'm not losing you, Jana. Either of you. It's too late for Cass, but you two? I am getting you two out. You're going home."

Chapter 33

Captain Wulfe wandered the square alone, the bustle of the 12th Corinthinan Long Rifles fading in his mind as they salvaged what they could from the remnants of the battle. Bodies were laid out in orderly lines, rebel on one side, legionary on the other.

Fifteen. Fifteen more dead, all for...

He paused, both in step and thought, stooping slowly to pick up a shell casing that lay discarded amongst the rubble. He stood there for a moment, turning the casing over and over in his hand. On the base a number had been stamped, a twelve-digit serial number followed by a production date.

Sihyld 2177.

One month after he had been denied further supplies.

Slowly, Captain Wulfe pocketed the casing, frowning thoughtfully.

A crowd had begun to gather in the cavern. There was a strange tension in the air, Jana could sense it immediately. A kind of electricity, crackling from person to person, setting everyone on edge.

A woman stood above the crowd, perched on the outset base of the ceiling support columns. She was pale and stocky, a thickness to her build and face unusual in the Warrens. Her voice rang around the cavern, rich and full, clearly audible despite the clamour of voices that surrounded her.

Jana saw Kristof's pace slow as his attention was drawn by the scene.

"It's been nearly four days." she said, stopping beside him. "I can see why they're scared."

Kristof didn't reply, stopping to watch the show with a bemused expression hovering about his features.

"They can't keep us here, trapped like animals." the woman shouted, one arm wrapped about the pillar, the other raised defiantly in the air. "We are citizens of the Ashkan Union, same as them! They have no right!"

A murmur went up from the crowd. A voice broke above the others, old and wavering.

"But what can we do?" an elderly man called out from near the back of the crowd.

Jana heard a wry chuckle from beside her as Kristof folded his arms, a small smile playing about his lips.

"That one's a plant." he muttered. "And a bad one. No-one asks questions like that." He shook his head, his voice rising to a mocking tenor. *"But what can we do?"* he scoffed.

There was another low murmur from the crowd around them. Jana looked back up at the Woman perched precariously on the pile of earth. She had said something about fighting back.

Kristof looked around at the crowd, eyes flicking from face to face, slowly drinking in the details.

"She's pushed them too hard." he said quietly. "Look at them. They're scared, not angry. Anger takes time to build."

There was a strange edge to his voice this time. Jana looked up at him, trying to disguise the motion by brushing some dust off her jacket's shoulder.

The bemused smile was gone, replaced by a troubled gaze. Occasionally the gaze would shift, sweeping across the fraying crowd, but it always returned to the woman at the front. His expression became bleak as the voice washed over him once more, his gaze becoming unfocussed for a moment.

"She's armed, too." he murmured. Jana wasn't even sure if he was talking to her any more.

"Look at the way her coat sits." Kristof continued, half to himself. "It's not hidden well and its hard to reach... I'd bet anything that she's never had to draw that thing before."

The woman shouted again, her voice lost this time as the crowd dissolved into a dozen separate conversations. The edges of the group began to flake away, until the woman stood alone amidst a gaggle of individuals.

"Maybe she's new to this?" Jana ventured.

"She is." Kristof sighed, and glanced at Jana. "How about you go and find Wulfe? He'll be trying to find that cave you mentioned, I guess." He glanced up, the bemused expression falling from his face. "I just want to have a quick word."

"Its fine, I can wait." Jana said, watching him carefully as he wordlessly started forwards, making his way towards the woman.

She had sat down on the column's base, legs swinging freely as she reached into a pocket for a cigarette. She looked up as Kristof approached, and shuffled aside to make a little space.

Jana watched the two of them curiously, too far away to make out words. She saw them exchange names, she could read that much on Kristof's lips. They spoke quietly for a moment, in short sentences, nonchalantly. The way strangers usually spoke. The woman offered Kristof a cigarette, which he took. He made a short comment and the woman laughed, coughing up a cloud of white smoke. Their faces turned sombre as the conversation continued, the expressions on their faces thoughtful, almost wistful at times.

Jana stepped a little closer, trying her best to appear disinterested as she strained her ears for the slightest wisp of conversation.

"It's all too big." Kristof was saying, his voice low and... comforting, almost, the tone you would use to address a disappointed child. "You could burn the city down, raze the whole thing to the ground, and the world would just keep on turning. People only know what they hear in the stories, and it's the ones you're fighting against doing the telling."

"Someone has to do something." the woman replied, speaking in the singsong accent of the Celthari. "All we want is..."

Kristof turned the cigarette over in his fingers, staring at the thin roll of paper thoughtfully.

"They won't ever know that you wanted fairness, or justice, or freedom. They'll know whatever the storyteller wants them to know."

He grimaced, placing the cigarette down on the plinth by his side.

"It runs on faith. Everything. Faith that things are best just the way they are. If you break it down, show people there's another way, they'll stop believing. So they fight and fight, tooth and nail, because if they back down they lose everything. And you..." he threw the woman a sidelong glance. "You do the same thing, for the same reasons. When you lose... and you *will* lose ...nothing will change. You will have lost everything, they will have lost nothing, and the world will just keep on turning."

Kristof looked around, eyes scanning the crowd briefly before turning back to the woman.

"You want to protect these people? You want what's best for them?"

He rose to his feet, wincing as his weight settled on his injured knee, before turning back one final time.

"Leave them alone." he said, flatly.

The cavern was pitch black by the time Kristof and Jana returned, what lighting there was seemed to have been turned off, the only light coming from a small open fire in the cave's centre. Figures stood around the fire, alone or in small groups, and the room was filled with the gentle chatter of voices. Children raced through the crowds, darting amongst the assembled people in a blur of laughter and colour.

Jana narrowed her eyes, squinting into the darkness, watching the ruddy glow of the flames play across faces. It was nice here. It reminded her of home, of the long nights spent out with the other pilots

Her eyes fell on a huddled figure by the far wall. Wulfe sat alone near the back of the crowd, his coat wrapped around his shoulders, a broad smile across his face as he watched the children at play.

He looked up as she approached, a look of faint embarrassment playing across his stony features.

"Where'd you get the bottle?" Jana asked, sitting down beside him.

"They gave it to me." The soldier said, waving a hand vaguely towards one of the nearby huddles. "Nice people down here." he muttered, almost to himself.

"Yeah." Jana smiled, nodding.

She looked up as a gaggle of children rushed past, shrieking and giggling as they chased eachother amongst their parent's legs.

"Always liked the sound, you know?" Wulfe said, gesturing again with the half-empty bottle as another group of children raced by, squealing with laughter. He smiled, fondly. "They don't even know there's anything wrong. Makes you feel like maybe things aren't as bad as they seem."

He shook his head suddenly.

"Sorry, rambling. I do that when I've been drinking…" he squinted at the label of the bottle, holding it up to catch the label in the ruddy orange firelight. "…whatever this is."

"Where'd you get that down here?" Jana laughed.

Wulfe gestured vaguely towards the small cluster of adults that stood by the cavern's central fireplace.

"Couple of Celthari were giving them out. There's some traditional celebration back home, apparently." he smiled a little. "Very generous of them, considering the circumstances. Always liked a Celthar. Very... positive, I always thought. Upbeat."

He looked back at Jana. "Want some? Here…" He shuffled sideways a little, and Jana gladly sat down against the wall beside him. She reached out for the bottle, but Wulfe seemed to have forgotten, absently taking another swig as he stared idly into the darkness.

She followed his gaze, and saw Kristof standing against the opposite wall of the cavern. He had barely moved since he and Jana returned, simply standing, his eyes staring pensively into the fire in the cavern's centre.

Wulfe took a deep breath, tapping thoughtfully on the bottle in his hand.

"I think I pushed him too far." he muttered, his gaze unmoving.

"Sounds like its time for the big brave hero of Carth to take charge then, doesn't it?" Jana said, giving him a playful nudge. "Show him how its done!"

The silence killed her smile dead.

"You know how I feel about that." Wulfe murmured.

"What, because you've been running away from it?" she countered.

She paused, before reaching out and plucking the bottle out of the soldier's hand and taking a quick swig.

"Do you know why I lived in Verkat, Wulfe?"

"Since when did you tell stories instead of asking for them?" The soldier rumbled.

"Shut up and listen." Jana laughed. "It's my turn now."

"Alright." the old man said, shifting his sitting position a little and leaning towards Jana. "It'll make a change."

"Mum never talked about it much, but my dad was the reason." Jana said. "She signed up for the envoy scheme to the most remote, backwater planet in the Union just to get away from him. We arrived there with nothing, no skills, no training, no money. You know what she did, Wulfe?"

The soldier shrugged, waiting expectantly.

"She joined the Legions. Because of me. She wanted me to have something."

Jana smiled to herself as she spoke. The memories were somewhat bittersweet.

"I didn't see her for years at a time. All I had was little releases of what the legions were up to. I imagined her having all kinds of adventures." She leant closer to the soldier for a moment. "That's where I started hearing about you and the lady up there." she said with a smirk.

"But she made it back, and we did have something. It was pretty good, all in all."

"Look, Wulfe. She was running away from something terrible, just like you. But she turned it around eventually. The running away doesn't matter. It doesn't change who you are, or what you stand for, or anything. You can do it for as long as you need to, the world will keep turning." Jana stopped, taking a deep breath. "It's what you do when you stop running that really matters."

Wulfe was quiet for a moment.

"You tell a good story, you know that?" he said eventually.

Jana grinned. "Why thank you!" she replied, only slightly sarcastically.

For a moment the soldier lapsed back into thought. After a few seconds, he broke the silence once more.

"You talked to her, right? You saw her?"

Jana frowned, puzzled. "Who?"

"Atesca."

"The Inquisitor?"

"That's what I said."

"I was a little busy, Wulfe." Jana said with a faint chuckle. "She was trying to kill me."

"Yeah, but was she…" Wulfe hesitated, frowning with concentration, staring intently at the liquid in the bottle as he swirled it around. "Psh, I don't even know what I'm asking."

"How long has it been?" said Jana. "Since you saw her, I mean."

Wulfe was silent for a moment.

"Carth." he rumbled. "We didn't part on the best of terms."

Jana looked up at him, watching the firelight play across his features.

"You know, the stories said that you two left together after defeating the Butcher." She smirked. "They had this whole… love story and everything. That used to be my favourite book when I was a girl. Very flowery, but had some good action in it. They said you left the White City to find more wrongs to right, or something along those lines."

Wulfe grunted. "Well the stories were wrong. Never spoke to her again. Never even saw her 'til today."

"You never went back?"

Wulfe scratched his cheek, and grimaced. "Like I said, not the best of terms. I'd be lying if I said the thought hadn't crossed my mind though. She made for good company." He paused, and set the bottle down with a sigh.

"Still miss her sometimes." he muttered quietly.

Jana looked up at him sharply. "You said the stories were wrong."

Wulfe shrugged. "Not about everything."

He straightened his posture for a second, stretching. He rolled his shoulders with a grunt before settling back into his slouch against the wall. He spoke again, without looking up.

"Those stories… how did they end?"

"I thought we just established they weren't true?"

"I'd still like to hear it."

"I can't remember it too well. It was a long time ago. I think the two of you just rode off into the sunset together. Well, flew."

Wulfe gave a short, mirthless laugh.

"Wish I'd thought of that." he muttered.

They fell to silence again. A distant motherly figure had emerged from the darkness, ushering the children away from the fire. Jana watched as they left the cavern together, the echoes of their voices receding into the night.

She sat up, throwing a sidelong glance at Wulfe. The man was leaning forwards, forearms resting on his knees, staring intently into the flames, seemingly deep in thought.

"What's she like?" enquired Jana. "The Inquisitor. Is she like in the stories?"

Wulfe pulled a face, shrugging. "Who knows. Never read the bloody things myself. Couldn't stand them." He paused for a moment. "Atesca was… She was a strange one. Committed. Driven, you know? But she had that... that something. Fire. I felt like she was the only one who really *believed* it, believed all the stories about what we were, what we stood for. What the Union stood for. And in a way, that made them a little bit closer to being true."

Wulfe paused for a moment, drawing a deep breath.

"She's just doing what she's told. Following orders." He shrugged, gazing over the heads of the children into the crackling flames. "She's a fanatic, but she's still human."

Jana shot Wulfe a sidelong glance. The man was gazing into the flames, a fond smile playing about his lips.

"What was it? You know, that you two…"

"I… she… I don't even know how to describe it."

"Come on, there must be something. One thing?"

Wulfe stared pensively into the darkness for a moment.

"Her smile." he said, slowly. "It's a little thing but… That's always stuck with me. She didn't smile much, so when she did it was… something special, I guess." he chuckled for a moment. "She didn't half make you work for it though."

Wulfe shook his head suddenly. He glanced down at the bottle he still cradled, and handed it across to Jana wordlessly. As Jana reached out to take it, Wulfe nestled back against the wall, pulling the folds of his coat tighter about him with a sound somewhere between a sigh and a groan.

"Shit, talking about this stuff takes me back." he growled. "You might be the first person I've told about it in years."

"You and Kristof don't compare notes occasionally?"

"We had very different experiences of Carth. We don't talk about it."

Jana grimaced, taking another swig from the bottle, wincing as the taste hit her again. "Well, don't let me stop you. Tell your tales, old wolf." she added, a small smile on her lips.

Wulfe began to speak again, hesitantly at first, but with growing confidence as the words began to flow.

Maybe it was the flickering firelight, the exhaustion or the rapidly emptying bottle of spirits she held in her hand, but as she sat there gazing up at the soldier who sat beside her, wrapped in an old coat, hair and beard streaked with silver, eyes twinkling in the darkness of the cavern, she saw something else for the first time.

The Wolf of Carth.

Kristof watched the two of them carefully over the flames. He hadn't seen the old man like this in... well, ever. Not in-person, anyway. It was nice to see them happy, despite their grim surroundings

The voices of the Celthari around Kristof were loud and boisterous as they sung and danced, but he was all but deaf to them over the sound of his own thoughts.

...Varian Syndicate supplies 200 units for processing. Dockside Kings take 20. 50 units go to deep and upper warrens, minus 5 for the Spikes cut. That leaves 75 that need to make their way back to the surface...

Jana smiled, laughing out loud at something that the old soldier had said. Wulfe chuckled fondly to himself.

...a person could only safely conceal 3 units on themselves at a time. Ambrosia needles are an inconvenient shape, so call it 2.5. The Kings must have their own route to transport burnables, but they will only have one, maybe two, and they'll be guarded...

She's watching.

Kristof looked up, and caught Jana's eyes on him. He gave a quick smile. She waved back, before turning and whispering to Wulfe as Kristof's gaze wandered back to the flames.

...Nadir's blood coating your hands and forearms as you drag him back towards the...

Kristof blinked.

...the majority of the transport must be in Varian hands then. It made sense. No-one would look twice at a Council-Sanctioned Trade Company owning strategic land above the Warrens, nor at Varians occupying the lowest rung of Ashkan society. They have the economic power to sustain it and... and...

...the light draining from Cass' eyes as she drifts away in your arms...

Kristof shook his head.

She's watching.

He looked up again. Jana beckoned him over.

Smile.

He smiled.

It was time to find the Varians.

Chapter 34

27ᵗʰ Sihyl, 2094.69 Core Time – Electronic Messaging Certificate – Confidential

Commissary Atesca Seratov, Commissary 1ˢᵗ Class

You may consider your previous orders regarding the pursuit of the 'Butcher' to be reinstated. Find them and terminate the individual.

Tulharden square lay in ruins. The rich shopfronts lay in tatters, windows smashed, walls torn apart, blackened by fire and ash. The acrid smell of smoke and burnt plastic hung heavy in the air, thrown up by the dozens of small, sputtering fires that had been lit amongst the enormous cavern, their flames guttering even with the intricate ventilation systems that supplied the upper levels with vital oxygen.

The vast steel doors that blocked the chamber's exit were pitted and scarred, seemingly both by flame and through heavy impacts. From this distance, Jana even thought she could make out bullet scarring across the once-polished surface.

The crowd that stood at the gates' base had only grown since Jana had last entered the square. Hundreds of people now stood gathered together in small huddles, some bearing banners and boards, some simply standing as if waiting. Some seemed to be attacking the rocks and improvised clubs. As Jana watched, a bottle arced from the crowd, shattering against the vast structures in a roar of flame as a cheer went up from the ragged groups.

The doors weathered the barrage. Implacable. Immovable.

"Stupid bastards." growled Wulfe. He looked back at Jana, and gestured towards one of the nearby buildings. "Let's get inside. Mob like that is dangerous whichever side you're on, trust me."

Together they ducked under the ruined doorway into one of the shop-fronts. Wulfe hadn't liked the idea of coming up near to the surface again, but this was the only part of the warrens where news of the outside world was able to trickle in. That made the fifteen-minute climb towards the surface seem like a tempting proposition, especially to Jana. She could feel herself going mad down here, unable to see the sky or feel the air move. It wasn't natural. She had spent almost her entire life under the endless skies of Valmeer, the planet famous for its sweeping planes and unobstructed skyline.

Until a month ago, the largest building she had seen was the Ashkan spire in Verkat. Now she was sealed in a concrete tomb under the largest city in the known universe.

It was getting too much.

Kristof would find a way out, eventually. They all would.

She squatted down in the cover of the derelict storefront, and drew out her slate. They weren't far below ground here. She could almost certainly get network access.

"Are you sure that's a good idea?" Wulfe voice sounded from behind her. She looked back, nodding encouragingly.

"I want to know what's going on up there, and this is the only way we can find out. Atesca knows we're down here already, otherwise all this..." she gestured towards the great gates, wincing as another roar of flame echoed throughout the cavern. "...all this wouldn't be happening."

"They can't be certain. If they see your slate come online, they'll know for sure."

Jana lowered the slate for a moment, and turned to face the soldier, standing up so as to be able to address him properly.

"I know you're being careful." she said. "But we don't know what's going on up there. We're flying completely blind. We've just assumed Atesca is on to us but this *could* just be a coincidence, we can't be sure."

Wulfe paused for a moment, seemingly in thought. Jana stared up at her childhood hero, who still towered over her despite his age. A month ago she had thought this man little more than a myth, now she was giving him encouraging pep-talks. The world was a strange place, despite its dangers.

"You're right." the soldier said. "Go on."

It took Jana a few minutes to sift through the local update feeds, with Wulfe hovering just over her shoulder the whole time. There were news stories, media releases, articles filled with speculation and discussion, and almost two dozen live video feeds of the outside world. As she brought the feed up on screen, Jana felt her heart leap.

"Marija." Wulfe muttered under his breath. "Would you look at that…"

The port at the mouth of the warrens was filled with people. Hundreds. Thousands, even. The image jumped and flickered strangely, but what it showed was clear even to Jana.

"They're protesting too." she whispered. A smile spread across her face, as if feeling the happiness in her voice. "Wulfe, this is wonderful! With pressure from both sides they'll have to let us out eventually!"

Wulfe gave a faint smile, although he seemed to Jana to be only half-listening.

"Right, Wulfe?"

The man stared at the screen, the smile falling from his lips.

"Wulfe?"

At the bottom of the screen stood a line of figures, a blurry, indistinct line, stretching across the ground in front of the gates. The greyish-green of their coats, turned a strange incandescent yellow by the slate's damaged screen, set them apart from the others, a thin line of monochrome against the roaring crowd. There were vehicles amongst them, too. Towering, box-like armoured transports dotted the line. Centurions stood too, unmoving, like vast iron statues looming above the masses.

And at the centre of all this stood a single figure. Atesca watched the crowds silently, hands clasped behind her back, head held high as she surveyed the scene unfolding before her.

Jana stayed quiet, watching Wulfe carefully.

The soldier stood silently, staring down at the slate, his troubled gaze fixed on the scene in front of him. Jana watched him silently. *No harm in allowing him a moment. Poor guy.*

She gave him space, handing him the slate wordlessly and wandering off to sift through some of the more remote areas of the ransacked shop-front. There was little to nothing of value left, now, as she had expected. Another slate would have been nice. She still didn't feel good about that, but maybe he was right. Currently all they had were two pistols, around ten rounds of ammunition and a slate she'd stolen from an unconscious thug.

Kristof had been taking care of their interactions with the Ashkan underworld for the past two days. He was secretive about it, possessive of what little information he had. There were hundreds of small gangs and cartels that operated out of the Warrens below Ashka, but only the heavyweights with money to throw around had managed to create structurally sound routes to the surface. Being rare as they were, getting access was hard. Especially at a time like this. And especially with no leverage.

Jana picked up her bag, slinging it onto her back.

"We should probably go. Kristof said not to hang around."

She turned, stepping back out of the ruined doorway, watching Wulfe take a final, lingering glance at the slate before turning to follow.

As they reached their home cavern once more, deep in the depths of the Warrens, Kristof was already waiting for them. From his expression alone, Jana could tell something was different. He was smiling, for a start.

"I did it." he whispered almost breathlessly, drawing the two of them towards the walls of the cavern with the fewest prying ears. "I followed one of their couriers to an out-of the-way block around the third level. I watched that building for two hours. Fourteen people entered it during that time. Three left."

"So we know where they've hidden it. How do we get to it?"

Kristof grinned a little sheepishly. "I'm working on that."

"Do they ever leave it unattended?"

The man shrugged. "Not sure. I need to keep an eye on the place a while longer. Maybe if I can work out how they identify each other..." he paused, then shook his head. "I don't know. But I will. Give me another day or two and I'll work something out, promise."

"Don't rush it." Wulfe cautioned. "The Syndicate are dangerous types."

"I'll be fine." Kristof said. "Takes more than a few Varian to scare me off. One more day. Maybe two."

"You're not alone in finding something out." Jana said with a smile. "We were right, it is Atesca who sealed us in. But the locals seem to be putting up a fight."

"I thought as much..." Kristof said, his smile turning to an expression of concern as he turned to Wulfe. "This doesn't make sense for her. She should *know* this is a bad move. Sealing the warrens puts her under time pressure and is political suicide for anyone associated with her actions. At this rate, the Council is going to pull its support and then the Commission will recall her."

Wulfe shrugged. "Maybe there's more to it than what we know." he said, non-committally.

"I'm serious, Wulfe." Kristof said again, a trace of anger in his voice at the man's apparent apathy. "This isn't like her, you should know that. She's more subtle than this. This feels... I don't know... *desperate.*"

Jana spoke up. "If she's on the clock then that implies she has something in the works. If she's as smart she's reputed to be, she wouldn't make a move like this without a plan."

"Either way." Wulfe rumbled. "We need to get out of here soon."

"I'm on it." Kristof said. "Jana, keep watch on Atesca as best you can. We need to know if she so much as breathes while she's up there."

Chapter 35

The Varian leant back against the wall and grinned disarmingly at Wulfe.

"So... what?" he said, his words cut strangely by his thick accent. "You want me to kill him? You think better people than me haven't tried?"

"No killing. Just find him. Talk to him. Find out what he wants. What his endgame is. Not a word about me."

The Varian ran a hand through his long, oily black hair for a moment, deep in thought.

"Same price as agreed?"

"Same price."

He grinned, and grabbed Wulfe's hand in his own.

"Then you have a deal, Wolf."

It was early morning when Jana awoke. At least she thought it was early morning. There were more people about, anyway.

It was quick to get up, at least. Wake up, brush the dust off your coat, brush the dried blood off your hands... she could have saved so much time on Valmeer if she'd picked up this morning routine, she thought drily.

She watched the other two as she worked. Kristof had fallen asleep propped up against the wall of the cavern. Wulfe had vanished, but his coat still lay sprawled across the stonework next to her, so she assumed he couldn't have gone far.

Eventually, she rose to her feet, straightening her jacket a little as she glanced around the cavern.

How Kristof heard her she would never know. It was uncanny.

"Where are you going?" he asked quietly, glancing down at Wulfe as she spun about. He raised a finger in a shushing motion.

"Doing the job you gave me." she said. "Heading up to keep an eye on Atesca."

"You just be careful, alright?"

"Alright, sure." Jana laughed. "I'm not a child, you know?"

"Last time I left you alone you fell off a building."

She rolled her eyes theatrically. The wounds were still fresh, but she was well enough to joke about them, it seemed.

"That was a strategic manoeuvre." she snarked back.

Kristof chuckled.

"Leave the strategising to the soldier." he said.

They both glanced across the now-crowded cavern, where Wulfe sat alone, weary eyes fixed on the people around him.

"He's not been the same since he saw her." Jana said. "I think it really tore him up. Have they met since..."

Kristof made a noise somewhere between a sigh and a growl. Jana looked up questioningly.

"What?" she asked.

The man responded with a shake of the head.

"Nothing."

Jana gave him a hard look. "It's not nothing though, is it? Don't you think we're past having secrets now?"

Kristof shifted, sitting a little more upright against the wall. Jana realised she had been leaning against him slightly, catching her balance with an undignified scramble.

"First of all, no-one is ever past having secrets." he murmured. He glanced up at Wulfe again, and for a moment Jana thought she saw the briefest of sneers ghost across his features.

"Secondly," he added, quietly. "You can safely ignore anything that man tells you about his partner in crime."

Jana frowned.

"I think he likes her, Kristof. He seems really hurt about it."

"Sure."

"You don't think so?"

"'Course not." Kristof spat. "You've met her. Does she seem like the lovebird type to you?"

"I mean no, but…"

"Commissaries aren't like that. They aren't like us. They're fanatics, Jana, raised from birth to believe in everything the Union stands for. Maybe he likes her. Maybe he really, truly likes her and hasn't just been cynically manipulated into it. But she sure as hell doesn't care about him."

"You can't *know* that, Kristof."

"This is who Atesca is, Jana. She manipulates, she *reads* people. That's what a first class commissary is trained for all their life. Reading those tiny, instinctive signals in your movements, your gestures, the way you speak, walk, stand, and react. That's what makes her the hunter she is. It's what inquisitors are *for*." he caught Jana's expression, and frowned.

"You don't believe me." he said flatly.

Jana hesitated. "It's not that, I..."

"How did you feel when you first met her in Verkat?"

"I was... scared, I guess. I was worried I would get in trouble for what I did, especially when I found out she was a Commissary."

"What else?"

"I was excited. I didn't really believe she was who she claimed to be, but... you know... meeting your heroes. I was tired too. It had been a really long day."

Kristof sat back against the wall for a moment.

"Let me guess: She was authoritative, yet gentle. She sympathised with you about the long process you went through. She limited your appreciation of her history, but denied none of it and allowed it to open you up a little."

Jana opened her mouth to speak.

...Commissary, First Class, although you may simply refer to me as Atesca if you wish...

...It is always a pleasure to meet a follower of my work, but I do not wish to talk about it. There is too much to do in the present to dwell on the past...

...I can promise you my questions will be extremely brief, Miss Schliefer...

She closed it again, wordlessly.

"I can't read people like she does." Kristof continued. "I'm not sure if anyone can. But that's what it takes. Just *understanding* people and knowing how and when to apply pressure until they break. You told her everything you could remember."

Kristof paused, taking a deep breath as he stared across the cavern at his comrade.

"You spoke to her for minutes, Jana. Imagine if she had years."

He grimaced, his anger dissipating into hapless despondence.

"It hurts that I can't help him, even after everything he's done for me. She's in his mind, and he doesn't want to get her out. He thinks it was all real, what the two of them had, but Commissaries don't work like that. They don't think like we do. They aren't human the way we are."

Kristof sighed.

"I tried helping him. I've tried to tell him. He won't listen to me. He won't listen to anyone. I owe him everything I have, and he hates me because I cost him everything he loved."

The two of them lapsed into silence for a while. Eventually Jana stood up again, gently pulling her flight jacket past her injured fingers and shrugging the now-battered garment into place.

"I'll head up top then." she said. "What are you two doing?"

Kristof looked up, tearing his gaze away from his fellow soldier.

"I need to watch the Syndicate a little longer." he said. "Maybe they have more exit tunnels, or maybe there's a time they leave it unguarded. I need more information to know for sure."

"Alright then, good luck. Where do I meet you?"

"Back here." Kristof said, also rising to his feet. "Good luck, and stay out of trouble if you can."

Chapter 36

The Legionary outpost bustled with life. Couriers ran back and forth, carrying weapons, armour and ammunition to the readying soldiers. A strange kind of electricity hung in the air, the kind that always brewed before major offensives.

Amidst this commotion strode Captain Wulfe, armed and readied for war. He crossed the ground between the Legion and Commissary command bunkers quickly, not wanting to be out in the cold air any longer than necessary.

The Hawk of Carth was already watching the door as he entered.

"You know you aren't allowed in here, Bastian." she commented, archly.

"I felt I should wish you luck, commander to commander." the captain responded.

And he felt his heart lift as a warm smile spread across her face.

Jana found herself deep in thought once more as she ascended towards Tulharden Square and the warrens' entrance. She made her way through the twisting caverns with ease now, accustomed to the strange environs after almost six days in this subterranean web. Even as she ascended and the caverns began to widen, forming into crowded streets and alleyways that thronged with life, she was able to navigate almost without thinking.

She was having a hard time separating fiction from reality. She had had a lifetime of dreaming about these characters... these people. She had believed for years, no, she had *known* with utmost certainty, that the Wolf and Hawk of Carth were safe. That they were together. That they were happy. She had been told, time and time again, the stories of their adventures, their trials, their escapades.

Somehow the reality of the situation just wasn't setting in. She just wasn't sure what to believe. It certainly wasn't beyond reason that a trained Commissary could wield that kind of manipulative power over her fellow man, but the stubborn twelve-year-old in Jana's heart of hearts was refusing to accept it as ultimate truth.

She sighed as she ascended yet another level, pushing her way through the thronging crowds towards the surface. Perhaps she would find out the truth one day. A small part of her hoped she wouldn't have to.

Minutes later, she stepped out into the ruins of Tulharden Square. She wasn't sure if the crowd by the gates had grown larger, but it certainly hadn't diminished. She could feel the nervous energy of a hundred trapped Ashkan citizens in the air. She could almost taste it.

Heeding Wulfe's advice, she worked her way amidst the dilapidated store fronts and rubble-strewn pathways as she skirted the edge of the square. There was something different about the crowd this time. She could hear raised voices echoing throughout the darkened confines of the cavern. Cries of anger, pain and hatred bounced off the steel gates of the warrens, their sound only amplifying as they rang off the hollow stone walls of Tulharden Square.

...They're scared, not angry. Anger takes time to build...

With Kristof's words echoing in her mind, Jana nestled herself semi-comfortably amidst the debris-strewn interior of one of the square's former outlets. The walls around her were blackened and scorched, and there was a clear smell of spirit smoke in the air. The place had clearly been firebombed recently.

Jana frowned. She wasn't sure when she'd worked out what a firebomb smelt like, but she really wished she hadn't. It wasn't the kind of thing she felt she should know.

She spent a few minutes rebinding the wrappings on her left hand, as she listened carefully to what sounds managed to drift through the flame-warped wreckage that surrounded her. She grimaced as she did so, as it was clear even to her unpractised eye that the hand was not healing well. The open wounds had largely scabbed over, but the severe bruising and strange ridges in her fingers still remained. She could still barely move the hand despite the almost a week of healing. It was the curse of her extremely limited medical training: She knew that things were going wrong, but didn't know how to fix them.

Much like the rest of her life right now, come to think of it.

With a wry smile, she pulled her battered slate out of her pocket and began to work through the connection process.

She felt the sound before she heard it: a low, yet thunderous rumbling that seemed to shake the building in which she sat to its very foundations. Dust was shaken free from the ceiling, and Jana watched as one of the thick polymer plates detached and hit the cracked marble with a dull clatter. She scrambled to her feet, stuffing her slate hastily back under her jacket as she dashed for the front of the shop, peering out from between where the street-facing display had toppled sideways, providing a small window into the world beyond.

The great gates that had sealed the warrens shut for almost six days were grinding open, sliding aside with surprising smoothness considering their vast bulk.

A ragged cheer went up from the crowd around the door, figures already pressing forwards as the first shafts of daylight began to pierce the gloom of the square.

Jana breathed a deep sigh of relief. It was over. She knew they'd have to give in eventually. Give the people their freedom. She scrambled to her feet, staring through the wreckage into the dying late-evening sunlight that filtered down the tunnel into the square.

"We made it." she whispered to herself, raising a hand to shield her eyes from the light that seemed almost blinding after so many days in near-blackness.

Then a tremor ran through the crowd.

The first figures to press through the gaps in the door had re-appeared, some walking slowly backwards, hands raised, others scrambling away in terror of the figures that pursued them. The crowd hesitated as the rear ranks pressed forwards, even as those at the front tried to turn and run.

The Legionaries marched in lockstep as they passed through the gates. They moved with weapons raised, on high alert, their sights training on the nearest individuals in the crowd as they pressed forwards. Their visors covered their faces now, the atmosphere shielding lowered, only a thin band of red light at their eyeline giving any indication of life beneath the mask.

The crowd withdrew as the legionaries advanced further, driving the people like sheep back down into the square. Even as Jana watched, more legionaries filed through the mouth of the warrens, marching in three columns down into the square behind the main line.

Jana ducked back into the wreckage of the building, throwing a glance at the street that left the square only a few hundred feet away. Slinging her bag back over her shoulder, she began to make her way towards it ducking and scrambling through the ruined shopfronts, one eye on the front of advancing legionaries as she moved.

There was an uneasy silence from the crowd now. Occasionally an angered shout would break the silence, but the crowd watched almost sullenly as the troops continued to file in, cowed by the show of force. As the legionary line reached the square it began to fan out, pressing out into a defensive square that blocked the mouth of the Warrens. The crowd was forced back, pushed away until it formed around the square. It was growing too, as people filtered in, trying to see the cause of the commotion.

Jana ducked under a collapsed doorframe, scrambling awkwardly on her one good hand and knees as she tried desperately to stay out of sight of the troops. She didn't know what was happening. To be honest, she didn't care either. All she wanted was to be far away from it.

She slung her bag through a narrow gap between two shelving units, squeezing through after it. She emerged on the far side, stumbling a little as her foot caught something. She reached down for her bag, and froze.

A voice echoed around the square. A familiar voice.

"My name is Atesca Seratov, Commissioner First Class, Acting Executor of the Quarantine of the Ashkan Warrens."

The inquisitor stood in the centre of the square of troops, head held high, seemingly oblivious to the crowds that flowed around her. She held a small red-leather notebook in one hand, and she read from the pages in a voice devoid of warmth or emotion.

"Five days ago, this illegal settlement was placed under quarantine due to the suspected presence of a severe viral outbreak. This has, after investigation by the Ashkan Commission ultimately proved false."

There was a ragged cheer from the crowd.

"Ordinarily, the quarantine would now be lifted. However, under recent scrutiny a document has been retrieved from the archives, dated 15ᵗʰ Sihyl, 2094.74, ordering the dismanteling of the illegal excavations beneath Ashka."

A figure stepped forwards out of the crowd. A ragged man, his clothing dishevelled and his hair awry. "Excavations? That was twenty years ago! You locked us up here to die you bitch!"

He hefted a rock in his hand, raising his arm as he stepped forwards to throw.

A sharp crack echoed out around the cavern as a legionary swung his rifle up and, without a second's hesitation, fired. The bullet punched through the man's skull, sending him tumbling to the ground in a lifeless heap. The crowd shrank back, several members turning and dashing back across the square, away from the soldiers.

Atesca continued, eyes fixed on the page she held open in front of her, seeming not to notice the corpse lying mere meters from her.

"A decision has been reached."

Atesca paused, eyes still fixed on the book in front of her. Jana turned, backing as fast as she could towards the street mouth.

"By this order that I hold, sector 23B2, this illegal settlement will be destroyed and dismantled. Those present will be permitted to leave after vetting and a thorough search. Those who refuse will be moved by force. Those who resist will be considered in breach of Ashkan law, and will be executed."

The legionaries, as one, took a step forwards, raising their rifles to their shoulders. Shouts of confusion and terror began to rise up from the crowd. Its edges began to fray as figures broke and ran, scattering across the square.

"My name is Atesca Seratov, and with a heavy heart I hereby carry out the orders of the Ashkan Council."

Jana never saw who fired the first shot. The deafening blast of a weapon discharge echoed around the chamber, and as she turned back Jana saw one of the Legionaries beside Atesca crumple slowly to the ground in a ragged heap as medicae rushed to his aid.

In a deafening chorus, the front rank of Legionaries fired. Screams and cries filled the air as figures crumpled under the barrage, mown down in the open ground even as they ran for the cover of the side streets. Within seconds, the square descended into anarchy, as several shots from amongst the crowd struck the tightly-packed Legionary formation. The air filled with the sound of gunfire, terrified screams and cries erupting from around Jana as she leapt from cover and dashed for the square's exit.

Atesca looked up, her cold eyes roving across the carnage. The small leather book in her hand snapped shut, and she tucked it inside her coat.

"For the good of humanity."

The legionaries began to fan outwards, fanning out across the square as more troops filtered into the cavern, stepping across the broken and shattered bodies as they moved.

Atesca's voice remained level, emotionless, lent a strangely metallic edge by the throat mic as it echoed amongst the screams of the dead and dying.

"United as one."

Chapter 37

"Unity is everything. Without unity, how can one have strength, or valour, or progress? Without the peace and stability of the Ashkan Union, we are nothing, and we will return to nothing."

> *- Captain Bastian Wulfe to the Butcher of Carth, 'Heroes of the White City'*

Jana ran, her feet light with terror, her breath running ragged as she dashed through the narrow streets. She could hear the sound of gunfire behind her, screams rising above the confused babble of the crowd around her.

Panic was spreading ahead of her, as the first of the fugitives reached the milling crowds in the tunnels surrounding Tulharden Square. Rallying cries mingled with those of despair and terror in the darkness. The once almost orderly confines of the upper warrens descended into chaos. Some residents retreated into their homes, barring their doors as best they could. Others fled, stampeding deeper into the tunnels like herds of terrified cattle, seeking nothing more than to escape the carnage of battle.

Jana watched, horrified, as the crowds swept past her. She pressed herself against the wall of the cavern, moving as fast as she could whilst avoiding the mad, claustrophobic crush as the tide of humanity pressed itself towards the exits. She could hear the sound of battle approaching now, the tramp of legionary boots and the thunder of their guns seeming to almost reverberate off the very stone she was backed against.

What would Wulfe do? she thought desperately. *What would Kristof do?*

She ducked around the corner as, almost silhouetted against the fire and smoke of Tulharden Square, the first of the legionaries pressed into the chamber. The air seemed to grow dense, a hideously oppressive sense of dread settling over the chamber's occupants as the air seemed to almost fall silent.

A silence that was almost immediately ruptured as a series of deafening gunshots rang about the chamber.

Two of the legionaries pitched forwards, their blood spilling across the concrete as the other scattered for cover. New figures rushed from the darkness. A man took two steps out of the crowd, pitching a bottle of burning spirits towards the nearest soldiers with a defiant cry. One of the legionaries stood up, his visor flashing in the darkness as he took aim. Two sharp *cracks* rang out. The first bullet shattered the flying bottle, detonating it in a flash of light and a hail of glass shards. The second took the rebel in the throat.

More shots rang out from above Jana as she ran. The rabble-rouser from the previous day stood in the window above, a battered old repeater in her hands. She screamed defiantly as she raised the weapon again.

"Free…"

The word was cut short as another shot punched through her skull, her body flung backwards into the building by the force of the impact.

Jana ran now, darting and weaving through the terrified crowds as best she could, carried as much by the momentum of the tide as she was by her own feet. It was like a stampede: a directionless charge soaked in terror and death. More screams echoed out, more gunshots carried on the wind. The air filled with tear gas as the legions launched it towards the terrified crowds, the hollow *thunk* of the launches underlaying the staccato cracking of rifle-fire.

There was no stopping this, Jana realised. This wasn't a fight that could be won. The Ashkan Warrens were falling, and soon.

Kristof stared out across the stampeding crowds as they entered the cavern. He could hear it descending upon them. The stonework around him, the very foundations of Ashka and its warrens, seemed to tremble with fear.

Find her.

He screwed his eyes shut for a moment, forcing himself to wait patiently. Hoping she returned was the only chance in this chaos.

She has to be here.

He looked out again, scanning the crowds. He could taste it in the air. Desperation. Fear. Something was very, very wrong.

Find her.

He shook his head, grinding the base of his palm into his eye-socket as he willed himself to focus. He couldn't think. His gaze roamed the panicked crowds once more, their faces, their voices all seeming to combine into an amorphous mass in his mind, defying reason, understanding and logic. He was lost. He couldn't *think.*

Find

New noises had begun to rise above the clamour of the horde. Gunshots.

Her

"Hey!"

Wulfe's deep voice thundered above the chaos of the crowd. The soldier was pushing his way toward him, one arm wrapped protectively around the shoulder of the figure who stumbled along at his side.

Kristof felt his heart almost skip a beat. His mind became still once more, the voice reassuming its usual dry monotone. He rushed forwards as the pair hurried to meet him.

"Jana!" he gasped, almost breathlessly. "You're... What's happening?!"

"Atesca! She's got orders to destroy the Warrens. Kristof, they're killing everyone!"

He could feel it in the crowds around him now. A palpable fear, a dense, oppressive energy that seemed to build and build, like a dam waiting to burst.

The Ashkan Warrens are home to five hundred thousand people.

"No. She wouldn't..."

Five hundred thousand families, contacts

"She's coming, Kristof! I've seen her with my own eyes..."

Five hundred thousand voices

"No." Kristof heard his voice murmur, lost in an overwhelming wave of his own thoughts. "No. Its suicide. She's... She's better than this. A quarantine is justifiable. You have deniability, you have reasonable justifications. She wouldn't... This..."

He turned to Wulfe.

"This doesn't make any sense."

"We need to stop her." the soldier rumbled sweeping the crowds with a troubled gaze. The tide of civilians flooding into the cavern had ebbed, but even as they watched a group of armed figures, Varian gangers by their clothing, hurried into the cavern, dragging one of their wounded with them. They let they wounded man down gently, and turned on eachother as an argument broke out within their ranks.

Kill her.

The gunfire was closer now, accompanied with the screams of terror and death. As the first wisp of tear-gas curled into the chamber Kristof grabbed the soldier by his sleeve and pulled the man around to face him.

"We need to get out, Wulfe. We don't have time. A bunch of gangers with side-arms won't even slow them down."

"She's..." The soldier cast about helplessly, lost for words. "Someone needs to..."

Kill her. Kill her. Kill her. Kill her.

Kristof snarled, grabbing the larger man roughly by the front of his greatcoat.

"Listen to me, Wulfe: We can't stop this!" he brought his face close to the soldier's. "You *know* we can't."

Jana's voice cut through the rage.

"Help these people, Wulfe. We know a way out. We can help them."

They all looked up together as a cry went up from the gangers by the cave mouth. One raised his weapon, stitching a line of erratic white pinstripes across the mouth of the tunnel and into the dense fog of ash and gas that begun to seep forth from without. From the smoke a returning volley lashed back, striking the firer once in the midriff and crumpling him to the stonework.

"Get them out, Wulfe! Show them the way!" Kristof grimaced, drawing his pistol from his pocket and priming it with a faint hiss as he thrust the soldier away.

The old soldier hesitated, the anguish of indecision etched into his weathered features.

"Do what you do best, Wulfe." Kristof said, turning back one final time. "And I'll do the same."

And without a second glance he plunged toward the tunnel mouth.

Kill.

Chapter 38

Captain Wulfe knelt over the body of one of the rebels. They were younger than he had imagined. Emaciated faces, sunken eyes… no condition to be fighting anyone, let alone Ashka's Finest.

He felt a hand at his shoulder.

"Could be worse Captain. At least we won." Kristof Richter muttered wryly.

The Wolf of Carth looked up at the dozen or so bodies that littered the street about him.

"Did we, sergeant?"

The cavern echoed with a series of sharp cracking noises, and Jana heard the hiss and whine as a flurry of bullets tore past her. A man beside her crumpled to the ground, clutching at his stomach and chest.

"Go, all of you!" Wulfe's voice thundered above the din as he ushered the remaining stragglers towards the door, shielding them with his body as they ducked from cover to cover.

Legionaries began to emerge from the far cave mouth, weapons discharging into the crowd indiscriminately. Jana dived behind one of the benches as a line of bullets stitched across the ground towards her. The sound of tearing wood filled her ears, and for a moment her world was nothing but a whirling cloud of splinters and metal. She curled up, hands covering her ears, eyes screwed shut as she desperately tried to shut out the sound. Screams washed over her, the crack of bullets and Wulfe's voice echoing around the cavern melding into a hideous maelstrom of noise.

She felt a hand on her shoulder, turning her over. She stared up, shell-shocked, her ears ringing from the detonations around her.

Kristof barely spared her a second glance, his face an emotionless mask, as he spoke. "Go, I've got you." His hand gave her shoulder a reassuring squeeze before she was pushed hard towards the far exit. She broke into a shambling run, ducking and weaving what cover remained in the cavern.

More legionaries had entered the chamber now, huge arcs of fire streaming out from their weapons towards the houses that surrounded it. Kristof raised his pistol, firing off a shot that took one of the soldiers in the throat, sending him staggering backwards into his comrades in a spray of crimson gore.

Wulfe backed towards Jana, staggering backwards a little as a bullet nicked the wall by his head. He held a rifle in his hands now, clearly something he had grabbed from one of the slain resistance fighters.

"Are they all out?!" he roared, raising the weapon to his shoulder and sending the Legionaries scattering for cover with a hail of bullets.

Jana looked around, watching as the last of the figures disappeared down the far tunnel.

"Are they out, Jana?!" Wulfe shouted again.

"Yeah!" she reached out, placing a hand on his shoulder and pulling him down beside her. "We need Kristof!" she shouted, wincing as a bullet splintered off the ground beside her foot.

"He'll catch up! We need to stay with the others and show them the way!"

For the briefest of moments Jana was torn, but she steeled herself. Kristof could handle himself. The people of the Warrens needed her more now.

The soldier stood up, and together they lunged for the exit.

The tunnels were in chaos. Thick black smoke clogged the air, the smell of ash and seared flesh riding on the wind. Figures dashed this way and that, every man for himself in the chaos. Children screamed, the pleas and cries of the injured and dying echoing through the claustrophobic tunnels. And the gunfire, the sharp crack of shots, the searing whine as the bullets tore through the air nearby.

Jana pressed through the tunnels as fast as she dared, terror lending speed to her steps. The smoke stung her eyes, and she stared out through a veil of tears, not knowing whether the others were still with her or not, simply trusting that they would be.

It was all over now. The terrified citizens of the warrens were fighting tooth and nail for their home, and the Legionaries were growing increasingly remorseless as the tight twisting passageways of the warrens threw them into disarray. It was carnage.

She stopped at an intersection, feet scrabbling for purchase on the damp stonework as she screeched to a halt, staring desperately through the chaos. Figures were dashing towards her though the smoke. Dozens of them, a crowd of terrified, panicked figures bearing down on her in the darkness. Jana hesitated, taking a step back as the first of the people reached her. They flooded past, crashing over her like water, knocking her off balance and almost dragging her with them in their desperation. One of the figures cannoned into her, sending her sprawling backwards on the cold stone of the tunnel floor, letting out a shriek as her injured hand slammed against the unyielding stone. She stared up through the murk as the man scrambled to his feet, dashing away without a backwards glance. More figures rounded the bend in the corridor, cries of terror echoing through the tunnel towards Jana.

A plume of fire leapt from the cave mouth, engulfing the fleeing figures. There was a moment of intense white light, a moment that blinded Jana, filled with screams of agony and death. She scrambled backwards, half blind, stumbling to her feet as she dashed back towards the others.

"Kristof!" she called into the darkness, her ears straining desperately for any reply. She glanced over her shoulder, watching as figures began to round the corner behind her. Muzzles flashed as the Legionaries stepped forwards, the anguished screams of their victims ending in hideous gurgling sounds as the bullets struck home.

"Wulfe!" she screamed, pawing at her eyes as she stared into the smoke, willing herself to see further. Her heart thundered in her chest, blood pounding in her ears as she ran.

A figure staggered out of the smoke, its green greatcoat singed and tattered, its gait that of exhaustion. Jana's heart leapt for a moment, before plummeting as the Legionary stepped forwards out of the darkness. A heartbeat passed as the two simply stared, a moment of absolute silence amidst the carnage.

In that heartbeat, Jana saw the Legionary's rifle twitch. She scrambled backwards, realising it was hopeless even as she turned to run.

...and cannoned into Kristof as he lunged past her, weapon raised. The two soldiers fired simultaneously, and for a moment Jana's eyes were filled with blinding light and her ears rang with the deafening booming of close-range gunfire.

Kristof's step faltered as the Legionary's bullet struck him in the midriff, an expression of mild surprise crossing his features. His first shot took the Legionary in the side, just below the armpit. His second took him in the shoulder. His third took him in the neck. As the man crumpled under the remorseless fire, Kristof pulled the trigger until his weapon clicked dry, eyes wide in a blood-soaked frenzy.

Jana stared up at her saviour, ears ringing, eyes weeping from pain and fear. As the soldier turned his eyes on her, a small part of her drew away from the cold hatred in his gaze. Then, in an instant, it was gone. She visibly saw the pain take him, and leapt forwards as his legs gave way beneath him, throwing herself under his arm to catch him.

He looked at her unclearly, his gaze drifting almost as if drunk on the agony. He smiled at her in an oddly detached way. Before raising a hand to point at a sharply inclined section of tunnel to their rear.

"Back this way." he murmured. "Wulfe is there."

"Let me help you down."

"Just go."

She couldn't argue with that voice of finality.

Jana slipped and scrambled down the short incline, her descent sending a flurry of rocks and earth tumbling after her as she slid. She stumbled as she struck the stonework at the bottom, finding herself at the intersection between two of the larger arteries of the lower warrens. The tunnels were packed. The clamour of voices assailed Jana's ears, some voices raised in anger, some hoarse with fear and anxiety, all speaking at once.

An avenue like this was the closest thing the deep warrens got to a street. Buildings had been cut into the stonework on either side of the main channel, with a high, arched ceiling sweeping across the main thoroughfare. The large, cheaply reproduced lighting arrays that usually bathed the would-be street in a dim neon glow now lay dark, and what light there was in the tunnel was being emitted from a thousand individual sources as the crowd stirred restlessly.

As Jana stared into this twilight, the sound of panicked voices from in front of her mixing with the screams of terror from behind, that she heard a scuffle from the top of the slope. Kristof was descending quickly. Too quickly. Jana could see it coming almost before it happened, but even as she opened her mouth to warn him she saw the man's cracked knee buckle beneath him, sending him tumbling down the steep slope in a shower of dirt and, to Jana's horror, blood.

"Kristof?!" she dashed forwards, dropping to her knees beside him. The man had begun to climb to his feet, rolling over with a strangled groan, pulling himself up slowly against the wall. One hand was clutched to his side, but Jana could just make out a faint trickle of blood oozing out from between his fingers.

Kristof caught her gaze, looking up at her with a breathless grin as she hauled him to his feet.

"Just grazed me, the bastard." he hissed. "Bit unsteady. Let's…" the sentence ended in an agonised gasp as he straightened up, and for a second Jana felt his weight rest heavily on her shoulder as his legs gave way once again.

"Still fucking hurts though." Kristof snarled through gritted teeth. "Come on, it's not far now."

They broke into a run, staggering through the smoke and chaos. Jana ran ahead, listening intently to Kristof's directions as they stumbled through the smoke-filled tunnels. His hand was still on her shoulder. She could tell he was hurt; his voice was strained and he was struggling to keep up, judging by the weight his grip was placing on her.

She reached up as they hurried through the densely-packed avenue, placing a hand on his as she spoke in what she hoped was a reassuring tone.

"We can do it. We're nearly there!"

Even she could hear the tremor in her voice.

Kristof grimaced back at her, eyes bright with pain. "I know."

Chapter 39

"They won't give up, not anymore." the Varian said, shaking his head thoughtfully. "Not anymore. I've never seen a group so dedicated to their leader."

"Son of a bitch." Wulfe swore, standing up from his chair suddenly. "The Butcher and his fanatics are determined to grind us all into the dirt before they give in, aren't they? Bastards don't care who they have to toss into the firing line, just trying to... to drag it out, to wear us down and drown us all in fucking blood! Why can't the bastard just admit he's beaten and surrender?!"

The Varian was silent for a moment. He grimaced, then spoke.

"You see, Savri, there's the problem."

"Hm?"

"They have been trying. For months."

Jana heard Wulfe before she saw him. The deep rumble of his voice cut across even the raucous clamour of the huddled masses around him.

"...Back, I told you!" the commanding voice rung out. "Give him space!"

She saw him then, standing almost a head above the rest of the crowd, hands raised as he addressed them earnestly. A man sat at his feet, clearly badly injured, his breathing shallow and his posture hunched. What was most notable was the legionary greatcoat that hung around the man's shoulders, its usual deep green stained a sickly brown by the blood that oozed from the soldier's chest and back.

Wulfe whispered something in the man's ear, before turning back to the people around him.

"We need bandages." he said. "Does anyone have anything we can use?"

No response was forthcoming from the sullen crowd. With a snarl of frustration Wulfe began to tug at the greatcoat that hung around his shoulders, slipping the battered garment off and pressing it to the man's side. As the soldier looked back up, he made eye contact with Jana across the crowds, and a momentary look or relief swept across his craggy features.

"Jana!" he called out as they pressed through the crowd to his side. "You made it!"

He followed Kristof's gaze to the man at his side, before sweeping a wary eye across the men around him.

"He got separated and took a bullet to the chest." he said, before lowering his voice to a near whisper. "These people were going to tear him apart. Nobody deserves that."

"We don't have time for this." Kristof murmured, casting a curiously intense eye over the wounded man. He knelt down suddenly beside the injured soldier, and reached towards him. Jana saw Wulfe visibly flinch at Kristof's sudden movement, but he restrained himself.

With a gentle motion, Kristof reached out and pulled the visor from the legionary's face. He looked at the small device curiously for a moment, turning it over and over in his hands, lips moving silently as he did so. Then, without warning, he cast it onto the stonework at his feet and ground it beneath his heel, seeming almost to savour the crack and splinter of fracturing plastic.

"She knows we're here." he said flatly, looking back up at the other two. "Those things transmit a live feed."

"We don't have much time at all. If he's here, then they're close." Jana said, cutting in. "Wulfe, stay with him. Me and Kristof can get the passage open."

She would never forget the proud smile that crossed Wulfe's features for that fraction of a second. The soldier nodded, his expression turning grim once more as she half-guided, half-followed Kristof across the avenue.

"That man is dead." Kristof muttered as they stepped into a narrow alley off the main thoroughfare.

"You don't know that." Jana said. "If they can get to him quick then..."

"Trust me." Kristof spat. "He's dead and Wulfe knows it."

The alley in front of them ended in a narrow wooden door, sunk a short way into the stonework. Kristof stood up unsupported once more, and drew his pistol from his pocket.

"If there are more than two of them we're in trouble." he muttered wryly as he checked its contents, snapping the barrel back into place with a sharp *crack*.

As it turned out, the smuggler's den was entirely deserted. The cabin consisted of a single room, barely the size of the Siren's hold. There was no furniture, the concrete walls and floor bare except for a few small blankets tossed carelessly into a corner.

Kristof staggered at the far end of the room, hands scrabbling frantically at a man-sized metal plate that had been bolted to the wall just below eye-level. He looked up as Jana entered.

"Jana? There's nothing here to lever it off with, give me a hand!"

Jana nodded hurriedly, rushing across the room to help. She could see where the plate had been left slightly out of place, its surface not entirely flush with the wall. She dug her fingers into the crack and glanced at Kristof.

He gave a worried grin. "Count of three?"

She nodded.

"One, two…"

They heaved together. Jana felt the sharp edge digging painfully into her fingers as she hauled at the plate. With a shriek of metal on stone the plate began to bend outwards, until with a final shuddering groan the metal gave way, clattering to the ground as the two of them leapt back.

Jana ducked, glancing into the tunnel that they had opened. The passage continued upwards, a low incline of steps cut into the stonework that climbed and climbed until it ascended into darkness. She turned back towards Kristof, a faint hope blossoming for the first time in days.

"We did it…"

She stopped. Kristof stood, leaning heavily against the far wall, almost doubled over, hands clutching his side. He caught her gaze, and straightened up a little.

"Probably should have got Wulfe to do that." he muttered, raising a hand to ward her away as she stepped towards him. His breathing trembled for a second as he straightened up.

Jana looked him straight in the eye.

"You're hurt." she said, flatly.

"What gave it away?"

Kristof turned away from her, moving back towards the open door, hand still clutched to his side.

As the two of them reached it, the door swung inwards, forcing Jana back a few steps to avoid its swing. A figure stood in the doorway, a young woman, clothes blackened with soot and ash. She stepped forwards, glancing about the room, a look of desperate hope in her eyes as they fell on Kristof and Jana.

"You've got a way out?" she asked.

Jana nodded, with a reassuring smile. "Through there. Go, quickly!" she gestured over her shoulder towards the tunnel. The woman nodded curtly, before scrambling through the entrance and disappearing into the darkness.

She was the first, but she was not the last. Kristof and Jana watched as the crowds thickened, dozens upon dozens of individuals following Wulfe's guidance as he directed them towards the way out. The door was narrow, especially for such a large number of people, and the presence of the young, sick and weak only slowed progress further. Jana ushered as many through as she could, almost pulling people through the doorway as the pressure from the crowd outside intensified. Some thanked her, heartfelt and earnest, whilst others simply pushed through unresponsively, their expressions haunted and their postures huddled. Jana barely had time to acknowledge the thanks anyway. They had to keep everyone moving. The alley was beginning to fill up.

Kristof stood to one side, staring out through the doorway, a look of deep concern clouding his features. Jana helped the next group through the doorway, a family, her hand pointing them towards the tunnel even as her eyes watched Kristof carefully.

"What's up?" she asked as she stepped aside for a moment, letting the crowd drive itself through the narrow entrance unsupervised.

He shook his head grimly. "There's too many. Far too many."

"Then we save as many as we can, right?"

Kristof grimaced. Jana opened her mouth to speak once more, and stopped suddenly as a new sound reached her ears over the clamour of the crowd.

Gunfire.

Chapter 40

"It is not our duty to do what we think is right. The Union cares."

"It isn't…"

"Remember what I told you, Bastian, all that time ago?" Atesca shook her head fondly. "Have faith. Don't think. Just do what they need you to do. What we all need you to do."

She smiled.

"Be the best man you can be, my Wolf."

Jana rushed to the doorway craning her neck to see over the heads of the crowd. Kristof had evidently heard the sounds too. He strode forwards, trying to push his way out through the inrushing crowd as best he could.

"Wulfe!" he roared. "Get in, now!"

They could both make out Wulfe's silhouette at the mouth of the alley. At the sound of Kristof's voice, the soldier turned, leaping down from the rubble pile that he had been standing on and hurrying towards the throng that had now formed at the doorway to the cabin.

"This way, all of you!" he shouted as he ran, beckoning several stragglers to keep up with him.

Kristof turned to Jana. "The moment he gets here, be ready to go, alright?"

Jana nodded furiously.

The crowd had heard the sounds now too, and had begun to push forwards with renewed vigour. Scuffles broke out as people tried to push past each other. Cries of pain and anger began to ring out as the crowd crammed itself together to fit down the narrow corridor and the doorway beyond.

Jana looked up, watching with rising terror as figures dashed past at the end of the street. One staggered, dropping to its knees as something struck it from behind. The crowd surged forwards again.

Kristof slammed a fist against the wall in frustration. He leaned forwards, staring helplessly out of the doorway as the crowds flooded in. Jana could hear his voice, see his lips moving as he muttered under his breath.

"Come on. Come on. Come on."

He drew himself up, still staring at Wulfe over the heads of the crowd.

"All of you, in! Now!" he roared, his voice lost amidst the terrified clamour of the crowd.

The people paid him no heed, figures already pressing forwards as fast as they could, fighting and scuffling to be the first through the narrow doorway.

Jana had lost sight of Wulfe now, as more and more people fought their way through the doorway, blocking her view. She looked up at Kristof.

"Is he close?"

"Not close enough." snarled Kristof, teeth gritted with frustration. He raised his voice, bellowing across the crowd. "Move! All of you!" He began reaching out, bodily pulling people through the doorway and thrusting them towards the exit.

A ripple ran across the crowds, a singular tremor of fear that seemed to send the entire mass pressing forwards as one.

As Jana craned to see above the heads of the crowd, figures began to appear from the dust-soaked haze that now made up the end of the alley. First one, then two then four, then dozens upon dozens. Small clusters of humanity appeared out of the mists, rushing heedlessly away from the source of their terror. Some carried weapons, some carried children or loved ones in their arms, all running with the kind of speed that only terror could grant.

Behind these figures, materialising like ghosts out of the mist and the fire, strode the Legions of Ashka.

Ash and blood clung to the once vibrant green coats that they wore about themselves. Their ranks were ragged now, the organisation from the start of their assault hampered by the web of tunnels. They moved in packs, like wolves, advancing in groups of twos and threes, harrying the fleeing citizens as they ran.

Shots began to ring out, and the air filled with the snap and whine of bullets. A fleeing man turned, raising his rifle on his pursuers before two shots punched through his chest and he collapsed to the ground in a twitching pile.

The crowd stampeded, pressing forward in terror now. Screams of anguish filled the alley as people were trampled underfoot or crushed against the alley walls. Only a single figure in the crowd stood still, unmoving as the tide of humanity flowed around him.

Amidst the carnage, Jana saw Wulfe turn his head, staring back down the alley towards where the legionaries were advancing, bringing their rifles to bear on the fleeing people. Figures fled from them, men, women and children, stragglers left behind by the crowd's flight.

Another figure had emerged from the smoke and flames at the end of the street, walking amidst the blood and fire of battle without a trace of fear or hesitation. A woman, tall and gaunt of face, a long, coal-black greatcoat about her shoulders.

Wulfe looked back towards the doorway, staring across the crowd that still separated him from it towards Kristof and Jana. Time seemed to slow, almost, as for a moment their gazes met his. A gaze full of sorrow and resignation.

Kristof started forwards, a look of horror spreading across his features.

"Wulfe!" he roared, lunging towards the doorway, trying desperately to fight his way through the stampeding crowd towards the old soldier.

Wulfe stood silently for a second, his gaze lingering on Kristof as the man tried in vain to push his way towards him against the terrified mass of humanity that opposed him. No longer did his gaze carry sorrow and resignation. It carried a fire that Jana had seen only once before.

"Wulfe! Please!" Kristof's voice echoed down the alley, his anguish lost in the clamour of the crowd. "Listen to me!"

Wordlessly Wulfe turned aside, pushing his way back through the crowd towards the legions of Ashka.

The soldiers advanced slowly, moving in a controlled formation down the gently tapering alley walls. Those of less iron resolution had long since succumbed to the claustrophobic chaos and terror of the warrens conflict, and now only the grimly committed remained.

Atesca Seratov, Commissary First Class, the Hawk of Carth and strode in their midst, implacable and fearless as she advanced into the line of fire. She paused for a moment as the legionaries reformed ranks, removing her visor to allow the waves of terror and death to touch her senses more closely. The acrid smoke stung her eyes, the terrified clamour of the crowd now all the clearer as she drew a deep breath, drinking in the atmosphere.

He has to be here.

She knew who stood beside her instinctively, just by the taste in the air. The sergeant was nervous. He was worried about his position, about potential future retribution. He was concerned for his safety and future freedom. The way he moved. The way he stood. The way he spoke. The way he breathed. The Commissary could read him like a book without a second glance.

But in the end, *why* he was afraid was quite irrelevant. For now, his fear of the Hawk outweighed his fear of the uncertain future. The Hawk of Carth was very certain indeed.

"Orders, Commissary?" he asked, his voice lent a metallic edge by his visor.

Atesca stood silently for a moment, eyes searching the crowd hungrily.

Where are you?

"They're escaping. Give them a volley, if they do not surrender then repeat it until they do." she said, turning away. Her quarry must be elsewhere.

Orders snapped out, and the legionaries drew up into close formation, their rifles levelled at the huddled mass that tried to desperately press itself through the single narrow doorway.

Stop

The commissary raised a hand sharply, and the Legionaries halted, their training snapping them into place like statues of the coldest stone.

Something was wrong. The way the crowd moved. The way it *flowed*. Something wasn't right.

Atesca turned back, sweeping her gaze across the crowds one final time before she felt her heart skip a beat.

A shudder ran through the legionary's ranks. The young sergeant stared first in confusion then in awe.

"It can't be..." he murmured. Without looking up, he spoke to the Commissary. "Orders?"

Disarray spread like a virus amidst the legionaries. Orders were being barked back and forth across the line, some Legionaries lowering their weapons, others looking to the Commissary for leadership.

"Commissary! What do we do?"

But no orders came. As the young sergeant looked up, he saw true emotion cross her usually iron mask. Falling silent, he followed her gaze, staring back down the street towards the tunnel's end, where from amongst the terrified crowds strode a figure of legend incarnate.

The Wolf of Carth stepped slowly from the terrified crowds, walking with measured pace across the intervening ground towards the soldiers. The faint orange glow of the caverns played across his face, sending flashes of firelight across his silvered hair and beard as the terrified people of the Union streamed past him. His expression was placid, though a steely determination lingered in his sorrowful gaze. He stopped as the final stragglers passed him, standing quietly as the wind drawn up by the fires whipped at his coat and hair.

The Legionaries stood in disarray. Orders were barked, but none were obeyed. Some rifles were raised, some fell, but none fired upon the man who stood alone against them.

And for a moment, that was all. The Wolf stood silently, a look of defiance playing about his weathered features, staring with level gaze at the soldiers in front of him.

Wordlessly, two of the soldiers drew aside, revealing the figure who stood behind them.

Atesca stepped forwards, hesitantly almost. The aura of authority and command that usually surrounded her had vanished, as frost melting away in the morning's sunlight. She seemed older, almost, as if whatever iron will that had driven her all these years had suddenly begun to wilt.

"Bastian?" the voice rang out, hollowly.

"Stop this, Atesca." Wulfe replied flatly, his gaze unwavering.

"I did what I had to, Bastian." she responded. "I had my orders. You know I will do whatever is necessary to carry them through."

"I thought better of you. You believed in something greater than this senseless slaughter. You believed in the Union. You believed in its values, its soul, its *people*. Never this." He shook his head sadly. "And if all it takes to stop this bloodshed is me, then here I am."

"You were never the cause, Bastian, you know that." the Inquisitor replied, coldly.

For a moment the air was silent, filled only by the faint rush of wind through the warren's now hollow shell.

"Why, Bastian?" Atesca's voice had an edge to it, a slight tremor barely at the cusp of hearing. "I've asked myself every day since then. Why?"

"A Union that fights the people it should be serving? That's something I could never be a part of."

"You don't understand, Bastian! You never understood." Atesca said, taking another step forward. "We do what had to be done. For the greater good of humanity as a *whole*."

Wulfe's gaze played across the floor of the tunnel, the broken, twisted bodies, the charred wreckage, the ever-present scent of blood that still hung in the air.

"If you really believe that *this* has anything to do with greatness, goodness or humanity," he said, slowly. "Then you have lost everything that ever made you human."

Atesca spoke again. Her voice had softened, the commanding edge it had carried gone.

"What you did can be forgiven, Bastian."

"Maybe." Wulfe looked around, then shook his head sadly. "But I don't think I can say the same to you."

"Come back to us, Bastian." Atesca continued. "Come back to me. Everything can be forgotten."

She smiled then. Comfortingly. Hopefully.

Wulfe's gaze grew troubled for a moment. His lips moved silently for a moment. Then his gaze fell on the carnage about him, and when it rose again it was filled with sorrow.

"I'll have no part in this. Any of it."

"Bastian." A heartbeat passed. "Please…"

"No."

The two of them stood silently for a moment, their eyes locked. Wulfe looked back over his shoulder, watching as the last of the crowd vanished into the house behind him, a sad smile ghosting across his features for the faintest of seconds.

Atesca's voice rang out, one last time.

"Goodbye, Bastian."

Wulfe nodded, sadly, lowering his gaze.

Atesca's lips moved almost silently.

Three shots rang out from amongst the Ashkan ranks. Three precise, staccato cracks that echoed around the silent cavern for what seemed like an age. The Wolf of Carth stumbled for a moment, his body rocked by the impacts. His mouth opened as if to speak, but no sound emerged as his legs gave under him, toppling him sideways into the dirt.

A scream of rage and anguish tore from Kristof's throat as he lunged through the doorway, pushing free of what remained of the crowd. Jana reached out, trying desperately to stop him but he broke free, breaking into a dash towards the oncoming soldiers. He raised his pistol, a snarl of wordless defiance on his lips.

Two further shots rang out from the legionary ranks, a pair of brisk detonations against the silence of the tunnel. Kristof staggered back, his head kicking backwards in a spray of bright blood as he fell, mere feet from Jana, his weapon clattering from nerveless fingers.

Chapter 41

Jana sat with her back to the doorframe, frozen in terror, her mind reeling with the enormity of what had just happened. She struggled to breathe, her the cramped cabin seeming to press in on her as she stared sightlessly at Kristof's motionless form sprawled in the doorway beside her.

Footsteps were approaching. Two pairs, it sounded like. Jana looked across the room, staring fixedly at the far tunnel.

Run. Get away. Every fibre of her being screamed at her to run. Her blood pounded in her ears, her heart racing. With a shaking hand she reached out, picking up Kristof's weapon from where it lay beside his still form. She held it in front of her, clutching it desperately in both hands as she threw another fleeting glance around the corner.

She shuffled sideways, placing herself beside the door, the pistol pointed at eye-level. Sweat slicked the grip of the weapon as she gripped it tightly, slowly turning to point it towards the doorway. She could see Kristof from where she hid, his body silent and unmoving. Jana gave a muffled sob, tightening her grip on the gun as she forced herself to focus. Her breath was ragged, her hands shaking even as she desperately tried to keep them steady.

A shadow fell across the doorway. The Legionary's armoured form loomed over her in the confines of the cabin, the blackness illuminated by the sickly white light emanating from his visor as their eyes met.

Neither moved. Jana's hand trembled on the trigger, her whole body tensed to the point of agony as the soft white light washed over her.

She could see now, from this close, the man's features through the tinted black glass that obscured the better part of his features. He was young, barely older than she was. Ashkan, too. He had the same kind of soft olive tan that the emissary troops on Valmeer often developed. Green eyes, it looked like. Mum had had green eyes. They were common on Taynia, apparently.

She could see her terror mirrored in those eyes. She could see the way his hands trembled as his whole body tensed to the point of agony.

Slowly, Jana drew a breath. With glacial slowness she lowered the gun to her side.

The Legionary stood silently for a moment, his gaze still locked with Jana's, his expression almost unreadable as a myriad of thoughts and emotions played across his features. A voice rang through from outside, two sharp exclamations in tac-speech. The soldier responded, the distorted, frequency-scrambled sound of his voice echoing around the silent room.

The faintest of whispers in the back of her mind was enough to tip her off. Something in the man's posture, the way he shifted his feet, the most minute change in expression as he set his jaw... As the Legionary raised his rifle for the kill she had already brought her hand up, slinging the solid kilogram of shaped steel straight at the man's face. She lunged forwards, grabbing the rifle by the barrel as the man reeled back, forcing it up towards the ceiling. As his grip reflexively loosened on the weapon to protect his face Jana twisted away, swinging the weapon by its barrel to bring it cracking against the man's temple.

And with a sickening crunch, it was over. Jana stood in the silent room, breathing hard as the rifle clattered from hands that now shook out of adrenaline, not fear. She looked about hurriedly, straining her ears to the sounds of the Legionaries outside. Then, heart still pounding, her gaze fell across Kristof's still form.

She dropped to her knees, scrambling past the fallen Legionary until she knelt beside him.

"Kristof?!" she asked, hesitantly, reaching out for him. There was no response.

"You are not fucking dead." she muttered, reaching out with both hands now as, with a grunt of exertion, she rolled the man onto his back. "You are not. I won't let you be. Kristof?!"

She gasped with horror.

Kristof's chest was matted with blood, a pair of deep wounds just below his ribs oozing with a continuous stream of dark blood. The left side of his face had been hit just above the cheek, the whole left eye-socket a mass of ruined bone and blood. The other eye stared blankly upwards, unfocussed and unseeing.

Jana felt his chest swell slightly as the man drew in a shuddering breath. She fell silent and still, willing her thundering heart to remain silent as she listened intently. The breaths were slow, a horrible wheezing noise barely on the cusp of hearing, but they were there. Kristof was alive, if barely.

Jana looked around helplessly, her eyes falling on the fallen Legionary beside her. She couldn't stay here, she knew that. She had seconds at worst, minutes at best.

"I've got to get you out. I'm sorry." She reached out, placing her hands under his arms, and slowly lifted the man into a sitting position. His head lolled forwards as he rose, the pool of blood that hand been welling in the eye-socket spattering the ground in front of him. A horrible, punctured wheeze escaped his lungs, and Jana found herself almost pleading as she braced herself against the body.

"I'm sorry. I'm sorry. I'm sorry." she repeated as she pulled the body forwards, ducking under it so that Kristof's form lay draped across her. She shuddered as she felt the warm sensation of blood trickling down her neck, Kristof's ruined eye-socket only inches from her own. He was heavier than he looked, and Jana felt herself buckling under the weight as she stumbled towards the tunnel, half carrying, half dragging her injured friend across the room.

Progress was slow, every metre feeling like a hundred, Kristof's faint, laboured breaths mingling with her own as they climbed up the rough-cut stone steps of the passageway. Smoke and sweat stung her eyes, the weight of Kristof's body across her shoulders seeming to grow with every passing second.

There was barely a thought in her head now, only the pure animal instinct to survive, to hold on to what you have and to never let go. As she climbed higher she began to hear voices, shouts, cries, the faint hum of engines, the faint kiss of fresh air against her face.

She broke into a staggering, lurching run as she pressed towards daylight. Her back aching, her shoulders numb, her neck slick with the blood of her friend, her broken hand sending sharp stabs of agony shooting up her forearm, Jana burst out into the streets of Ashka once more.

The alley was deserted. Empty. A broken ventilation grating lay tramped into the dirt by her feet, the last remaining evidence of the concealed passageway that lay hidden beneath the building.

She leaned forwards, sighing with relief despite herself as Kristof's weight slid from her shoulders. Carefully, as gently as she could, she dropped him into a sitting position against the wall of the alley. She stretched, rolling her shoulders, taking care to keep one hand pressed against Kristof's chest as his body lolled forwards against it.

She paused for a moment, drawing in a shuddering breath to calm herself. There was only one place to run now.

The door to the waterfront was heavy, and Jana was forced to throw her full weight against it, slumping against its surface in an attempt to force it open. The door swung inwards, and she staggered forwards into the darkness.

"Help us." she stammered, almost toppling forwards with exhaustion, barely catching herself on one knee. "Please."

In the dim light of the coffee house, she saw a familiar face look up at her from behind the

Kozlov frowned. "Who the fuck are…" He paused, his gaze falling on Kristof's body as Jana let it slump to the floor, and his expression lit with recognition. "Kristof, right? And you're… you're the other one. What happened to him?"

Jana swayed a little, the adrenaline that had carried her this far already beginning to fade. It was like running on water. You had to keep moving, or you'd sink.

"The warrens." she said, her words slurring with exhaustion slightly. "We were there."

Suddenly, Kozlov was at her side, his eyes intent upon the hideous wounds that covered Kristof's body. He drew in a sharp hiss of air through his teeth, and looked at Jana.

"He needs help. Real help." he looked down again, dabbing at the wounds with his hands. "Marija's grace, this isn't something I can deal with."

"Can't." Jana said. It was all she could do to stay upright. "Not now."

The man glanced up at Jana, thoughtfully chewing on his lip, his features tensed with the agony of indecision. Then he shook his head, scowling with irritation.

"Get him on the counter. Quickly!" He stood up, quickly stepping over to the door, the lock closing with a low clicking sound. Jana summoned the last of her strength, forcing her weary muscles into motion as between the two of them they lifted Kristof's still form onto the countertop, glasses clattering to the floor as Kozlov swept them aside with his forearm.

Jana slumped forwards, resting heavily on the counter, drawing in deep gulps of air as the weight lifted from her shoulders. Her vision faded for a moment as the exhaustion overcame her, and she found herself kneeling on the ground beside the counter, blood dripping from her collar on to the white, glass-worked tiles beneath. She closed her eyes, resting her head against the counter's cool metallic front, letting the silence of the room wash over her.

She felt numb. She didn't think. She couldn't. Not now.

She jerked awake from her momentary stupor, staggering to her feet as she heard a door open and shut, glancing back over the countertop as Kozlov disappeared through the doorway. She stood, swaying slightly, her vision swimming from fatigue and exhaustion, staring after the man as the door slid slowly shut behind him. Slowly, her gaze wandered, down to where Kristof lay, motionless, the faint wheezing gasp of his breaths the only sound in the room.

She reached out, only half conscious of her actions, idly tracing her fingers around the blood that welled and pooled on the dented countertop. Nothing had really sunk in yet. Not Wulfe. Not the Warrens. Not even Kristof, she thought, as she stared with a kind of bemused detachment down at his ruined features.

"I'm sorry." she whispered. "I…"

She stopped. She reached out, silently placing a hand on Kristof's shoulder.

"We made it." she said quietly, gently brushing an errant strand of hair from his face, drawing it free from the matted blood that stained his features. "That's something."

She jumped slightly as the door slammed open and Kozlov backed into the room, his hands filled with a variety of equipment.

"Wasn't planning on taking this stuff anyway." he muttered to himself as he dropped the items onto the counter beside Kristof's head with a clatter.

"This is going to take some serious surgery, and I've never known how to do that. I can get the shells out, do some stitching maybe, but it's going to be a mess and I definitely can't do it while he's conscious."

He looked down, an expression of concern breaking across his features. "This stuff won't help with that, but it might knock him out cold for a few hours. That's the best we can hope for."

Jana watched as the man raised the narrow plastic tube to the light, watching as the liquid swirled about inside. He paused, glancing at Jana.

"This could be…" Kozlov nodded towards Kristof's body. "Get a hold of him."

Jana stepped forwards, placing her hands on Kristof's shoulders. "What does it do?"

"It hurts." the man gave the tube a practiced twist, sliding the two halves apart and exposing the complex needle mechanism beneath. "Like hell."

Before Jana could say another word, Kozlov brought the device down hard onto Kristof''s exposed forearm. Almost immediately, she felt Kristof's shoulders tense. His hands clenching reflexively, on fist slamming spasmodically against the metal countertop.

Jana leant forwards, her whole weight pressing down on Kristof's shoulders as his body bucked and kicked. She could feel his muscles clenching with the agony, his single eye, wild and bloodshot, staring unflinchingly past her. His jaw clenched, a faint, high pitched keening emerging from between his gritted teeth.

Jana stared down helplessly, watching him twist and writhe in her grip. She lowered her head onto her arms, her body covering his as it trembled spasmodically beneath her.

"I'm sorry." she whispered over and over again, as she felt the seizures begin to subside. "I'm so sorry."

She didn't know if it was the exhaustion, the memories of the day, or a combination of the two, but as she felt Kristof movement stop, his breathing slowing, she felt tears beginning to roll down her cheeks. She stayed, head and arms rested on his chest as the shuddering stopped, Kristof's body falling horribly still.

She didn't know how much time passed there, it could have been seconds, minutes or hours. But eventually, as she stood with her head buried in her arms, listening to the faint sounds of Kristof's laboured breathing, she felt a hand on her shoulder pulling her gently but firmly away from the man's body.

"Is he going to be ok?" she whispered, her gaze never leaving his still form.

"Best get out of the way for now." Kozlov said, not unkindly. "You'll be no help to me in that state anyway. Go." he jerked a thumb over his shoulder. "Everything's packed up in there, but I'm sure you can find something to rest on."

"Is he going to be ok?!" Jana repeated.

Kozlov gave a wry smile. "Truthfully? No. Right now I'll settle for keeping him alive."

Jana nodded sadly. She had suspected as much. She shuffled around the countertop, heading for the door behind Kozlov. She pushed the door open, her hand shaking with the exertion, glancing back over her shoulder at Kozlov as she paused in the doorway.

The man had stepped up to the counter, rolling his sleeves back, staring thoughtfully down at the dying man that lay on his bar.

"Thank you." Jana whispered, her voice hoarse, barely audible even in the silent room.

Kozlov snorted derisively, a wry smile hidden somewhere in that thick black beard.

"Don't thank me yet."

"I want to. Thank you."

Chapter 42

"This isn't a war, Atesca, it's a slaughter! They don't stand a chance any more, and still they throw themselves in front of our guns. I can't solve this."

"You have done more than anyone ever dreamed, Bastian."

"But I haven't won. It still isn't over." The Wolf said. "I can't stop this war. I don't even want to win anymore, I just want it to end. But it won't, because… because…"

"Because what, Bastian?" Atesca spoke, her voice suddenly cold.

"Nothing."

Jana woke, slowly. Every muscle in her body ached, the pain from her ruined hand flaring again as she shifted her position on the narrow, poorly padded bench she had collapsed on the night before. She felt something shift around her as she moved, becoming aware of the weight of a blanket around her shoulders. Still half asleep, she pulled it in tighter, eyes staring blearily at the room around her.

It was sparsely furnished, a single large table against the far wall, a few cabinets and containers scattered about the floor. It was silent too, for a place on the surface, only the faint, persistent hum of the ventilation system making breaking the stillness.

Jana groaned as she swung her feet off the bench, her shoulders and back screaming in protest. She paused for a moment, staring at the far wall, waiting for her senses to stop swimming as she shrugged the blanket tighter about her shoulders.

"Good morning." muttered a voice, coarse and gruff in its speech, but not unkind.

For the faintest of moments, Jana expected to see Wulfe when she sat up.

"How is he?" she asked, as Kozlov put down the case he had been carrying. "Is he ok?"

"He's alive." the shopkeep said, nodding slowly. "Not much to look at, but alive."

That was all Jana needed to hear. Within moments she was out of bed and through the door into the main hall of the coffee-house.

Kristof lay still, his only movement the slow rise and fall of his chest. The blood had been cleaned from his face, the set of greying bandages wrapped around his head barely covering the gaping wound beneath. Already the blood had begun to seep through, staining the sterile white of the bandages with a deep crimson. The rest of Kristof's body was covered with a long coat, concealing the worst of his wounds from Jana's view. She glanced up at Kozlov, who shook his head.

"It's not pretty. Had to clamp most of the wounds shut to stop the bleeding. His face and side are about 20 percent pins now." He grimaced. "Don't envy the person who has to get them out if he heals."

He turned to Jana, reaching out to turn her away from Kristof's body.

"There's something you need to know though." Kozlov said, his voice low. He drew Jana aside, gesturing for her to sit.

"This isn't going to make him 'better'." the man continued. "Injuries like that don't get better, not with the kind of help I can give him. You want to save him, you get him somewhere that he can see a real medical, and you do it soon."

Jana nodded solemnly. Kozlov placed a reassuring hand on her shoulder.

"He's getting better for now though. In a few days he should be on his feet again, if a little unsteady. You two are welcome to stay here as long as you like."

"Won't we get in the way?"

Kozlov shrugged. "I won't be here anyway."

"Why not?"

The shopkeeper shook his head with a dry chuckle, and turned to the monitor that hung from the eastern wall. There was a gentle clicking sound, and the image sprung to life.

It was like a punch to the gut. Jana was back in the warrens. Smoke filled her vision, scenes of chaos and battle flitted across the screen, the sound of cheers, anguish and suffering seemed to surround her. She recognised certain shots too. Tulharden Square. The Port. Unity Plaza. The Council Halls of Ashka. And over all this, a monotone voice seemed to done, growing louder and louder by the second...

...the past six hours the violence has escalated still further. The Varian representative Councillor Siddarth Vress has called for an immediate assembly of the Ashkan Council, but has otherwise refused to comment further on the happenings. Councillors Saskia and Ovan have also barred any commentary, although Councillor Song has claimed that the commissary has 'significantly overstepped her authority' and suggested that many of the reactive elements are 'justified' in their...

The screen went dark.

"Whole place is going up in smoke." Kozlov said. "So I'm leaving. This much anger in the streets, sooner or later something is going to give." He paused, shaking his head sadly, throwing a mournful glance around the bar's interior. "I love this place. Been here most of my life. But I'm not getting myself caught in the middle of another Aceh or Carth."

Jana was taken aback. "It's not that bad, surely?"

Kozlov shrugged. "Who knows? The Union has built itself a lovely tinderbox and I'm not waiting around to see if someone throws a match on it. Pioneer's leaving in a few days, heading to Taynia and Sirrus. Then Varia, from what I remember. I'll get myself on board if I can. Otherwise it's just a matter of finding a skimmer that can take me far enough away."

Jana licked her lips thoughtfully, taking another sip from her glass. She found her gaze straying across the room, towards where Kristof lay. "Maybe you're right." she mused, quietly.

"'course I am." Kozlov retorted with a short chuckle. "Anyone who chooses to stay in a place like this needs their head examined. Take my advice," he said, gesturing with the empty cup. "find yourself somewhere new. I hear Valmeer is nice." He rose to his feet slowly, his chair scraping backwards across the rough tiling on the floor.

Jana gave a non-comittant shrug, still staring thoughtfully at Kristof.

"It's not all it's made out to be."

Kozlov gave another mirthless laugh. "Can't be worse than here."

Chapter 43

The Wolf's foot slipped on the slick ground, plunging him down into the mud as bullets whipped past him. The clatter of automatic rifle fire filled the air around him as he lay there for a moment, stunned.

He felt a hand on his shoulder.

"Up you get, Captain." Kristof muttered, pulling Wulfe slowly to his feet. He turned, calling back to his men.

"Forwards, all of you! The Wolf needs our…"

He crumpled around the bullet as the sniper's shot found its mark, punching through his chest in a spray of bright arterial blood.

One day passed. A day during which Jana barely left Kristof's side. She watched Ashka smoulder through a screen's filter, with the volume muted. She didn't want to hear those sounds again.

There wasn't anything to do but worry now. Kozlov had left them enough food for maybe a week. The Pioneer left in a few days. She'd be damned before she went out into that city alone. So she just watched.

It was a surreal experience. She would see things in the broadcast that she could see from the window. She would see Legion skimmers take off in the background of a shot and hear them roar overhead moments later. It was like nothing she had ever imagined.

And then she saw a face she recognised, if only for a moment.

Councillor Song stood grim-faced before a crowd, at the steps of the Halls of Ashka. Her resplendent features were flawless once more, and she stood as a pillar of confidence as she spoke. By the time Jana had brought the sound up to listen the speech was over, and the sounds of cheers, shouts, screams and gunfire once more filled the room as the broadcast switched to footage of Atesca's "heroic defence of the high city".

Jana flinched and looked away. Her nerves were still too raw. She could still almost taste the blood in the air as she stared at the grisly scenes.

And her eyes fell on Kristof.

The soldier lay still, his single eye roving slowly about the room. It stopped, settling on Jana. Kristof drew in a breath, a deep shuddering seeming to pass through his whole body. His eye twitched for a moment, his lips moving as the faintest whisper tried to escape them.

"What?" Jana leant closer, gently pressing Kristof back onto the table as he struggled to sit up to speak. "Try again."

She leaned forwards, placing her ear close to his mouth. She felt the warm sensation of breath on her cheek as he spoke again, his voice still barely at the cusp of hearing.

"Wulfe."

It didn't sound like a question.

Jana stepped back, crossing her arms as she gazed sadly down at Kristof. For a moment everything came back to her, she felt herself once again standing amidst the acrid smoke as the terrified crowds streamed past her, watching as the lone man faced down the Legions of The Hawk. She felt a wave of sadness wash over her, folding her arms tighter as she stared wordlessly down at Kristof, hopelessly trying to find the right words to say.

The injured man stared up at her silently, the single, slate-grey eye searching her face for any trace of expression. Jana opened her mouth, and hesitated.

She could have handled an expression of anguish. She had been ready for tears, or anger, or hatred. But the expression that fell across Kristof's face froze her heart like ice. The resignation, the passive acceptance settling across his face like a mask.

It took until the following morning for him to be able to speak properly. Jana managed to scrounge together a hot drink for him, which seemed to help somewhat. It was the little things.

He struggled to rise, and Jana reached out quickly, grasping his upper arm to steady him. He glanced sideways at her, drawing another shuddering breath.

"Thank you."

She gave what she hoped was an encouraging smile. "How are you feeling?"

Kristof raised a shaking hand, gently touching it to the dressing that covered his eye. He winced as his fingertips touched the fabric, flinching away from its touch. He lowered his hand, staring at the faint crimson smear across his fingertips.

"Kristof?" she said, placing her hand across his. He looked up with a start, the single eye boring into her, his expression an unreadable mess of emotions.

"You're alive." Jana laughed, the tension of the last few days suddenly banished as the realisation overcame her. She lunged forwards, tentatively placing her arms around him. "I told you we'd make it." she whispered.

Chapter 44

Sergeant Kristof Richter, Posthumous Equipment Retrieval Report – 26th Sihyld 2193

Cothiq-Pattern Long Rifle — *Retrieved*

47 Rounds of A.503 Shells — *Retrieved*

Cothiq-Pattern Body Armour — *Damaged in Action*

Mess Kit — *Retrieved*

Legion Sergeant Ident Badge — *Retrieved*

Civilian Identification — *Missing or Damaged in Action*

Days passed.

The city of Ashka smouldered. From the Council hills to the Varian enclave, all were up in arms at the atrocity that had taken place on their doorstep. The streets were in disarray, with protests, rioting and looting occurring almost daily. Segments of the city stood on the edge of armed insurrection, with only the fear of armed reprisal keeping the people of Ashka contained. Members of the Ashkan Council spoke daily; initially addressing crowds from the sloped stairway at the base of the council halls, but eventually retreating behind screens and radio broadcasts as the city that had conquered a solar system turned its eyes on them.

Kristof was recovering, in some ways. By the third day he could move again, managing a few tottering steps across the Waterfront's main room before his weight came crashing down on Jana's shoulders once more. By the fifth he could carry himself, although he seldom did. By the seventh his breathing had begun to recover, losing the hideous scraping noise that had been Jana's constant companion for almost an entire week.

And still he barely spoke a word.

Outside, Ashka was burning. The floodgates had been opened. Every day a new insurgency broke out, and every day another was stamped out beneath the boots of Atesca's Legions. Fools dying for a fool's cause, Kozlov had said before he left. The Jana who had arrived in the city two months ago on the Pioneer would have agreed wholeheartedly. The Jana that now stood alongside Kristof on the 51st floor of the Waterfront stack staring out across the devastation? She wasn't sure.

"What do we do now?" she said softly, watching the smoke curl lazily from the industrial segment far to the south.

Kristof stared wordlessly for a while. A long moment passed, drawn out almost as long as Jana could bear. Finally, with a faint rasp of indrawn breath, he spoke.

"What can we do?"

"I don't know." Jana admitted. She sighed. "But someone needs to do something."

Kristof said nothing. Jana stared straight ahead, pretending to watch the city burn as she carefully eyed his reflection in the misted glass of the window in front of them.

His gaze was on her. Beneath the bloodied gauze and the strands of matted hair his expression seemed almost thoughtful for a moment. He spoke slowly, softly, his voice barely more than a whisper.

"Not us. Not this time."

"I just..." Jana hesitated. "We know things. We must be able to do something. Atesca can't get away with this. And there's Song. ...And whatever was in that Vault."

She paused helplessly, grasping for a solution, for words that simply would not come.

"We just have to do something." she finished weakly.

"Jana, I've seen where this ends. You run, and you might live a little longer. You fight, and you die. Everyone dies."

"There must be some way..."

"This isn't your fight."

"You made this my fight. It was you who got me involved in the first place!"

"And now I'm getting you out."

"I don't *want* to be out, Kristof! I want to help you! You don't have to do everything by yourself. Listen to me..." She stepped closer, pulling him around to face her. The single, slate-grey eye bored met hers for a moment.

"I don't care if we die. We are getting to the bottom of this. We are finding out what happened in the Vault. We are dealing with Atesca. We are going to prove that the reality of Kristof Richter is so much more than the fiction."

"Jana, if you want to help…"

"I can. Anythi…"

"Just go." The words cut through, sharper than the sharpest blade. "Please. Walk away, somewhere far away from here, and find somewhere to be happy. That's all I want."

"Listen to me, you stupid bastard! You are going to *die*!" she shook her head, her hands clenched with frustration. "What the hell am I doing? I barely even know you! But this? After everything I did for you? After everything you did for me? You're going to kill yourself because you're just too fucking stubborn to back down!"

"It needs doing. You saw what Atesca is capable of. You saw what that thing in the Vault is capable of."

"Did *you* see what it was capable of? That's not something you can fight. I'm not letting you die. Not alone." She stepped in front of Kristof again, staring up at him with as much defiance as she could muster. "If you're going to do this, I'm coming with you."

"No."

"I wasn't giving you a choice, Kristof."

"You'll die."

"I don't care. I am not just going to stand by and watch you kill yourself over… over whatever this is!"

Kristof stepped forward suddenly, looming over Jana. His face was bleak, the single grey eye meeting her gaze with such intensity that she faltered for the slightest of moments.

"You're everything I have left."

"I don't care. I'm not letting you die alone. What we do next is up to you, but we're doing it together."

"I don't want you hurt."

"Then leave. We have a chance now. If we walk away, they might just let us go." "Remember what we talked about on the Pioneer? A home? A new life? We can still do that." she stared up at him hopefully, watching the play of emotions across his face. "All of it. You just need to *walk away*."

She stared up at him, mustering every last shred of her defiance to meet that awful, empty gaze.

She felt bad for him. Really bad. She missed Wulfe, Cass and Nadir, and she'd only known them for… what? A few weeks? A month, maybe? She could barely imagine what he must be feeling.

A flurry of emotions passed across Kristof's face. His hands trembled for a moment, clenching into fists as he caught her gaze. The one mad eye roved across her features, searchingly, almost pleading in the intensity of its stare. He started, several times, as if beginning to speak before biting down on the words.

Then he sighed. His gaze softened, and he glanced down at his feet, shaking his head sorrowfully.

"You're right. You're always right."

Chapter 45

The Pioneer was leaving. One final set of shuttles was going up before it left the planet for its nine-month round trip across the Ashkan Union.

The streets of Ashka were near-empty this early in the morning. The scent of rain hung in the chill air.

Valmeer. she thought. *I'm going home.*

Kristof had been near-silent since they left, shuffling along beside Jana like a walking corpse.

"Hey." she whispered, taking his hand in hers. She smiled up at him, eyes searching that hollow gaze for any sign of the man she had met months before. "It's better this way. Second chances, right?"

The single grey eye bored into hers for a second as their gazes met.

"Don't worry about me." he gave a weak grin, and for a moment Jana saw a brief flash of something familiar in that ruined face. "I'll make it through, one way or another. As long as you're safe."

Jana smiled with relief, turning away from Kristof as she fiddled with the door of the chamber. "Well I don't want to be too hasty, but…" she looked away, glancing up at the vast craft that hung in the sky hundreds of miles above. "…I think we're going to be safe for at least the next few months."

Kristof smiled weakly.

He looked up as the vast mouth of the shuttle loomed above them. Jana could hear the chatter of voices ahead of them in the crowd, as the legionaries processed the passengers.

"We shouldn't be together." Kristof muttered, eyeing the Legionaries nervously. "Idents don't have any relation."

"I know, I know." Jana said, giving his hand a squeeze. "Take care. I'll see you inside." she whispered, before slipping away through the crowds. She could feel his eyes on her back as she darted away, slipping through the meandering crowds towards the line of soldiers.

"Ms. Ester Lindova?" the Legionary asked in brisk, no-nonsense voice as he looked up from the ident she had handed him.

"Yep." Jana beamed.

"Destination?"

"Valmeer. Verkat."

"Really?" the soldier grimaced, and tapped something out on his slate. "Reason for travel?"

"I'm a medicae. I heard they are in need of doctors out there."

"Brave of you." the Legionary smiled tightly. "Probably still safer than here. On you go."

"Thanks." Jana said, smiling again as she brushed past.

And just like that she was out.

She sat herself on the base of one of the support columns and rested there for a while, legs kicking in the air as she watched the crowds go by. The shuttle was larger than the others she'd been on. Jana grinned to herself. She was becoming quite the connoisseur.

She could almost taste the feelings of the crowd now. Fear. Relief. Above all, excitement. Some stood and talked. Others had already begun to trickle out of the main bay into the depths of the shuttle.

Minutes passed. She stood up on the base of the column, clinging on with her good hand as she stared out over the heads of the crowd.

Sirens sounded. The vast doors at the mouth of the shuttle began to slide slowly shut. Jana dropped off the column and began to push her way towards the glass screen that separated the inside of the shuttle from the outside world, a hideous sinking feeling forming in her chest.

She threaded her way to the front of the crowd as the launch sirens began to sound. The Legionaries stepped forwards together, holding back the press of the excited crowd as they pushed forwards to shout their goodbyes at their loved ones beyond the glass.

And there he stood, motionless amidst the crowds that thronged about him on the landing platform below. His single, slate-grey eye bore a sorrowful gaze as he stared up her, riddled with fear, longing and remorse. His ruined features twitched, drawing back into a fond smile for the briefest of moments. Then, with a final, lingering glance, he turned away, limping back towards the city of Ashka. Within seconds, the broken husk of a man that she had known as Kristof Richter had vanished into the crowds below.

Jana Maria Schleifer watched silently, mutely, the sounds of the crowd fading to nothing as the engines roared above them. She wanted to scream, with rage, with anguish at the betrayal she felt inside, but she knew it was pointless. There was nothing she could do. Not now. Not anymore.

Epilogue

"Bastian, stop. Do not go after him alone. He's dangerous."

The Wolf of Carth stared quietly around the room, ignoring the voice that crackled over the comms. He stood hunched, limping slightly from the heavy bruising down his right side. His clothes were tattered and worn, streaked with blood and grime, his skin and hair matted with dust. Dead eyes stared into the darkness, their lustre a long-forgotten memory.

"This is an order, Bastian. I am ordering you to wait for us." He could hear exertion from the end of the line.. Voices could be heard in the background, shouting, screaming. The voice came again, distant this time, as if speaking to someone far away.

"All of you, follow me! Now!"

The Wolf of Carth stood motionless, his face locked in the agony of indecision. Seconds passed. Hours. Days. He closed his eyes in resignation.

The voice returned. Pleading.

"Bastian. Please."

The Wolf paused, thinking of all the things he could say. That he should say. There were too many to choose from.

At last, he decided.

"Goodbye, Atesca."

"...Bastian?"

The radio crunched underfoot as the Wolf stepped into the chamber.

The room was dark and sombre. No decoration adorned its bare concrete walls, the only light breaking in a single beam from the large bay windows at the room's end.

The Butcher of Carth sat beside the window, his body slumped against its frame. He stared vacantly out across the city, watching its ashes as they smouldered.

He flinched as he heard The Wolf's footsteps. He looked back, staring up as the Wolf of Carth stumbled towards him, eyes full of anguish and sorrow.

His mouth opened, his voice weak from exhaustion.

"I never..." he stopped. "I didn't want this."

He fell silent, recoiling as The Wolf of Carth approached. Resigned, he lowered his gaze, screwing his eyes shut and turning his head away from his killer.

Silence fell across the room. The Butcher of Carth sat silently, waiting for the shot that would end his life.

But it never came.